THE DRAGO

BO

Rising from the Ashes

BOOKS BY CAREN J. WERLINGER

NOVELS:

Looking Through Windows
Miserere
In This Small Spot
Neither Present Time
Year of the Monsoon
She Sings of Old, Unhappy, Far-off Things
Turning for Home
Cast Me Gently

SHORT STORIES:

Twist of the Magi
Just a Normal Christmas
(part of Do You Feel What I Feel? Holiday Anthology)

THE DRAGONMAGE SAGA:

Rising From the Ashes: The Chronicles of Caymin

COMING SOON:

The Portal: The Chronicles of Caymin
The Standing Stones: The Chronicles of Caymin

THE DRAGONMAGE SAGA
BOOK 1

Rising from the Ashes

The Chronicles of Caymin

Caren J. Werlinger

Rising From the Ashes: The Chronicles of Caymin
Published by Corgyn Publishing, LLC.

e-Book ISBN: 978-0-9960368-3-2
Print ISBN: 978-0-9960368-4-9

E-mail: cjwerlingerbooks@yahoo.com
Web site: www.cjwerlinger.wordpress.com

Cover design by Patty G. Henderson
www.boulevardphotografica.yolasite.com

Cover photo: Jane Morrison
Questions of Light Photography

Book design by Maureen Cutajar
www.gopublished.com

For all who still believe in magic...
and dragons

Contents

Caymin's Map of Eire

Enat's Village

Ulaid

the Mystical Forest

Connacht

the Sett

Gai's Clan

Laigin

Munster

Caledonia

Gwynedd

PROLOGUE

The New Cub

Broc lay still under a heavy thicket. Up in the sky, a ring surrounded the cold moon. Snow was coming. She could smell it. Normally, she didn't venture so close to the two-legs, but this night she did. She'd felt a trembling and vibration in the earth that she'd felt before, and she knew what it meant.

The birds that flew near the edges of the land told tales of various bands of two-legs that came over the endless water in strange hollowed logs to their land. They said when the logs settled, out spilled more two-legs than they could count, and when the different bands met, they nearly always fought. Broc had never been so far from her sett as to see the water, but she remembered other days, when she was a cub and had unwisely ventured too close to a village and she had seen them fighting. She never forgot the screams and the fire, and the smell of blood and fear.

Now, she flattened her body even lower under the thicket, her bright eyes glittering as she watched a band of two-leg males stealthily approaching this village from the forest. The badger sow sniffed the air as they approached, all wearing tunics and cloaks bearing the same design, all carrying weapons of metal, and the scent of the animal skins that the two-legs wore in place of fur of their own came to her on the cold night air. She shivered and retreated deeper into her thicket, her smooth fur shielding her from the prick of the thorns. Silently, she turned and began to retrace her steps back to her own hunting.

She froze as sudden yells and screams rent the night air around her. Two-legs crashed through the underbrush near her. Digging quickly, she made a shallow hole under the tangled roots of a yew tree and burrowed into it, watching their heavy feet stomp the earth just beyond the roots where she hid. She preferred to hide, but if any of them saw her and tried to get to her, they would be sorry.

Broc stayed hidden for a long time as the sounds of their fighting filled the night – the blows, the sounds of bodies falling, and all the while, their voices raised. It went on and on until, at last, she heard the pounding of footsteps running away from her. It sounded as if the two-legs from the village who survived the attack had fled and were now being pursued by their attackers. She emerged from her tree roots, ready to scamper back to her sett. A new sound made her stop. Her keen ears and nose often picked up what her poor eyes could not, and now she heard a mewling cry, "*Mam! Help me.*"

Startled, she paused. She shook her head as if ridding herself of an annoying fly. "*It is not to do with me.*"

She turned again in the direction of her sett, but a renewed crying stopped her. Cautiously, she crept to the edge of the forest where she could see what remained of the village. She detected no movement of other two-legs, though many of them lay still on the ground. Shivering as she crawled among them, she followed the sounds of the cries to the burning remnants of one of their dwellings. She had never understood why the two-legs built their shelters aboveground instead of digging warm, safe setts as her kind did.

There, thrashing and crying in pain at the edge of the fire, was a two-leg cub. Broc warily crept nearer and grasped the cub by the cloth that covered it. She dragged it back out of the fire. Not much bigger than a badger, it whimpered pitifully. Sniffing, she curled her snout at the smell of burned flesh and hair. It was a girl-cub. She freshened her grip on its covering and, using her powerful legs and strong claws, she dragged it farther away from the heat. She waited to see if any other two-legs would come to care for it. None came. She dragged it closer to the forest.

"Broc?"

She lifted her head and whickered at her mate's call.

"I am here, Cuán."

A large badger boar pushed his way through the underbrush, followed by two of Broc's sisters.

"What are you doing?" he asked.

"This two-leg cub was in the fire," she said. *"A girl-cub. She is hurt."*

"Leave her," said Broc's older sister. *"She will die in the cold. We would all be better if the two-legs left this forest to us as it should be."*

Broc looked back at the girl-cub. *"This one is different."*

The boar sniffed, wrinkling his snout in distaste as Broc had done. *"Different how?"*

"She speaks to us," Broc said. *"Listen. I heard her call to me."*

The four badgers became silent, and they could hear a tiny voice calling, *"Do not leave me,"* though no sound was made.

The younger sister backed away. *"How is it that this two-leg speaks as we do?"*

"I do not know," Broc said. *"But I wish to take her back to our sett. Help me to move her."*

"This is not wise," her older sister said.

"I cannot explain," Broc said, but she ached in sorrow, remembering her own cubs from last season, taken by wolves when she was away hunting. She had mated again, but would not give birth to new cubs for many moons to come. *"I feel it. We must not leave her. Help me."*

"We cannot drag her to the sett," said the boar. *"We will hurt her more and she will die."* He cautiously approached one of the fallen two-leg males, ignoring the sickening smell of the blood. He pawed at a wooden disc clasped around the two-leg's arm. It had been

pierced by a weapon, but was still intact. The two-leg was dead. Cuán dared to draw nearer until he could use his teeth and claws to part the leather straps holding the disc fast, and then dragged it to Broc. "*We must put her on this, and then we can move her safely through the forest.*"

The four badgers crept close enough to grasp the girl-cub by the cloth covering her. The older sister shook her head, wiping her tongue with her paw. "*She tastes like ash.*"

They pulled her onto the disc.

"*Wait,*" said Broc. She went to another of the fallen two-leg warriors and chewed loose the clasp holding a heavy cloak. She brought the cloak back to the girl-cub and covered her with it. "*She has no fur of her own. We must keep her warm.*"

Working together, the four badgers hauled her back to their sett.

CHAPTER 1

The Ghost-Child

Ash prowled the edge of the village, keeping to the shadows, though there was no real need. She wore a dark cloth stolen by Cuán from another village long ago, and her hair was interwoven with twigs and bits of moss so that, if she stood still against a tree, she became nearly invisible. Winter's hold was loosening, but small pockets of snow remained at the base of the trees. She carefully placed her feet so as to leave no trail and make no noise. She cocked her head as she listened to the two-legs' speech. It was odd that she could understand it still, though, if she had ever spoken it, it had been long ago, when she was a cub, before the fire. Sometimes, when she was alone, she tried to speak their words, but they felt strange on her tongue. Talking with Broc and the other four-legs was much easier, as she could hear their thoughts and they hers.

"Go *around*," she said now to one of the dogs that accompanied her.

She crept a little closer to where a man and woman sat beside their fire in front of their dwelling, and she let herself be seen.

"What's that?"

"Where?"

"Over there, just beyond the firelight."

The man strained his eyes, trying to pierce the veil of darkness beyond their fire. "'Tis just the ghost-child. Can't talk or hear. Leave her be. She does no harm."

"Poor thing," said the woman. "And no one to look after her."

"We've enough babes of our own to care for." His strong teeth bit into the meat clinging to the bone in his roughened hand.

"I know," the woman said. "But she looks so hungry." She took a few tentative steps toward the girl, holding out a hand. "Won't you come closer?"

But Ash backed away, drawing their attention, just as she'd planned. Behind the people, unnoticed by either of them, the dog crept close enough to grab a bird roasting on a spit over the fire.

"Give her just a wee bit," the woman said.

Scowling, the man tossed what remained of the bone in the girl's direction. She snatched it and scampered away into the underbrush.

Ash was neither deaf nor mute, but it served her purposes for humans to think she was. The dog who had stolen the bird came to her, dropping it at her feet.

"*Good,*" she said. She gave him the bone with the meat left on it and picked up the bird, still hot and greasy from the fire.

Within a few heartbeats, she was surrounded by the village dogs, who sat or crawled near on their bellies, their noses twitching eagerly in the direction of the meat. She pulled a piece loose and put it in her mouth. It was the first meat she'd had in many days. She ate another couple of mouthfuls, and then tore other bits off, handing them out to the waiting dogs.

Some nights, the dogs fed them, stealing hunks of meat from the fires when the two-legs weren't paying close enough attention or bringing down a fawn or a rabbit. They always shared with Ash, as she did with them if she was able to scrounge food. She preferred the cooked meat, but food was food. Many days, her only option was to paw through the remnants of the fires while the humans were sleeping or away hunting, looking for something that wasn't so rotten it would make her sick. Ash could always dig for roots or look for berries in the right seasons, but the dogs couldn't eat that. She ate a bit more and let the dogs have the rest. She glanced up at the moon as the dogs tugged on what remained of the bird carcass, growling at one another. Broc would be back from her hunting soon.

"*Tomorrow,*" she said as she got to her feet.

She limped through the forest, the scarred skin of her right leg stretched so tightly behind the knee that it couldn't straighten completely. It had been that way for as long as Ash could remember, from the night Broc pulled her from the fire.

"*You whimpered and cried like a new-born cub.*" Ash had asked Broc to tell her the story again and again. "*You were no bigger than I am. I licked your wounds and bit away the dead flesh until you began to heal.*"

"*And what did you feed me?*" Ash asked, though she knew the answer.

"*I tried to feed you earthworms, like I feed my cubs,*" Broc said every time. "*But you would not eat them. I did not know what two-leg cubs eat, but you finally ate roots and berries I brought you.*"

Ash slowed as she approached the sett, sniffing the night air and listening to make sure no wolves or foxes were near before pushing aside the curtain of moss that hid her entrance. She crawled on her hands and knees down a long tunnel to a larger cavity lined with more moss and leaves.

"*Broc? Cuán? Is anyone here?*"

There was no reply. They were still hunting. Ash wrapped herself in her cloak, the one Broc had covered her with the night of the fire. Her fingers traced the frayed threads that made a design in the cloak. She knew Broc's stories of that night, but had no memory of it, or of anything that came before. Absently, she touched the scars that ridged the side of her face. Sometimes, while she slept, she thought she could remember being held by a two-leg woman, being sung to as she had heard them sing around their fires in the village, but when she woke, it was all gone, vanished like smoke.

"*Ash?*"

"*Here,*" she replied.

Within the darkness of the sett, Ash made out the darker shadows of Broc and three nearly grown badger cubs as they waddled through a badger-sized tunnel on the other side of the larger sleeping chamber that had been dug to accommodate Ash as she grew. One of the cubs came to her and deposited a bird egg in her lap.

"*For me?*" Ash reached over and scratched the cub behind his ears. He groaned in enjoyment and flipped over so she could reach his belly. She cracked the eggshell open and tipped the contents into her mouth.

"*Did you hunt?*" Broc asked as she licked her paw and washed her face.

"*Yes. The dogs worked with me and we got meat from the two-legs.*"

Broc looked up from her cleaning. "*Were you careful not to be seen?*"

"*I let them see me,*" Ash said.

Broc sat up taller. "*It is not safe.*"

"*They call me ghost-child in their speech. They will do me no harm.*"

"*Two-legs always do harm,*" Broc said.

Ash lay down with her head resting against Broc's broad, warm body, larger now with the new cubs she would soon give birth to. "*How many winters ago did you find me?*"

"*You know, little one,*" Broc said, snuffling as she licked Ash's face.

"*Tell us again.*" The cubs crowded near, curling up against Ash as they listened to the story they all knew as well as their own names.

"*It was a cold night, eight winters past. Snow was almost upon us...*"

Cuán and the others waited until nightfall to crawl out the tunnels and begin their hunting. Broc was nursing three new cubs, their pink skin only just covered by fine, silvery fur. Their eyes were not yet open.

"*I will return quickly,*" Ash said. She scraped together the soiled bedding from under the new cubs. The disturbance made them cry and wriggle. She carried the debris up the tunnel and out to dispose of it at some distance from the sett. Working quickly in the dark, she gathered more moss and leaves and brought them back inside. She gently lifted the cubs as Broc settled on the fresh bedding with a contented whicker. Ash placed the mewling cubs where they could get to a nipple.

"Thank you."

Ash pressed her forehead to Broc's. *"I will hunt for both of us tonight."*

Once out in the forest, she moved silently, despite her lame leg. She used a stick to dig for wild rutabaga and turnips. She knew the villagers grew these things, but she never took from their crops unless she was desperate. She rubbed the dirt off and munched on one as she dug for more. She gathered up all the earthworms and grubs unearthed by her digging and placed them in a large leaf for carrying. When she had enough, she stood with her prizes gathered in a fold of the cloth she wore. Walking more slowly now, she made her way back toward the sett.

Suddenly, the usual sounds of the night forest – the scuffling noises of mice and voles, the hoots of owls, the squeaks of bats – were drowned by screams. Badger screams. Ash dropped her gathered food and ran as fast as she could in the direction of the screams. Topping a small knoll, she saw four wolves surrounding three badgers. One wolf lunged, teeth bared, and a badger screamed in pain, but all three snarled and bared their teeth as they held off the wolves whose teeth snapped again and again as they tried to get hold of one of the badgers. Ash picked up a large fallen branch and launched herself down the slope, yelling as she did. She swung the branch, catching one wolf in the shoulder and sending it tumbling. Pressing their unexpected advantage, the other badgers advanced, snarling fiercely while Ash continued to swing her stick and yell. The wolves backed away, circled for long heartbeats, and then slunk off into the dark.

Ash dropped her branch and knelt. The injured badger was Cuán, his side covered in warm blood. She gently wrapped her arms around him and picked him up. "*Keep watch. They may return,*" she said to the others as she struggled to stand with his extra weight.

Limping and short of breath with the exertion, she carried him back to the sett. Once inside the entrance, she set him down. He managed to crawl into the room where Broc waited anxiously with the new cubs. There, he collapsed.

"*What happened?*" Broc asked.

"*Wolves.*" It was too dark for Ash to see anything, but her fingers probed the wound in Cuán's side. He barked in pain, gasping. Her fingers were sticky with his blood.

Broc crept near, nudging him with her nose. His breathing was growing shallower. "*Do not die,*" she said.

"*I do not wish to go,*" he gasped.

Ash placed one hand over Cuán's heart and her other over the wound in his side. A white glow began to emanate from under her hands, so that the blood in them and on them glowed red and hot. The light grew until it was blinding to the other badgers. They closed their eyes and backed away as the underground room became brighter than daylight. The light seemed to go on and on until Ash fell to the side, her energy spent. The light went out, leaving the sett darker than ever it was before. Broc crept close again, nuzzling Cuán who stirred and lifted his head. She licked his side where the skin and fur were healed.

Broc turned to Ash who was still and cold. The badger prodded her cheek. "*Little one?*"

Ash opened her eyes, but could not yet sit. "*What happened?*"

"*I am whole again,*" Cuán said. "*How did you do that?*"

Ash lifted her hands, though she could not see them. "*I do not know.*"

Broc placed a paw on Ash's leg. "*Have you ever done that before, little one?*"

"*No. Never. I do not know what happened.*"

The other badgers still cowered in a far corner.

"*Do not be afraid,*" Broc said. Slowly, they came near and nudged Ash and Cuán, sniffing them both.

"Do not tell of this," Cuán said. *"I do not know what it means, but we must keep it secret."*

Deep in an ancient forest, an old woman paused where she knelt, gathering herbs and mushrooms. Cocking her head, Enat listened. She left her basket and got to her feet. She hurried through the forest and came to an enormous ash tree, covered in lichens and moss, its trunk bigger around than six men could encircle. Laying her gnarled hands on the tree, she closed her eyes and stood quietly for a long time.

"At last," she breathed.

CHAPTER 2

The Reaping

Enat stopped to survey the village below her. It was like countless others – a small grouping of perhaps a score of dwellings – some made of stacked stone, others of wood daubed with mud and moss to keep out the cold and wet. She rested her staff against a tree and chewed on an early stalk of asparagus while she watched the activity for a while. The village was situated in a broad, shallow valley. In the distance, a herd of sheep and cattle and goats grazed, tended by older children. There was a large plot of cultivated land outside the cluster of dwellings, the soil in neat rows even this early in the year. It was near a stream for ease of carrying water. Some of the dwellings had smoke rising from a central smoke hole in the roof, but most had fire pits outside their doors. She saw a mix of women and young children below, but only a couple of old men. She hadn't passed any signs of war parties, so most likely, the other men were off hunting for the celebration. Several dogs roamed the village, sniffing and digging for any leftover bits of food near the fires. She hitched the ropes of her basket higher onto her shoulders, grabbed her stick, and began the trek down the hill. As she neared, she bent over and began to hobble, leaning on her stick as if she were lame.

"Herbs? Shells?"

She called out as she entered the village, and the women paused to watch her. She slipped the ropes off her shoulders and set her basket down, sitting on a log pulled up near a fire.

"Welcome, grandmother," said one of the women, her belly large with new life. "May we offer you some cold water?"

"Thank you, daughter," said Enat, honoring the hospitality accorded her. She accepted a gourd filled with water and drank deeply. "That makes an old woman feel refreshed." She reached into her basket, soft and pliable, woven from reeds, and pulled out a purple shell, already strung on a woven cord. "For you and the wee one to come." She placed a hand on the woman's belly. "Health to you both."

"Thank you," the woman said. Her face lit up as she turned the shell over in her hands.

Other women gathered around, looking to see what the old woman offered. They had little to trade: some bone needles and gut thread, dried meat and salted fish from their stream. Soon, all Enat had brought with her to trade was gone, all but her salves and potions.

"Have you a healer?" she asked the women.

"We did, grandmother," said the woman who had offered her water. "But she was very old and passed on this winter past. Are you a healer?"

Enat nodded. "I am. Tomorrow eve is Imbolc. It will be a full moon as well. A good omen for the spring." She smiled at the woman's bulging abdomen. "Not that you need more. Brighid has been good to you?"

"Aye, grandmother," said the woman. "My man and I have five others. All have lived, praise Brighid."

"You are blessed," said Enat. She looked around. "Are there others here, anyone your healer was training?"

"None. None here have the gift." The woman sat beside Enat on the log, grunting a little with the effort of lowering her bulky body.

"Oh, many of us know a little of healing herbs and roots, but none have magic."

Enat smiled. "I will stay through the celebration of Imbolc, if you like."

"We would be honored to have you," said the woman. "I am Rós."

"I am Enat." She reached deeper into her basket and retrieved a heavy woolen cloak. "I am weary. I am going to rest in the sun."

She made of her cloak a pad to sit on and placed it at the base of an oak tree standing on the edge of the village. She sat with her eyes closed, her face tilted to the warmth of the sun, just now moving toward spring where it would soon give life to all. As she sat, her hands rested on the roots of the tree, and she listened. She cast her mind out, probing. Nothing for the moment. All was quiet. *You will come.*

Ash huddled in the sett, her knees hugged to her chest as she listened. The day before and through the night, she had heard something, almost a whisper on the wind. She was afraid. It spoke to her as the four-legs did, but it was different. She knew it was a human voice - the first that had ever spoken to her like this. She had never questioned how she could speak to Broc and the others when no other two-leg seemed able to.

All the day long, she had listened. Cautiously, she had crept from the sett and made her way into the forest, taking care to remain hidden. From deep within a thicket of holly, she watched an old woman move through the forest, gathering white snowdrops from where they bloomed in patches, pushing their way up through the forest loam. She watched as the woman cut stout branches from the blackthorn, placing all of her gatherings in a woven basket she wore on her back. Once, the woman straightened and seemed to look straight at the place where Ash was hidden. Ash had remained frozen in place until the old woman wandered off to look for more snowdrops.

Only after she had disappeared from view did Ash crawl from her thicket and return to the sett where Broc was still nursing her cubs.

"Did you not hunt last night?" Broc got up from the nest. Her cubs cried at the loss of her heat and milk. She came to rest against Ash's leg.

"No."

"I heard it."

Ash laid a hand on her wide back. *"It is an old two-leg female. Do you know what she wants?"*

"No. But I think you must go see, little one." Broc raised her head. *"She calls for you."*

As darkness fell, Ash left the sett. She made her way to the village by a circuitous route so that she came to it from the far side. From above the village, she watched the humans below as they gathered together around a fire lit in the center of the village. The old woman she had seen earlier lit a torch from the fire and went from dwelling to dwelling, hobbling along with her stick, which Ash found curious, as she had walked quickly and without difficulty through the forest. Using her torch, she lit small fires that had been prepared in front of each, and she passed out bunches of the snowdrops and blackthorn branches she had gathered. One of the men began hitting a stick against a stretched animal skin, and the others began moving, all in rhythm with the beating of the stick.

Ash watched them in fascination. She forgot to watch the old woman and suddenly realized that she was no longer visible down in the village. In alarm, Ash looked about, scanning the outskirts of the dwellings, but the woman was nowhere to be seen. She backed out of her hiding place and stood.

"I know you are here."

Ash froze at the sound of the woman's voice in her head.

"I have come to speak with you. Will you not come to me?"

Ash looked around in terror. She could not tell from which direction it came. Silently, she crept through the forest, retracing the same route she had taken. Moving farther away from the village and the continued beating of the stick, she rounded a heavy thicket and nearly stepped on the woman who was sitting with her back against a tree.

The light of the full moon was nearly as bright as daylight to Ash's eyes, and she could see the woman's eyes fix her with a gaze that was not unfriendly.

"I mean you no harm," the woman said aloud.

Ash feigned deafness.

"I am Enat. I know you can hear and speak, though you pretend you cannot. The women in the village told me of the ghost-child, and I knew you were the one I seek."

Ash looked around for the best escape route.

"I mean you no harm," Enat repeated. "I have come to find you because you have power. I have felt it."

Ash turned back to her, but said nothing.

"Who raised you?"

Ash looked at her in puzzlement.

"Who cared for you, when you were younger?"

Ash's eyes reflected her understanding, but she was not willing to speak aloud to this two-leg. *"My clan. Broc and Cuán saved me and hunted for me."*

Enat nodded. "I would be honored to meet your clan and speak with them. I will not harm them."

Ash looked back down toward the village where the sounds of the humans celebrating had grown louder.

"They will not trouble us," Enat said, as if she could read Ash's mind. "None will follow."

She got to her feet, and Ash noticed that here again, she did not lean on her stick and hobble, but strode along swiftly as Ash limped beside her.

Ash called out ahead as she approached the sett. *"Broc? Cuán? I am not alone."* But she was certain they already knew that.

Enat paused and said, "I will wait here. You may speak to them and bring them to me, if they will so honor me."

Ash went on ahead, glancing back once to see that Enat had settled on the ground again, waiting. Even so, she did not enter the sett. She would not take the chance of exposing the hidden entrance to this two-leg, no matter that she spoke their language. She waited and, before long, heard the snuffling of Broc and Cuán as they approached, their heads high as they sniffed the air, the white stripes on their heads gleaming brightly in the moonlight.

"*She asks to meet you,*" Ash said. "*She speaks as we speak.*"

Cuán snorted. "*I do not trust any two-leg. It is a trap.*"

Broc nuzzled him. "*She came looking for Ash. I have heard her. I will meet her.*"

Cuán huffed his displeasure, but shuffled along behind as Ash led them to where Enat sat.

Enat looked up at their approach. If she was surprised to see Ash accompanied by two badgers, she did not show it. She bowed her head. She reached into her pocket and retrieved a handful of shelled nuts and berries. "*I bring an offering of friendship to those who cared for a human cub.*"

Cuán backed away suspiciously, but Broc approached, sniffing tentatively at the berries she had left on the ground. Enat reached out and plucked one of the berries, placing it in her own mouth. "*You do not have these in season here.*"

Broc nibbled on one of the nuts. "*We offer thanks.*"

Enat smiled. "*I am called Enat. You wonder why I am here.*" She gestured to Ash to sit. "*I have felt the stirrings of power in this one for a long time.*" She settled comfortably against a tree. "*Tell me of how you saved her.*"

She listened as Broc, with a little help from Cuán, told the tale of the night they had found Ash. Enat frowned, looking more closely at the ridges on Ash's face. Ash pulled her arms and legs more tightly under the cloth she wore as Enat's sharp eyes probed her.

"*But there was something, something stronger, something different last moon, was there not?*" Enat asked.

The badgers looked at each other.

"*Tell her,*" Cuán said.

Enat nodded as Broc told of how Ash had healed Cuán's wound. "*This is what I felt that night, and I knew it was time.*" She looked at Ash. "*Your power is growing as you grow. Now, you are like a storm that blows up without warning and without control. I can offer the teaching to control and use your power.*"

"*How?*" Ash remained suspicious.

"*You would come with me,*" Enat said. "*To a very ancient part of the forest.*"

Ash watched her. "*Are there other two-legs?*"

Enat nodded. "*Yes. There are others. But all are like us. When we feel the stirrings of magic, we leave to reap, to gather young ones like you, who have shown signs of power, and bring them back to be trained in our ways. We are not like the villagers.*"

"*How long would I be gone?*"

Enat's gaze rested on Broc's bright eyes. "*Long. If you come, you will not return to see Broc and Cuán.*"

Ash's eyes blazed. "*No!*"

Broc lifted her head. "*Hush, little one. Let us speak. When do you leave?*"

Enat spoke gently. "*You are wise, Broc. I leave tomorrow at mid-day.*" She looked at Ash. "*If you do not come to me, I will take that as your answer, and I will not trouble you again.*" She got to her feet. "*Thank you for speaking with me. You have newborn cubs. May I give them a blessing of health on this night when we celebrate life?*"

Broc bowed her head. Enat raised her staff, and her lips uttered words Ash did not understand. The staff glowed like the moon. Ash gasped and backed away.

"*There.*" Enat lowered her stick, and it looked again like ordinary wood. "*I cannot promise they will not be hunted, but they will not die of illness.*"

"*Thank you.*" Broc looked up at Enat. "*We will speak of what you have said.*"

Enat turned and left them, moving away on feet as silent as Ash's own.

Broc and Cuán led the way back to the sett. The cubs whimpered for Broc and settled contentedly to nurse when she lay down beside them. Ash lay down as well, resting her head against Cuán.

"*I will not leave you,*" Ash said.

"*I want you to listen to us, little one,*" Broc said solemnly. "*Though we have raised you and you are part of our clan, you are a two-leg. You will live much longer than badgers. If you stay with us, Cuán and I will still leave you. We are already in the second age for our kind. We will never make you leave, and you may stay with the clan all your days. But you should consider what Enat offers you. With her, you will not be an outcast, as you would be among other two-legs.*"

Ash's eyes filled with tears. "*I do not want to leave you. I love you.*"

Cuán nudged her. "*And we love you, little one. But Broc is right. Even if you stay, we will leave you one day. You should think on what Enat said while you hunt.*"

Ash turned her head, wiping her tears against Cuán's sleek fur. "*I do not want to hunt tonight.*"

Broc whickered. "*Let us all stay here for our last night together.*"

Ash woke early and went to gather food for a last meal with Broc and Cuán, plus some extra for her journey. She had not asked Enat how far they would travel. She could think of nothing to say as she tried to eat.

"*I will not tell you to not be sad, little one,*" Broc said. Badgers could not cry, but her voice in Ash's head was muffled.

The other badgers came to join them, the cubs squirming into Ash's lap and nuzzling her ears. When she could stand it no longer, Ash crawled out the tunnel of the sett – for the last time, she realized – and stood.

"*Take this,*" Cuán said, dragging out her old cloak, the one they had wrapped her in the night they found her. "*You will need it.*"

Ash draped it over her shoulders and then dropped to her knees to give them a final hug. "*I will miss you.*"

"*And we you, little one.*"

With a cry that sounded as if her heart were being ripped out of her chest, Ash pushed to her feet and ran. She refused to look back, for she knew, if she did, she could never leave them.

Ash did not know where to find Enat, so she simply climbed a hill above the village and waited. Her eyes were swollen with crying. She was still crying when Enat found her. "Come." She led the way, letting Ash weep as she followed. They walked for a long time, as the sun traveled across the sky and began to settle behind the hills. Only then did Enat say, "I know it was hard to leave your clan, but I'm glad you came."

Ash said nothing, only wiped her nose with the edge of her cloak. Enat did not speak again until darkness had fallen. She found a clearing under an overhang of rock.

"This will offer us some shelter."

Ash thought it offered no shelter at all. *"We should look for a tunnel where we can take shelter."*

Enat shrugged her basket from her shoulders. "You will have to learn to speak aloud. Not all can hear as you do. Gather some wood and we will make a fire."

"Why?"

Enat looked at her.

"Why?" Ash said again, aloud this time. Her voice sounded strange to her ears.

"For warmth," said Enat. "It is cold above ground this time of year. I have food the villagers gave me in thanks."

Ash went off to gather wood, but, never having built a fire, she brought only twigs and brush. Enat shook her head.

"We need some of this, but we need more like these." She picked up a branch as thick as her arm. "Find more of these."

By the time Ash returned, Enat had a fire kindled. She showed Ash how to add wood to it. Fascinated, Ash held her hands out to the heat. She had only had fleeting visits to the villagers' fires to steal food. Not since Broc pulled her from the fire had she been this close to one.

"Do they hurt?" Enat said.

Ash looked up in question.

"Your burns. Do they hurt?"

Ash opened her mouth, but no sound came out as she searched for words. "I do not know... hurt."

Enat reached out to touch a fingertip to Ash's face. "Is there pain?"

"No."

"Show me your leg."

Ash pulled up the cloth she wore, and Enat took Ash's leg in her hands. Turning it to the fire, she saw the pink skin behind the knee, stretched tightly so that the knee could not straighten. She then took Ash's arm and did likewise. The elbow was bent, the skin there looking as if it had melted, pink and shiny in the firelight. When she tried to straighten the elbow, Ash gasped and pulled away.

"I'm sorry. I did not mean to hurt you."

Enat turned to her basket and retrieved a bundle wrapped in cloth. "This is bread." She tore a chunk loose and handed it to Ash who sniffed it curiously. She touched her tongue to it, and then pulled a piece off and put it in her mouth. Her eyes widened as she chewed. She quickly stuffed another piece into her mouth. The only bread she had ever had had been the burned or moldy chunks tossed away by the villagers. This was nothing like that. Enat reached for another bundle, similarly wrapped in a cloth. "And this is cheese." This time, Ash took a bite without hesitation. "Good?"

Ash gave a low growl of contentment. Enat looked up from her food.

"Among humans," she said, "that sound would not be comforting, though I'm guessing among badgers, it's a happy sound?"

Ash lowered her head.

"Don't feel bad." Enat reached out and patted her knee. "You have much to learn. You haven't lived among two-legs since you were very small."

Ash tilted her head as she listened to Enat's speech. She swallowed a large mouthful. "Will you teach me?"

Enat nodded. "I and others. You will learn from many of us. We each know different things, different kinds of magic."

Ash glanced at her. "How did you find me? Did four-legs show you?"

"We call them animals. You will learn the human names of the different kinds of animals," Enat said. "But no. The trees told me of you."

Ash was so astounded, she forgot to eat. "The trees?"

Enat smiled. "Yes." She reached out and placed Ash's hand on the trunk of a gnarled pine tree. "Listen. Reach out with your heart and mind."

Ash listened. From under her hand, she became aware of a vibration and a very faint pulse, as if the tree had a heartbeat. It did not speak in thoughts or words, not as the badgers and the humans did. But gradually, she became aware of feelings, images – a great storm, a flood, the passage of time – and she gasped.

"Trees do not bother with small things," Enat said. "To them we are no more than ants, but they sense the big changes that occur, and they can tell of magic and power, for they are of that power. Do not ask a tree where to find a fish, but if you wish to know what happened long before you were alive, a tree might be willing to tell you if you know how to listen."

"Cannot all humans do this? The ones with magic?"

Enat shook her head. "Only some of us. Others can move wind and water. Some can call fire from the earth. We all have certain gifts that we were born with; others we have to learn how to use, but they will never feel as natural. All of us learn to heal, to call up the elements, and we can learn to hide things." She waved her hand and, suddenly, was not there.

Ash cried out and scrambled away. With a word, Enat was once again sitting before her.

"Will I learn to do that?"

"If you wish." Enat narrowed her eyes. "But what we do, we do only when necessary. To do magic requires energy. How did you feel after you healed Cuán?"

Ash thought back. "I do not remember. I think I was weak."

Enat nodded. "What you did took a great deal of energy, especially for someone untrained. If you exceed your energy, you must draw upon other sources. That is never something we do lightly, for it might take a life. All of this, you will learn."

Ash drew closer to the fire, as the night was growing cold. She stared into the flames, thinking about everything Enat had said. Loneliness pressed upon her as she thought about Broc and Cuán in the warm, safe sett. Tears pricked her eyes again.

Enat must have seen, for she said, "I'm sure they are missing you as well. We should sleep now. We have a long journey ahead of us."

CHAPTER 3

The Forest

If Ash had thought Enat would wait until they reached their destination before beginning to teach her, she was wrong. They moved slowly, as Enat kept pausing to pluck plants and roots from the ground, teaching Ash their names and uses.

"They will look different when they have leaves," Enat told her, but she insisted Ash needed to know what they look like in all seasons.

It wouldn't occur to Ash until much later to wonder whether Enat took so much time because Ash couldn't walk as quickly as she. Though Ash's bent leg was strong, she had never walked this long or this far from the sett before. They walked from sunup to sundown for days and Ash was exhausted each night.

She was fascinated by Enat's clothes – leggings and a woolen tunic. She thought her own loose cloth was more practical, as she could move freely enough, but when the wind blew, the cold air chilled her body, and she could not get warm. She missed having other badgers to cuddle up to for warmth. Her feet were tough as horn on the bottoms, but they, too, got cold as they traveled over hills still covered by snow. Enat wore leather boots, but Ash shuddered as she touched them.

"Skins?"

"Yes," said Enat. "We hunt animals sometimes and keep a small flock of chickens. But we always honor the spirit of the animal for feeding us and providing us with skin and bone."

Ash did not look convinced. She knew the villagers hunted, and she had stolen meat from them many times, but she did not wear animal skins. "The skin and bone are better left with the animal."

Enat laughed, a sound that startled Ash at first. She had heard the villagers do this thing sometimes, but she had never laughed herself. She tried to emulate what Enat did, but it sounded like a crow's screech.

"Never mind," Enat said with a smile. "Not all humans laugh. You will, if something moves you to it."

The more time Ash spent with Enat and the more Enat spoke of things about which Ash knew nothing, the less certain she was that she belonged among other two-legs. "I will not be like them."

"No," Enat agreed. "You will be like you. And that is good enough."

Ash did not understand this.

A few times, Enat paused when they encountered other two-leg settlements. She studied them from afar for a bit before choosing to detour around them. This puzzled Ash, as Enat had willingly gone into the village near the sett, but she obediently followed as they gave these settlements a wide berth.

On their fifth day of traveling, they climbed the largest hill Ash had ever seen. As they reached the summit, she gasped. "What is it?"

Enat's eyes crinkled in amusement, a look Ash was beginning to recognize, as she did it often when Ash expressed surprise over something she had never seen or heard before. "That is a lake."

"Is it the endless water the birds speak of?"

"No." Enat pointed. "See? There is land on the far side. At the ocean, you cannot see any land."

Ash had never seen so much water and she could not imagine more water, so wide that no land was visible. Enat pointed to another range of hills, so far in the distance that they were little more than a purple smudge against the sky. "That is where we are going. Beyond those hills is our forest."

Far from being reassured, Ash felt an emptiness inside her. As Enat had talked of leaving her clan and never seeing Broc and Cuán again, Ash had still harbored a tiny hope that it might not be so final. But this was so very far… Never had she imagined such immense distances.

Ash was quiet as they settled for the night. She knew now how to strike metal against flint to create sparks and kindle a fire. Enat found some wild onions and shoved them under the coals to roast. They tasted good with a bit of the dried meat she had in her bag.

That night, Ash lay watching the fire until Enat slept and the fire grew low. She got to her feet, wrapped her cloak around her and crept away into the dark. The moon was waning, but there was still enough light to see by as she made her way back down the hill. She no longer wanted to learn magic. She did not want to live among two-legs. She wanted the comfort and warmth of those she loved. As she walked, she heard the scuffling of small animals in the underbrush. She realized she had not spoken with a four-leg since she and Enat had begun their journey. She called out.

"I am one of you."

There was only silence for a long while, then a timid voice said, *"We do not know you."*

"I am of a clan far from here," she said. *"I will not harm you. Will you not show yourself?"*

The bushes rustled and a young vixen peeked out, her nose twitching as she sniffed. *"How is it that a two-leg can speak to us?"*

"I do not know." Ash squatted down. *"I have always. My clan of badgers raised me from a cub."* She held a hand out, but the vixen backed away.

"You are not of us." With a flash of her white-tipped tail, the fox was gone.

Ash sat there for a long time, listening. She could hear small voices whispering around her, and she knew that other animals watched her, but none would approach. At last, she stood and squared her shoulders and made her way back up the hill to the fire where Enat still slept. All flame was gone. Only the coals remained, pulsing with a red glow as if they breathed. She placed more wood on them and watched as flames began to lick at the bark. She looked across at Enat and saw that her eyes were open.

"I thought you might not come back."

"I thought I might not, as well." Ash returned her gaze to the fire. "I do not belong anywhere."

Enat said nothing for a while. "It's true. You are different. You are not fully animal or fully human. That is not a bad thing. But you will have to find your own way."

Ash said nothing, but lay down, covered by her cloak.

Enat pulled her cloak more tightly under her chin. "I'm glad you returned."

The next day they traveled down the far side of the hill, pausing near the lake. As she had when she came to find Ash, Enat began hobbling, leaning on her staff as they entered the tiny village at the edge of the lake. She spoke to a man there, handing him something, and then turned to Ash.

"We've time for a little diversion," she said.

Enat got into a small boat and gestured to Ash to get in. She rowed Ash out onto the water. Ash gripped the sides, her hands tightly clenched as the boat moved in rhythm with Enat's pulls on the oars. Gradually, she relaxed, enjoying the rocking motion of the boat. Silvery fish darted below them.

"Can you call them?" Enat asked.

Ash had never tried talking to fish. She reached out with her mind and looked up at Enat with a gasp. "They heard me!" Several fish approached the surface of the water, their mouths opening and closing as they stared up at her. With a sudden splash, they leapt from the water and dove again. Ash leaned over the boat to watch them.

"Stop!"

Enat stopped rowing, and the boat stilled on the water. As the ripples of their movement faded, the water became smooth. Ash raised a hand to her face, touching her scars.

"Have you never seen yourself?" Enat asked gently.

"No. All the water near the sett moved. It was not still. Not like this." Ash fingered her hair, matted and tangled with twigs and moss. She looked at Enat, whose silver hair was smooth, tied back with a woven leather cord. "I used a sharp stone to cut it when it got too long. It does not look like yours."

"No, it doesn't." Enat reached out. "I can cut it for you."

Ash touched her scars again. "But you cannot change this."

Enat said nothing, but picked the oars up and rowed them back to shore where the owner of the boat waited.

They journeyed on, skirting the lake and leaving it far below them as they climbed the hills on the far side. That night, sitting near their fire, Enat pulled a silver knife from a sheath on her belt and cut Ash's hair.

"How much more?"

Ash reached up and felt the rough ends at her shoulders. "All. Cut it all."

"Are you sure?"

"It will grow back."

Enat cut the rest of Ash's hair, leaving only stubble all over her head, everywhere except where her scars extended over her right temple. There, no hair grew. "Your hair is red," she said in surprise. "Like a fox," she added at Ash's questioning look. "I did not realize."

Ash picked up the matted tangles of hair lying on the ground and lifted them to her face. They smelled of badgers and, suddenly, she was lonely again for her clan.

"We will arrive at the forest day after tomorrow," Enat said. "You will have to ask permission to enter."

Ash looked up sharply. "The trees?"

Enat nodded, a gesture she had had to explain to Ash, who did not understand at first. "The trees, but also the animals there."

"What if they say no?"

"They will not," Enat assured her. "But the forest is theirs to grant permission or no. We must never assume we are welcome." She was quiet for a while. "There is one thing more you must know. Once the forest grants you entrance, you may not leave it again until your training is complete, or you will not be permitted to re-enter."

"How long?"

Enat shrugged. "As long as it takes. It is different for each of us. But the forest knows when we are ready."

"Have others left before they were ready?"

"Yes." Enat poked the fire with a stick. "They live in villages, healing and making potions. They still have magic, but it is weak."

"Why do they leave?"

"Different reasons," Enat said. "The lessons are hard. They miss their families. Other reasons sometimes."

Ash was quickly learning that Enat did not answer all questions completely, and that further questioning was of no use. She reached out to pluck the sleeve of Enat's tunic.

"Will I have clothes like yours?"

"Would you like to?"

Ash remembered to nod. She looked down at the cloth she wore. "Cuán took this from a woman who was washing clothes in a stream. He brought it back to the sett for me. He said I was like a newborn cub, with no fur, except I would never grow fur."

"Broc and Cuán were very wise," Enat said. "They raised you well. You will honor them among the creatures of the forest."

Ash felt the forest before she saw it. She hadn't wanted to admit to Enat how weary she was as they climbed yet another hill, clambering over low rock walls and following deer trails through patches of woods. A sudden wall of fog awaited them, which Ash found odd. Fog usually settled in the low places, not the high. Cuán had taught her how to use it to hide and move silently through the mist. She approached, her head tilted as she listened. She looked at Enat to find that she had stopped a few paces earlier, and was watching with a small smile. Ash turned back to the wall of fog and stepped nearer. She held out her hand and reached into the cool droplets. They immediately parted to create an opening in the curtain of mist, and Ash stepped through, with Enat following.

Ash gasped as soon she passed through the veil.

"You hear it?" Enat asked softly from beside her.

"Yes," Ash breathed, not wanting to disturb. All around her, lower than her actual hearing, but somehow audible nonetheless, was a hum of life such as she had never felt. Everything around her, the very ground upon which she stood, thrummed and pulsed. For the remainder of her life, she would recall the wonder of that first meeting with this mystical forest as it welcomed her.

All around stood the largest trees she had ever seen in her life, surrounded by many smaller ones – yews and oaks and ash and others she did not know. The ground beneath them was covered in ferns and more white snowdrops and small purple flowers. Ash squatted down to take a closer look.

"An early orchid," Enat said, kneeling next to her, holding the delicate purple flower.

Ash closed her eyes and placed her hands on the earth, digging her fingers in a little. "Why?"

Enat looked at her. "Why what?"

"Why is it like this here?" Ash opened her eyes. "Why are there so many voices?"

"This is a sacred place," Enat said. "The things that live here carry the wisdom of all who came before. There are other places like this. You will know them when you meet them, for they will speak to you, also." She placed a hand on Ash's shoulder. "Come. We are nearly at our journey's end."

Ash's weariness was forgotten as she got to her feet and followed Enat. Every now and again, she paused to lay her hands on a tree, listening for a moment before trotting after Enat.

Though Enat had said they were nearly there, it seemed to Ash that they walked on and on before at last coming to any other sign of people. A shallow valley held a small cluster of stone dwellings, some built entirely of rock, their cone shapes pointed at the top, others thatched to keep rain out. A stream ran nearby, tumbling and gurgling over rocks. At their arrival, a few people appeared, mixed older and young, male and female.

One man, enormous, with a wild head of black hair and a beard covering most of his face, stepped forward. "Enat." He greeted her by placing his huge hands on her shoulders and bending to touch his forehead to hers.

He turned. "Who have you brought?"

Enat rested a hand on Ash's shoulder. "This is Ash." Enat gestured toward the man. "This is Ivar."

Ivar looked at her curiously, his black eyes raking her face, taking in her scars, her naked head. His nose twitched as he sniffed, and he suddenly reminded Ash of a bear she had seen once, snuffling as he trundled along, hunting grubs.

"We should have known you were coming by the smell alone," he said.

Enat was unperturbed. "We have had a long journey. We can both use a bath." She nodded to him and the others, and led Ash away, back into the forest.

"Will we not live there, with them?" Ash hurried to catch up.

Enat shook her head. "My cottage is a wee bit farther on. I prefer solitude." She glanced at Ash, her eyes twinkling. "I guess you would prefer it as well."

Ash was filled a sense of relief. Through all their journey, she had been fretting silently about having to live among a group of humans. She still felt a little ill at ease even with Enat, who had been only kind to her. She had watched the villagers near her sett enough to know that they sometimes fought, especially the children. She had seen several of them beating up on one child, yelling and jeering, far out on the hills when they were supposed to be tending the cattle and goats and sheep, and there were no grown humans nearby. Again, Enat seemed to read her thoughts.

"The other young ones who are here for training live together in separate houses – one for the girls, one for the boys. You'll meet them, but not just yet."

She led Ash around a twist in the trail to a small cottage, thatched like the others, but with plants growing along the walls. Enat pushed open the wooden door and Ash followed her inside. Daylight came through the openings in the walls, but the cottage was dark and cold. Enat pointed to the hearth.

It was unlike anything Ash had ever seen. Built of stacked stone, it contained a deep cavity that was blackened, with a circle of stones sitting amid the ashes. A metal rod was suspended in some way from the stone so that it could swing over the fire. Strangest of all was a tall column of stone that went through the cottage's roof. Ash stuck her head inside and craned her neck to look up.

"It's called a chimney," Enat said. "It allows us to have a fire inside and yet channel all the smoke out through the hole in the stone. Will you light a fire for us?"

Ash found a pile of twigs and shredded bark for tinder, but no wood. She turned to Enat in question.

"Use the peat," Enat said, pointing again to blocks of dirt stacked next to the hearth. She came over. "We don't cut wood here. Even the fallen trees are sacred. Only the branches that fall do we use and sometimes we ask permission to cut live branches and flowers for medicines. The trunks of the fallen become homes for other life. All of the wood we build with or make things from comes from outside the forest. This..." She held up a brick of peat. "This is dug from the earth. When it's dried, 'twill burn." She showed Ash how to stack the peat bricks around the tinder and watched as Ash struck a steel to her flint to light it.

Almost immediately, the cottage began to warm. Looking around, Ash saw that the rafters were hung with bunches and bunches of dried plants and flowers.

"Now, for our baths," Enat said.

She gathered up an armful of folded cloth and led Ash deeper into the forest, to another stone building that housed a small pool of water. Nearby was a stone fire pit already filled with blocks of peat. Rather than using steel and flint, Enat waved her hand and the peat ignited into large flames. The interior of the building quickly warmed.

"Where does the water come from?" Ash looked around for a source.

"A small stream has been blocked for our use here," Enat said, stripping off her travel-stained clothing. She plunged into the water. Ash stood on the edge, unwilling to follow.

"Have you never taken a bath?" Enat asked.

"No," Ash said, dipping her foot into the icy water and withdrawing it immediately. "Not like this. Only with my hands." She dipped a hand into the water and rubbed it on her arm to show Enat.

"That is not good enough. You can't wash your hair like that. It's only cold when you first jump in." Enat picked up a handful of sand from the bottom of the pool and rubbed it on her arms.

Ash pulled off her cloak and the cloth she wore and jumped in, immediately sinking over her head. She sputtered and coughed as she came back up. The water stung like a thousand nettles pricking her everywhere at once, but, as Enat had said, the stinging lasted only a little while, and then the water felt almost warm. Emulating Enat, she used sand to scrub her skin, though the sand had quite a bit more dirt to scrub off in her case. Soon, Ash was pink as a newborn cub.

"Let me do your back," Enat said.

After some scrubbing that left Ash wondering if she would have any skin left, Enat inspected her work. "That will do."

She reached for a small jar Ash had not noticed and scooped out a fragrant handful of thick liquid that she rubbed all over the short hair on Ash's head and then she did her own. She showed Ash how to duck under the water to rinse her head. With more sputtering, Ash wiped the water out of her eyes.

"This is not worth saving," Enat said, lifting Ash's old cloth. "But this is." She pulled the cloak into the water, scrubbing it and rinsing it. As she lifted it, the colors woven into the cloth had new life, red and blue and yellow. Enat inspected the design more closely, and looked at Ash. "This will do as well."

They clambered out of the water and wrapped themselves in the clean cloaks Enat had brought from the cottage. Ash was reluctant to leave the warmth of the bathhouse, and her teeth chattered as they made their way back to the cottage. On the way, Enat pointed to yet another small building.

"It is called a latrine. We use them to relieve ourselves. Of course, we do not have them everywhere in the forest, but we use them when we can."

Ash nodded. "Badgers, also. We do not soil our setts once we are no longer nursing cubs. We always have a place far away for such things." She looked at Enat. "But I have never seen things such as these among the villagers near our sett. Nor your chimney."

Enat smiled. "Some of our kind have traveled to far-away lands, and have brought back here the best of what those people have discovered or built."

Enat hung Ash's cloak to dry and sat her on a stool pulled up close to the fire while she rummaged in a carved wooden trunk sitting in a far corner.

"I think these will fit you," Enat said, holding out some clothes.

Ash pulled on a pair of leggings and a tunic. The tunic hung to her knees, but Enat cinched it with a length of braided leather and nodded.

"Better." She donned clean clothing of her own and joined Ash at the fire where she put a kettle on the hook and swung it over the flames. "Now, we can have some things we could not have while we traveled."

Soon, Ash held a steaming cup of tea. Her eyes widened at the aromatic liquid that warmed as it slid down her gullet.

"Good?"

Ash nodded, taking another sip. "It tastes of… of summer."

Enat laughed. "It does. It has many grasses and herbs that grow in summer. I will show you how to make it."

She mixed water with some ground flour and nuts and, explaining as she worked, placed the cakes on a flat stone and slid it into the hot coals. Ash's stomach growled hungrily as this new aroma began to fill the cottage. At last, the cakes were baked.

"Be careful," Enat said. "These will be hot."

Despite the warning, Ash burned her fingers picking a cake off the stone. She blew on the hot oatcake until she could take a bite. Never had she tasted anything like this. She gobbled it down, quickly followed by three more. Warmed by the fire, clean and dressed in new clothes, and now with her belly full, Ash's eyes began to close and her head to nod as she sat there. She thought maybe Enat was saying something, but her voice sounded very far away....

"She looks like a runt."

"She was rescued by a clan of badgers and raised by them."

"You jest."

"No."

Ash listened from where she lay on a warm mat, covered with a heavy woolen throw. She had never slept on anything so soft and comfortable. She inhaled and recognized the scent of lavender. The shaggy shadow of a bear-like man moved over the wall next to her as he approached. She closed her eyes and lay without moving. He was silent for a moment.

"Are you sure about her?"

"Ivar, I felt her power. From here."

"From here?"

"Yes. All natural. She's had almost no contact with humans. I've never encountered another so strong at such a young age. I think it may be because she's used her power to communicate with them ever since they saved her."

She heard his big feet shuffle away and opened her eyes.

"What –?" Ivar's shadow pointed. "Where did that come from?"

"It's hers," Enat said. "The badgers took it from a fallen warrior the night they rescued her. She's had it ever since."

Ivar's shadow disappeared from the wall as he went to Enat. "Does she know?"

"No. I didn't realize myself until I washed it last night. And I think it best if it stays that way. At least for now."

Ash lay very still.

"Hmmm." Ivar cleared his throat. "We'll see how she progresses."

"Ivar, she shows great promise, but she will make mistakes. We must give her a chance."

CHAPTER 4

Fire and Crow

For several days, Enat was the only person Ash saw. The girl was still fatigued from their journey, and she found her days and nights turned around. Living with the badgers, she had been in the habit of sleeping during the day and hunting at night. Since leaving with Enat, she had had to learn to change that pattern, but night seemed a strange time to sleep when so many animals were about. She looked longingly at her soft sleeping mat – filled with feathers, Enat had told her – while Enat was trying to teach her about herbs and medicines. Enat must have seen, for she said several times, "Go and rest. We will talk more later." Never had Ash slept so much or so deeply. Within a few days, she felt more rested and began to take a greater interest in her surroundings as Enat took her for walks through the forest around their cottage.

"Why did you pretend to be lame?" Ash asked as Enat strode quickly through the forest. "With the villagers where I first saw you and again at the lake. You pretended to be lame."

Enat glanced at her. "Why did you pretend you couldn't speak or hear?"

"It was safer if they thought I could not understand their speech."

"Even so. Not all believe now in the old ways. They fear magic, and I seem less of a threat as a crippled old woman," Enat said.

"Why do they fear it?"

Enat did not answer immediately, but paused to pluck some plants, shaking the dirt off the roots before placing them into her bag. "There are men who have come to our land. They want others to believe in their god. They don't believe in magic, and they have taught some of the people to fear it. The village near your sett was not such a village. The women there did not fear what I offered. Until I know how the villagers feel about it, I pretend to be a harmless old woman."

Ash did not know much about magic, and she did not know what a god was, but it had never occurred to her that not all humans believed in the same things. "Is that why we did not go to those villages on our journey?"

"Yes. The monks and their followers control those villages. For myself, I'm not afraid, but you haven't enough magic yet to defend yourself if there would be trouble."

"They would fight?"

"Yes, sometimes." Enat walked on. "Sometimes they fight over differing beliefs, sometimes over land, sometimes for no good reason at all."

Ash thought about this as she followed, pondering what had led to the destruction of her village, for Broc had told her many times about the raid. She'd never thought before about why it had happened, and wondered now why she had not.

She had expected to be doing magic with Enat and others as soon as she arrived, but she was wrong. Most days were spent like this one, with Enat putting her to work gathering roots and plants, teaching her how to prepare them and hang them to dry. Some they cut up, some they ground into a fine powder, some they steeped in water and placed in containers unlike anything Ash had ever seen the villagers use.

"This is glass," Enat said. She held one up to the light so Ash could see through the thing, glowing green. "It does not absorb the liquid as clay would. Another thing we learned and brought back from invaders of a neighboring land."

While they worked, Enat spoke of ordinary things. She told of growing up, one girl among ten brothers in a fishing village on the coast. Rapt, Ash listened to her tales of being out on the sea – Ash still could not envision endless water or waves. Sometimes, she thought she could almost remember what it was like to live among humans, to have music and dancing and laughter – she still couldn't laugh. As she listened, she learned without realizing. She found herself using the new words Enat was teaching her, adjusting to life with another human. Adjusting too well. Sometimes, for brief bits of time, she forgot what it was like to live with Broc and the others in the sett.

"What's wrong?" Enat looked up to see that Ash had stopped stripping the bark off a large bunch of willow branches they had picked. She stared at the stone bowl in her lap.

"Ash?"

"I do not want to forget." Her voice was barely a whisper.

Enat came to her and sat. "You won't. You'll become accustomed to living among two-legs..." Ash smiled. "But you will never forget the ones who loved you and cared for you." She placed a hand over Ash's chest. "You carry them with you. Always. Here."

Enat returned to her mortar and pestle, where she was grinding other leaves into a powder. "I've told enough stories. Tell me of Broc and Cuán."

Ash thought for a bit and began to tell the familiar story of how Broc did not know what to feed a two-leg cub, and tried to feed her earthworms. Enat laughed as Ash went on, telling tale after tale, and soon, Ash forgot her fears of forgetting. It felt as if her clan were here with her.

The days passed, and the moon waxed again. Before Ash knew it, a full moon was upon them – a whole moon cycle since Enat had come to the village and found her.

"Tonight," Enat said that morning as they broke their fast, "we will join some of the others."

"For what?" Ash's eyes opened wide.

"Just a gathering to listen to a bard sing," Enat said. "It is time for you to meet some of the others."

Ash grew very quiet. "I am going to go for a walk."

"As you wish."

Ash got to her feet and took a now-familiar path through the forest. It had rained overnight, and droplets of water still hung from every leaf and branch, shimmering in the morning light. Ash moved silently through the mist rising from the damp ground. She heard and felt all the life about her as she made her way to an enormous tree that had fallen on its side. Its roots stuck out at all angles, and the trunk had been hollowed by time. It was so large that Ivar could have stood inside it without having to bend. Ash, being very small, crawled deep into the trunk. She found a cache of nuts, left there by some animal. She sat, her knees hugged to her chest, pretending she was back in her sett, waiting for the badgers to come back from hunting. She reached out with her mind.

"Who is there?"

"Who is asking?"

She smiled, recognizing the familiar voice of a crow who had befriended her. *"It is Ash."*

There was a flapping of wings, and the crow came strutting into the hollow. Ash had never really talked much to the birds in her forest with the badgers. Since the badgers often stole eggs, the birds had never wanted anything to do with her, but this crow was different. She had spent much time around humans and knew Enat.

"Greetings, Beanna."

The crow cocked her head, looking at Ash with her bright eye. *"Have you anything?"*

Ash reached into her pocket and pulled out a handful of seeds. She held them in her hand, and Beanna approached, gently plucking the seeds from her palm without poking with her sharp beak.

"What news of the forest?" Ash asked as the crow took the last of the seeds.

"*Much is happening,*" Beanna said. "*Young are birthing or hatching everywhere. All are busy hunting to feed them.*"

"*Have you no nest? No young hatching?*"

Beanna tipped her head again, watching Ash. "*I am old. I have raised many broods. My mate is gone on, now. No more eggs for me.*"

"*Well, I am glad. It means you can visit with me,*" Ash said with a smile. The crow hopped into her lap, rustling her feathers and settling down as if she were sitting on eggs.

"*How goes it with you, little two-leg?*"

Ash stroked the sleek feathers. "*Tonight, I am to join the others for the first time.*"

Beanna clicked her beak. "*That troubles you?*"

"*Yes.*"

"*You are a two-leg.*"

"*Yes.*"

"*You told me you came here to be among them.*"

"*Yes, but I have never been among two-legs. Only Enat.*"

"*They are your kind,*" said Beanna. "*They will accept you.*"

Ash shifted, picking Beanna up gently and lying down on her side with the crow tucked against her stomach. "*I wish I could just stay here.*"

A tiny grub wriggled in the rotten wood near them. Beanna pounced and swallowed the grub. She waddled back and settled again against Ash. "*That grub may wish I had not just eaten it. Wishing does not make it so.*"

The moon was bright as Enat led the way. When they arrived at the small village where Ash had met Ivar, the others were already gathered around a large fire lit in the center of the dwellings. They nodded greetings to Enat and Ash and shifted over to make room for them. Ash looked around and saw that she was an object of great curiosity. The others craned their necks to get a glimpse of her. Scattered among the grown humans were other young ones, some who appeared to be about her age, and some who were a few winters older. Ash assumed they must be here to learn as she was. Enat had told her that there were about ten apprentices living in the village, four others who were recently arrived, and a handful of older ones who studied separately.

One woman got to her feet and began chanting a song of a man named Cú Chulainn. She was younger than Enat, with yellow hair and a pretty face. She moved as she sang, and Ash found herself also swaying with the rhythm of the words. Ash had never heard such a tale, but the others seemed familiar with it, nodding and clapping at the telling of his exploits. Ash looked around in puzzlement at their enjoyment, especially the young ones, who seemed to like it especially. After listening a while, Ash stirred restlessly.

"What is it?" Enat whispered.

"Do all human stories tell of killing and fighting?"

Enat looked back for a moment at the woman chanting. When she came to a pause in her tale, Enat interrupted, saying, "Thank you, Neela, but my old heart is in the mood for a more gentle tale. Would you honor us with such a one?"

A few frowns were cast in Enat's direction, but Neela obliged by reaching for her small harp. She sat with the harp in her lap and began to sing a tale of two humans who loved each other. Ash listened raptly. Something about the harp sounded familiar to her. The younger apprentices soon became bored and wandered off.

"Go with them," Enat whispered. "Talk to them."

Reluctantly, Ash got up and followed to where they had gathered around another fire pit lined with stones and stacked with peat, ready to be ignited.

"Show us, Fergus," one girl was saying to an older boy.

He flung his hand toward the pit, and flames suddenly rose from the peat as it burned fiercely. They turned to glance curiously at Ash as she hung back.

"Come sit with us," said the girl. "I am Cíana."

"I am Ash." Ash sat next to her as the others settled around the fire.

Another boy snorted with laughter. "What kind of name is Ash?"

"Gai!" Cíana frowned at him. She shook her head. "Ignore him."

The boy called Gai scowled.

"It's your turn, Méav," Cíana said to one of the older girls. "Let's see what you can do."

Méav lifted her arm, twirling her hand in the air. The flames leapt, twining and twisting, following her movements. The others clapped and then took turns showing their skills. A girl named Una levitated some of the sticks piled next to the fire pit and then a boy they called Ronan wrung his hand in the air and water poured from his closed fist.

As amazed as Ash was by the magic, she was even more fascinated by the other apprentices. It was the first time she'd ever had the opportunity to be this near to two-leg young – like her, no longer cubs, but not yet grown. Méav had eyes the color of a summer sky with hair as black as Beanna's feathers, gathered in many braids under a leather band around her head. Ronan's chin was covered in sparse hairs the same red-brown color as his hair. Cíana's hair was the color of the sun, long, pulled back into a twisted strand hanging down her back. Gai's hair and eyes were almost black, but his face was pale, like the moon. Una's hair was dark, and she looked a lot like Gai. Another older boy, Niall, was so fair, he looked as if he had no color at all, with his pale eyes and white hair.

The younger ones tried to mimic what the older could do. Cíana succeeded in sparking a twig into flame and Gai could briefly levitate the sticks. Daina was able to extinguish Cíana's flame with a thought. Diarmit, a heavyset boy with thick, brown hair tried to move the sticks as well, but only succeeded in toppling the pile. The others laughed.

At last, they turned to Ash.

"Show us what you can do," said Gai.

Ash knew there was an owl sitting on an overhanging branch, watching a mouse hiding in a nearby clump of moss. She knew the mouse was quivering under the moss, watching the owl. There were many animals about, and she could hear them all, but she was not going to call them to her for Gai's enjoyment.

"I do not know how to do anything," she said.

He stared at her for a moment. "Nothing?"

Ash shook her head. "Not like you. I cannot make fire or smoke do my bidding or move things."

Cíana turned to look at Ash more closely, taking in the scars on her face and her bare feet. Ash lowered her head. "You live with Enat," Cíana said.

Ash nodded.

"How old are you? You look too young to be here."

Ash poked a forefinger in the dirt and drew a pattern. "I do not know."

There was laughter from the circle. "How can you not know how old you are?" Diarmit asked.

Ash looked up sharply as Cíana hissed for them to be quiet. "I do not know how many winters I had when my clan found me. I was with my clan for eight winters before Enat came."

"What clan?" Cíana asked.

"Badgers."

"Badgers?" Niall looked as if he did not believe her.

"Yes. Badgers saved me when my village was burned." Ash looked at them. No one was laughing now. "They raised me and taught me."

"How could badgers teach you?" Gai's tone was challenging, but the others looked intrigued.

Ash looked from him to Cíana to some of the others. A new feeling pricked at her, one she had never felt before and, forgetting for a moment that she was not going to call animals to her for Gai's entertainment, she reached out. *"Beanna? Are you awake?"*

The others looked from one to another, casting furtive glances behind them in the dark as Ash looked over their heads into the woods. Nothing happened for a moment, then a great flapping of wings and a loud caw signaled Beanna's arrival. She landed on Ash's shoulder.

"What do you wish?"

"They do not believe I can talk to you," Ash said. Beanna tipped her head, looking at Ash with her bright, black eye. She then turned and looked at the other humans.

"Do you want me to peck their eyes out?"

Ash snorted. *"No. That would not help them to like me."*

Beanna hopped down from Ash's shoulder and strutted around the fire pit, pausing a moment in front of each human, looking each in the eye before moving to the next. In front of Cíana, she said, *"This one shows great promise."*

Ash translated, and Cíana smiled, looking proudly around at the others.

To Diarmit, Beanna said, *"This one eats enough for three."* The others laughed raucously as Ash told the group what she had said.

"So you have a trained crow," Gai said.

Beanna hopped onto his knee, and Ash was pleased to see him jump. *"Tell this one I have seen him in the forest, practicing his magic. He knows of what I speak. Tell him the forest is restless and will not allow him to continue."*

Ash repeated Beanna's words as the crow flew back to her shoulder. Patches of scarlet rose in Gai's pale cheeks.

"What does that mean?" Cíana turned to him. "What is the bird talking about?"

"It's nothing," Gai said, but he looked at Ash and Beanna shrewdly.

"So that's how the badgers taught you?" Méav asked. "You can talk to them?"

Ash nodded, reaching up to stroke Beanna's feathers. *"Thank you."*

The crow gave her ear a gentle tug with her beak and flew off into the night.

The others looked at Ash with new respect. Cíana reached up and ran her hand over the short hair covering Ash's head. "Did you keep it short when you lived with badgers?"

"No," Ash said, smiling. "I had no means of cutting it. I asked Enat to cut it for me."

"Ash?"

They all jumped at the sound of Enat's voice.

"It's time for us to leave."

Something in Enat's tone made Ash feel she had done something wrong. In silence, she followed Enat back to their cottage.

"Sit," Enat said, indicating a stool near the hearth. She stirred the fire and took an adjacent stool. "What happened tonight?"

Ash told her all that had occurred. She frowned in puzzlement. "I have never felt anything like what I felt when Gai did not believe me."

Enat watched her through narrowed eyes. "You were angry. I felt it."

"Angry?"

"You were annoyed, displeased. You wanted to make him sorry for what he had said."

Ash looked at her, realizing Enat was right. "Yes. I had never felt that before."

"And you used your power, your ability to communicate to call a creature to you and prove him wrong." Enat's voice was gentle, but Ash hung her head in shame.

"Yes."

Enat was quiet for a long time, staring into the flames. "Ash, you'll be tempted many times to use your power to impress people, to make them fear you or like you. You may even be tempted to use it against others." Ash opened her mouth to protest, but Enat held up a hand. "You must learn when to use your power and when not to. Animals like the badgers you lived with are simple creatures. They care for their own; they are hunter or hunted; they raise their young and send them out to raise more young. Humans are more complicated than that. We can choose to do good or evil. We can –"

She stopped at the blank expression on Ash's face. "Never mind. Go to bed. It's late."

Ash went to her sleeping mat and pulled her old cloak over her. As she drifted to sleep, she wondered what Beanna had meant, what she had seen Gai doing.

Ash woke to the sound of a soft rain falling. She lay there, still feeling troubled by all that had occurred the evening before.

"You are awake?" Enat was at the fire, stirring a pot. "Come and eat."

She dished out some porridge into a bowl. This new delight had become one of Ash's favorites, sweetened with a bit of honey. She sat next to Enat, dipping her fingers into the porridge. Enat cleared her throat and held out a wooden spoon. Ash scowled. Eating with her fingers was so much easier than this awkward implement. She grasped it in her fist and scooped some porridge into her mouth.

They ate in silence until their bowls were empty. Ash scraped the last of her porridge from her bowl while Enat poured tea into two cups. Handing one to Ash, she said, "Tell me what troubles you."

Ash stared into the fire. "The others can do things I cannot."

"And you can do what they cannot," Enat said. "You will all learn. Méav, Ronan and the other older ones have been with us two or more winters. They have had time to study. Cíana, Daina and Gai are a little older than you. They have been here since last summer. Diarmit only arrived four moons ago. You will find your way with your magic."

Ash cocked her head. "Beanna said she had seen Gai in the forest, practicing magic that made the forest restless. What did she mean?"

Enat looked at her sharply. "Did she say more?"

Ash shook her head.

"Gai is a king's son," Enat said.

"What is a king?"

Enat sighed. "There is so much you don't know." She paused. "Among humans, there are clans, like yours. They gather together to protect what they have, but they often want what others have – land, wealth, crops. And they will fight to take it from one another."

A distant memory flashed through Ash's mind – shouts and the clanging of weapons and screams of pain – and then it was gone.

"The leader of a clan is a king, or a woman may be queen," Enat continued. "So Gai is the son of a leader. His older brother will become king in his time, and Gai will be expected to return and help him rule with his magic."

Ash looked at her. "He would use magic to control other humans?"

"He might. This is what I was trying to explain to you last night. Evil is when you use your power to deliberately harm others rather than help them. And not just those with magic. Those without magic can also be evil, using force to make others do their will."

"Is Gai evil?"

"No," Enat said quickly. "Not yet. But there is an emptiness in him. He was not raised with love as you were. His mother died when he was born, and his father and brother had little time for him. He has had to make his own way, and he feels a need to prove himself. Gai may even become king himself if his brother dies."

She looked at Ash with thoughtful eyes and reached for the empty bowl sitting at the girl's feet.

"When this bowl is empty, there is room to fill it with anything – porridge or muck. Good or bad. But if I fill it first with porridge, there is no room left for anything bad. Gai is like this bowl right now. If we can help to fill him with goodness, there will be no room for evil."

Ash looked puzzled. "How can we do that?"

"You feel you are missing something compared to the others because you were not raised in a human family, but you also were not tainted by the bad things people can do to one another. You are different, in a good way. You can help the others, including Gai, to see things differently. Teach them the way Broc and Cuán taught you."

CHAPTER 5

Elements

Ash's training began in earnest after that night. Neela and Ivar were their teachers most days, taking the young ones into the forest and teaching them more of the herbs and plants there, teaching them how to control their magic.

"It will be different for each of you, how you tap into your power, but one thing is true for all. You'll find it easier here," said Neela. "The life-force of the forest will aid you. If you were to go out into the world as you are now, it would be difficult for you to harness your power. You probably could only perform magic by accident."

Ash was reminded of the night she had healed Cuán, and knew that it had only been in the terror of that night that she had been able to channel the ability to heal him.

Neela took them this day far from the village. As they walked, Ash wondered again how extensive this forest must be. Neela led them deep into a grove of oaks, and asked them each to go to a tree. They spread out while Neela herself went to the largest tree in the center of the grove.

"This tree is the mother of this grove," she said, laying her hands on the massive trunk. "All of these trees are her children. All came from acorns she dropped over the winters. Listen."

She closed her eyes. Ash sat at the base of her tree and laid her hands on its roots. She knew what these ancient trees felt like from her lessons with Enat, but even she was surprised to feel echoes of Neela's touch come to her like a tiny shiver of awareness in the tree she clasped.

Cíana next to her gasped as she felt it also. They smiled at each other.

"Each tree is still connected to the mother tree and to the others," Neela explained. "They communicate with one another, much as we do. We cannot cut one without doing harm to the others. This is true in every forest."

The other apprentices looked perplexed as they struggled to feel something. Neela went from one to the next, whispering, laying her hands over top of theirs, guiding them. Ash watched as Neela went to Gai. Remembering what Enat had said to her, she was curious to see whether he would feel the power of these beings. She could not hear what Neela said to him, but Gai closed his eyes and laid his hands again on the tree where he stood. His pale face at first was expressionless, but as he felt and listened, his features softened. A look of wonder came over him, and when he opened his eyes and met Ash's gaze, for just a moment, it was like looking into the soft eyes of a deer. Almost immediately, the softness was gone, replaced by his usual hard expression.

"That was amazing," said Daina a short while later as they began their trek back to the village. "It reminded me how small we are."

"It reminded me how hungry I am," said Diarmit.

Cíana laughed. "You're always hungry."

Diarmit shrugged. "Aye." He eyed Ash as they walked. "Why do you limp?"

Ash felt heat rise in her cheeks.

"Leave her alone," Cíana said.

"Why? I'm only asking," Diarmit said.

"My leg was burned," Ash said. She pulled up her legging and showed them. "It will not straighten. Nor my arm."

Cíana winced. "Does it hurt?"

Ash shook her head. "Not unless I try to force it."

"Can you run?"

Ash grinned at Diarmit. "I can beat you back to the village." And she took off with her strange lopsided gait that nevertheless was light as a rabbit as she ran through the underbrush rather than along the trail, scrambling under branches and hopping over roots and rocks, arriving back at the village well before Diarmit and the others.

"Now I'm hungrier than ever," Diarmit huffed as he bent over, his hands braced on his knees.

"We thought you might be."

Ash turned to find Enat standing at the door to the largest building. No one lived in it. It served as a space for teaching or meetings of the elders of the village or a place to tell stories if the sky was raining or snowing. Today, a large pot hung over the fire and lured them inside with the smell of food.

The older apprentices were already gathered. Ash had not spoken to them since the night of the full moon, and she eyed them curiously.

Diarmit hurried over and spooned a large portion of stew into a bowl. The others followed. A platter of freshly baked loaves sat on a table long enough for all of them to be seated on benches on either side. Ash stood and waited until Enat was seated with a bowl before taking a seat herself.

She raised her spoon to her mouth, glad now that Enat had insisted she learn how to use it, but paused as she sniffed. "Deer?"

Enat nodded. "Yes."

After the lesson of the morning, a few of the others paused their eating.

"Did you hunt?" Ash asked.

Ivar frowned. "Aye, we hunted."

"Why?" Gai asked from down the table. "Don't badgers hunt?"

Ash looked at her bowl and did not respond.

"You told me you ate meat," Enat reminded her. "We have honored the spirit of this deer, giving thanks for his sacrifice in order that many may eat. We'll make use of every bit of him, so that his death is not a waste. When we die, our bodies will likewise go to replenishing the life of the earth. So 'tis for all living things."

The eating gradually resumed, and Ash ate silently. In her mind, she thanked the deer again for his sacrifice. She had never thought about this when she and the dogs scavenged meat from the village. The hunting was already done, and she was doing what she had to to live, but she had never killed. She had stolen eggs. She supposed the birds she'd stolen from considered that killing. She wondered if she would ever be asked to kill, and she wondered how she would respond.

Ash's mouth gaped as she stared at the map Ivar had laid out on the table. It was drawn on a large animal skin and depicted a land completely surrounded by water.

"You are saying if I walk far enough in any direction, I will reach the endless water?" Ash found this impossible to comprehend. She and Enat had walked for many days but, looking at where their forest was drawn on the map, were still nowhere near the edges of the land. How far would she have to walk to get there?

"Éire is an island," Ivar said. "So, yes. If you walk far enough, you will meet the sea. That is how invaders come to our island from other lands. But they are not the only threat." He pointed again to the map. "A hundred winters and more ago, we had only four main kingdoms: Uladh in the north, Laigin in the east, Munster in the south and Connacht in the west. But over those hundred winters, clans have been fighting for land, and the four kingdoms are now broken into many smaller ones. Our forest sits on a boundary between kingdoms. This is why you must all know how to fight."

"Only to defend," said Neela. "Defend our forest, and those who are weak and cannot defend themselves."

"If we know magic, why do we have to fight?" Ash asked.

"Are you afraid to fight?" Gai challenged her.

He had bragged many times of being taught fighting skills by his father's warriors when he was young. Ash knew that Cíana and some of the others already had been taught some of these skills.

"I do not know," Ash replied. "I have never fought. Do humans know how to do anything but fight?"

Cíana hid a smile. Ivar stepped forward and said, "You're right, Ash. We should avoid fighting whenever we can. But our island has been invaded by many tribes from other lands – from the north, from the east." He pointed on the map. "When they come, they come to kill. This forest is protected with enchantments to keep non-magic folk from finding it. Most would encounter fog and mist and wander about lost on the boundaries until they gave up. But some of the invaders have their own magicians, and they sense the power of this forest. They might lead the invaders in and allow them to do harm. We must be prepared to protect our home. The forest cares for us, and we must care for it."

Though Ivar's reasons were sound, that did not make Ash feel better. Smaller than all of the others and hampered by her scarred leg and arm, she knew she would be at a disadvantage and was not looking forward to learning to fight.

Fortunately, there were other things to learn first. She spent days listening to Neela tell them tales of the gods and goddesses who protected their land – the Dagda and Danu, Morrigan, Aonghus, Brighid, Arawn – the list went on and on until Ash's head swam with the names and deeds.

"Do you believe in the gods?" she asked Enat one evening as they sat outside their cottage. It was a gentle night. The new warmth of the spring lay heavy on everything, and the scent of flowering bushes and trees perfumed the night air. Ash lay on her back, watching the stars wheel slowly through the dark sky, listening to the activity in the forest around them.

Enat smiled as her fingers deftly wove a basket from reeds, working by feel without the need for light. "I believe people need something to believe in. They need a way to explain what they cannot understand, and they need to feel that there is something bigger than themselves."

Ash thought about this. "Animals do not do this."

"No, I would guess that they don't."

Ash sighed impatiently. "Life with the badgers was much simpler."

Enat smiled. "I'm sure it was. Would you go back?"

Ash was quiet for a long time. "I have learned much, yet I miss them."

Enat set her basket down and came over to sit beside Ash and pointed to the sky. "You are like the evening star, one with all the others and yet apart, brighter than the rest."

Ash shook her head. "I am not brighter. The others – Cíana and Gai – they all know more than I. Even Diarmit does."

"Not more. At least, not more important," Enat said. "You know things that cannot be taught. One day, you will understand how rare that is."

At last, the day Ash had been dreading arrived.

"Today, we will go to the sparring ground." Ivar led them to a clearing not far from the village. There, a three-sided lean-to sheltered a forge. A fire was already lit. Ivar had Diarmit pump the bellows, each gust of air shooting flames and sparks high as Ivar moved a bar of metal sitting in the fire, glowing red. When it was soft enough to mold, his thick arm wielded a hammer, hitting the bar with blows that rang in Ash's ears.

"Are we going to make our own weapons?" Daina asked, raising her voice over the clanging of the hammer.

"No," said Ivar, his face glistening. "But you should know where they come from."

Nearby was a small stone building that held weapons of all types: long and short sparring sticks, round discs of wood nearly as large as

Ash, and an array of actual weapons, their metal edges gleaming in the half-light coming into the storehouse. Ash's nose wrinkled at the sharp odor of the metal. Ivar appraised her for a moment and handed her a short stick. He handed fake weapons out to the others as well.

"These are your swords," he said.

Gai protested. "I can handle a real sword."

Ivar looked at him. "Until I'm sure you can handle real weapons, these are what you'll use. You'll watch and learn."

He took them all through slow-motion moves with their sticks: blocking, slashing, stabbing. He left them to practice while he went to supervise some of the older apprentices who were fighting with long sticks on the other side of the yard.

Ash and Diarmit and Daina sat together watching Gai and Cíana spar with their wooden swords. Ash winced as she listened to the sharp clack of their sticks as they parried. For a long while, they seemed evenly matched, but gradually, Gai, being taller and heavier than Cíana, forced her off-balance with a thrusting push with his stick. Ash groaned as she watched Cíana fall backward, certain that Gai had won. Cíana quickly rolled to one side, using her legs to sweep Gai's feet out from under him. He landed heavily on his back and lay there, gasping for air as Cíana stood over him, her stick held to his throat.

"Well done!" Ivar came over to them.

"He'll be angry as a wet wasp over that," Daina whispered as Gai pushed to his feet.

"Why?" Ash saw no reason to be angry if an opponent bested her. When an animal lost a fight over a mate or territory, it was best to retreat and fight again another day. Staying only led to injury and death.

"He's told us so many times how he was taught to fight by his father's warriors, and he thinks he should never be beaten."

Ash frowned. "Can anyone never be beaten?"

Ivar gestured to Ash and Diarmit. They took their places as Gai and Cíana sat to rest. Ivar showed them again how to hold their fake swords, and took them through slow-motion moves, some attacking, some defending. He then stepped back to allow them to practice what they had been taught. Diarmit advanced, and Ash stumbled backward, falling to the ground.

Gai laughed, and Cíana elbowed him to be quiet.

"Again," Ivar said.

Ash scrambled to her feet.

A short time later, Diarmit knocked Ash to the ground for the twelfth time. She couldn't seem to move fast enough to get her sword in position to block his blows, and his greater size overpowered her every time.

"Enough." Ivar looked angry, his black brows furrowed over his fierce eyes. Ash stood, sweaty and panting, her fake sword hanging at her side. "Sit and rest."

He dismissed them. Dejected, Ash got a long drink of water and sat with the others to watch two of the older ones spar. Méav's long black braids whipped through the air as she spun, swinging her staff at Fergus. He moved just as fast, their staffs a blur of movement as they fought. Ash thought they looked like two of the gods in Neela's tales. Farther away, the other three – Una, Ronan and Niall – all practiced throwing long, thin spears that impaled their targets like needles piercing cloth.

"I will never be able to do that," Ash murmured.

"Not to worry," Cíana said, laying a consoling hand on Ash's shoulder. "It took me a long time as well."

Ash suspected that was not true, but her heart lightened a little at Cíana's words.

"Focus," Neela said. "Try and pull the smoke toward you."

What Ash lacked in fighting skills, she made up for in her other lessons.

"The elements existed long before us," Neela had told them. "They will exist with or without us. They do not depend upon us in order to be."

This Ash understood, intuitively, without really having to be taught. Living with the badgers, she had seen that humans could make fire, but so could lightning. Streams could overrun their beds, the earth could heave and move when wet enough.

"Fire and smoke can be used to create a protective screen," Neela said. "Water is harder, but it can be manipulated to allow you to cross a stream to safety or to create a flood to keep your enemies on the other side. Earth is very difficult and takes a tremendous amount of energy. You must be careful. Once you start a spell, you may not be able to stop, and the energy it demands can kill you."

Each of them sat with a candle. Ash stared at hers, feeling the power build inside. With a flick of her hand, the wick sparked and lit. She made the flame grow and then shrink, and then made smoke rise densely from the flame, twisting and coiling sinuously.

She felt the energy draining from her the longer and the more intricately she tried to control it, but it left her with a feeling of exhilaration that here was something she was good at. Closing her eyes, she imagined herself one with the fire, asking it to assume the shape she desired.

"How do you do that?" Diarmit asked in frustration as Ash made the flames rise in the shape of a crow.

"You cannot force anything to do your bidding," Ash told him. "You must ask; you must become the fire or the smoke."

Diarmit frowned, clearly not understanding what she meant.

"No," said Gai. "You must exert yourself. If you are strong enough, you can force it to do your will. Like this." His brows knitted in concentration as his flame twirled, spinning faster and faster.

Ash laid a hand on Diarmit's arm. "Close your eyes," she said patiently. "Put yourself in the fire. Feel it move, feel it sway with the breeze. Now, ask it to move with you."

Diarmit screwed his face up in concentration, swaying where he sat.

"Look," Ash whispered.

Diarmit opened his eyes to see the flame writhing and dancing. "I did it!"

Immediately, as he lost his focus, the flame returned to its natural size and shape, but Diarmit did not care. "That was the first time I could do it!"

"None of us could do it as quickly as you," Daina said to Ash. She whispered loudly, "It took Gai ages and ages before he could force it to do his will."

Gai, who had been watching them closely, frowned, but Ash glowed with Daina's praise.

As much as she excelled in controlling fire, able to do so almost without thinking, it was the exact opposite when it came to learning to read and write. Ash struggled, trying to figure out how the symbols scratched into the dirt translated to spoken words. She was fascinated, looking at the scrolls and pages of writing kept by the elders in the meetinghouse, shelves and shelves of them. Some of them had pictures, beautiful drawings with inks in vibrant colors, intricately knotted creatures and lines. Enat sat and read to her for ages, letting Ash trace along with the words. Slowly, she was learning.

"Be patient," urged Enat when Ash grew frustrated. "This is not magic. No power can help you, and in this you are not behind the others. Most of our apprentices come from humble beginnings and have never seen writing in their lives. Diarmit has not. Neither did Daina or Cíana before they came here."

"Gai has," Ash said resentfully. "He said his father's house had many books and scrolls. He had a teacher when he was young."

Enat looked at her with some amusement. "Gai had many things growing up that most of us have never had. I certainly had never seen a book or writing before I came here to learn."

Ash swallowed her retort. "I forgot. You said you grew up in a family that did not have much."

"We've few wealthy people in our land." Enat carefully rolled up the scroll she had been reading from. "You watched the people in the village near your sett. They were farmers and hunters. They did not have wealth. They most certainly did not have books. That is why we tell stories and sing songs. Neela studied for a long time to learn our stories. When most do not know how to read or write, and books are scarce, 'tis the only way we can pass our knowledge and traditions along."

Ash was silent as she thought about this.

"Do not envy Gai the things he had," Enat said. "He would be the first to say they don't make up for the things he did not have."

Ash snorted. "I do not believe Gai would admit any such thing. Not to me."

"Why is there this feeling of ill will between you?"

Ash opened her mouth to answer but then shut it again. "I do not know."

"Could it be that you are jealous?"

Ash frowned. "I do not understand."

"Envious," Enat explained. "Wishing to have what the other has."

Ash flushed. "Perhaps. Gai comes from wealth I cannot imagine."

"I did not mean only you," Enat said. "I meant jealous of each other. Do you think Gai could be jealous of you?"

Ash's mouth fell open, and Enat smiled.

"Why would Gai be jealous of me?"

"Can you not see why?" Enat tucked the rolled-up scroll securely on its shelf and gathered up her bag. Ash followed her as they made their way back to the cottage.

"No," Ash said. "I cannot see any reason why Gai would be jealous of me."

Enat walked on in silence for a bit before saying, "You are learning quickly, and this after you started with so much less."

"But... but I cannot fight," Ash sputtered.

Enat gave an impatient wave of her hand. "Fighting. Bah. 'Tis necessary to know how to fight, yes, but it's the least important thing we teach you. I don't care if you never defeat an enemy with a sword or staff."

Ash laughed and immediately clapped her hand over her mouth at the unexpected sound. Enat smiled.

"That is good," Ash said, lowering her hand. "Because I probably never will."

"All the better. Those who can, tend to rely on physical force to get their way. I would be very happy if you never do that."

They reached their cottage. Ash squatted to light the fire – "without magic," Enat reminded her. Ash grinned and struck the steel to the flint. The spark ignited the tinder, and flames began to lick at the little branches and fibers she had piled up. As the flames grew, she added a few blocks of peat. When the fire was burning well, she took the pail to the stream to fetch water for their dinner.

When she got back to the cottage, Enat poured some of the water into a kettle on the fire to heat. She ladled more of the water onto some ground flour to make some loaves while Ash chopped carrots and turnips, dropping them into the kettle.

"It would be a worthwhile thing," Enat said as she kneaded the flour mix, "if you could find a way to be friendly with Gai."

"That is easier to say than to do."

"Many things are."

CHAPTER 6

Provocation and Promise

Weeks passed, and still Ash could not overcome any of the others when they sparred. Time and again, whether it was Diarmit or Cíana or Gai or Daina, Ash was forced off-balance, unable to raise her weapon quickly enough to counter their blows.

Ivar fumed as he watched. "She is hopeless."

"She is not," Enat said sharply. "You have simply not learned how to get the best from her."

Enat rarely came to the sparring ground, but she began to appear more regularly. While Ivar coached the apprentices in the use of sword and staff, Enat taught them how to use a bow. There were bows of varying thicknesses and weights with the other weapons, but Enat's bow was beautiful, made of smooth black wood, carved with intricate designs.

"This is a woman's weapon," Gai said, dropping his bow and picking up a sword, hefting it with both hands.

Enat whirled, shooting an arrow at Niall's feet, a hundred paces away.

"It is much more effective to keep your enemy at a distance if you can," she said with a reproving glance in Gai's direction. "By the time he gets close enough for you to use a sword or staff, you may have already lost your advantage."

Ash struggled with this as she had with sword and staff. Her scarred right arm wouldn't straighten enough to allow her to draw the bow as the others did, with the left arm already extended, so she learned to nock the arrow and grasp the bowstring first, and then push the bow out with her left arm.

"It's not the right way," Gai complained.

"It works," Enat said. "That's all that will matter if she ever has to use it."

Ash's arms trembled trying to hold the draw and aim. Even using the lightest bow, she could only hold the draw for a heartbeat or two, and her arrows flew wildly. She practiced every chance she got, raising welts on the inside of her left elbow from the twang of the bowstring. Enat made her a leather guard to tie around her arm. Despite Ash's reluctance to wear anything leather, the relief the guard offered was welcome. For days and days, she practiced, gradually getting stronger until she could hold the draw, her right thumb resting against her jaw as she settled to take aim.

"Well done," Enat said as Ash loosed an arrow and it joined the others bristling from the center of the target. Ash smiled as Enat walked on.

Ivar and Niall came over from where they had been practicing, using real swords. Breathing hard, they joined Enat and Neela who were watching from the edge of the archery range.

"That is fine, from a distance," Ivar said, leaning on his sword. "But she'll never defeat an enemy who has made it close enough for hand to hand fighting."

Enat eyed him. "You think not?"

"Have you watched her spar?" Ivar laughed. "She can't best anyone here."

Enat shrugged. "I told you, you've yet to find the right way to motivate her."

"And you have?"

Without warning, Enat seized Niall's sword and swung it at Ivar, forcing him to leap back and defend himself. She allowed him no time to question her, but began fighting in earnest, the clang of their swords resounding through the sparring yard. All stopped to watch, including Ash. Blow for blow, Enat met Ivar, blocking his sword, he blocking hers as she attacked, but his greater size began to tell as Enat was forced to retreat step by step. She suddenly stumbled and fell. Ivar raised his sword over his head.

With a scream, Ash fired an arrow at Ivar. It tore through his beard, startling him as he cursed. She ran and leapt between him and Enat, crouching and snarling like an animal, her teeth bared. She raised a hand, and Ivar was thrown backward, the force of her power lifting him off his feet. He soared through the air and landed on his back with a sickening thud.

All was silent, and it seemed no one dared move for a moment. Enat and Ivar both sat up.

"I told you," Enat said. She got to her feet and went to Ivar, whose face had gone from white to a furious red, and offered him a hand. She pulled him to his feet as he glared at Ash. "She only needed the right motivation."

"She shot an arrow at me!"

"She missed you."

"By a hair's breadth."

"A hair is as good as an arm if it misses."

"Enough."

Ash sat with the younger apprentices outside the meetinghouse where the elders and the older apprentices argued her fate. Ash listened to the voices. One was unfamiliar. It belonged to an old man, much older than Enat to judge by his wizened appearance. His name was Timmin. He had been summoned by the others when Ivar and Enat continued arguing Ash's punishment, or whether she was to be punished at all. Patiently, they had sat and waited for him to come from some distant part of the forest.

"Timmin is First Mage and prefers to live alone," Enat had murmured to Ash while they waited. "He studies the stars and the skies, looking for portents as to the future."

Ash frowned. "Can anyone see the future?"

Enat shrugged. "I've never known anyone who could. But Timmin is very old and very wise. Perhaps he can."

When Timmin arrived, Ash watched him with great curiosity. He walked straight despite being very old, supported by his staff. He had a long, white beard, but sharp eyes, black as Beanna's, and Ash had the feeling he could see through her when he glanced in her direction before going into the meetinghouse.

"Summon the girl," he said now.

Enat's face appeared in the doorway, and she gestured to Ash. Ash entered, and Enat stood her before Timmin where he sat in a chair while the others occupied the benches on either side of the long table.

"Come." He held out his hand, and Ash approached. His hand, when she placed hers in it, was surprisingly warm and gentle. He held it, looking long into her eyes.

"Do you remember what happened?"

"How can she not remember –?"

Timmin silenced Ivar with a look and turned back to Ash.

"I remember some," Ash said. "I remember watching Enat and Ivar fighting. I remember Enat falling, and Ivar raising his sword." She paused, biting her lip. "Then I do not remember anything until Enat was helping Ivar to stand."

"You don't remember shooting an arrow at me?" Ivar shoved angrily to his feet.

"Ivar –"

"She lies!"

Ash did not know what that meant but understood it to be an insult. She stood as tall as she could, but before she could speak, Enat said calmly, "She doesn't know how to lie."

Ivar opened his mouth to retort, but Enat continued, "You forget – all of you – that Ash was not raised by humans. She has not been taught in the ways of guile or deceit. She does not know how to fight when there is no reason to, but she will defend when threatened. Because that is how her clan raised her." She turned to Timmin. "If there is fault, it is mine. I knew that Ash would act to protect me, and I allowed myself to be made vulnerable so that we could see just how strong her instinct to protect would be. I confess, I did not expect it to be so… potent."

A few chuckles came from those around the table. Ivar glared at them.

"Sit, Ivar," said Timmin. He returned to his regard of Ash. "Enat tells me you were raised by badgers after they saved your life."

"Yes."

"May I?" Timmin gestured to Ash's face.

She nodded and stepped closer. He reached up to touch her scars and lifted her sleeve to inspect her arm. Ash could see movement from the table as others, curious about her burns, craned their necks to see as well. Timmin, who still held Ash's hand, placed his other hand over top of hers and looked into her eyes. At last, he released her and turned to the others.

"I've no right to order you to keep her here, but I sense no malice in what she did. I would suggest a more prudent approach to teaching her in future." He gave Enat a wry smile.

"Thank you, Timmin," Neela said. She stood, and the others rose as well.

"Enat, a word, if you please," said Timmin.

The others glanced back curiously as Enat stood with Ash in front of Timmin.

Timmin waited until they were alone before saying, "Do you remember anything from before the badgers rescued you, child?"

Ash shook her head.

He looked at Enat. "It is time she had her name."

Enat inclined her head. "I've been waiting for her to settle in with us, as everything was so new to her. You feel it's time?"

"I do."

"We'll see to it, Master Timmin. Thank you."

Ash looked back and forth between them, not understanding. Enat laid a hand on her shoulder and led her from the meetinghouse. Cíana, Daina and Diarmit were waiting. Off to one side, Gai sat by himself.

Enat nodded. "Go to them."

Ash trotted over. "I do not have to leave."

"Oh, good," Cíana said, taking Ash's hand. "I was so afraid for you."

"I've never seen Ivar so angry," Diarmit said, his eyes wide.

Ash glanced toward Gai. "He will be disappointed."

"You are wrong." Daina got to her feet and went to where he sat. "Come and join us. We should celebrate. Ash is not going to be dismissed."

Gai glanced in Ash's direction. "I don't –"

"Stop pretending you don't care what happens," Cíana said impatiently. "We want you to join us."

"She doesn't."

They looked over and it was clear from Ash's expression that Gai was right.

"Stop it, both of you!" Cíana stomped her foot. "We're all here to learn together. We can help one another if you two would stop picking at each other. Now come join us."

Gai obediently followed her back over to where Ash sat with Diarmit and Daina.

Diarmit, lowering his voice, said, "Did you see how far she threw Ivar?"

For a tense moment, everyone was silent, then they all burst out laughing.

"How did you do it?" Daina asked.

"I do not know," Ash replied.

"Have you ever done that before?" Gai was looking at her with an expression Ash had never seen on his face before. She shook her head.

"Only one time did I do something like it, when Cuán was attacked by wolves and I healed him."

"What?" Cíana and the others gaped. "Tell us."

Ash told the story of that awful night. "That was what led Enat to me. I do not know how I did it. And I did not mean to hurt Ivar."

Diarmit snorted. "Hurt his arse more than anything."

"And his pride," Cíana said seriously. "That, he will hold against you."

"It was like watching a badger," Gai said. "You were snarling and hissing at him. I thought you were going to bite him, and then... you –" He gestured with his hand. "And he went flying. It was brilliant."

Ash swelled with his praise as the others retold what they had seen and asked Ash to tell the story of the wolf attack again. Not until later, as she was making her way back to the cottage, did it occur to her that Gai's one and only compliment had come after she used her power in a way that could have injured someone, even if she hadn't meant to.

Ash and Diarmit crawled along, reaching under bushes and thickets for eggs. Chickens roamed freely about the village, sometimes roosting in the small shelter built for them, but just as often laying their eggs under any handy bush. Hens clucked at them, surrounded by dozens of young chicks as they flapped in the dust.

Once every moon, two of the elders journeyed outside the forest to trade salves and potions and metalwork for provisions such as meat and cheese and salt and wool, things they could not produce for themselves in the forest.

"We do not keep cattle or goats or sheep," Ivar had told the younger apprentices. "There is not enough grassy land here in the forest for them to graze, and we don't have time to milk and make butter and cheese, but there is a clearing large enough to plant crops."

As the weather warmed and spring turned to summer, it was time to plant. Cabbage had been another delight that Ash had discovered since coming to live with Enat. She had occasionally nibbled on stolen cabbages from the villagers when she was living with the badgers, but she had never eaten it cooked.

After the eggs were gathered for the morning, all the young ones followed Neela to the clearing, ringed by apple trees, their branches still bursting with white blossoms. Bags of seeds waited to be placed in the furrows they were soon digging. Once Neela was satisfied with their work, she left them to it.

The older apprentices came by to watch.

"You could help us," Cíana said.

"We did this before you came," said Ronan as Fergus leaned an elbow on his shoulder.

Una sat with Niall and Méav as they watched. "Niall and I did it the last few springs, before we moved up. You'll do the same with the ones who come after you."

"Do it right or do it again, wee ones," said Méav. The others chuckled and gave one another knowing glances.

Ash set to work, pulling a metal hook fastened to a long stick through the dirt to dig a furrow. Daina came behind her, placing seeds at regular intervals and then covering the furrow with her foot.

The older five soon got bored with poking fun at them and wandered off, leaving the younger ones to their work. They spread out around the clearing, everyone hard at work.

Almost everyone, Ash thought as she watched Gai standing off to one side, leaning on his digging stick.

"This is servants' work," he said.

Cíana straightened. "That's what you say every time you don't want to do something. I'll tell you again what I told you before; we're not your servants. I didn't hear you complain about having turnips and beans to eat during the winter. So if you expect to eat again this winter, get to work."

Diarmit sniggered, his chubby face red and sweaty from the effort of digging.

"I do not mind," Ash said. "Badgers and squirrels and other animals gather food all the time to store through the cold."

"Well," Gai said, stepping forward. "If we must do this, at least we could use magic to get it done more quickly."

He waved his hand and seeds flew down the row, plopping into the openings in the soil. With another wave of his hand, the soil shifted to cover them.

Ash stood upright, her own back aching from being bent over. She wished she could do that, but she had not yet mastered the art of moving things through the air. No one else had been able to do this like Gai could.

He strode over to the others. "I can do the same for you, and then we can go do something more fun than this."

The others straightened, looking at one another, no one willing to reply.

"All right," Diarmit said at last. "I can't do that yet, so I'm willing."

Gai walked to each of them, waving his hand similarly, dropping seeds into the ground and covering them with soil. When he was done, they trooped together into the forest to a stream where they spent the rest of the day wading and splashing in the water. They overturned stones, looking for small crayfish and tadpoles, catching them and letting them go.

The sun was on its downward path when they returned to the village, laughing and talking. As one, they stopped when they saw Ivar and Neela waiting for them. Ash saw the older five sitting back by the meetinghouse, grinning and nudging one another.

"You finished your work quickly," Neela said.

Gai's pale cheeks colored with bright patches of scarlet as he jutted his chin out. "We used magic. Why should we toil like –" He glanced toward Cíana. "Like oxen when magic gets the work done so much faster."

Ivar stepped forward, his brows drawn together. "And did your magic plant all the cabbage seeds far enough apart? Did it plant the bean and carrot seeds at the proper depth? Because if it didn't, the plants will wither in the soil and we'll all go hungry this winter."

Gai opened his mouth to retort, but Ivar silenced him with a gesture.

"Your excuses are meaningless."

Neela laid a calming hand on Ivar's arm. "Magic is a wonderful thing, and it will serve you well in many tasks in your life, but there are some things that must be done by the sweat of your brow. If magic were the answer, do you not think we would have done it that way without your help?"

All of them hung their heads, staring at the ground. Even Gai looked somewhat abashed.

"To thank you for your work, we had planned on taking you all on the morrow to a special place in the forest, a waterfall such as you have never seen. But now we can't," Neela said.

"Tomorrow," said Ivar, "you will all go back to the clearing. You will dig up everything and replant it properly so that it has time to grow."

His gaze challenged Gai to argue, but Gai only nodded and turned away.

Neela and Ivar left them.

Daina rounded on Gai. "You told us it would do no harm to use magic."

"Don't blame Gai," Cíana told her. "He didn't force us. We were all eager to get done quickly. We're all to blame."

Gai looked at the older ones resentfully. "You could have told us."

Ronan cocked his head. "It seems to me we did. It's not our fault if you're too dense to listen."

"Don't rub it in," said Niall. "We did the same thing."

Fergus laughed. "That's why it's so funny. We all try it. They know we will."

"And now, we get to do it all again," Diarmit said with a sigh. "Let's eat. We'll need the energy for tomorrow."

"I am going to eat with Enat," Ash said. "I will meet you at the clearing tomorrow."

She suspected Enat would have heard about what happened, so she was not surprised when Enat greeted her by saying, "I trust you had an educational day?"

Ash snorted. "A lesson I will not forget."

Enat smiled. "A good lesson, then."

CHAPTER 7

Claiming Her Name

"We should go this way."

"No, it's this way."

The planting was done – "and properly," Neela had said with a nod of approval after the younger apprentices replanted all the crops. She had sent them out into the forest to find a selection of plants and roots for her. She had given each group a list written out on a small piece of parchment. Ash was working with Cíana and Diarmit, while Gai was with Daina somewhere else in the forest.

"This is not a contest," Neela had warned, but Ash saw the gleam in Gai's eye and knew he did not see it so. Ever since the planting, Gai seemed to have felt the need to prove himself.

The things on Neela's lists were for the celebration of Bealtaine that night. Like Imbolc, when Enat had first sought Ash, this celebration was something all the other humans knew well, while Ash knew nothing of it.

"It marks the start of summer," Diarmit said as they walked through the forest. "In our village, we had a huge bonfire and all the cattle and sheep were decorated with wreaths of flowers and led around it."

"Why?" Ash tried to picture this strange custom.

"To bless them and keep them healthy."

Cíana nodded. "And all the fires in all the houses are doused and then relit from the Bealtaine fire."

She pointed to a clump of tiny purple flowers and led them over. "Let's pick these. Comfrey is on the list. Be sure to get the roots."

Ash dropped to her knees and dug. She placed the flowers in a woven bag Diarmit carried over his shoulders.

On and on they walked, collecting the things on Neela's list. They crossed a stream, Diarmit and Cíana stepping on stones to stay out of the water, while Ash splashed through.

"Don't your feet hurt?" Diarmit looked down at Ash's bare feet.

"No. I have never worn shoes."

"Not even in winter?"

Ash giggled. "Badgers don't wear shoes."

Diarmit grinned. "You could have made little shoes for them."

They all laughed as they pictured this.

"I wish we could meet your clan," Cíana said.

Ash sobered. It had now been more than three cycles of the moon since she had left them. "I do, as well."

"What's left for us to find?" Diarmit asked, rubbing his stomach. "I could eat a whole cow."

Cíana consulted her list. "We need only mushrooms."

They stopped abruptly at the sound of something large moving through the forest. Ash held her breath as an enormous antler appeared around a stand of trees, an antler so broad she could have lain upon it with room to spare, the prongs as big around as her good leg. The three of them looked up into the eyes of an elk, the largest four-leg Ash had ever seen. She had seen other deer and elk, but none like this. His shoulder stood higher than she could reach, and his hooves were as big as her head. He saw them and stopped, sniffing the air, his black nose quivering.

"*Greetings.*" Ash stepped forward and inclined her head.

The elk inclined his as well. "*Greetings, small one. I am Ríordán.*"

"*I am Ash. These are my companions, Cíana and Diarmit.*" She gestured back toward them.

Cíana and Diarmit stood, looking puzzled.

"*You are all here to learn from your elders?*" Ríordán asked.

"*Yes.*"

"*And you speak to us?*"

"*Yes.*"

He lowered his great head, and the shadow of his immense antlers shut out the sunlight filtering through the trees. "*Ash? That is not your true name.*"

"*I do not know my true name.*" She reached out and laid a hand on his jaw as he nuzzled her scars.

He raised his head and surveyed them once again. "*Until next time, Ash. I think, by then, you will know your true name.*"

He walked on, leaving the three humans dumbstruck.

"What did he say?" Cíana whispered.

"His name is Ríordán. He... he asked if we were here to learn." Ash watched him disappear. She didn't know why, but she did not wish to share the other things he had said.

"He's a giant elk," Diarmit said in a hushed voice. "We thought they only existed in the songs and tales told around the fire. No one has seen one, not for ages and ages. And you talked to one!"

A loud grumbling sounded from the direction of Diarmit's stomach.

"Mushrooms. I saw some back this way." Cíana led the way.

Ash followed, turning once to look back in the direction Ríordán had gone.

By the time they got back to the village, preparations were well underway for Bealtaine. Gai and the others had already returned. They took their finds to Neela, who thanked them.

"What took you all day?" Gai asked.

Diarmit looked up from where he was stuffing his face with an oatcake. "We met a giant elk. Ash talked to him."

Neela looked over at these words. “You met Ríordán?”

Ash nodded.

Gai came nearer. “And he spoke to you?”

Ash nodded again.

“He honored you,” Neela said. “We rarely see him or his mate, Osán. It’s always a great thing when they come to our part of the forest.”

Gai looked at Ash. “What did he say?”

“He told me his name and asked if we were being taught by our elders,” she said.

Neela watched her for a moment but remained silent.

They all spent the remainder of the day preparing for the celebration. Even Timmin joined in the preparations. Ash found the others’ enthusiasm contagious and was soon looking forward to nightfall.

The sun settled far beyond the trees, and the sky was turning a deep indigo. A feast was laid out on a long table: roasted venison and last year’s parsnips and carrots, different kinds of breads and cakes, asparagus drizzled with cream, cheeses and berries. Ash tried some of everything. She laughed as she saw Diarmit trying to balance two plates piled high with food.

Night had fallen completely as they finished feasting. The torches were doused, and the four elders gathered around the bonfire pit, positioning themselves at the compass points. As one, they raised their staffs and magically ignited the wood piled there, the flames roaring high into the dark. The elders chanted in a language Ash did not understand, sprinkling handfuls of herbs and plants into the fire. The air shimmered and her skin tingled. The atmosphere felt charged, as it did during a thunderstorm. She could feel the power of all those gathered, building on itself. The village had no cattle or sheep to bless, but the elders blessed the apprentices, all ten of them, wrapping their heads in garlands of wildflowers.

“Like a crown!” Cíana said.

Ash did not know what a crown was, but she reached up to touch the flowers adorning her own head. Cíana was beautiful, with her golden hair and her flowers. Gai was beautiful, as well. The flowers on his dark head glowed, as did his pale face. Méav and Ronan and the others looked again like gods. Even Diarmit seemed to shine with an inner light. They joined hands with the elders and were led in a circle around the bonfire. Cíana laughed and twirled Ash around and, for a little while, Ash felt as whole and beautiful as the others.

After dancing a while, Ash backed away from the circle of light cast by the fire and sat, breathless, as the shadows of those still gathered around the fire danced over her.

Enat approached, holding a torch lit from the bonfire. "Come. It is time we went home. Tonight, you shall have your name."

Enat used the torch to light the fire when they got back to their cottage. She gestured to Ash to sit as she murmured more words and tossed more flowers into the fire. She filled the kettle and swung it over the flames before sitting next to Ash.

"When you spiritwalk in your sleep, do you ever recall where you've been?"

"Usually, I am back in my forest with Broc and Cuán and the others," Ash said.

"Do your spiritwalks ever take you to places with other humans?" Enat reached for a few bowls of dried leaves and herbs, and sprinkled some of each into the water in the kettle. She stirred the mixture.

Ash thought. "Sometimes, I can almost see a gathering of people. But it all fades, like smoke, as soon as I wake. I cannot hold it."

Enat nodded. She filled a cup from the kettle and held it out. "Drink all of this. It will help you to sleep deeply. Then I will guide you on a spiritwalk to find the answers you seek. Bealtaine is a good night for this. Your power is great on this night."

Ash took the cup and drank. It was bitter, and she made a face as it went down. Enat led her to her sleeping mat and placed stones and crystals on her forehead, her chest, her belly, and then covered her. "These will help you on your journey."

"How long will this take?"

Enat smiled. "As long as it takes." She laid a hand on Ash's shoulder. "Sleep, child. I will not leave you until you wake."

Ash felt certain she would not be able to sleep with Enat sitting over her, but the potion she had drunk began to work almost immediately. She felt as if her body were drifting slightly above her mat. She thought how odd it was that she could look down on her sleeping self with Enat sitting beside her, humming a low, calming tune. She turned and wandered out the cottage's door.

Immediately, she was surrounded by fog so thick she could see nothing. She kept walking, following a path only just visible in front of her, as if it was forming itself, step by step, leading her to some unknown destination. She reached out to touch the mist, but it parted before her hand, always just out of reach. Trusting that Enat would not allow her to come to harm, Ash followed the path. She walked for she knew not how long and, suddenly, the mist cleared.

She was standing on the outskirts of a village obscured, not by mist, but by smoke. She gasped as she saw that it had been plundered. The remains of buildings burned, and bodies lay everywhere, pools of blood lying dark beneath them. The vacant eyes of some stared up at a sky they would never again see. Others lay with their faces pressed to the earth, hidden from Ash's sight. She stepped warily among them, wondering why she was here. She heard a whimper and turned toward the sound. Something small writhed on the edge of one of the smoldering dwellings. She started at unexpected movement from the edge of the forest.

Broc.

Transfixed, Ash watched as Broc approached the squirming thing on the ground, and she understood. This was the night Broc saved her. She watched Broc drag her from the fire, wincing as she saw the raw, burned flesh on her face and arm and leg. She raised a hand to her own face.

"*Broc?*"

But Broc could not hear her. This was not a normal spiritwalk. Ash understood that she was an observer here. She watched Cuán and the sisters come to Broc, listened to them, watched them retrieve the shield and the cloak and drag her away to the sett.

The mist came again, and Ash was again led along a path she could not see. This time, when the mist cleared, Ash stood on the outskirts of a village that was whole and undamaged. It took a moment before she realized it was the same village.

Fascinated, she walked among them, unseen, as the villagers laughed and worked. The men had brought down a deer and were butchering it a distance away, portioning some to each household. The women were tending their babes and grinding flour and mending clothes as they watched the older children.

This village was much like the one she had watched from the safety of the woods when she lived with the badgers, the one where she and the dogs had worked together to get food. The badgers could not have dragged her so very far, and she suddenly wondered if the village that knew her as the ghost-child had been rebuilt on the same location as the one she had been rescued from.

She heard a woman's voice and turned. There stood a woman with hair the color of a fox, long and flowing gently about her shoulders. She was laughing as she held a small girl with hair the same color as her mother's, struggling to get down out of her arms. She set the child down and watched as she toddled about on unsteady legs. Nearby, a man sat, sharpening a scythe with a stone and smiling at her.

"No, you don't," the woman said as the girl immediately made for a nearby dog, grabbing at its tail. She produced a small doll made of cloth. "Here, Caymin, play with this."

Ash's hands flew to her face.

Enat sat quietly, allowing herself to fall into a kind of waking trance. Occasionally, Ash twitched as she wandered in her sleep. Though she could not see what Ash saw, she felt the girl's emotions as she progressed along her spiritwalk, felt her horror followed by joy. Then, she felt nothing for a while but waited patiently. Time in the spirit world did not move at the same pace as time here. There was a shift, and Enat became more alert. The girl had reached her destination.

She roused herself and kept a closer eye on Ash as she lay there. There was a surge of emotion, and she saw a tear leak from the corner of the girl's eye.

Enat clasped her hands together and pressed them to her lips as she whispered a prayer of thanks.

Enat was asleep when Ash woke. Silently, she got to her feet and crept from the cottage. The night was still dark and moonless, but Ash did not need light. Sure-footed as she had been when she lived with her clan, she strode through the forest. To all she encountered, she reached out with a reassurance. On and on she walked, as she had in her spiritwalk, not sure where she was going, but confident that she would know when she arrived.

Through the canopy of the trees, the stars watched her as she made her way. She knew that the animals of the night marked her progress as well.

As she walked, she tried to recall every detail of the things she had seen, afraid they might disappear as regular spiritwalks usually did, but this one had been different, and she soon realized she would never forget the one she'd had this night. Her mother. She had seen her mother and father. Memories she hadn't known she possessed flooded her, and her eyes filled with tears. Memories of being held and sung to, memories of her father, laughing as he carried her on his shoulders.

She came at last to a clearing in the forest, a clearing with a circle of ancient stones, some standing, connected by stone lintels laid upon them. Others of the stones had collapsed, their lintels fallen.

All were covered in moss.

This place was old, older than any place Ash had ever been. She felt the power emanating from the stones as she stepped inside the circle and stood, her face to the sky, her arms held wide.

"I am Caymin."

Back at the cottage, Enat sat by the fire. She had awakened to find the girl gone, but she was not worried. A ripple of energy moved through the air, moved through the very earth. She lifted her head. *Caymin*. It suited her, but Enat knew her heart would always have a special place for the girl named Ash.

CHAPTER 8

An Arrow Through the Heart

For two days after Bealtaine, Caymin avoided being with the others. Enat let her be, allowing her time to walk in the forest or just sit quietly, lost in her thoughts.

"It is strange," Caymin confided. "I feel exactly the same and completely different – all in one. How is that?"

"Not so strange," Enat said. "You're the same as you've always been, but you know something about yourself now that you never knew before. That's bound to change how you see yourself."

"Will it change how others see me?"

Enat considered. "It may. You are no longer the nameless orphan, raised by badgers."

Caymin frowned. "But I do not wish to leave my badger family behind, as if they never existed."

"No." Enat smiled. "You will now have two families to think on. You are blessed to have been loved by both."

That thought warmed Caymin as she walked through the forest. She came to a stream and crouched down. Moving her hand in a circle over the current, she murmured a calming charm and a portion of the water became as still as ice. She was pleased to notice that she felt almost no energy leave her. Leaning over the water, she gazed at her reflection. She nearly didn't recognize the face staring back at her. She had asked Enat to keep her hair short, cutting it every moon with her silver knife, but her face was rounder, fuller than it had been the first time she'd seen herself. Her leggings were shorter, so she knew she was growing. The scars, though, were the same. And always would be.

Beanna flew down and perched on her shoulder.

"Caymin, is it?"

"How did you know?" Caymin released the charm and the stream gurgled on its way. She got to her feet.

"The whole forest heard." The crow tilted her head, looking at Caymin with her bright eye. *"How did you find your name?"*

"Enat guided me on a spiritwalk. I saw my village the night the badgers saved me, and then I saw my mother holding me. She called me by name."

Beanna's head bobbed up and down. *"Powerful."*

Caymin thought about this. *"It was powerful. A powerful memory."*

"No. I meant you."

Caymin stopped so suddenly that Beanna had to flap her wings to keep her balance. *"I do not understand."*

"There is strong magic in this forest," Beanna said. *"Small things like the magic you have been learning, these do not affect the forest. But the night you claimed your name, all heard it. All felt it."*

"What does that mean?"

"I do not know, Caymin who was Ash. But it means something."

Beanna pushed off from Caymin's shoulder, cawing as she flew away.

When Caymin got back to the cottage, Enat was waiting for her. "Is it time?"

Caymin nodded. "It is."

Enat held out a bowl of porridge. "Eat first. Would you like for me to go with you? To help you tell them?"

Caymin ate a couple of bites. "No. I am ready to tell them."

"Very well. I'll see you this evening."

When Caymin got to the village, she found the others gathered with Neela and Ivar in the meetinghouse.

"Welcome back, Caymin," Neela said with a nod.

"Sit here." Cíana slid over on the bench to make room.

Caymin sat and could feel the curious glances of the others as Ivar continued talking about how to create a summoning spell.

"It's similar to levitating something," he was saying. "But it takes more concentration to draw something to you. Of course, the greater the distance and the larger the object, the greater the strength it takes, so take care before you think about using this spell. Once you summon something, the spell will hold until the object comes to you, and if you deplete your energy in doing so, you will either have to draw from another source, or it will kill you."

He called Daina forward to try summoning a scroll from the far end of the room. They watched as she frowned, muttering the words. For long heartbeats, nothing happened, but then the scroll slid off the shelf and moved through the air to her waiting hand. Daina looked around proudly as the others gasped and cheered. Diarmit tried next, screwing up his face as he tried.

"He looks like he's laying an egg," Gai whispered from Cíana's other side.

Cíana elbowed him, trying not to laugh.

All Diarmit succeeded in doing was getting the scroll to flop over.

"Enough." Ivar stepped forward. "You'll try again another time." He pointed. "Gai."

Gai strode forward and, almost lazily, murmured the incantation, holding out his hand. The scroll immediately flew to him. He handed it to Ivar and sat back down. Cíana had to murmur the incantation three times before the scroll came to her. Caymin sat until, at last, Neela pointed to her.

She got up. Though she had quickly learned to control the elements with things like the calming charm she'd used on the stream, she had never been able to get anything to levitate before and was not looking forward to failing at this task with everyone watching. Concentrating, she whispered the words of the spell. For a moment, nothing happened, as she'd expected, but then, she felt a curious tingle of energy leaving her. The scroll flew so quickly through the air that she was unprepared for it. It hit her in the chest and knocked her backward.

The others burst out laughing as Neela stepped forward and pulled her to her feet.

"Well, that's one way of doing it," she said as she brushed Caymin's backside off.

Dazed, Caymin sat back down. Like at the stream, the fatigue had passed, replaced by a feeling of euphoria. She'd never felt as powerful doing magic before.

When Ivar dismissed them, the others crowded around her.

"Tell us what happened, Ash." Diarmit grinned. "Sorry. I mean, Caymin."

She told them of Enat guiding her through her spiritwalk the night of Bealtaine, of seeing her village and her mother, and learning her name.

"You really saw all that?" Gai asked.

"I did."

"We felt it," Cíana said. "We didn't know what it was, but we felt it. Almost as if the earth shivered."

"Maybe you'll be able to channel your magic more strongly now," Diarmit said. "Now that you have your true name."

Caymin rubbed her backside. "If it gets any stronger, I may need to carry a pillow with me everywhere."

"Show me again."

Caymin leaned over the miniature map of Éire she had copied onto a spare bit of parchment. She was trying to figure out where everyone was from. Enat had shown her approximately where the badger sett was, and the village nearby, located in the northcentral part of the island, not too far from the lake they had rowed upon. She had also shown Caymin where she'd grown up, in her fishing village on the northwest coast, in a sheltered bay. Cíana and Diarmit were both from the southern part of the island. Cíana's family lived on a lake, and Diarmit's were cattle farmers, living in the hills.

"Ivar came for both us of us," Diarmit said. "I was to begin schooling with one of the monks near our village. The only magical thing I'd ever done was when my little sister fell into the river, suddenly she was with me on the bank. I couldn't remember how I'd done it. But Ivar said I should come be trained."

Daina was from the north, where Méav and Niall were also from. "When I was old enough, the mage near our village brought me to meet Neela."

Gai's family lived near the west coast.

"My father's keep has held off invaders for ages," he told them. "These clans are all loyal to us." He pointed to the entire southwestern part of the island.

"How could they protect that much coast?" Cíana asked. "Invaders could come in anywhere."

Gai shook his head. "Much of it is steep cliffs, straight down into the sea. It's said the cliffs used to be protected by dragons, but I don't believe that."

Caymin looked up, frowning. "What are dragons?"

Diarmit went to the shelves and shuffled through the scrolls there. "This is a dragon." He unrolled the scroll to reveal a brightly colored drawing of a fantastic creature with enormous wings and flames erupting from its mouth. "But they don't exist."

"Is not that what you said about the giant elk?" Caymin asked.

Cíana laughed. "She's right. Who knows? It could be dragons do exist."

"Well, if they do, I've yet to see one," Gai said.

"Enough of this," Diarmit said. "Let's play a game."

Caymin looked up from the map. "What is 'a game'?"

A short while later, she and the others were on the sparring ground, chasing a small leather ball about the size of her fist with sticks, called hurleys, that looked like long spoons, flared on one end, trying to hit the ball between two of the archery targets. Diarmit used his bulk to shoulder others out of his way as he worked the ball along the ground with his stick. He passed the ball to Caymin. She saw Gai coming toward her, and she quickly dodged, using Daina as a block, and slapped the ball toward the targets.

"Yes!" Diarmit yelled, thumping Caymin on the back as the ball rolled through.

"Lucky," Gai said, frowning.

Caymin grinned, but the grin soon faded as Gai had the ball, feinting left and right, easily out-maneuvering Caymin and Daina to send the ball between the opposite set of targets.

"Ha!" He shouted, thumping his fist against his chest.

They played until they were breathless, and then flopped on the ground, panting.

"Let's do something that requires real skill," Gai said, sitting up.

"Like what?" Cíana looked at him.

"Like shooting arrows at a moving target."

Gai went to the storehouse where the weapons were kept and emerged with a handful of bows and a quiver full of arrows.

Diarmit sat up. "What are you going to shoot at?"

"It's no challenge to hit these straw targets," Gai said, stringing one of the bows. A sly smile slid onto his face as he nocked an arrow. "How about you?"

He drew and let the arrow fly. Diarmit yelled and jerked away. The arrow pierced the ground where just a moment before Diarmit's hand had been.

Cíana stormed over and shoved Gai in the chest. "That's not funny!"

Diarmit jumped to his feet, his face a furious red. "Why did you do that?"

"I didn't hurt you," Gai said, but his eyes glittered. He looked around. "If I can't shoot at him, maybe..."

Just at that moment, a pheasant exploded from a nearby bush with a loud flurry of wings. Gai loosed another arrow, catching the pheasant through the breast.

"NO!"

Caymin ran to the bird which lay panting where it had plummeted to the ground, its beak opening and closing as its wings fluttered against the ground. Blood pooled under it. The others hurried over, and she looked up with tears in her eyes. "Why?"

Gai's face was lit up with a kind of malicious joy as he watched the bird's struggle grow feebler.

Caymin seized his hand, her other on the bird's breast. She closed her eyes. Gai's face went ashen, and he tried to pull his hand free, but Caymin held him fast. He began to pant. He dropped the bow he still held in his other hand and grabbed at his tunic, over his chest.

"Look," said Daina.

Overhead, black clouds gathered, low and menacing as they circled and the wind whipped to a frenzy.

"He can't breathe," Cíana said, looking from Gai to Caymin. She laid a hand on Caymin's shoulder. "Stop."

Gai sank to his knees, his eyes rolling back in his head.

"Stop it!" Cíana grasped Caymin's hand and pulled it free from Gai's.

Gai fell onto his side, gasping for air. Caymin cradled the bird in her lap, the arrowhead protruding from the bird's breast. She snapped the shaft and gently pulled the arrow through until it was free. Her hands, placed over each hole in the bird's chest, glowed red and hot. She went stiff, and the cords of her neck stood out, her eyes screwed shut. Day turned to night and the wind howled.

"She's having a fit," Daina whispered, taking a step back, looking fearfully at the sky.

"No," said Diarmit. "Look."

Caymin suddenly went limp, slumping over the bird, her hands no longer glowing. The pheasant wriggled free and flapped furiously away into the trees.

Caymin slowly sat up, looking very pale. She looked at the blood on her trembling hands. The wind calmed and the clouds began to disperse, letting sunlight through once more.

The sound of heavy footsteps made them all jump as Ivar, Neela and Enat came running.

"What happened?" Neela asked.

The apprentices looked from Gai to Caymin.

Gai pointed with a shaky hand. "She tried to kill me."

"What?" Ivar hauled Caymin up by her tunic, lifting her as easily as if she were a rag doll.

"No." Cíana stepped in, laying a hand on Ivar's arm. "That's not what happened." She told them of Gai's wanting a moving target – "He shot at me!" Diarmit sputtered – and of his shooting the bird. "And then..." She paused. "I'm not sure what happened then."

They all turned to Gai who had pulled his tunic up and was probing his chest. "I thought there would be blood," he muttered. "She tried to kill me."

"No." Caymin pulled loose from Ivar's grasp, straightening her own tunic. "I only wanted him to feel the bird's pain and terror. I made him feel everything she felt."

"And then," Daina said, her voice hushed, "the sky got dark and you healed it. You healed the bird. Like you did the badger after the wolves attacked."

Enat laid a hand on Caymin's shoulder. "Is this true?"

Caymin nodded. "I had to. It was not an honorable death. She was not shot because we needed to eat. She has a nest of young ones that need her."

Neela rounded on Gai. "You shot a live creature because you craved sport?"

Telltale scarlet patches rose in Gai's pale cheeks. "Our hunting parties used to bring in scores of birds. This was just one."

"Just one." Enat's voice was gentle, but even Caymin winced at the pain in her voice. "Have we taught you so little?" She squatted down and placed her fingers under Gai's chin, making him look at her. "There is no such thing as 'just one life'. All life is sacred. You are just one human, but you are sacred to us, Gai."

"We've all had enough to think on for one day," Ivar said. He picked up the bows and arrows lying scattered on the ground. "Go. All of you."

When Caymin got back to the cottage with Enat, she slumped on the floor next to the hearth. Enat laid a hand on her forehead.

"You're feeling weak?"

Caymin nodded, wiping sweat from her face with a trembling hand.

Enat swung the kettle over the fire and selected some herbs from her pots. When the water was hot, she poured it into a cup with the herbs and handed it to Caymin. "Drink this. You took the bird's pain as well, didn't you?"

Caymin nodded again. She sipped the tea and felt strength returning to her.

"You must be more careful. If her wounds had been more grievous, you might have died, taking her pain and trying to heal her, your life for hers."

"I had to try," Caymin said. She sipped more of the tea. "This is good."

Enat nodded. "You have some color again. You were white as death for a wee bit."

A shadow fell across the doorway, and they looked up to see Gai standing there.

"May I come in?"

"Of course," Enat said. She poured another cup of tea and handed it to him as he sat cross-legged on the floor.

For a long moment, he stared into his cup. Enat and Caymin glanced at each other as they waited.

"Would you like to speak with Caymin alone?" Enat asked.

Gai looked up. "No. I need to speak with both of you. I'm... I'm ashamed of what I did. Shooting that bird. I'm sorry."

"Thank you for saying that, Gai." Enat frowned toward Caymin, who was watching him.

"Why did you do it?" Caymin asked.

Gai drank some of his tea before saying, "When I was young, my father's men took me hunting. I shot my first deer. It was a bad shot, and I only wounded her. When we found her, we probably could have removed the arrow and she would have lived, but they told me I had to kill her." His pale face was paler than usual. "I hesitated, and they laughed at me, said I was weak. One of them cut her throat." He swallowed hard. "And then they left her lying there. Said we had enough venison and didn't need to haul the carcass back."

Caymin didn't know what to say. She felt sick to her stomach – for the deer and, curiously, for Gai.

"When we got back, they told my father and my brother what had happened. My father grabbed me by the throat and pinned me against the wall. He said if I ever failed to kill again, he would disown me. He wanted no part of such a weakling for a son." Gai's mouth twisted into a snarl as he said this last. His eyes glittered with tears when he looked up at them. "I was never anything but a disappointment to him."

"You're better than that, Gai," Enat said softly. "Strength does not come from hurting or killing others. Strength comes from knowing yourself and doing what you know in your heart is right."

He nodded, wiping a hand across his eyes. His gaze lowered as he swirled the tea in his cup. "I've never felt anything like what that bird felt." He glanced up at Caymin. "What you made me feel."

"I should not have done that," Caymin said.

"No." He leaned forward. "I'm glad you did. I want you to teach me how to talk to them. To animals."

Whatever Caymin had expected Gai to say, this was not it. "I do not know if I can teach you," she said. "I have always known how to do it."

"And it may not be a matter of learning," Enat cautioned. "Animals will decide for themselves who they will and will not speak with."

Gai pulled back and his expression hardened. "You mean they might not want to speak with me."

"I mean," Enat said, "that we must respect that they can make their own decisions. Learning that is the first lesson."

The hardness disappeared from Gai's face. "You're right, Enat."

Caymin felt a stirring of pity for him. "We can try."

He smiled, and Caymin thought it transformed him into something beautiful. "Thank you," he said.

"You might want to offer to teach the others as well," Enat said.

A flicker of displeasure passed over Gai's face, but he forced a smile. "Of course. We should include them."

"We can do this," Enat said. "But it will have to wait until after Lughnasadh. You have other important lessons to master between now and then."

CHAPTER 9

Lughnasadh

"Hold steady now."

Caymin held her hand out as Méav passed a ball of fire from her own hand. The younger apprentices had been paired with the older ones to practice more advanced skills.

"Ouch!"

Next to them, Diarmit flinched as Ronan passed him a similar ball of flame.

"You have to brace yourself," Ronan said impatiently.

"I did," Diarmit said. From the corner of her eye, Caymin saw him shaking his hand.

Her ball of fire, sitting now in her palm, tingled and was warm, but it didn't burn. She had sat, mesmerized, next to Méav as she conjured the flame out of nothing. She could now easily spark a candlewick or a fire when there was something to ignite, but this pulling flame out of nowhere eluded her.

"Again," she had begged, watching her do it over and over. Méav taught her the incantation, but Caymin hadn't been able to do more than create a spark until today.

Nearby, Gai also held his hands out, but instead of fire, as he worked with Fergus, they were causing ruts to appear in the dirt as if they were dragging a hoe through the earth. With a sweep of their hands, the loose dirt shifted and filled in the ruts.

On the other side of the empty fire pit, Una and Niall were teaching Cíana and Daina how to conjure water out of the air, gathering it into a clay bowl and then causing it to shoot into the air, arcing gracefully back into the bowl.

"Why are they different colors?" Caymin asked. Her ball of flame, as she accepted it from Méav, was a pale blue while the flames produced by Ronan were a deep red-gold.

"Every spell we do carries a bit of us, our energy," Méav said, watching the flame burn steadily as Caymin fed it. "Your energy sustains it now, look."

Caymin gasped as the flame turned from blue to a brilliant white.

"Pass it from one hand to the other," Méav said.

Caymin carefully passed the flame to her other hand. The flame began to gutter.

"Feed it," Méav said.

Caymin concentrated, and the flames exploded into her face. With a cry, she dropped the ball of fire and shielded her face with her hands.

Diarmit's flame went out with a pop. Everyone stopped to watch her as she lay on her side, her arms wrapped around her head.

Méav laid a hand on her shoulder. "You're fine, now. You're fine."

Slowly, Caymin loosed her arms and sat up, feeling her face. "I am not burned?"

"No."

"That's not exactly true," said Cíana. "You're just not burned again."

The tension broke as Caymin laughed shakily. Embarrassed, she turned back to Méav. "I am sorry."

"No need to be," Méav said. The others returned to their practice. She pointed to Caymin's face. "Do you remember it?"

"No. I was very young."

Méav's icy blue eyes glinted angrily. "I can't imagine, even in the middle of a raid, how anyone could throw a wee baby into a fire." She tilted her head. "Ready for another go?"

Caymin nodded.

"Hold your hand out and try to make the fire yourself then."

Caymin closed her eyes and held her hand out.

"Center yourself," Méav said. "Find your power and bring it up slowly, under control."

Caymin whispered the incantation and a ball of white fire appeared in her palm.

"Good," Méav murmured. "Now, feed it; make it grow, but control it. You are in control."

The ball of white flames grew, licking the air, then shrank to a pinpoint, and then grew again.

"You did all that?"

Caymin nodded, smiling.

"Hmm. You should scare yourself more often." Méav pulled a wooden bowl near. "Now, we work on water."

The day of Lughnasadh dawned warm and sultry with the full heat of summer. The sun was not fully up when Caymin and the other younger apprentices were sent out to gather bilberries.

"Why do we need these?" Caymin asked through a yawn.

"For tonight," said Daina. "They're part of the feast of Lughnasadh."

"But why do we celebrate this? It is not a solstice or an equinox."

"It's the harvest festival," Diarmit said. "Didn't you ever celebrate any of these things?"

Caymin shrugged. "I watched the villagers when they had celebrations, but I never knew what they were for."

They found a patch of bilberry bushes full of the almost-black berries. They picked them, placing them in baskets to take back.

"Later, we'll have contests," Gai said.

Caymin glanced at him. "What kind of contests?"

"Running, sparring, archery."

"Don't worry," said Cíana. "You don't have to participate in everything. But you should do the archery. You're better than all of us."

"I just want to get to the feasting part," Diarmit said, stuffing a handful of bilberries into his mouth. "And there had better be more to eat than these berries."

By the time they returned to the village, the older apprentices had set up targets for archery and spear-throwing contests, while the elders had prepared a running course.

"What are you doing?" Daina asked when Caymin sat on the edge of the weapons ground.

"Watching."

"Why aren't you competing?" Diarmit asked.

Caymin tilted her head. "Why do we need to compete?"

"We don't need to," Cíana said. "We like to. It's fun to see if you can best the others."

Gai sauntered over. "And it's good practice, for when we need to do this against enemies." He looked at her. "Unless you're afraid."

Caymin's eyes glittered at the challenge. "I am not afraid."

"Well, then." Gai crossed his arms as he looked at her.

She got to her feet as Neela called everyone to the archery targets. Instead of the fixed straw targets they usually shot at, five discs of wood had been hung by different length ropes from a long pole.

"That doesn't look so hard," Gai said just as Neela walked along, setting the discs to swinging back and forth and spinning on the ropes suspending them.

Cíana smirked. "And now?"

Fergus stepped up first with one of the heavy bows. It creaked as he drew, holding the string to his jaw as he followed the movement of the first disc. He loosed the arrow, but it glanced off the edge of the disc as it spun, ricocheting toward the sky. He drew another arrow from his quiver and struck the second disc, though not in the middle. He moved down the line, ending with three targets struck.

"Not bad," Ivar said, pulling the arrows free and setting the discs to swinging again for Cíana.

She, too, ended with three targets hit. Méav and Ronan each hit four discs. Gai stepped forward.

He nocked his first arrow and drew, following the motion of the disc. When he loosed the arrow, it struck the disc nearly in the middle. He smiled and drew again, and again hit the second disc and the third. His fourth grazed the edge of the disc, veering off wildly. Clenching his jaw, he drew his fifth arrow and let it fly. It hit the edge of the last disc, quivering where it struck. He threw his bow to the ground with the others as he stalked away.

Diarmit stepped up next, but only managed to hit one of the discs. With a shrug, he turned to Caymin. "Your turn."

She stepped to the bows and found the one she preferred. She checked the string and gave it a tug as Ivar set the discs to swinging again. She nocked her first arrow, drawing the string and setting her hand against her jaw as she pushed the bow away with her left arm. She took a breath and held it as she followed the movement of the first disc, watching the rate of spin, and let loose the arrow. It struck the target in the center, but she wasn't watching. Her second arrow was already nocked and the bow pushed into position as she followed the movement of the second disc. She had her third arrow drawn almost before the second struck its disc. She let the third fly and reached for her fourth, and heard the third hit as she aimed and released. Dimly, she heard exclamations from the others watching as the fourth also struck the disc. She reached for her fifth arrow and barely looked at the target, feeling the motion rather than watching it. As she released the arrow, she turned away before the sound of its impact reached her ears.

"All five!" Diarmit stood and pounded her on the back, almost knocking her to the ground.

Cíana pulled her down to sit as Ivar yanked all five of her arrows from the middle of the discs. "And you didn't want to compete," she said with a smile.

Caymin grinned.

"I'm not looking forward to going after that," Una said as she stood.

Caymin glanced toward Gai, who sat, stony-faced, scarlet patches on his cheeks and her grin faded away.

"Come on," said Diarmit. "Spears next."

"You go. I will watch," Caymin said, sitting where she could see the action as the others lined up.

Enat sat next to her. "You shot well. Why are you looking so glum?"

Caymin glanced at her. "It hurt Gai's pride that I beat him."

Enat pondered for a moment. "Yes, it did. But wounded pride can be a good thing for some people."

"But it did not matter to me. I should have let him win."

"Letting Gai win would have wounded him in other ways – more than beating him."

Caymin frowned. "I do not understand."

"Gai wouldn't have wanted you to let him win. If you had and he'd found out, it would have made him feel worse than being outdone by your best effort. Always give your best, Caymin. Always."

Caymin thought about Enat's words after Enat left her. By the time Neela announced that they were ready to begin the running course, Caymin had made up her mind to do her best as Enat had said.

She lined up with the others, and took off when Ivar gave the signal. To her surprise, the course was laid out in a way that evened the competition. There were open stretches where her scarred leg put her at a disadvantage as she fell behind, but then the course moved into the forest where it wound through thickets and over or under fallen logs – places Caymin could scramble through more easily than the others, so that she ended up finishing in fifth place, coming across the finish line on Gai's heels.

Diarmit came in last, flopping on the ground, his chest heaving. When he sat up, he declared, "I'm not moving another muscle unless it involves eating."

Neela laughed and said, "Eating is exactly what we're doing next."

Everyone gathered for a small meal of barley cakes and smoked venison.

"Isn't there more than this?" Diarmit asked, reaching for another barley cake.

"There will be more at the feast tonight," Enat told him. "But it's important for all of us to go there hungry."

Caymin looked up. "Where are we going?"

That question was answered late in the day as all of them gathered to carry baskets filled with food: the bilberries picked that morning, along with more baskets of meat and bread. They carried empty baskets as well.

"What are the empty baskets for?" Caymin asked.

Enat leaned on her staff. "You'll see."

They proceeded to the clearing planted with all of their crops. To Caymin's surprise, Timmin was there, also holding a staff, waiting for them. They gathered near as he drew a silver knife from his belt, like the one Enat carried, and used it to cut a sheaf of barley from the stalks that had grown almost taller than Caymin. That first sheaf was carefully set aside, and then a few people harvested some of the beans and cabbages, placing them in one of the empty baskets, while Caymin and the rest dug up onions and carrots and turnips, depositing them in yet another basket.

When they had enough, the baskets were slung over their shoulders and carried in a procession up a steep hill. The sun had sunk behind the mountains to the west as they set their burdens down and gathered together. The five older apprentices led the five younger to make a circle. Méav and Caymin stood together and waited as Fergus and Gai worked with Una and Cíana, murmuring incantations and pointing to direct the shallow ditches that began to appear in the earth, connecting each pair of apprentices until the lines in the ground joined together in the pattern of a pentagram.

"It's our turn," Méav whispered. She and Caymin raised their hands, whispering words of power, and fire ran like a living thing along the ditches, illuminating the lines of the five-pointed star.

Darkness fell in earnest as Timmin stepped inside the pentagram, holding the first sheaf of barley. He raised it overhead, murmuring more words of blessing, then tapped the end of his staff on the ground. A hole opened up. He bent over and placed the sheaf inside it, tapping again with his staff to bury it.

Niall and Daina held their hands to the skies, speaking the incantation for water, and doused the fire in the ditches. Then Ronan and Diarmit shifted the earth to heal the scars, leaving it untouched.

The elders all stepped into the center of the pentagram, raised their staffs until they glowed brightly in the darkness. As one, they brought their staffs down and the ground trembled under Caymin's feet, seeming to spread out from the hillside like ripples in water.

"Please say it's time to eat," Diarmit whispered.

Enat chuckled and pointed her staff at a pile of wood that had been stacked off to one side. It burst into flame as the others retrieved the baskets of food. "Now, we eat."

They feasted late into the night, laughing and listening to Neela sing a song about the god Lugh and his funeral feast in memory of his mother, Tailtiu.

"This tale is the origin of Lughnasadh," Cíana whispered to Caymin, who was hearing it for the first time.

The others told stories of their villages' traditions for the harvest celebrations.

"We always slaughtered a young bull," said Una.

"This was when all the matches in our village were made," Diarmit said, his cheeks stuffed with bread.

"Ours, too," said Daina. "My sister was matched last year. I would have been next year, but…"

Caymin looked around, realizing something for the first time. "Do all with power stay alone? Do they not take mates?"

"Some do," Fergus said. "The mage in our village had a man and children, but many wander from place to place. Can't easily do that with a family."

"What of our mages, Enat and the others? They are alone," Caymin murmured.

Méav leaned close and whispered, "Neela and Ivar are not always alone. They spend nights together when they wish. The apprentices before us told us that Enat had a mate, a woman named Sorcha. She died long ago, and Enat came here to be mage to us."

Caymin looked at her to see if she was serious. "Two women can be mates?"

Méav smiled. "Two anyones can be mates if they love each other. There are more reasons to be mates than just to make young."

Caymin thought about this as Neela began another story. Among the badgers, there had been some of both sexes who had paired up, mated for life, but not to breed. She had never thought about taking a mate of her own one day. Being the only two-leg among the badgers, she had always pictured herself thus, alone among her clan.

Later, trudging back to the village under a blanket of stars, Enat said, "You're very quiet, little one."

Caymin shrugged. "I am tired."

It was true, all the activity and excitement of the day had exhausted her body, but still, Caymin lay in the dark, unable to sleep. Nearby, she heard Enat's gentle snores. All the others had memories of growing up with family – a human family. In recent weeks, her mind had drifted more and more to the mother and father she had only seen once in her spiritwalk. And more and more, she wondered what her life might have been if she'd lived with them. She felt a powerful ache of loneliness for Broc and Cuán and the other badgers – the only family she had known. She drifted into a restless sleep, remembering snuggling with Broc for warmth.

She felt herself flying through the night sky, soaring over hills and lakes until, at last, she was walking through familiar woods. Approaching the hidden entrance to the sett, she lowered herself to hands and knees and crawled inside. There, in the room deep under the earth, was Broc. Her cubs were big now, no longer nursing. They had just returned from hunting, and were grooming one another. Broc licked her front paws and wiped her muzzle.

"Broc?"

None of the badgers stirred at the sound of Caymin's voice. She reached out, but her hand passed through Broc's solid body as if she were merely smoke. She understood, then, that this was also a spiritwalk, though it felt different than her usual ones. This felt more real, as if she were actually there.

"Broc, I wish you could hear me. How I long to speak with you."

Broc raised her head, her nose twitching as she sniffed.

"Can you feel me?" Caymin reached a hand out again and rested it on Broc's side. Broc swung her head around, nosing the place where Caymin's ghostly hand lay.

"What is it?" asked one of the cubs.

"I thought... I have been thinking of Ash, missing her," Broc said.

"I miss you, too," Caymin said. *"How I wish I could be with you again."*

Broc curled into a tight ball, resting her chin on Caymin's hand.

Dawn was breaking when Caymin woke in her bed in Enat's cottage. She rolled over and tucked her hands under her head. She sniffed her hand and smiled as she realized it smelled of badger.

CHAPTER 10

The White Worm

As Enat had promised, once Lughnasadh was over, she gathered all of the apprentices together.

"Gai has asked for lessons on communicating with animals," she told them. "Caymin and I are willing to try and teach any of you who wish to learn, though, as I explained to Gai, only part of it is learning to talk to them. This is a gift not all can ever learn, but we must always remember that they may not choose to talk to us."

"But all the animals speak to Caymin," Daina said.

Caymin shook her head. "Not all. On my journey here with Enat, the animals I encountered would not come to me. They did not know me and were suspicious of my ability to speak with them. It was never something I thought about growing up with the badgers, as it was something I did from the time they saved me."

Enat looked around. "Do any of you know how to do this already?"

Niall nodded. "I can sense when animals are near, or in pain, but I've never spoken to one."

Enat glanced at Caymin. "We'll need help with this. Can you call Beanna?"

"Beanna? Are you busy? We have need of you."

The others looked around as nothing happened for a long time. A caw and a sudden flapping of wings announced Beanna's arrival. She landed on Caymin's shoulder.

"You called?"

"Yes. The others wish to learn to speak with four-legs and winged ones like yourself," Caymin said. *"Are you willing to help?"*

Beanna cocked her head, her bright black eye looking from one to another of the students gathered in a circle. Her head bobbed in a clear sign of amusement. The apprentices glanced at one another.

"I will help," she said. *"Though they may not like what I have to say."*

Enat smiled. "She has agreed to help."

"So you can hear and speak to them?" Cíana asked.

"I can." Enat reached out to stroke the sleek black feathers of Beanna's breast.

"And can animals understand us when we speak like this?" Daina asked.

"Beanna can. She has been a friend to me for many seasons. Other animals may pick up the odd word." Enat turned her attention to the circle. "Close your eyes and just listen for now. Not with your ears. Listen with your mind."

Diarmit frowned at this, but closed his eyes along with the others as Enat and Beanna carried on a conversation about nothing in particular – Beanna's recent flight to a distant valley beyond the forest, the Lughnasadh celebration. For several heartbeats, Caymin listened as they spoke. She watched the others. Méav gave a small gasp and her eyes fluttered open as she heard. Ronan also smiled as he heard them. Diarmit's face was screwed up in concentration, but Gai's was a mask.

"Some of you heard and understood?" Enat asked them aloud.

There were nods from the few who had heard, but frowns of discouragement from the others.

Beanna hopped down from Caymin's shoulder, waddling to face Daina. Fixing Daina with her gaze, Beanna said, *"Listen to what I say."*

Caymin watched as Daina strained to hear while Beanna repeated the phrase over and over. Daina shook her head, but next to her, Cíana suddenly smiled. Beanna looked at her.

"You heard?"

"Yes."

"Now, you must learn to speak with your mind, not your mouth."

Cíana laughed and then scrunched her eyes shut as she concentrated. *"I will try."*

Daina gave a sigh of exasperation as she could only watch this, to her, silent exchange.

Beanna moved on to Méav and Ronan, speaking with them both for a little bit. Caymin watched Gai as he listened, but she couldn't tell if he heard or not.

Beanna hopped over to stand on Gai's knee. She tilted her head, looking at him. *"You, I remember."*

To Caymin's surprise, Gai answered.

"Yes."

"You remember what I said the last time we met?"

Gai's gaze flickered to Enat and back. *"Yes."*

Beanna considered him for a long moment. *"Many two-legs make the mistake of believing they are the only thinking creatures in the world. Remember, that everywhere you go, in the forest and beyond, your movements and actions are being noticed."*

Gai bowed his head. *"I will remember."*

Beanna fluttered over to face Una and Niall. Niall was able to communicate with her, but Una could not. Lastly, Beanna hopped onto Diarmit's knee.

"Have you heard anything we have been saying?"

Diarmit blinked as he looked down at her.

"This one has a head of stone," she said.

"But a heart that is true," Caymin replied. Her brow creased as she noticed that Diarmit's cheeks flushed though his expression remained blank.

Beanna flew back to Caymin's shoulder. *"Not badly done for their first time."*

"Thank you, Beanna. May we call upon you another day?"

The crow gently tugged on Caymin's ear. *"You may."* She turned to Enat as the others chatted amongst themselves. *"One thing more. When I flew beyond the forest, I heard whispers of invaders approaching from the open water to the west. Beware."* With a loud caw, she flapped her great black wings and took to the air.

Enat frowned for a moment and then returned her attention to the circle.

"I'd say that was well-done," she said. "More of you could speak with Beanna than I expected. 'Tis a rare gift and not one to be swept aside lightly. Much can be learned from non-humans if we but take the time to listen."

Enat, Ivar and Neela spent the next two days huddled with Timmin in the meetinghouse, leaving the apprentices on their own.

"What do you think they're talking about?" Una wondered.

They listlessly practiced archery and sparring but, with their attention diverted, the practice was haphazard at best.

Caymin wasn't certain if any of them had caught Beanna's parting warning and, as Enat had said nothing aloud about it, she had thought it best not to say anything, either. Nevertheless, she felt certain the elders were discussing the reported invasion.

Sure enough, when Neela emerged from the meetinghouse late on the second day, she called the apprentices to them. They filed inside to find the other elders seated around the table with the large map laid out in the center. The apprentices sat on either side of the table.

"We've learned," said Ivar, "that there may be invaders coming to our island from here." He pointed to the west side of the map, where the land was indented in several places. "These bays make easy landing places from the sea, and this is most likely where they're coming ashore if the reports are true."

He pointed next to the upper middle of the island, near a long, narrow lake. "Our forest sits on the boundary between Uladh and

Connacht. The power of our forest should protect it, but as we've told you, if the invaders travel with their own mages, then they may breach the magical protections that are in place here."

Ronan looked up. "How can we help?"

"We want you to go in pairs," Neela said, pointing to a different map, one that showed the forest in greater detail. "Ronan, you and Caymin will go here. Stay for two or three days, find a vantage point that will allow you to see any smoke. If they've come, they'll likely be burning villages as they move. Remember, all of you, you cannot leave the forest or you will not be able to re-enter. The birds and other animals can cross the boundary. Ask them to help you. Ask if they've seen anything."

She assigned the other apprentices two by two, older and younger together, distributing them along the western boundary of the forest.

"You'll leave as soon as you're packed. Bring enough food for three days; take steel and flint," Enat told them. "If you see anything, ask a bird to fly to us and give us the news. We'll come to you."

"Take weapons as well," Ivar said.

Enat opened her mouth to protest, but Timmin spoke for the first time, saying, "It's what they've been training for, Enat. The forest is theirs to protect as much as ours."

They all left the meetinghouse.

"I'm going to get a spear," Ronan said to Caymin. "Do you want me to get a bow for you as well?"

She nodded. "I will gather food and fire starters. Get a cloak to sleep on and meet me back here."

Enat accompanied her to the cottage and helped to pack a basket of food along with fire starters and some tinder. "I know you can start a fire now without these, but save your energy. You may need it for other things."

Caymin rolled up an old cloak and stuffed it into the basket. Enat took her by the shoulders.

"Remember all you've learned, but don't forget who you are."

Caymin frowned at those words.

By the time she returned to the village with a basket slung over her shoulders, Ronan was ready with a bow and a quiver of arrows for her, a spear for himself, and a cloak rolled and slung across his chest. He had a bulging water skin tied to his belt, and she noticed a small roll of parchment tucked into his belt.

"A small map," he said. "In case we need to send word back to the elders." He pointed to the basket. "I can take that."

"Later," Caymin said, hoisting the straps higher on her shoulders. "I will take it for now."

He looked at her as if to argue, but she turned so he could strap her bow and quiver to the basket.

When he was done, they set out, going in a direction Caymin had never been. Ronan, she thought, looked like a warrior, tall and agile, carrying his weapon off to meet a potential enemy. She limped along beside him.

They walked well past sunset as a bright moon rose in the sky to light the way. Caymin grew tired but didn't want to complain or ask to stop.

"Enough," Ronan said at last. "I don't know if you're tired, but I am. We need to stop for the night."

Caymin dropped the basket and slumped to the ground, rubbing her shoulders.

"Were you just going to keep on?" Ronan asked, reaching into the basket and grabbing a couple of oatcakes. He stuffed one into his mouth, holding the other out to Caymin.

"I do not want to hold you back," Caymin said, accepting the oatcake gratefully.

Ronan laughed. "I can barely keep up with you. You've nothing to prove to me. Tell me when you need to rest. Chances are, I do, too."

He eyed her as she ate. "You don't say much, do you?"

Caymin shrugged. "I had nothing to say." She glanced at him now, the moonlight gilding his head. "Do you want a fire?"

"Aye. I think a fire tonight, for we'll not be able to light one when we get to the forest's boundary tomorrow. You light some tinder and I'll gather wood."

Soon, they sat beside a cheerful fire. She felt the presence of many animals around them. Probing with her mind, she asked them if they had seen any sign of invaders, but they all replied they hadn't. She returned her attention to the fire and Ronan.

"How old are you?" Caymin asked.

"I have sixteen winters. I've been here since I was your age." He looked around. "I should be finishing my studies here soon, going back to my family. But this forest has become home. I don't really know my family any longer. I expect my brothers and sister have all made matches by now." He frowned as he snapped a branch in half. "It won't be the same."

Caymin had never considered that the others would return to homes and families much changed in the time they were studying here in the forest. She, who had no human family to return to, could go anywhere she liked when she finished here. As they bedded down for the night, she wondered for the first time where she would go and what she would do.

"This is as far as we go."

Ronan set the basket of food down as they stopped. Caymin felt a subtle shift in the energy of the forest, though it looked as if it went on and on.

"This is our boundary," Ronan said, looking down at her.

"But we cannot see anything."

He pointed. "We can up there."

They spread out, climbing trees that gave them glimpses of the world beyond the forest. Caymin, being smaller and more agile, climbed higher into the canopy of her tree than Ronan could. She felt as if she were atop the world, looking down on a sea of leafy trees that gradually thinned, interspersed with bits of cleared land in the distance. She saw tiny people in the fields, and small clusters of dwellings, thin plumes of smoke rising from them, but no large fires or smoke, nothing that looked to be disturbed.

She spoke to the birds who shared her lofty vantage point, asking them if they had seen anything in their travels beyond the forest, but they had not.

She stayed there until her bum began to go numb sitting on a branch. Restlessly, she looked toward Ronan's tree, though she couldn't see him. To her relief, she heard him call her and began the long climb down.

They met on the forest floor and broke out some dried venison and cheese.

"Nothing," he said, passing her the water skin. "We'll rest a bit and climb back up later. If they're coming, they won't move fast. They'll burn and pillage as they go."

"Why do they do that?"

Ronan shrugged. "Some have run out of room in their land, and so need to find new land to occupy. Others are looking for prisoners or wealth to take back to their land. Fat chance they'll find any of that here. The folk around here are simple farmers and herders. I suppose they could steal the cattle and sheep, but that's about all."

Caymin gnawed on a strip of venison, wondering not for the first time what had led the pillagers to her village. She supposed she would never know.

They rested a bit after eating and then climbed again, staying until late in the day. Still nothing. They climbed back down before it got fully dark, just as a cold rain began to fall.

"I don't fancy spending the night in this," Ronan grumbled.

"There is a small cave over there." Caymin pointed from where she huddled under her cloak. "I found it earlier."

Ronan reached for the food basket. "Lead the way."

He followed her to the low mouth of a cave. "I never would've seen this."

"Wait," she said, holding a hand out. "There is someone in there already."

She probed. "I cannot fully speak to... whatever it is, but I sense it."

"Is it dangerous?"

"I do not think so. It is afraid."

"Tell it we won't hurt it, we only want out of the wet."

She reassured whatever was inside that they meant no harm, and led the way, crawling on hands and knees. Ronan had to get almost on his belly to get through the opening in the rocks.

Inside was dry. There was a rustling from the rear of the cave.

Caymin produced a ball of flame, holding her hand out to illuminate the dark recesses of the cavern. There, recoiling from the light, was a... a...

"What is it?" Ronan asked, his mouth twisted in disgust.

"I do not know." Caymin had never seen anything like the white worm-like creature writhing against the rocks.

It had a long snout and short legs that didn't look as if they could hold up its long body. Its eyes were large and milky, as if it was blind or accustomed to being in dark places.

"We need a fire," Ronan said. "I'm going to get some wood." He pointed at the worm-like creature. "Is it safe to leave you?"

"Yes," Caymin answered.

Ronan crawled back outside, and Caymin examined the creature more closely, noting strange dark marks on its white skin.

"*We will not harm you,*" she said to it. She crept nearer. "*Are you injured?*"

It didn't respond in words or thoughts as she was accustomed to when speaking with animals, but she could sense what it was feeling. The injuries were old and, though they still caused pain, they were no longer serious. She reached a tentative hand out. The creature shrank from her touch, but didn't respond aggressively. The moment her hand came in contact with it, she felt a tingle. Gasping, she saw an explosion of images – flashes of light, the creature writhing in pain, escape to the welcome dark of an underground tunnel. So powerful were the images that Caymin felt her own side, expecting to feel blood and pain, but there was nothing.

By the time Ronan returned with a large armful of wet wood, pushing it ahead of him as he crawled back into the cave, Caymin had ignited a small pile of twigs that had blown into the cave, and she was running one hand over the worm-creature while still holding a handful of flame in the other.

"What is it?" he asked.

"His name is Péist," Caymin said. "He is injured."

"He told you his name?"

"No." Caymin frowned. "I just know." She started to lay her hands on the creature.

"Hold on," Ronan said. "The last time you healed something, it nearly killed you. Is it – is he gravely injured?"

Caymin shook her head. "He says no."

"Then it's staying warm we need to worry about. We'll have to feed this fire to ignite the wet wood and keep it burning. Save your energy for this."

Caymin agreed, her teeth chattering. They gathered some of the wood Ronan had collected and added it to her twig fire. She and Ronan together fed the flames, forcing the wet wood to dry enough to catch fire and burn.

She took off her wet cloak and held it up to dry.

"Here." Ronan whispered an incantation and moved his hand over the cloak, drying and warming it.

"I must learn that," Caymin muttered, wrapping it back around her shoulders.

They were startled by a rustling sound behind them as Péist crawled nearer the fire, his milky-white eyes shielded from the light by semi-transparent inner lids.

"He likes the heat," Caymin said.

Ronan shrugged, though he still looked with some disgust at the wriggling creature. "He's welcome."

The cave quickly warmed and Caymin stopped shivering. Her eyelids drooped and her head bobbed as she sat.

"Sorry," she said, her head snapping up.

"Not to worry." Ronan fed a few more branches to the fire. "Lie down and sleep. I'm going to sleep as well. We'll keep an eye on the fire." He glanced toward the white worm. "You're sure?"

Caymin smiled. "I am sure. He is harmless."

When they woke, the rain had stopped and Péist was gone. Caymin looked around the cave, but there was no sign of him other than undulating tracks in the dirt. Strangely, she could still sense him from a distance.

She and Ronan spent most of that day up in different trees, spreading out to observe a wider vista for any signs of danger. The birds all told her they had seen no disturbances.

"Nothing," Ronan said that night when he got back to the cave. Caymin already had a large pile of firewood gathered and was roasting a few turnips in the coals.

"What I wouldn't give for some stew," Ronan said.

"This is better than earthworms," Caymin said.

At Ronan's puzzled expression, she said, "It is what the badgers tried to feed me when they first rescued me. They did not know what two-leg cubs ate."

He chuckled. "And you just always knew how to talk to them?"

Caymin nodded. "Broc said I called to her." She looked at him. "You said the invaders sometimes take prisoners. So that means they do not kill everyone?"

"That's what I've been told. Some of them take captives and haul them back on their boats to wherever they came from." He paused. "You're wondering if your ma and da might still be alive?"

She shrugged and didn't reply.

Ronan used a stick to prod the turnips out of the coals. "Here," he said, tossing one to Caymin. They both had to hold the turnips in their cloaks for a moment until they cooled enough to eat.

"Do you know who attacked your village?"

Caymin shook her head. "No. I cannot remember."

"Too bad. If you did, you might have a chance to find out if they're still living." He looked at her sympathetically. "'Tis not likely though." He pulled out a knife to split his turnip and then handed the knife to Caymin.

"I know." Caymin cut her turnip.

"We'll stay one more day," Ronan said. "If there's nothing tomorrow, we'll head back."

When Caymin lay down to sleep, she could still feel Péist. She had never had a connection like this to another. Usually, the animals she could talk to were like talking to other people, and the connection ended when it ended. This connection, though, didn't use words and felt almost as strong as it had when he had been in the cave with them. He was hunting, feeding hungrily on grubs and mice, as he hadn't eaten the night before when they had entered his cave.

When at last she slept, she saw again her mother and father as they had appeared in her spiritwalk.

CHAPTER 11

The Invaders

When they were still some distance from the village, Ronan and Caymin felt something and paused. They listened, but there was absolute silence in the forest. Not a bird or animal moved or spoke. They placed their hands on an ancient tree and waited.

"I don't hear anything," Ronan said.

"Nor do I."

They approached the village cautiously, the nearly empty food basket slung over Ronan's shoulders and his spear held at the ready while Caymin had her bow strung, an arrow nocked. They were startled by Beanna, who came cawing and flapping toward them. She landed on Caymin's shoulder.

"*Did you see anything?*" the crow asked.

"*No. Nothing.*"

"*Two of the others did. They have all left for that part of the forest. Enat left instructions for you.*"

Ronan understood and broke into a run, Caymin following on his heels while Beanna took to the air at the sudden jostling.

A piece of parchment was nailed to the door of the meeting-house with a map of which direction the invaders had been spotted nearing the forest.

"Let's go," Ronan said.

"Enat said you are to pack more food," Beanna told them. *"And bring more weapons."*

"She is right," Caymin said, pulling the basket off his shoulders. "You go get the weapons you want, and I will pack more food."

He soon returned with a sword buckled at his side and a bow slung over his shoulder. He had a second sword, which he held out to Caymin. She shook her head.

"You know I cannot defeat anyone with that."

He looked at her darkly. "If they make it into the forest, a bow may not be enough."

Reluctantly, she strapped the sheath to her side.

She had stuffed two baskets with bread, cheese, turnips, carrots, more dried meat, "and oatcakes," said Ronan gratefully as he crammed one into his mouth before shouldering one of the baskets. "Ready?"

Caymin nodded, the other basket slung over her shoulders.

"I will come with you," Beanna said, flying circles around them.

They settled into an easy lope, Ronan taking care not to outpace Caymin as she trotted along with her lopsided gait. The slap of the sword and sheath against her leg was bothersome, but she kept up with him.

Beanna flew ahead and then back to them as they traveled. For what seemed like an age, she reported nothing, but then, *"They are just there."*

She flew to where Enat and Neela were hidden in a dense copse of rowan trees, armed with both their staffs and swords. Breathlessly, Caymin dropped her basket and sat, her legs trembling.

"Where are the others?" Ronan asked, breathing only a little more easily than Caymin.

Neela pointed up. "The other apprentices have all taken positions that will give them vantage points for their bows or spears if the invaders get this far."

Caymin looked around. "Where is Ivar?"

"He went to the closest village to warn them," Enat said. "If they're capable of fighting, he'll organize them."

"And if they are not?"

Enat glanced at her. "Then he'll try to hide them."

Ronan turned at this. "But that means there'll be no one to stand between the invaders and the forest."

Neela nodded. "We don't yet know if they have mages with them. It may be that the forest will turn them away without our help."

"Timmin?"

Enat smiled grimly. "Timmin is preparing his own defenses if the invaders make it into the forest."

"What do you want us to do?" Ronan asked.

"Spread out and take up positions that will allow you to use bows first," Neela said. "We want you out of harm's way unless it becomes necessary for you to use swords or spears."

Caymin and Ronan strung their bows and moved off. Caymin found an aged elm tree that offered her hand and footholds for climbing. She didn't climb high, but looked for a gap in the leafy branches that would afford her a view of any who might be approaching their position. She settled in the crook of two branches. Beanna flew to the branch beside her.

"Now, we wait," said the crow.

All was still eerily quiet, as if the entire forest held its breath. Caymin felt the undercurrent of energy from the tree she sat in. *"The trees know."*

Beanna fluffed her feathers. *"The whole forest knows."*

Hours dragged by. All remained silent. There was no stir of movement, no word from Ivar. Darkness began to fall. Caymin heard Enat's voice in her head.

"Come down. We will eat and decide who will stand watch through the night."

Caymin climbed down from her perch to find Diarmit, Cíana and the others already gathered together.

Speaking in whispers, they explained that Daina and Fergus had been the ones to sound the alarm.

"We saw an enormous plume of black smoke in the distance," Daina whispered.

"Did you actually see the invaders?" Ronan asked, helping himself to some cheese and bread.

Fergus shook his head. "We didn't wait for them to get that close. We sent word back and waited for everyone to join us here."

"What do you think is happening with Ivar and the villagers?" Diarmit looked worried as he bit into a strip of venison.

No one replied.

"We'll need to divide the watch through the night," said Neela. "The forest will help to sound an alarm if they cross the boundary."

She assigned Niall, Cíana and Gai to the first watch. "The rest of you get some sleep. We'll switch at moonrise."

Caymin spread her cloak on the ground and lay down, listening for any sound. Her eyes snapped open at every creak of a branch. She could feel the animals sheltering as they, too, waited, but none were speaking. She forced herself to close her eyes.

She wasn't sure what time it was when something pushed through her sleep. She opened her eyes to find the moon high overhead, and realized the first switch of the watch must have been made. As she listened, she felt Péist – his fear and alarm.

She jumped up, searched for Enat and shook her awake.

"They are coming in from another direction."

Enat sat up. "How do you know this?"

"I heard it."

"I've heard nothing."

"It woke me."

Enat reached out to wake Neela and, together, they placed their hands on a tree, listening.

Neela quickly shook Ronan, Méav, Una and Diarmit awake.

"We'll go to meet them at the place Caymin knows," she said to

Enat. "You and the others stay here in case it's a trick. Ask Beanna if she'll carry a message to Ivar."

Enat gave Caymin's shoulder a squeeze. "You're sure?"

Caymin nodded as she gathered her bow, quiver and her sword.

"Take care."

Neela asked Caymin to lead the way. Shafts of moonlight filtered through the trees to light their way, but Caymin wished it were dark to cover their movements.

"Where are we going?" Neela asked.

"West."

She told Péist they were coming, and followed the thoughts she sensed from him as she led the others through the forest.

"How does she know where to go?" Diarmit whispered as he tripped over a root.

"Shhh."

Caymin had never been to this part of the forest, but Péist's presence drew her surely as an arrow shot from a bow. She slowed her pace and the others followed suit.

Crouching, she peered through the tree trunks. She sensed the boundary of the forest.

"They came across the lake," Neela breathed in Caymin's ear.

Below them, they could see five long, wooden boats pulled up on a grassy shore. A score of men gathered there. Puzzled, Caymin wondered why they were standing about, doing nothing. Then she saw them. Two men, their light hair gilded by the moonlight, their shoulders draped in fur capes, walked along the edge of the forest. She saw that their hands were raised and saw their bearded mouths moving, though they were too far away to hear what they said.

She felt a shiver run through the ground beneath her feet. The others felt it, too.

"Move back," Neela whispered.

They crept back the way they had come.

"The two are mages," Neela said. "They are using their power, looking for a way through the protections around the forest."

"Why?" Una glanced at the others. "What do they want here? There are no villages to plunder."

Neela shook her head. "They may not know that. They may want sacred wood from the forest, or plants we have here that don't grow in their land. I only know they do not come as friends."

She looked at the apprentices. "There are too many of them for us to fight with weapons alone. We will watch at first, to see what they do. If they bring any harm to the forest or to us, we must protect what is ours. Use what you know, but only use your weapons if you've no other choice."

They spread out, climbing trees or hiding in clumps of undergrowth. Caymin pushed into a dense thicket and found a position that gave her an opening she could shoot through if needed.

"*We are here,*" Caymin said to Péist. She wasn't certain where he was, but she knew he was near. "*Stay hidden.*"

Silently, they waited. Another shudder ran through the earth beneath her, and she knew the strangers had found their way in. Barely daring to breathe, she heard them before she saw them, and listened as they drew near. Their speech was strange, guttural and harsh. They tramped along, not bothering to move quietly.

She glanced right and left, and saw the shadows of Méav and Ronan in neighboring trees readying their weapons. She knew Neela, Una and Diarmit were probably doing the same in other clumps of undergrowth.

The invaders halted their progress at a stand of rowan trees. By shifting just a bit, Caymin could see them as they pulled out knives, collecting berries and cutting branches, tying them in bundles. One of them called out, and the others joined him at a nearby yew – an ancient and gnarled tree. Moonlight flashed of the broad blades of the axes they hefted. A few of them began hacking at stout branches while others used their axes to shave the bark.

Again, Caymin felt a shudder, almost of pain, from the forest. Neela had said not to use weapons, but they were attacking the trees. Caymin drew her bow, took aim at the stranger nearest her and let loose. Her aim was true, and the arrow hit the handle of his axe, causing it to go spinning from his hand. With a cry, he whirled, looking for the one who had shot at him. From all around them, the invaders were suddenly besieged by arrows and balls of flame flying from every direction. Caymin joined in, flinging balls of fire at their feet as they bunched together, shouting and looking for their enemies.

With a raucous screech and the thunder of many flapping wings, a flock of birds swooped down, diving with beaks and talons at the invaders. Caymin saw owls and hawks and other crows. The strangers yelled in fear, covering their heads with their arms as the birds pecked and scratched at them.

A mighty wind whipped the air and a great creaking rose up from the forest floor. What moonlight there was, was obscured. New shouts of terror came from the invaders as the very trees seemed to close in around them. Someone among them roared a word and they all began running back the way they had come. The birds pursued them until all were out of hearing.

Slowly, the wind ceased and the moonlight filtered once more through the leaves of the trees, and all was as it had been. Caymin crawled out of her thicket to join the others who were emerging from their hiding places.

She looked around, staring at the ground around the trees, but all was as before. Nothing looked disturbed; no trees were uprooted. But she could have sworn...

"Did you see that?" Diarmit asked, pointing. "The trees... the trees banded together!"

Neela turned to him. "Don't be daft. Trees can't move."

But Caymin noted that she smiled as she said it.

Suddenly, they heard a harsh cry. They crept through the forest, staying behind trees for cover until they saw that one of the invaders was writhing on the ground. His companions had left him behind. In the distance, the long boats could be seen pushing off from the shore and gliding back across the lake.

Neela approached the stranger, her bow held at the ready, flanked by Méav and Ronan who had spears aimed at him.

Peering around Neela, Caymin saw that the man's leg was injured, pierced by one of their arrows.

Still aiming an arrow at his heart, Neela said, "Why have you come here?"

The man stared at her, his expression in the moonlight one of panic as he looked hopelessly around for help. Seeing that he'd been left, he calmed himself and faced Neela.

"Vi mener ingen skade."

She frowned. "I don't understand you."

"Do you want me to heal his leg?" Caymin asked.

Neela shook her head. "No. You'll not use your energy healing the likes of him." She jerked her bow up, indicating she wanted him to stand. He got up, balancing on one leg, leaving his axe lying at his feet.

"Search him for other weapons," Neela said, keeping her bow drawn and aimed at him.

Ronan stepped forward and found two knives, one in his belt, the other tucked into his boot. He handed the knives to Una and placed the stranger's arm over his shoulder.

"Let's go," Neela said.

Dawn was tinting the sky to the east with pinks and purples as they got back to the village. Exhausted, the small party collapsed to the ground, the invader grunting in pain as Ronan dropped him. He grabbed his injured leg.

They dug into the food baskets. Caymin handed the injured man a hunk of bread and a piece of cheese. He sniffed them cautiously, and then, seeing that they were all eating from the same baskets, jammed the food into his mouth.

Before long, they were joined by Enat and those apprentices who had stayed with her.

They stopped when they saw the injured stranger on the ground. Enat squatted down next to him, running a hand over the smooth fur of his boots and the rough, thick hair of his cape.

"A northman," she said. "Can you understand me?"

He looked at her blankly. "Vi mener ingen skade."

"That's what he said before," Neela said. "I don't know what he's saying."

He looked from one of them to the other. "Vi hørte der drager her."

Enat turned to Daina. "Get the map. The large one."

Daina was back in a moment. Enat laid the map on the ground. "Show us." She pointed at him and then at the map again. He nodded his understanding and pointed to a place far to the north.

"How many?" Again, she pointed at him and then held up her hands, ticking numbers off with her fingers.

He held up both of his hands four times.

"We didn't see that many coming in from the lake," Neela murmured. "Where are the others?"

Enat stood. "Tie his hands behind his back," she said. To Neela, "We need to summon Ivar and Timmin."

She stood and closed her eyes. Within a few heartbeats, an owl and a hawk landed on her outstretched arms. Caymin heard her ask them to fly, the owl to Ivar and the hawk to Timmin. She lifted her arms and they spread their great wings and took off.

Ronan produced a length of braided leather and tied the invader's hands tightly.

"What happened?" Cíana whispered, sitting beside Caymin. "We felt... something." She pointed her chin at him. "And who's he?"

"Four of their boats came across the lake," Caymin said. "They had two mages with them and they got into the forest. They had axes and were cutting some of the trees, when..."

"The trees moved," said Diarmit through a mouthful of oatcake. "They did. I swear."

"'Twas amazing," said Una. "It was as if the forest came to life. More than it normally is."

Caymin ripped loose a chunk of bread for herself and passed the loaf to Cíana. "It was unlike anything I have ever seen."

The prisoner groaned, and Enat knelt again beside him. "I need a couple of you to hold him." Fergus and Niall grasped him by either arm while she snapped the shaft of the arrow still protruding from his leg. "Brace yourself."

The man seemed to understand what she meant, for he nodded and screwed his eyes shut as she pulled the arrow from his leg. He gave a strangled cry, panting in pain.

Enat turned to Caymin. "Go to the cottage. Get what we need."

Caymin ran, collected a roll of cloth for a bandage along with some healing herbs and brought them all back to Enat. She quickly packed the wounds in the man's leg with some of the crushed leaves, and then wrapped it all with the cloth. From the rest of the herbs, she made a tea and held it to the man's lips. He drank it with a look of gratitude.

Almost before he finished his tea, he was getting drowsy. He slumped back against the wall of the meetinghouse, sleeping heavily.

"He'll be asleep for quite a while." Enat turned to Neela. "Start at the beginning."

Neela told what had happened, and then Enat gestured to Caymin.

"It's time we heard what led you there. How did you know?"

"Someone called to me in my sleep. Told me the invaders were coming from that direction."

Neela frowned. "Who called to you?"

"His name is Péist. He is..." Caymin glanced at Ronan. "I do not know what he is."

"He was in a cave when we first were sent to watch the forest," Ronan said. "He looks like a... a white worm. Has short legs, but kind of wriggles about. Caymin can talk to him."

"Not like I can talk to others," she corrected. "With Beanna and other animals, it is like talking to one of you. This was different. He was hurt, and when I touched him... there was a connection unlike anything I have ever felt before. No words, but I felt things, saw things."

"What things?" Diarmit stared at her.

Caymin closed her eyes, trying to remember. "Flashes of light, pain, someone attacking him, hurting him." Her eyes fluttered open. "But that is all."

Neela looked at Enat, bewildered. "What is she describing?"

Enat glanced at the stranger where he lay sleeping. Her eyes narrowed. "I don't know for certain, but I've an idea."

"Well, I never saw anything so disgusting," Ronan said.

"Is he speaking with you now?" Enat asked Caymin.

She listened. "Not speaking. I always feel him now. Like a quiet breeze that you do not always notice, but always there." She frowned. "He is sleeping, somewhere dark. He does not like the light."

Heavy footsteps signaled Ivar's return. He ran into the village, red-faced and panting. "What happened? I was already on my way back when the owl found me." His mouth fell open at the sight of the sleeping prisoner. "And who is that?"

Just then, the hawk flew to Enat, landing lightly on her shoulder.

"Timmin is weak. He needs you."

Neela gasped. "It was his magic. We should have known."

"We must check on him." Enat pushed to her feet. "Come, Ivar, we'll tell you on the way." She pointed to Fergus. "Come with us. The rest of you stay here, and stay away from the prisoner."

Caymin and the others watched them leave.

"Why? What is wrong?" she asked.

"The energy it must have taken to work such a spell from such a distance," Una said.

"The forest? That was his spell?"

"What else could it have been?" Niall said.

"They're afraid he won't be alive," Cíana said solemnly.

Diarmit turned to her. "It might have killed him?"

"Magic takes energy," Gai reminded him. "You know that. If it demands more than you have, it can kill you."

A somber silence fell over the group. Caymin looked from one to the other, bewildered. "Timmin is old," she said tentatively.

"Yes," Daina said. "But because he is old, he is the wisest among us. It will be a great loss to us if he dies."

Caymin fell silent. All her life, she had lived with death. Badgers, foxes, hawks, owls – they all hunted. For them to live, something else had to die. It was simply the way things were. There was a sense of loss, of course. Other badgers had died in the winters she lived with them, and she missed them, but she knew, if Broc or Cuán had died, she would have felt a keen grief.

Cíana must have been watching her, because she said, "You told us about the night the wolves attacked. You would have died fighting them, to save the badgers."

Caymin nodded.

Cíana dipped her head. "The same with Timmin. He fought the invaders with magic, and he may have died doing it. We honor that."

This, Caymin understood.

The day wore on with no sign of the elders. The prisoner stirred and sat up. He looked longingly toward a nearby pail of water.

"He is thirsty," Caymin said.

Méav stood over him with her spear as Caymin filled a gourd with water and raised it to his lips. He gulped it down, plus a second gourd-full of water. They eyed him curiously.

"What kind of animals did those skins come from?" Méav wondered.

"I do not know," Caymin said. So many things about him were strange and wondrous, like the brooch he wore at his chest, fastening his furred cape. It was made of metal, worked with intricate designs. She leaned forward for a closer look.

"Take care," Méav warned her.

Caymin glanced into his pale blue eyes, but he was smiling. He nodded and she reached out to touch the pattern – a long, sinuous creature with wings spread.

"Drage."

She frowned. "Dragon?"

His eyes widened. "Ja!"

"Caymin," Méav said in a low voice. "Come away."

Caymin backed away from the man and waited with the others.

The sun was on the far side of the sky by the time Enat and the others returned to the village, Ivar carrying Timmin in his arms.

They brought him into the meetinghouse, and Caymin got a glimpse of his face, nearly as white as his beard. Someone fetched a sleeping mat from one of the dwellings and they made Timmin as comfortable as they could.

The apprentices were shooed outside while the elders worked. Enat emerged after what seemed like a long time and called Caymin to accompany her to their cottage to gather herbs and roots she needed.

"Will he live?" Caymin asked as Enat loaded her arms with pots and jars.

"I don't yet know," Enat said. "He's very weak. The spell took nearly all he had. And he had a great deal."

"But it worked. The invaders left. They are gone."

Enat's expression darkened. "Not all are gone. And now they know we're here."

CHAPTER 12

Back Into the Mist

For the next days, Caymin barely saw Enat. She slept alone at the cottage, making the porridge and oatcakes she liked so much. She brought some to the meetinghouse, leaving them outside the door for the elders who were still tending to Timmin. Neela thanked her tiredly, and then closed the door again. No word came as to whether Timmin was improving or not.

The apprentices were left on their own to speculate what would be done with the stranger. He had been brought into the meetinghouse as well so that the elders could heal his leg.

"They're trying to talk to him," Diarmit whispered, listening at the door. "He just keeps saying the same things over and over."

"Come away from there," Ronan said.

"What do you think they'll do with him?" Diarmit asked as he joined the others.

The older apprentices looked at one another darkly.

"What?" Daina looked from one of them to the next.

"Well, they can't just let him go now, can they?" Méav said.

"He knows too much about us and the forest, now he's been here,"

Fergus seconded.

Caymin sat up. "What would they do with him?"

"There are ways," Una said. "Spells that can take away someone's memories, but it's near impossible to only take the memories you want. It might leave him completely addled."

"In the meantime, we've work to do," said Ronan. "It's past time we should be finishing the harvesting. The crops have been ready."

Gai scowled. "Can't we hunt? We need meat as well." He glanced at Caymin. "You can speak to them better than we can. You can call something to us."

She looked at him, aghast. "I would never. Hunt if you must, but you cannot hunt animals who trust you enough to speak with you."

"She's right," Una said. "No matter how skilled any of us ever becomes at speaking with them, we can't call animals to us. It isn't sporting or right. We hunt by stealth, and we'll honor the spirit of any we kill."

Fergus and Una shared a meaningful look. "I'll go with Gai to hunt," he said. "If the rest of you don't mind harvesting."

They left to get bows and spears while the others collected baskets and headed to the planted clearing. There, they spent the rest of the day gathering the last of the barley and wheat and oats, digging up parsnips and turnips, pulling carrots and onions, cutting cabbages and picking beans. They filled two baskets with apples.

Caymin tried to block the occasional stabs of fear she felt from animals in the forest where she knew Fergus and Gai must be in pursuit. Underneath all, she felt Péist, faint and indistinct, but there. Always there. She smiled.

When they had gathered all they could carry, they shouldered the baskets and carried them back to the village. To their surprise, they found Ivar, Neela and Enat sitting around the fire outside the meetinghouse, a pot of stew hanging over the flames.

"How's Timmin?" Méav asked as she set her basket on the ground.

"Finally better," said Enat.

Caymin noticed how tired she looked. "He will live?"

Ivar nodded. "He'll live. But he's still weak. That spell cost him dearly."

The others deposited their baskets and joined the group at the fire.

"And what of the stranger?" Ronan asked.

"He's well enough to walk," Neela said. "In a few days, we'll remove all memory of the forest and his days here, and take him where others can decide what to do with him."

She dished out bowls of stew for each of them.

"What happened when you were at the village?" Cíana asked Ivar as she passed a bowl to Daina.

"They were ready to fight," Ivar said. "I was organizing them to go meet the invaders at a valley beyond their village, but the invaders stopped on the far side and never advanced. We could see them camped there. We didn't know what they were waiting for, why they didn't attack. Then, they just retreated back the way they came." He glanced at Caymin. "Not until I got back here, did I realize they were just a ruse to distract us while the others came across the lake."

"Thank the goddess you were warned that they were coming from that direction," Enat said to Caymin. "When things are calmer here, I would like to meet Péist." She looked around at the harvest baskets. "But for now, we have more work to do, getting everything you harvested stored away and picking the rest tomorrow. It's nearly the equinox."

A triumphant shout diverted their attention as Gai and Fergus appeared with the carcass of a stag slung over their shoulders.

Ivar got to his feet. "I'll help them skin and then butcher the meat."

Neela sighed. "Well, let's get the bowls cleaned and back to work."

Caymin gathered an armful of bowls to wash while the others took the harvest baskets to the storage cellar dug on the outskirts of the village. Diarmit accompanied her.

"You really can talk to the worm-creature?"

Caymin shrugged. "As I said, it is not really talking so much as I feel his thoughts."

"But he didn't show you who hurt him?"

Caymin knelt at the edge of the stream. "No. Why?"

"No reason."

Diarmit knelt beside her and they scrubbed the bowls in silence. As they carried the clean bowls back, Diarmit said, "Only, we know someone who enjoys hunting and hurting things, don't we?"

She looked at Diarmit as, from somewhere in the trees, they could hear Gai telling Ivar about their hunt.

Within a few days, Timmin was well enough to be moved, "but not well enough to live by himself," said Enat. "So he will be staying here with us for a bit."

Caymin helped set up a sleeping mat for him near the cottage's fire. He leaned heavily on his staff as Enat accompanied him. A chair from the meetinghouse had been carried by Ivar and padded with a sheepskin. Timmin groaned a little as he settled his frail frame into it.

"Caymin, would you make Timmin a cup of tea?" Enat said.

Caymin pulled the kettle from where it hung over the fire, and mixed the hot water with some herbs and leaves to aid healing. She glanced questioningly at Enat, who nodded. Holding her hand over the cup, she whispered words of power to enhance the healing.

Timmin thanked her, and sipped at the tea. "I couldn't have made better myself."

Caymin beamed with the praise. She peered at him. "Can you tell me more about the magic you used against the invaders?"

"What did you see?"

"We were all hidden, watching the invaders as they began to chop at the trees with their axes," Caymin said. "I could almost feel the pain from the trees. Suddenly, it seemed the trees moved, surrounding them. The moonlight disappeared and a great noise rose up. It felt as if the forest was fighting back."

Timmin nodded. "The forest did fight back."

"But the trees did not actually move. Or did they?"

"Yes and no." He looked at her. "If you can probe the minds of your enemies, you can sense what they fear most. Those strangers come from a land of great superstition. They knew this forest has ancient power and they feared it. All I did was use their fears against them."

Caymin frowned. "But we saw it also."

Timmin smiled grimly. "It was a costly spell."

"The distance he cast the spell and the number of people he made feel it," Enat said. "Don't ever attempt such a thing again."

Timmin shrugged. "Aye, but it worked. We can hope they'll never come back."

Enat pursed her lips, but said nothing more on the subject. Instead, she said, "You should get some sleep."

With a heavy sigh, Timmin agreed and allowed her and Caymin to help him to his makeshift bed.

"Sleep well, Timmin," said Enat, covering him with a blanket.

"You as well," he said with a yawn.

Caymin wandered through thick mist, swirling about her so heavily that she could not see her outstretched hand. She knew this mist. It was the same that had surrounded her when Enat guided her on her spiritwalk. She followed, letting the mist choose her path for her. When it parted, she was unsurprised to find herself on the outskirts of her village again.

There, as before, was her mother, her red hair tied back as she cut carrots into a kettle of hot water, while she watched little Caymin laughing as she sat on her father's lap, plucking at the small harp he held.

All around them, other villagers called to one another, cooking over their fires or chasing their own toddling children. In the distance, she heard older children calling from the field where they tended the cattle and goats and sheep, bringing them in for the night.

Caymin smiled, looking at the peacefulness of it all. She sat, watching her family in wonder, listening as her father plucked the harp and sang a song.

Too soon, the mist swirled around her once more, and she walked on, following the path it laid before her. When next the fog parted, it was full night, with fires burning in front of some of the dwellings, others with plumes of smoke rising from smoke holes in their roofs. It seemed most had retired for the night, though a few men still lingered at one fire and Caymin saw a woman leaning close to another, using its light to sew a torn garment.

Suddenly, the night air was filled with screams and yells and the sounds of chaos as warriors swarmed the village. Swords flashed and more screams followed. Thatched roofs were set afire and ignited bottles of oil were thrown through doorways. Soon the entire village was ablaze and a pall of smoke obscured what was happening. Warriors entered dwellings, hauling people outside where most were put to the sword. She saw bodies falling, heard women scream as they were dragged by their hair. Caymin watched as her father ran from their burning cottage, armed only with a scythe. He used it well, keeping two warriors away from their door, but when a third warrior joined the fight, her father could not swing the scythe fast enough to keep all three at bay. He dropped the scythe and lunged at one of the warriors, grabbing at his sword, but one of the other warriors moved in, plunging his sword into her father's back.

Her mother emerged from the cottage as he fell. She ran to him, catching him and clutching him to her. Behind her, a crying Caymin stumbled out of the cottage as the roof and walls collapsed, sending a geyser of sparks into the night sky. Her mother reached one arm toward her to shield her even as she clung to her dead husband, but the warriors wrested his body from her arms and pulled her to her feet.

As her mother struggled to free herself, one of the warriors knocked little Caymin into the flames, taking no heed of the little girl's screams of pain as she writhed.

Caymin stood torn between her younger self, burning and screaming in the flames, and her mother being dragged away by cloaked warriors....

The mist swirled about once more, and she heard a voice in her ear.

"Come away now."

She felt herself rising through the mist into wakefulness and opened her eyes to find Enat kneeling beside her.

"I saw..."

"I know." Enat wrapped her in her arms and held her, rocking her as she cried.

When she quieted, Enat released her. Caymin sat up, wiping her face with her blanket. "How? How did I have this spiritwalk tonight? I did not have the potion."

Enat glanced toward the fire where Timmin lay sleeping. "You've been wanting to go again since that night, wanting to see more. I think Timmin's presence, his magic, opened the door for you in your sleep."

"They did not kill her."

"What?" Enat turned back to Caymin who had reached for her old cloak.

She stared at the design woven into the cloth – a blue wolf with red eyes, holding a yellow sword in one paw. "They killed my father, but they took my mother." She held up the cloak. "If I can find the ones who wear this, I may find her."

Enat was silent for a long moment. "It's not likely, little one, that she could still be alive."

But Caymin wasn't listening. She lay back down, holding the cloak in her hands while Enat went back to her bed.

From far away, Caymin felt Péist's concern at her distress. *"I am unharmed."* That wasn't exactly true, she knew. As much as she had wanted to see her family again, to know what had happened to them, she almost wished now she hadn't seen. Her fingers unconsciously went to the scars and ridges on the side of her face, and she closed her eyes against the image of her father's death. But her heart held fast to the knowledge that her mother had not died that night.

When she opened her eyes again, she saw that Timmin was awake, watching her from his bed.

"Focus," said Ronan to Caymin as she tried to levitate a rock he held in his hand.

Frowning, she concentrated harder.

"Stop. You're not going to frighten it into moving by glaring at it. Pull the power from deep inside you," he said. "Feel it rise, and with it, the stone."

The stone rocked in his palm and slowly began to rise, spinning in the air.

"Well done," he murmured. "Now feed it, just enough to hold it steady."

"Look at Caymin," said Diarmit, who was working with Méav and hadn't succeeded in getting even a feather to levitate.

"You'd do better to look at this feather," said Méav. "And get the wretched thing to lift."

Diarmit reached for the feather and tickled her under the chin with it.

"Bah." She slapped at his hand and got up. "I've had enough of this one."

"I've had enough of this altogether," Gai said, dropping the stone he was levitating under Una's tutelage. "What do you think they did with him?"

The meetinghouse door stood open and the elders were nowhere to be seen, nor was the prisoner.

For days, the elders had ensconced themselves in the meetinghouse with the northman. Occasionally, their raised voices could be heard as they argued about what to do with him.

"They agreed to alter his memory," Fergus said. "They're probably taking him away to the villagers to let them decide what to do with him."

Caymin frowned. "But will they let him go?"

Méav turned to her. "What would you do with him? Let him go back to his land and take the chance he'd tell them all about us if his memory comes back?"

Daina looked troubled. "Surely, they wouldn't kill him..."

"The invaders came here with one goal," said Fergus. "They wanted our land, our forest. We have to do what we must to protect it."

"My father would have had him executed after he told us all he knew," Gai said. He glanced at Caymin. "I'm not saying it's the right thing, but it's what must be done."

"Well, our elders are wiser than that," Una said. "They did what they could to learn what he knew, they removed his memories of what he's seen and heard here, and they'll let others decide what to do with him." She turned back to Cíana and held out a small clay pot. "Now, back to work. See if you can move this pot over to that table."

When the elders returned, they returned one by one from various directions. Timmin had insisted on accompanying them to see the stranger off.

"They were checking different parts of the forest to make sure no one else is here," Niall told the others.

Nor did they elaborate on what had happened with the stranger once they were all back.

"But you live with Enat, and Timmin is still staying with you," Daina whispered to Caymin. "Haven't they said anything?"

"No. And I have not asked." Caymin shook her head. "I have learned I will not get answers to all questions."

One such unspoken question was how long Timmin would be staying with them. Where she and Enat often sat in companionable silence for long periods of time, or could talk about almost anything, things were different with Timmin there.

When she first met him, he had seemed kindly and wise, but now, Caymin found his presence unsettling. She often looked up to find him staring at her, and his probing gaze made her uncomfortable.

"I understand you made an interesting friend in the forest," Timmin said to her one evening.

Caymin sat near the warmth of the fire, as the nights had grown cold. "Yes. Péist. Do you know him?"

"I don't, no. But Enat said he's the one who warned you the northmen were coming across the lake."

"Yes."

Enat sat nearby, mending a tear in a woolen tunic, as he filled a pipe with crushed leaves and lit it with a flick of a finger. Smoke puffed from both the bowl of the pipe and from his mouth. "Enat said you have connected with him in a way that lets you feel him at all times?"

Caymin nodded.

"Do you know where he is now?"

She shook her head. "I do not get such specific images from him most of the time. He is hunting."

Timmin nodded, looking into the fire. He said nothing more, but Caymin had the feeling he was not done with asking about Péist.

To everyone's surprise, Timmin began teaching the apprentices.

"We've never had lessons with him before," Méav whispered. "He never left wherever it is he lives."

Enat had taught them much about herbs and roots and barks and leaves and their various properties, but Timmin showed them how to make more than just teas and powders for different ailments.

"One sip of this potion, and someone will sleep for many hours," he told them as he carefully measured his ingredients into a cauldron heating over a fire. "Useful if you ever need to slip past someone, or escape an enemy. And if you add just a few yew needles, it will put them so deeply asleep they will appear to be dead."

"Yew needles are poisonous," Cíana said.

Timmin nodded. "All of the yew tree is poisonous. But if you know how to brew this potion – and it only works in a very few recipes – you can use the poison to your advantage."

Caymin had to admit these lessons were more exciting than learning to make simple salves and healing potions. Not as exciting as learning to control the elements or levitate things, but it was fascinating to watch him create different potions. He added the ingredients almost tenderly, as if the potion were a living thing.

"Anyone care to try it?" Timmin smiled as he dipped a wooden spoon into the pale green solution.

"I think not at this moment," said Neela.

The apprentices all turned in surprise at her unexpected arrival.

"I have other work for them today, and it doesn't involve sleeping."

"I should have taken the potion," Diarmit grumbled a short while later as they all shouldered square metal shovels and walked to a low, boggy area of the forest.

"We need to replenish our stock of peat," Neela told them. "We'll be spending the next few days working here."

Gai looked around with a scowl. "This is –"

"We know," Una interrupted. "This is servants' work. But since we've no servants here and we need enough peat to keep the fires burning all winter, stop complaining and get to it."

Caymin grinned at her and pushed her shovel into the soft, moist earth, thick with bits of rotted plants and roots. She welcomed the hard work and the sleep she hoped would be hers that night, as sleep had been hard to come by lately... ever since the night of her last spiritwalk.

Sometimes she woke in the night, fragments of that terrible night fresh in her mind, sometimes all mixed up with images of Péist and how he'd been hurt. She still couldn't tell who had hurt him and wondered if Diarmit could be right about Gai. Always, when she woke, she turned to find Timmin awake on his bed, watching her as he had that night. And she knew he knew what was in her mind. In fact, she sometimes wondered if he didn't cause her to go there in her sleep. She'd considered asking Enat how much longer he would stay with them, but Enat was kind. She'd taken her in, letting her invade her nice, quiet cottage. Caymin didn't feel as if she had any right to complain.

They dug peat all afternoon, the heavy wet earth eliciting groans of fatigue from all of them. Daylight was fading as they returned to the village. Enat and Ivar had a hearty meal awaiting them – a chicken stew with cabbage and carrots and onions, and fresh bread.

Diarmit filled his bowl almost to overflowing, spooning stew into his mouth before he even sat. "Oh, this is so good."

Caymin had to agree as she filled her own bowl. The day's work had stirred her appetite. Enat looked at her legs.

"You've grown. Those leggings were down to your ankles when you first came here," she observed. "They're halfway to your knees now."

Caymin looked down in surprise. Enat was right. She hadn't noticed how she'd grown.

Cíana smiled at her. "You're not a badger runt any longer."

"Still a human runt, though," Gai said. Cíana glared at him. "What? I'm just saying she's still the smallest one here."

Caymin shrugged. "He is right. I am the smallest."

"Maybe," said Ronan. "But don't make her angry."

Ivar scowled as the others burst into laughter. Daina asked Neela to tell them a story and she told a story of the Morrigan, challenging Cú Chulainn and predicting his death in battle.

The apprentices listened raptly to her tale.

"Does she really turn into a crow?" Daina asked when Neela finished.

Beanna chose that moment to fly down and land on Caymin's shoulder. *"And why would she not become a crow?"*

The ones who could understand her chuckled. Caymin offered her a bit of bread.

She accepted it, cocking her head to look around at them all. *"Why do humans sit and tell tales?"*

"They are enjoyable to listen to," said Enat.

Beanna nibbled gently on Caymin's ear. *"One day, they will tell tales of you, little one."*

Caymin flushed as Enat and some of the others turned to look at her. Diarmit suddenly choked on his stew, apparently oblivious to the unspoken conversation taking place around him.

"What did she say?" Daina asked.

"Nothing," Caymin said quickly, giving Beanna a sidelong glance as the crow bobbed her head, laughing silently. "She said nothing."

CHAPTER 13

The Worm Who Isn't

"W*here are you?"*

Caymin wandered through the forest, only starlight to guide her in the darkness. She felt Péist and knew that he was near, but he would not come to her. Something compelled her to keep walking, keep searching, but, "*Stay away,*" she said to him. She struggled against the thing that made her continue, fought with it....

She started awake, finding herself back in her own bed. She refused to look toward where Timmin lay. He stayed on at Enat's cottage, though Caymin was sure he was better and could have gone back to his own dwelling.

The equinox had passed, and daylight came later and later. She lay in the dark and heard Enat stir before dawn. Caymin joined her at the fire.

Enat spoke in a low voice so as not to wake Timmin. "Neela and I must travel to a village outside the forest. We've need of salt and flour and a few other things, so we'll take things to trade. I should be back before nightfall. You and the others may have the day to yourselves. Ivar wants to look after our weapons, sharpening the swords and making new arrows in case the invaders return. You may help him if you wish or have the day to do whatever you would like."

She packed a bag with pouches of herbs and roots, small pots of salves, along with food for her journey.

The sun was up when Timmin woke. He found Caymin outside the cottage, bent over a piece of parchment spread on a flat stone in her lap as she wrote with a sharpened quill dipped into a small pot of ink.

"What are you working so hard at?" Timmin asked as he came out, holding his staff.

She kept her eyes on her work. "I am writing down some of the potions you showed us."

He leaned over to peer at her scroll. "You've a good memory. These are all written down in the scrolls in the meetinghouse."

"I know. But this helps my writing."

He chuckled. "So it does." He stood and looked around. "I fancy a walk. Need to build my strength up a bit. Care to go with me?"

She looked up at that. Timmin never asked the apprentices to accompany him anywhere. "Yes." She set her parchment and quill aside but then paused. "I should leave a message for Enat."

"No need," he said. "She knows."

Caymin was a little puzzled, since Enat had not said anything of this before she left. Timmin, as if sensing Caymin's hesitation, placed a hand on her shoulder, propelling her along with him.

They walked past the large hollowed tree, lying on its side, where Beanna had found her many months before. Caymin tried calling out to Beanna but heard nothing in response.

Timmin kept her in front of him, guiding her along forks in the path by placing his hand on her shoulder again and again to indicate which way she should go. As they walked, he spoke of trivial things, leaving Caymin to wonder where they were going and why. Twice, he made her pause, listening for a moment, and then continued on their way.

They walked for a long time, and it struck Caymin that Timmin was not tired, nor was he stooped and walking feebly as he had been since the invaders had come, but upright and with a purpose.

She was surprised to find them approaching the ring of stones she had found the night she claimed her name. The power of them pulled her even before they stepped inside.

She stood there, looking at Timmin who was staring at her.

"Call him."

She wasn't certain what he meant. "Call who?"

"Péist. Call him."

"Why?"

Timmin grasped his staff with both hands, leaning on it. "I wish to meet him. That is all."

She frowned. "But why?"

He looked at her appraisingly. "If he is the creature I think he is, I have never met one, and I must meet him."

She could feel Péist as she always did, but the feeling was magnified here. Tentatively, she reached out to him, asking if he was near. She was not surprised to find that he was.

"Timmin wishes to meet you, but I do not know if it is safe."

Timmin's eyes narrowed, and she knew he had understood. For a time, she felt nothing. Timmin stood patiently, watching her. Something rustled in the leaves from outside the circle and Péist appeared. He wriggled into the stone circle, his snout busily sniffing the air as he approached. His white skin still bore the marks of his injuries.

"You are well?" She laid a hand on him as he came to her side.

He replied that he was.

Timmin stared at the white worm, a hungry look in his eyes. *"You are Péist?"*

Caymin heard his question and felt Péist's hesitation, as he did not answer.

Timmin approached and dropped to one knee. *"I have long wanted to meet one of your kind."*

He held out a hand, but Péist recoiled, wriggling closer to Caymin, where she could feel him trembling as he nudged against her leg.

Timmin stood, and his eyes flashed. *"Do you not know what I could offer you? What we could be together?"*

His staff glowed red.

"Leave him alone," Caymin said. "If he wanted to go with you, he would."

"What do you know of anything, you witless girl?" Timmin glowered at them. "You know nothing. You don't even know what sits beside you. What he could mean for our kind."

He turned and paced around the circle. "While the monks with their Christ spread everywhere and convince their ignorant flocks that we are evil, while they hunt us down and destroy our sacred sites, we flee like cowards to hide away in the few strongholds left to us." He pointed. "Invaders from the north came here, looking for such as him. They know what he could mean, while our own people do not!"

He whirled and a sudden wind rose, whipping his hair and beard. "It is time we took back what is ours."

Ominous clouds gathered and darkened the day, blotting out the weak autumn sunlight. He brought his staff down and the earth trembled while the staff went from red to white.

Caymin fell to her knees beside Péist and wrapped an arm around him as he cowered next to her.

Timmin pointed. "He could save us! He could avenge us upon all who would destroy us! But you will never know how to use him and all he could bring us. I cannot allow this."

He raised his staff and aimed it at them. Caymin shielded Péist with her body as something like lightning shot from the end of Timmin's staff. She twisted away as the bolt hit her. An enormous clap of thunder shook the ground and she heard a cry. She looked up in time to see Timmin landing in a crumpled heap several feet away.

Caymin slowly sat up, checking to make sure Péist was unhurt. "Go," she told him, but he would not leave her.

Footsteps pounded, and she turned to find Enat and Neela running into the circle. They quickly took in the scene as Timmin lay motionless, blood running from his mouth.

"What are you doing here?" Caymin asked.

"Beanna warned me," Enat said, not removing her gaze from Timmin, her own staff held at the ready. "She said her ability to speak with you had been blocked when she saw you leaving with Timmin."

"But why are they here?" Neela asked, clearly perplexed. "What happened?"

Caymin glanced around. Péist was gone. "Timmin said he wanted to go for a walk. He brought me here. I did not know why until we got here." She looked at Enat. "What did you do to him?"

"We didn't do it," Enat said, leaning on her staff when Timmin remained still. "You did."

"But how could I...?"

"He wanted to meet Péist, didn't he?"

Caymin nodded. "He said something about Péist avenging us against those who force us to hide, against the followers of the Christ and the northmen."

"Was Péist here?" Neela looked around.

"He was. He came when I called him," Caymin said. "I should not have done it. I put him in danger."

"You trusted an elder," Enat said. "I, however, did not. He has shown much interest in you of late, and would normally have been eager to get back to his own cottage days ago. I asked Beanna to keep watch. I suspected if I was gone, he might make his intentions known."

They turned to look at him.

"He forgot how strong your magic is when you are protecting one you care about," Enat said. "You simply rebounded his own magic against him. I think he did not mean to harm Péist, as he values him so highly. But he thought to incapacitate you long enough to take Péist with him." She waved her arm toward the stones. "And he unwisely brought you to a place where your magic is magnified."

"I do not understand how he thought he could use Péist against anyone," Caymin said. "Péist is harmless. He is afraid."

"He is for now," Enat said cryptically.

Timmin stirred and sat up, looking around dazedly. When he caught sight of Enat and Neela, his expression darkened. He used his staff to push to his feet.

Enat flicked her hand and a small bundle appeared at Timmin's feet. "You will take your staff and the food I have provided. And you will leave this place."

Timmin's eyes blazed. "You've no right –"

Enat spread her arms wide, her staff held in one hand. "The magic of this sacred place gives me the right." The wind moaned again, whirling around them. Enat herself was more fearsome than Timmin had been. She seemed to glow with light. "You have broken faith with us, with the forest. You sought to harm a defenseless child entrusted to our care, and you have paid for underestimating her. Go."

With a last glance at Caymin, Timmin gathered up the bundle, walked out of the stone circle and disappeared into the forest. Enat lowered her arms and the wind calmed. She was once again just Enat as Caymin had come to know her.

"Follow him," she said to Neela. "Send for us if he delays at all."

Neela left the circle and Enat turned to Caymin.

"Come," she said, wrapping an arm around her shoulders. "Let us go home."

As they left the circle, Caymin cast a glance back. She knew Péist was watching, and felt his satisfaction that she was safe.

"It would be wise not to speak to the others of this," Enat told her once they were back in their cottage.

Caymin started to pick up Timmin's belongings, which had become scattered all about the cottage, but Enat said, "Today, we do this the easy way."

She waved her hand and removed all signs of Timmin's stay with them. In an instant, his bed, clothing, his pipe – all was gone and their cottage was as it had been.

"Oh, that's better. A house is much nicer when it's kept neat, and most men are not neat."

She built up the fire and placed a kettle of water over it to heat. "I'm sorry to have put you in harm's way."

"I was not afraid until I thought he might hurt Péist." Caymin sat, staring into the fire, watching the flames lick at the blocks of peat. "I did not know Timmin felt so much hatred toward others."

Enat was silent while she waited for the water to heat. When it was hot enough, she poured it and pushed a steaming cup of tea into Caymin's hands. "I must confess, I did not know he felt that way, either. I have long known of his frustration that the old ways are disappearing, and that fewer and fewer people believe in magic. He's right that the monks and their followers fear what they don't understand and in their fear, they believe magic and those who practice it to be evil." Her eyes narrowed. "For some of them, it's more a matter of control."

"I do not understand."

"If the people look to us for healing or wisdom as in days past, they don't look to the monks and their religion. They would never admit that it's power they seek, but they're human after all."

Caymin looked up at her. "I still do not understand why he thought Péist could help him."

Enat sighed. "I know you don't." She got up and went to her door, opening it to look outside. She closed the door and whispered words as she stroked the door with her hand.

Caymin saw the door shimmer for a moment.

"We may speak now without being overheard," Enat said, sitting again at the fire. "You've heard Gai and the others speak of dragons?"

"Yes." Caymin stared at her. "The northman spoke also of dragons. 'Drage,' he said."

Enat nodded. "Yes. It's said that once there were many dragons roaming the earth, many different kinds living in different lands. And the people of the north have long told stories of dragons."

"But what do dragons have to do with Péist? Gai describes them as being huge winged creatures, bigger than the biggest bird, fierce and able to breathe fire. Not... not helpless creatures like Péist, wriggling about in the dirt."

"Gai is right. The dragons people know to be dragons are as he described. We always thought they hatched from eggs, but now I'm starting to believe we were wrong."

It took Caymin a moment to realize what Enat was saying. "You mean they all start as creatures like Péist? Small and helpless?"

"Think of them as cubs."

"Do they not have parents to protect them? The way Broc and Cuán protect their cubs?"

Enat smiled. "It would seem not. We do not know much about dragons beyond what they have told those few humans they trust. We have stories and legends, of course, but those are often fanciful and exaggerated."

At Caymin's dubious expression, Enat said, "If you were so vulnerable, would you want others to know of it? Dragons have done their best over the ages to hide their beginnings from humans. Think what people like Timmin might do if they knew a young dragon was out there, helpless and easy to catch."

Caymin's mouth opened and closed a couple of times as she thought. "How does a creature like Péist become a dragon?"

"We don't know." Enat took a sip of her tea. "There's much we don't understand, much they have never shared beyond the one they bond to."

"As Péist bonded to me?"

Enat nodded. "From what I know, and it's not much, not all dragons bond to a human. Some are wild creatures their whole lives long. But the ones who bond, bond for life. It will span all distance and will last until one of you dies." She looked at Caymin appraisingly. "You should count yourself blessed that Péist chose to bond with you. Timmin knew. When you spoke of Péist waking you to tell you of the invaders, he suspected what Péist was, but the prisoner confirmed it. We couldn't understand most of what he said, but we believe they heard there were dragons here, and they came searching."

"Why would they think there are dragons here?"

Enat took a sip of her tea. "It is written that when people began to crowd the lands the dragons once roamed, they took refuge on islands across the sea. It may be the northmen interpreted that to mean our island."

Caymin thought about this. "Timmin thought he could make Péist bond with him?"

Enat appraised Caymin. "Yes. He wanted his power for himself. He should have known better. That bond, once formed, cannot be transferred to another."

Caymin stared into the fire again as she thought on this. She opened her hand and conjured a ball of flame. "And they really breathe fire?"

"So I've heard. I don't know how they do it, though."

Caymin looked at her. "This is why you do not want me to speak of it to the others?"

"Do you think it wise to let others know you've bonded with a dragon cub?"

A sly grin tugged at Caymin's mouth. "It might be useful the next time Gai makes me angry."

The younger apprentices sat huddled around a fire with Niall and Una, warming themselves against the frosty cold of the morning.

For days, their talk had centered around why Timmin had left so unexpectedly. Caymin sat silently, not participating in the speculation, since only she knew the reason. Neela had returned late that day, assuring Enat that Timmin had crossed the boundary of the forest.

"I think he went after the invaders," whispered Daina now. "Followed them north to their land to make sure they don't come back."

The others looked suitably awestruck at this suggestion. Without meaning to, Caymin snorted impatiently.

"Well, where do you think he is, then?"

Diarmit eyed her as she felt her cheeks burn.

"I do not know," she said, thinking quickly. "But I doubt he is strong enough yet to travel across the sea and take on the invaders single-handedly."

Gai looked toward the meetinghouse with its closed door. "What do you think they're doing in there?"

Fergus, Méav and Ronan had been summoned to meet with the elders.

"They're soon to be tested," said Una.

Diarmit looked up. "For what?"

"To see if they're ready."

"Ready for what?" Caymin's curiosity was piqued.

"Their final test in the forest." Cíana lowered her voice. "The healer in our village told me a little. When we've learned enough as apprentices, we go into the forest at Samhain, the night when the veil between worlds thins, when we can pass between worlds. She couldn't tell me what happens that night. All who undergo the test are sworn to secrecy, but she said, if the forest deems us worthy, we leave as mages, with our staff. Only then, can we come and go from the forest freely."

"What if they aren't deemed worthy?" Daina asked.

"They may return to us for more training or they can choose to leave with what they have," Niall said. "There are many with some magical training, and they live as healers. Not all become full mages." He glanced toward the meetinghouse. "But if they win their staffs, they'll leave the forest and we likely won't see them again."

Caymin watched the meetinghouse with renewed curiosity. She half-listened as the others began speaking of their traditions for Samhain – bringing the cattle and sheep in from summer pastures and slaughtering those that would feed their village through the winter. Caymin remembered watching the villagers participate in these rituals, relighting their doused fires from a central bonfire. But she had never heard of the passage from one world to another.

"My da swears he saw his da's da on Samhain," Diarmit said solemnly. "Talked to him, he did, though he'd been dead a score or more summers."

Caymin looked up at that. "You can see and speak to the dead on Samhain?"

Diarmit shrugged. "Some can."

Gai scoffed. "Tales for children and simpletons."

"No." Niall shook his head. "I saw my mam, one Samhain when I was ten winters, and she died when my younger sister was born, some five winters before. She looked just as I remembered her. We talked. 'Twas she who told me she'd had magic and had passed it to me, and that I'd be coming here."

Caymin tilted her head. "She had magic and still died?"

"Having power doesn't save us from everything," Una said, laying a hand on Niall's shoulder.

The door of the meetinghouse opened suddenly and the elders emerged with Méav, Fergus and Ronan. The others gathered round. Una and Niall embraced them, wishing them well. Caymin hung back.

Méav noticed and came to her. She pulled a silver knife and sheath from her belt. "For you, my brave little warrior."

Caymin looked into her eyes, remembering how fierce Méav had seemed to her when first she saw her sparring, with her black braids flying as she whirled and leapt. "I cannot take this. You may need it. In the forest, when you are tested."

Méav smiled. "If the lack of a knife keeps me here, 'twill be a sign I'm not yet meant to leave." She pressed the knife into Caymin's hands. "I feel certain we'll meet again."

Ronan joined them. He laid a hand on Caymin's shoulder. "If I don't see you after the morrow... well, thank the white worm for us all. If he hadn't warned you, who knows where we'd be now."

He gave her a pat, and then he and Méav joined Fergus to go pack their few belongings and prepare for the trial they were to face.

Caymin sat back down at the fire, holding the knife. She'd never seen anything so beautiful. The blade was honed to a fine edge, its leather sheath embossed with spirals and knotwork. In her limited dealings with humans, she had never taken leave of anyone. The pain of leaving Broc and Cuán had been almost more than she could bear.

Cíana joined her. She reached over and examined the knife. "A fine gift." She handed it back.

Caymin nodded, unable to speak through the lump in her throat.

CHAPTER 14

Samhain Trials

"It's time."

Enat turned to Caymin who was reaching for her old cloak, Méav's knife strapped to her belt. She held out a cloak of her own.

"Wear this one."

"Why?" Caymin laid her cloak on her bed and held up the one Enat offered.

"Yours is special to you," Enat said. She picked up her staff as Caymin fastened the cloak around her shoulders. "We'll keep yours here. If this one is damaged, it won't matter."

Full dark had fallen as they made their way to the same hill where they had burned a fire at Lughnasadh. Their breath puffed in front of them as they walked through the frosty night.

"A full moon," Enat said.

Caymin looked up at the orb, luminous in the night sky, gilding the edges of the clouds drifting by her. "There was a full moon the night you came to find me."

Enat chuckled. "There was. I could feel you, but I didn't think you'd ever speak with me."

"I was frightened of you," Caymin said. "You were the first two-leg I met who could speak without speaking."

"You've been here for eight moons, nearly a year. Are you sorry?"

Caymin limped along for a bit, thinking. "Not sorry. Sometimes, I think about what I would be doing if you had not come to me. I know I would still be with my clan, but..."

Her voice trailed off.

"You know Broc and Cuán would have wanted what's best for you. 'Tis natural to feel torn – to miss them and to be happy you're here – all at once."

Caymin was silent for a long while. "It is not just Broc."

"Your mother and father?"

Caymin stopped abruptly. "The others say that tonight, it is possible to speak with the dead."

Enat stopped as well and turned to look back at her. "This is a night when many things are possible. The veil that separates worlds parts on this night, and for some, it allows passage from one world to the other. But, as with magic, it comes with a cost."

"What cost?"

"When the ones we love leave this world, they do not truly leave us, for we carry them with us." Enat tilted her head up to look at the moon. "You weren't old enough to know and remember your parents, so you feel an emptiness when you think of them. But you must know, when people try to bridge the worlds, they risk losing themselves in what can never be."

"Did that happen to you?"

Enat became very still. "What do you mean?"

"With Sorcha? Did you try to join with her again?"

Enat stared at her. "How do you know of Sorcha?"

"I heard the others speak of her," Caymin said. She laid a hand on Enat's arm. "Did you love her very much?"

Enat blinked rapidly. "Very much indeed. And yes, I did see her one Samhain, many winters ago. She was as lovely as I remembered, but we could not touch, as we were in different realms. The sadness of seeing her thus was almost more than I could bear. It nearly destroyed me. Beware if you part the veil, Caymin, for it does not always bring happiness."

Caymin thought on this as they climbed the hill to where the others were gathered, standing around an unlit fire. If the elders were feeling Timmin's absence, they did not acknowledge it, except that Enat stepped into the role of First Mage. She produced a pouch of ashes from the Lughnasadh fire, speaking words of power as she held the pouch to the moon. She sprinkled the ashes onto the stacked wood of the bonfire. With a gesture, she invited the others near and they all held out their hands, igniting the bonfire as one.

It flared high into the sky, illuminating their faces. Neela uncorked a glass bottle full of some liquid. She raised it to her lips and passed it to Cíana who drank and passed it in turn. Each of them took a drink and handed it on. When Caymin raised the bottle to her own lips, she nearly choked on the liquid that scalded her throat, burning all the way down her gullet. She passed the bottle to Gai who passed it back to Neela, completing the circle. Neela then began to chant, something that had no real melody, but the singsong rhythm of her words worked their way into Caymin's mind. She found herself swaying in time with the chant. All joined hands and began to sway in unison as Neela's voice continued to work its way into her head.

She turned and stepped away from the fire, and was only mildly surprised to look back and see herself still swaying with the others around the fire. She walked through the clearing toward the forest and found Péist waiting for her. Without questioning, she followed him as he wriggled into the trees. She had no sense of time or distance as they moved through the forest, the moon throwing shadows through the trees. Sporadic pinpricks of light appeared along their path, and she knew wood sprites guided them.

Péist led her to a place she had never seen, a place where the trees were overgrown with vines growing thickly up the trunks, spreading out along the branches to join tree to tree so that they formed a tunnel. He stopped and turned to her. She reached out to part the vines and walked through the curtain of green.

When she emerged from the dark, leafy passage, she found herself standing in her village, outside her family's cottage. She waited a moment and her father stepped through the door.

"Caymin."

She looked up into eyes as blue as the sky on a bright summer day. "You are here."

He nodded. "I hoped one day you would come."

His eyes took in her scars, and a great sadness came over his face. "I could not protect you and your mother."

"But you tried," she said. "I saw. I watched you fight them. There were too many."

She looked around but, other than the two of them, the village was empty. "Is my mother here?"

He shook his head. "She is not."

"Do you know where she is?"

He turned and picked up his harp. "Do you remember playing it with me?"

"I do not remember, but I have seen."

He plucked the strings and sang the song Caymin recalled from her spiritwalk. His voice rang out, clear and strong. He finished, his head bowed.

"You must leave now," he said. "You do not belong here, but in the land of the living." He lifted his face to her. "But know that I love you more than my own life."

He stood and walked back into the cottage.

"Wait!"

Caymin stepped through the door of the cottage and found herself outside the wall of vines where Péist waited for her. She sank to her knees, crying. Péist wriggled closer, pressed to her side. Though he spoke no words, she felt his understanding of what she had seen.

When she was ready, he accompanied her back to the hill where she still danced with the others around the bonfire. She stepped into the clearing and looked back to find he had gone, but she smiled as she realized she could feel them both, her father and Péist, as she rejoined the circle.

Caymin awakened early after a restless night. Her head felt woozy when she sat up on her mat. She didn't fully remember coming back to the cottage.

She stoked the fire, adding blocks of peat and putting the kettle on to heat. She made a bit more noise than she needed to until Enat sat up, rubbing her own head.

Caymin opened her mouth to ask questions, but Enat silenced her with a look. She made tea instead, handing a cup to Enat and waiting until she had had time to drink before speaking.

"I do not understand how could I have been in two places at once."

Enat took another sip of tea, her eyes closed, before saying, "I told you last night, that is the magic of Samhain. Your body was with us around the fire – you never left. 'Twas your spirit that went into the forest."

"But it felt so real. I heard my father sing to me, and I felt Péist next to me."

Enat opened her eyes wearily. "Just because it was your spirit that spoke with your father doesn't mean it wasn't real."

"There were wood sprites, too."

Enat appeared more alert at this news. "You're sure?"

"I think so. There were points of light that stayed just ahead of us."

Enat nodded pensively. "You were blessed. They do not appear often."

Caymin stared into her own cup, saw her reflection staring back up at her. "Will they guide Méav and Ronan and Fergus in their trials?"

"They may. No one can ever predict what a wood sprite will do. Sometimes they help, sometimes they hinder. It depends on their mood, and they can be capricious."

Enat reached out and ran her hand over Caymin's head. "Your hair is getting long. Do you want me to cut it?"

Caymin nodded. "Use this." She handed over Méav's knife.

Enat smiled as she used the sharp blade to trim Caymin's hair. "'Tis a fine knife she gave you. A noble gift."

Caymin reached for the sheath, turning it over in her hands. "But why did she? I do not understand."

"We give gifts as a sign of affection or respect. Did you not ever give things to Broc or Cuán?"

"Fresh bedding or food, sometimes something special from the village." Caymin looked up. "But it is not the same."

"No. Badgers have simple needs. Humans are more complicated."

Caymin frowned. "Too complicated sometimes."

"Complicated or not, you have to learn to live with them."

Caymin stretched her feet out to the fire, enjoying the warmth on this cold morning. "I was thinking I might want boots this winter. Like yours."

Enat nodded. "A fine idea. We've enough deerskin to make you a pair. I'll teach you how. We may get them done today, since you have no lessons."

She tossed the cut hair into the fire and got up. "For waking me so early, I'll let you make me some porridge."

Caymin grinned and set about heating the water again.

The sun was not yet fully up as Caymin sat at the long table in the meetinghouse, hunched over a book flanked by two lamps to provide light.

She'd been too restless to wait for Enat, who was still grumbling and stumbling about even after her tea and porridge.

Cíana came in and looked over her shoulder. "Dragons?" She sat beside Caymin at the table. "Why are you looking at a book about dragons?"

Caymin looked up from the page filled with a drawing of a fearsome creature, flying over a village, burning it with its fiery breath. "Gai was talking about them, and I had never heard of them before. I was curious. What do you know of them?"

"Only what the elders of our village told us when we were children." Cíana smiled. "I think they did it to scare us. Told us dragons come in the night to capture and take away children who misbehave." She paused, squinting into the distance. "I heard them say that once, there were many dragons here. Some had riders, humans they were connected to – dragonmages, they called them – but most dragons remained wild."

Caymin's head snapped around. "Riders? Humans rode on dragons?"

Cíana nodded. "So they say."

"Did they attack villages?"

"Some did, according to the tales. Some of the wild ones, and even some of the dragonmages; they used their power over their dragons to rule people. They can speak. Dragons. The tales all say they have their own wisdom, passed down through the ages, and they can speak with humans when they wish." Cíana laughed. "But I'm sure I wouldn't want a dragon taking enough interest in me to speak with me."

Caymin frowned. "But, how do they pass down their wisdom if they are all alone when they are young?"

"How do you know they're alone?"

Caymin's cheeks burned. "I think I read it."

"Oh." Cíana shrugged. "I don't know. If you ever meet a dragon, you'll have to ask him."

Caymin intended to do just that.

They both jumped when the meetinghouse door burst open. Fergus staggered in and fell to the ground.

Cíana and Caymin rushed to him and turned him over. One side of his face was bruised, with a gash over his forehead, dried blood covering his face and clothing.

"Go get the elders," Cíana said.

Caymin ran to Ivar's cottage. He and Neela were both there, sharing a cup of tea and looking just as bleary-eyed as Enat had been. They looked up at Caymin's unexpected knock.

"Fergus. He is hurt."

Without asking questions, they jumped up and ran to the meetinghouse where they crouched on either side of Fergus. A moment after they got there, Enat hurried in, her arms filled with a stack of deerskin.

"What happened?" Enat asked. She dropped the leather on the ground and knelt beside Fergus.

Ivar helped Fergus to sit up. "Can you tell us?"

"I'm not sure," Fergus said shakily.

Cíana dipped a gourd of water, which he drank down.

"We three parted, each going a different way in the forest last night," he said. "Méav and Ronan headed in that direction." He waved his arm vaguely toward the east. "I went north."

He closed his eyes tightly, as if trying to recall. "For a long while, I could hear all of you at the bonfire, but the sounds faded as I walked farther. The forest..." He paused, looking at Caymin and Cíana. "There were tests, things I had to do to move on. I heard someone crying. I figured it was another test, and I tried to find the person. I thought I saw a girl – she looked like you." He looked at Caymin. "But then she was gone, and I saw only a ghostly creature, white and glowing in the night. I followed it through the forest, thinking it was leading me to my next test. I heard footsteps nearby, and thought Ronan or Méav was following the same creature. Suddenly, something hit me."

He raised a shaking hand to his head.

"The sun was coming up when I woke."

They all turned at the sound of more commotion from outside. Méav and Ronan charged into the meetinghouse, grasping Gai between them.

"We found this one sneaking around in the forest," Ronan said angrily, pushing Gai ahead of him.

Méav dropped to her knees beside Fergus. "We knew something happened to you. We felt it."

"Why are you here?" Ivar demanded. "You should have completed your trials."

Ronan shook his head. "Not like this. If we all must wait until next Samhain to complete our trials, so be it."

Ivar stood and faced Gai. "Explain yourself."

Gai stood stubbornly silent.

Daina, Una, Diarmit and Niall all came in.

"What's wrong?" Una asked. "Why are you all here?"

Niall saw Fergus's face. "What happened to you?"

"Someone hit me," Fergus said with a scowl in Gai's direction.

Niall flew at Gai, grabbing the front of his tunic and pummeling him with his other hand.

"It wasn't me!" Gai yelled as Ivar pulled Niall away.

"It wasn't me," he repeated, touching a hand to his bleeding lip.

Méav shoved him. "Then what were you doing out in the forest?"

Neela stepped between Gai and the others. "Stop. All of you." She turned to Gai. "This is serious. You knew the three would be in the forest for their trial. What were you doing there?"

"I wanted to see!" Gai jutted his jaw out. "I wanted to see what the trials are, what we'll be facing some day." He pointed. "But I didn't attack him. I heard someone, too."

Diarmit scoffed. "That's likely."

"It's true! There was someone else out there," Gai said. "I tried to follow the sounds, but lost them in the night. Then these two grabbed me." He shot a hateful glance at Méav and Ronan.

Neela looked at Ivar and Enat. "Do you think there could have been someone else out there? Could the invaders have come back?"

Ivar shook his head. "The forest would have alerted us."

"Timmin?" Neela asked worriedly.

"It's possible," Enat said. "He was angry when he left."

"You never really said why he left," Ronan said.

"Never you mind," Enat said. She shook her head. "He wouldn't need to hit the boy over the head to hurt him. He could do it magically from a league away if he wished. No, this was crude. But until we know who it was, I think it would be best if we make a pact to be with someone at all times in the forest and to be in the village or in our cottages by nightfall."

"Agreed," said Ivar. He glared at all of the apprentices. "And I'll be checking. So no wandering off at night."

CHAPTER 15

A Traitor Among Them

For days, the apprentices were kept under the close watch of the elders. Fergus's wounds healed and the decision was made to allow the three oldest to attempt their trials again at the next full moon.

"It won't be the same as doing it at Samhain," said Enat. "There won't be the power of the night, but, if the forest is willing, it will suffice."

The older apprentices sequestered themselves to practice in preparation for their trials, while the younger spent the next days learning about crystals and stones.

"Stones have power?" Caymin turned over a chunk of rock in her hand.

"Many do," said Neela.

"Is that why you used them at Bealtaine?"

Enat nodded. "Yes. Their power helped guide you on your spiritwalk the night you claimed your name."

Cíana held out a smooth green stone with veins of red running through it. "They come from the earth, so why wouldn't they have power? Bloodstone can help you with the circulation of your blood or things that block your energy."

Ivar reached into his tunic and pulled out a blue stone hanging on a leather string around his neck. "Some crystals can protect us from dark power, or enhance the light."

Enat suspended a rough stone in mid-air, and small flecks of glossy black within caught the light. "Some stones are already imbued with power, but many more can become receptacles of power. You can enchant them to hold a spell, and they will hold that power for ages. Often, we leave these with someone for healing or protection."

Diarmit turned a shiny black rock over in his hand. "Can we enchant it to bring us luck?"

Neela frowned. "That's a frivolous use of power."

Caymin looked at the stone in her hand. "You speak of dark power, but we have never seen this. How are we to know it or protect against it?"

"There are mages who revel in the dark," said Enat. "For it brings them a sense of domination to hold others bound to them in fear, to use their power to punish. We will not teach you the dark side of magic, for it is too easy to be lured into using it. It is seductive, pulling you deeper and deeper into it, until it owns you."

The apprentices stared at her with wide eyes.

"It is enough for you to know it exists," Neela said with a gently reproving glance at Enat. "If dark magic is ever used against you, you will know it, and you will know how to counter it with the light."

They spent days learning the properties of the large collection of stones and crystals there.

"Many of these were brought here from across the sea," Ivar told them. He held up a brilliant blue stone with tiny flecks of gold. "This is called lapis lazuli and it comes from a land called Mesopotamia. Some day, in your travels, you'll collect crystals and stones of your own. Mayhap you will bring some back to us."

They learned how to place spells of protection and healing on various stones to enhance their natural powers.

"I can feel it," Daina said when Cíana laid several stones along her spine. "I can feel the power in them. It tingles."

Caymin glanced over to where Gai sat by himself, studying some of the notes on crystals. He was different since Samhain, more subdued.

"He's ashamed," Daina had whispered when Caymin mentioned this. "Because he got caught cheating."

None of the older apprentices would interact with him. They clearly still believed he had been the one to attack Fergus. Watching him now, Caymin felt a stirring of pity, similar to the way she felt toward a wounded animal. She went to sit beside him.

Gai ignored her, continuing to read. Still, she sat. She pulled another scroll to her and read.

At last, he straightened and turned to her. "What do you want?"

She blinked. "I do not want anything."

"Then why are you here?" His lip twisted. "Why aren't you avoiding me like the others?"

She tilted her head. "Why did you do it?"

"I told you. I told everyone. I didn't hit him!"

"No, I meant going into the forest to watch them. Why did you do it?"

Gai turned back to his scroll, scarlet patches showing vividly on his cheeks. "You don't know, any of you. My father... If I don't earn my staff, if I leave here without becoming a full mage, he'll disown me."

"But he is your father." Caymin frowned. "Surely, he will welcome you back when you come, no matter what."

Gai scoffed and quickly turned away. "You don't know my father. I'm the younger son. My only value to him is if I can use my power. To him, if I don't return with a staff, I may as well not return at all."

Caymin thought about this. She had never had to worry about those she loved not loving her in return if she could not give them what they wanted. Broc and Cuán had loved her from the time when she was too young to do anything, and she knew Enat loved her as she loved Enat. She didn't know what to say.

"Go away." Gai turned his back on her.

Caymin got to her feet. "I do not believe you attacked Fergus."

Gai twisted around. "You don't?"

She shook her head. "No. You had no reason to hurt him if you wanted to see what his trials consisted of."

Gai smiled at her and she was struck again by his beauty.

"I am hungry," she said. "Would you like to eat with me?"

He stood. "Aye, I would."

The others watched as they walked together to the fire where a pot of stew simmered over the flames.

Days passed. The others slowly began treating Gai as they had before and the tension that had dogged them since Samhain diminished.

The moon waned and then waxed again toward full. The day of the full moon dawned. Caymin frowned at the stone in her hand, holding her other hand over it and whispering the words of a spell. She smiled when the stone grew warm in her palm and glowed green.

She draped Enat's heavy old cloak over her shoulders and went to find Méav who was at the weapons yard with Ronan, practicing with staffs, whirling and hitting each other as they sparred. She sat and watched until they stopped, breathless and red-faced. Ronan took the staffs to put them away, and Méav dropped down beside Caymin.

"I like your new boots."

Caymin grinned, wiggling her feet. "They still feel strange, but much warmer." She looked up into Méav's face. "I wanted to offer you this again, in case you need it tonight." She held out the knife.

"Do you not like it?"

Caymin flushed. "I like it very much. I have never had anything so beautiful."

"Then I want you to have it. To remember me."

"I would never forget you," Caymin said. She held out the stone, strung on a braided leather cord. "For you. I enchanted it with a protection spell, so what happened to Fergus last moon cannot happen to you tonight. If an enemy approaches, it will grow warm."

Méav took it and put it over her head. She held the stone so that it caught the light, glowing a deep green. "Jade. Thank you." She tucked it inside her tunic and pressed it to her heart. "I'll keep it with me always." She took the knife from Caymin, murmuring words as she moved her hand in a circle over it, then handed it back. "I told you before I felt sure we'd meet again. Last moon, during our first trials, I saw you. We were fighting side by side. I don't know what it means and I don't know where I'll be after tonight, but if you should ever need me, I charmed the knife to point in my direction. Just hold it in your palm and say my name, and it will show you the way."

Caymin stared at her in awe. "Thank you."

Méav gave her shoulder a squeeze as Ronan walked in their direction. "Take care, little badger."

As darkness fell, and the three headed into the forest for their trials, it seemed all the forest held its breath. The apprentices and the elders gathered together in the village where the main fire burned brightly.

"We'll all spend the night in the meetinghouse," Ivar said, looking around.

No one needed to ask why. Gai lowered his head as he felt the stares of the others aimed in his direction. Caymin moved to sit beside him at the fire as they ate. Neela distracted them with songs played on her harp.

Above them, the moon shone bright and round in her fullness. Caymin felt small tremors of magic – in the air, in the earth. She saw Enat smile in her direction and knew she felt the same.

As always, she felt Péist, hunting in the night. She reached out.

"The three are out again tonight, being tested. I do not know where they will be. Stay safe and stay hidden."

Though she felt certain none of them would do him harm, she knew it had been she and Péist that Fergus had seen at Samhain, and that Fergus had followed Péist, thinking he would lead him to his next trial. Whoever had attacked Fergus had likely been following Péist as well.

The fire burned low, and they all moved into the meetinghouse to bed down for the night. Enat closed the door, placing a charm on it to keep it sealed.

"But what if I have to get up in the night?" Diarmit asked.

Ivar glared at him. "That would not be advisable on this night."

Diarmit nodded and lay down, making himself as comfortable as he could, while the others did likewise.

Caymin wrapped Enat's old cloak around her, glad she had boots to keep her feet warm.

She slept fitfully, waking often to the restless turnings and snores from the others before she drifted off again.

When daylight broke, she lay there. No more stirrings of magic came to her and she knew the three were gone. She touched the knife lying beside her and wondered if Méav was right, that they would meet again one day.

Enat woke and Caymin sat. Around them, the others slept on. Enat got up to remove the charm from the door and gestured to her to follow.

Outside, they walked several paces from the meetinghouse before Enat said, "We must check on something. I should have thought of it before."

They stopped at the latrine first, and then Enat led Caymin deep into the forest.

"They all won their staffs last night, did they not?"

Enat smiled. "They did. The only time we take wood from live trees. Upon passing their trials, they each would have been led by wood sprites to a tree willing to give a branch for the making of a staff. It is a most moving rite of passage."

Caymin limped along beside her. "Where are we going?"

"To Timmin's cottage. I should have gone as soon as he revealed his true intent toward you and Péist."

"What do you expect to find?"

"We'll know when we get there."

It seemed they walked a long time. Caymin's stomach was growling with hunger by the time they approached a stone cottage, so covered in moss and ivy that it almost disappeared. Enat slowed and raised her hands, as if pressing on an invisible wall.

"What do you feel?" Caymin asked in a whisper.

"Just as I expected, Timmin guarded this place with magic." Enat moved sideways, still pressing with her hands. She walked all the way around the cottage, eventually coming back to where Caymin stood waiting.

"The protection is complete," Enat said, sounding relieved. "I thought perhaps whoever attacked Fergus might have found a way through, but the most I can detect is that someone tried to get in here." She pointed to a place where Caymin could now see that the leaves and dirt had been disturbed.

"Stand behind me," Enat said as she stepped forward, her hands raised once more. Her lips moved as she murmured.

Caymin felt a surge of power pushing back against Enat's magic, and then a sudden yielding.

"Here. We can get through here."

Caymin followed Enat through a gap in the charmed protections placed around the cottage. Cautiously, Enat pushed the door open, standing back as if she expected something to pounce out at them. When all remained quiet, she stepped inside.

"He thought no one would get through the outer protections," Enat said as Caymin entered after her.

With a small gasp, she looked around at the remnants of Timmin's life here. Arranged on a table with three oil lamps were several scrolls and books, some of them lying open. Even before she stepped to the table, she could see that they all had to do with dragons.

"He knew," she said, looking at Enat. "Even before he met Péist, he knew what he was."

Enat nodded. "He did. And he wanted to use him." She leaned over a scroll. "This is the story of an ancient mage who once ruled this entire land, he and his dragon. This was the cause of the last great dragon war."

Caymin saw something under one of the scrolls and picked it up. "Enat."

Enat turned to her.

"This is the brooch the northman wore." She held up the silver medallion, worked with its design of a dragon. "How? I thought you and the others took him...?"

"We did." Enat stared at the medallion. "We took him to a larger town, closer to the sea." She paused. "But we scattered when we got back, each going in a different direction to make sure no one had entered the forest while we were gone.

She reached out and took the brooch from Caymin. "The northman was wearing this the last time I saw him."

They stared at each other for a long moment before Enat turned to look around. She wandered around the cottage. Caymin stepped over to an array of stones and crystals lying on a table.

"Don't touch those!"

Enat came to her and suspended her hands over them for a moment. She gathered them up, taking care to use a cloth to handle them. "I think we should take those as well," she said, pointing to the books and scrolls. "We don't need anyone else learning what it was Timmin was after."

"You do not think he told anyone else?"

Enat shook her head. "Oh no. He wouldn't have wanted to share what he knew. He wanted to have Péist to himself."

Caymin collected the books, tucking them and the scrolls into a bag she found in a corner. "I have been thinking that the person who attacked Fergus at Samhain knew about Péist."

"I have thought the same thing," Enat said. "I still don't think it was Timmin, but it frightens me that someone else, someone living among us, knows what Péist is and is so willing to hurt someone else to get to him."

Caymin looked at her. "You think it is one of the elders or apprentices?"

"We've detected no other people within the forest this past moon. It cannot be a stranger. We would have felt it. It can only be one of us."

"But who? Gai?"

"Gai has not acted honorably, and I know others would suspect him."

"You do not."

"Nor, I think, do you." Enat studied Caymin. "You befriended him when the others turned from him."

"I felt sorry for him. He told me why he stole into the forest at Samhain."

"His father?" Enat smiled when Caymin gaped at her. "I know he feels duty-bound to become what his father wishes." Her expression sobered. "But if not Gai, then who?"

CHAPTER 16

Unexpected Tidings

ith the three eldest apprentices gone, the studies for the younger resumed in earnest. Ivar, Neela and Enat pushed them harder than ever.

Winter had settled in hard and cold, and Caymin often wished she were tucked snugly in a nice, warm sett with her clan, sleeping most of the winter away. Enat gave her a heavy wool tunic, but still she was hesitant to leave the comfort of the fire.

She huddled close to the flames she had conjured under her cauldron. The others did likewise where Enat had them gathered in the meetinghouse, teaching them to make a potion to staunch bleeding.

"The more you know about healing," she told them, "the more welcome you will be in any village you visit. You will not be working the land or learning a trade like most others. Some learn a craft such as metalworking, like Ivar did. For most of you, magic is your craft, and you must be versatile in many skills to make yourself as useful as possible."

She went from one to the other, watching as they mixed the ingredients for the potion.

"You added three crushed beetles instead of two," she said to Diarmit, whose potion had become thick and foul-smelling. She moved on to Daina and Cíana, dipping a spoon into their cauldrons. "Very good."

She came over to Gai and Caymin, who were working side by side. She leaned over Gai's cauldron as he stirred it. "This is perfect. Nicely done."

Gai looked up at her unexpected praise. "Thank you."

Caymin sat back as Enat spooned some of her potion, confident that she would win the same words of praise. She and Gai had followed the formula for the potion, step for step. Hers was the same pale yellow as his, the same thickness, so she felt a sharp sting of disappointment when Enat only said, "This will do."

She stared at Enat's back as she walked away. She carefully bottled some of her potion, sealing the stopper before cleaning the cauldron. Enat hadn't actually dismissed them, but she left to return to the cottage while the others were still chatting as they cleaned up.

She flicked an irritated hand and magically stoked the fire, taking some satisfaction in knowing Enat would frown at such a frivolous use of power. She was reading one of Timmin's books on dragons when Enat came in. She didn't look up.

Enat plucked the kettle off the hook and poured two cups of tea. She set one cup next to Caymin who remained silent.

"A blazing fire," Enat said. "Nice and warm."

Still, Caymin said nothing.

Enat sat back and sipped her tea.

Caymin's gaze was glued to the page in front of her, but she was not reading the words.

"You're angry because I praised Gai and didn't praise you."

Caymin sat stubbornly mute.

"Did you make mistakes with your potion?"

Caymin's head snapped up. "No."

"Did you follow the correct formula?"

"Yes."

"So, your potion was perfect and you knew it."

Caymin frowned. "Yes."

"Then why did you need me to say it?"

Caymin opened her mouth but then closed it.

Enat lowered her cup and smiled. "When you first came here, you doubted that you belonged because you hadn't been raised with other humans. You felt out of place. Despite that, you have proved yourself, again and again. Gai arrived also needing to prove himself, but for very different reasons. Gai has never known love or approval, not from his father or his brother. He speaks as if he does not need those things, but inside, he craves them more than anything. You know when you have done well, whether I say it or no. Gai does not. While he pushes people away, what he really desires is to be close."

Caymin bit her lip, thinking about what Enat had said.

"Lately, I've seen you make an effort to talk to Gai, spend time with him when the others turned from him. Why have you done that?"

"I felt sorry for him."

"I'm glad you are capable of feeling pity for someone who has made you angry in the past." Enat leaned forward to poke at the fire. "I told you before that Gai is probably jealous of you." Enat sat back and looked at her. "Don't be jealous of him now."

"I am sorry."

"There's no need to be sorry, Caymin. But always, always trust what you know of yourself."

"Why are we out here in the cold?" Diarmit complained.

Despite her woolen tunic and Enat's heavy cloak, Caymin shivered as she and the others wandered the forest with another list of plants and herbs they had to find.

"Neela said certain of these plants are most potent at this time of year when there is no growth," Daina said. "All their power is stored in their stems and roots."

"And Yule is coming soon," Cíana said. "We need mistletoe for the Yule night."

"What is Yule?" Caymin asked.

"The longest night of the year," Gai said. "The winter solstice. We always had a roaring fire with giant logs in my father's hall and spent the whole night listening to bards tell tales and sing songs."

Cíana nodded. "We did as well. 'Tis the turning point of the year, when Lugh, the sun god, comes back and the days grow longer."

"Our village is mostly Christian," Diarmit said. "We're supposed to celebrate the birth of the Christ at this time of year, not Lugh."

"The monks near us try to stop us celebrating Yule," said Daina. "But many still do in secret."

"Do the ones who celebrate Yule try to stop the believers in the Christ?" Caymin asked, spying a stand of wild cherry bushes.

They gathered most of the cherries that remained, leaving some for the birds. They also asked permission to cut some of the branches.

"You don't understand," said Daina. "The Christians are becoming more powerful, and it's dangerous in many places for people to admit they believe in the old gods and old ways."

Caymin shook her head. "Why does it matter if others believe differently? Does it stop them from believing as they wish?"

Gai laughed. "You speak like a badger."

Caymin grinned. "Sometimes I think badgers and animals have more sense."

"Mistletoe!"

Cíana pointed to a hazel tree with large bunches of mistletoe hanging from the branches, filled with clusters of white, waxy berries. Caymin climbed up, cutting the clusters loose and letting them drop to the others below who gathered them into a bag.

They were all startled by the loud and unexpected arrival of Beanna as she settled on the branch above Caymin's head.

"*Where have you been?*" Caymin sat up. "*I have not seen you in ages.*"

"*Roaming,*" Beanna said vaguely. "*I must speak to you later. What are you doing?*"

"*Gathering things for the Yule.*"

Beanna tilted her head. *"I have seen the two-legs celebrating on the longest night."* She glanced down at the others who were chatting amongst themselves. *"Meet me tonight at the hollow tree when the moon rises. Bring Enat."*

Caymin shifted on her branch and reached into the pouch hanging from her belt. She retrieved a strip of dried venison and offered it. Beanna took it in her beak and flew off.

"What did she want?" Diarmit asked as Caymin climbed back down.

"She wondered what we were doing."

They finished gathering the things on their list as the last of the weak winter daylight faded. They wandered back toward the village. Light snowflakes began to fall, floating first one way and then another on the cold breeze as if they would never settle to earth.

The apprentices brought their finds to the meetinghouse where Neela and Enat were making a thick salve.

"What's this for?" Cíana stuck her finger in, rubbing some of the salve between her thumb and finger. "It smells good."

"It heals skin damaged by cold and wind," Enat said. "It can also heal burns and blisters."

Daina glanced at Caymin. "Have you tried it?"

Caymin flushed. "I do not think anything can change my burns. They are too old."

Enat pursed her lips. "I'm afraid nothing can heal them." At Caymin's downcast face, she added, "But it might help to soften the scars so that they don't pull as much."

She used a wooden paddle to push some of the thick salve into a small, squat jar and handed it to Caymin who raised it to her nose.

"It smells of spring."

"I wish it were spring," Diarmit grumbled, hunkering down near the fire crackling on the hearth. "I hate winter."

They all rubbed some of the salve into their cold, chapped hands and cheeks.

"Winter is necessary," Neela said. "Without the sleep of winter, the death of the plants and the pulling in to rest, nothing would bloom come spring and summer."

The moon was not yet up as Enat and Caymin made their way through the forest. The snow that had started falling earlier in the day had stopped, leaving patches of ground untouched. They moved soundlessly and arrived at the hollow tree before Beanna.

"Why does Beanna need to speak with us?" Caymin asked as she crawled inside the tree and sat.

Enat followed her. "I asked Beanna to do something for me."

Beanna entered the hollow at that moment, the flapping of her wings bringing swirls of snow in with her.

"Greetings, Beanna."

"Greetings to you, Enat."

The crow hopped up onto Enat's knee and settled with a rustle of her feathers. Enat reached into her pouch and pulled out a handful of seeds and nuts. She and Caymin waited patiently while Beanna ate.

"My thanks. I have grown weary of the dried berries left on the bushes at this time of year, and finding worms takes more work in the frozen ground."

"What news?"

Beanna cocked her head, looking at Caymin with her bright eye. *"Have you told her?"*

"I have not."

"Enat asked me to try and track Timmin." She turned her gaze to Enat. *"You were right."*

"Right about what?" Caymin looked from Beanna to Enat and back.

Enat turned to Caymin. *"I feared that Timmin might seek another way to draw you from the forest, to force you to leave our protection and so open yourself to his power."*

"He is gone," Caymin said. *"How could he do this? Through what means could he get me to leave you?"*

Enat didn't answer immediately. She looked at Beanna. *"They are coming? You are sure?"*

Beanna bobbed her head.

Enat turned back to Caymin. *"When Timmin first left the forest from the circle of stones, Neela told us that he headed north. I suspected he knew he was being watched and deliberately led us false. I asked Beanna to fly to the south and wait."*

"I did as she asked," Beanna said. *"It took him days to make his presence known, but he began searching, asking other four-legs and winged ones if they had seen you."*

Caymin shook her head. *"I do not understand."*

"Not many two-legs can speak without speaking, and Timmin counted on the animals we encountered remembering that we had passed through on our journey here." Enat laid a hand on her shoulder. *"He is searching for Broc and Cuán."*

"What?" Caymin jumped up in alarm.

Beanna flapped her wings and Enat held up her hands. *"Be calm. Let me speak."*

Caymin sat back down, her heart racing.

"I feel responsible. When first you came here, I told the other elders more or less where I had found you living among the badgers." Enat folded her hands and stared down at them. *"He means to find them and use them, use your affection for them to force you to come to their rescue. Beanna was able to find them first."*

"Enat told me enough of her search for you to convince them to listen to what I had to say," said Beanna. *"Together with my stories of you, little one, I assured them they are in danger, and asked them to come to us, to make their home here."*

Caymin sat up straighter. *"They are coming here? The entire clan?"*

"Not all," Beanna said with a click of her beak. *"Some of the older ones are too feeble to journey so far, and some are too young. But they have been warned and they are smart enough to pretend they know nothing of you if Timmin should find them. They will be safe."*

"But where are Broc and Cuán? When will they be here?"

Enat looked to Beanna.

"They are traveling only at night," Beanna said. *"And they are speaking with none so as to leave no trail for Timmin to follow. They should be here by the next dark moon."*

Caymin reached out and ran her finger down Beanna's breast. "*Thank you, Beanna. Thank you for going so far to protect my clan.*" She looked at Enat. "*And thank you for thinking of them. I never believed Timmin capable of this.*"

"*I had my suspicions after the circle of stones,*" said Enat. "*But after the things we found in his cottage, I knew I was right to be afraid for them.*"

Caymin's jaw tightened. "*How could we have trusted him?*"

"*I knew him far longer than you and had no idea,*" Enat said. "*I don't believe he was evil or attracted to dark magic in the beginning, but something has changed. He is not the man I knew. Some people are easy to read.*" She smiled. "*I always know what you are feeling if you feel it strongly enough. But some have learned to mask what they think or feel. It would seem Timmin was one of those.*"

Caymin shivered in anticipation of seeing Broc and Cuán again, but her expression suddenly sobered. "*If he would do this, use them to get to me, he would do almost anything. The forest, all of you, you are not safe while Péist and I are here.*"

"*Do not worry about us, little one,*" Beanna said.

"*Beanna is right,*" Enat said. "*We will work together to protect you, protect the badgers, protect the forest, come what may.*"

She thanked Beanna again, and started to get to her feet when she froze at the sound of a branch snapping outside the hollow tree.

Enat ran out with Caymin on her heels and Beanna taking to the air to scan the area, but none of them saw anything. A quick search of the hard, frozen ground around the tree yielded nothing.

"*Perhaps it was a four-leg,*" Caymin said dubiously.

"*And perhaps I am a two-leg,*" said Beanna, landing on Caymin's shoulder.

Caymin glanced at her. "*You are a two-leg.*"

Beanna flapped her wing against Caymin's head. "*For a human, you are funny, little one.*"

CHAPTER 17

Reunited

Caymin waited anxiously, watching the moon each night as it seemed it would never wane to the dark.

"Remember," Enat had warned her after they had left Beanna, "you cannot tell the others the truth about why Broc and Cuán are coming without also telling them about Timmin. And that means telling them about Péist. I think it would be wise to keep this among you and the elders only for now."

"Do you trust Ivar and Neela?"

Enat smiled grimly. "I do. But we trusted Timmin, didn't we?"

"I wish I could leave the forest to go meet them," Caymin fretted.

"I know, but Beanna will fly out to meet them and escort them the rest of the way. We will know when they get here."

"What should I tell the others?"

Enat considered. "Tell them only that the badgers' forest has been overrun with humans and they wished to be someplace safer."

Caymin found it difficult to concentrate during their lessons.

"Would you pay attention!" Neela sighed in exasperation as Caymin haphazardly tried to turn a clay pot into a scroll.

She succeeded only in covering the pot with writing.

"Remember, all of you, you cannot permanently turn any object into anything else, you can only create the illusion that it has changed, and the change will only last as long as you feed the spell. Try again."

Neela moved on to where Diarmit hadn't been able to change his cup into anything.

Cíana leaned close. "You're anxious for your clan to get here?"

Caymin nodded. "I am. I have missed them greatly."

"We're all looking forward to meeting them."

Caymin smiled at her. "You will like them. They are kind and... honorable."

She tried again and the clay pot disappeared, replaced by a rolled-up scroll. Cíana reached out and picked it up.

"Nicely done."

Nearby, Gai was trying to turn a cup into a candle. Daina had already succeeded in this, but the candle wouldn't light.

Caymin looked at Cíana. "Do you miss your family?"

She nodded. "I do. Especially my mother. My brothers were all older and were making matches when Ivar came for me. I think it was hard for my mam to let me go, knowing I wouldn't be a girl any longer when I came back."

"Daina said she would have been matched this past Bealtaine," Caymin recalled. "Did you want to make a match?"

"I never thought about it before," Cíana admitted. "Making a match is what everyone does. No one asks whether you want it or no."

"But do you?"

"I don't know." Cíana frowned. "I don't want to have a man expecting to tie me to a home, filling me with baby after baby. Not when I've all this power that I'm just learning to use. I'll be taking the potion come the next moon. I've already spoken to Neela about it."

"What potion? What are you talking about?"

Cíana glanced over to see that Diarmit and Gai were listening. "Come outside."

They left the meetinghouse and wandered a short way into the forest, snugging their cloaks tightly around their shoulders.

"Hasn't Enat talked to you about this?" Cíana asked.

"About what?"

"Have you started to bleed yet?" Cíana asked in a hushed voice.

Caymin held out her arms, inspecting her hands for any blood.

"No." Cíana pulled her down to sit on the ground. "When girls get to a certain age, they begin to bleed, every moon." When Caymin still looked baffled, Cíana rolled her eyes. "Didn't Broc come into season, and then she and Cuán would mate?"

"Yes. Once a year."

"Well, human females do the same thing, every moon."

"Every moon?" Caymin looked indignant.

"But there's a potion," said Cíana. "Enat or Neela can show you. You drink it every moon and it will keep you from bleeding. If you ever want to have babies, you stop drinking the potion, and after two or three moons, your cycle comes back and you can mate."

"What if I do not ever want to have babies?"

"Then you just keep making the potion every month." Cíana nodded. "That's what I'm going to do."

"I will as well." Caymin couldn't imagine dealing with a baby. She made up her mind to ask Enat about the potion that evening.

A soft whirring of wings startled both of them as a thrush landed on Caymin's shoulder.

"Beanna says you are to come to the edge of the forest." The thrush flew off.

"They are here!"

Caymin jumped up and tugged on Cíana's hand as they ran through the forest, following the path Enat had taken when first she brought Ash there. She had forgotten how far they had journeyed after passing over the forest boundary. They were both out of breath as they felt themselves approach the protective barriers around the forest.

They dropped to the ground, panting.

"We are here," Caymin called out. She listened.

From a distance, she and Cíana both heard, "*We are coming. We will need your help.*"

Caymin got to her feet, pacing anxiously as they waited. At last, there were snuffling grunts and the noise of something moving through the forest, and suddenly, Beanna burst through the foliage. She landed on the ground, looking back in the direction from which she'd come. In a moment, a white-striped badger head appeared through the undergrowth.

"*Broc!*"

Caymin fell to her knees, but Broc backed away with a snarl.

"*Do you not know me?*"

Broc sniffed, edging nearer. "*It is you, Ash?*"

Caymin nodded, only now realizing how different she must look to the badgers, wearing human clothes, her hair cut short. "*It is I.*"

Broc crawled up her lap, nuzzling her face with whickers of happiness. Caymin wrapped her arms around Broc, hugging her tightly. Eight of the clan came in after her – older cubs from past seasons. They, too, crowded around Caymin. Lastly, Cuán staggered into the clearing, panting.

Caymin crawled to where he'd dropped. "*What happened?*"

"*We were attacked,*" Broc said. "*This is the first we have traveled during the day.*"

"*Who attacked you?*" Caymin scoured the forest growth, expecting Timmin to come crashing through the underbrush.

"*It was a clan of foxes,*" Beanna said. "*We were passing through their territory.*"

"*Are you hurt?*" Cíana asked anxiously.

Broc looked from Caymin to Cíana and back. "*This two-leg can speak as you do?*"

"*Yes. Some can here.*" Caymin echoed the question. "*Are you hurt?*"

Cuán turned to nuzzle his haunch. "*One of them bit me.*"

Cíana stopped Caymin who had started to lay her hands on him. "*Do you want to heal him here? Or take him back to the others? You don't know how much energy this will take from you.*"

"*She is right.*" Beanna hopped nearer. "*Can you carry him to the village?*"

Caymin nodded, wrapping her arms around Cuán and lifting him. The small group retraced the path to the village, and Caymin quickly realized she wouldn't be able to carry Cuán the whole way. She whispered words to partially levitate him.

Cuán lifted his head to look at her. "*What did you do, little one?*"

"*Just a bit of magic to make it easier.*"

"*You have learned much.*"

Caymin smiled. "*I have.*"

Beanna flew ahead to warn Enat and the others that Caymin was carrying an injured Cuán, so they were assembled and waiting for the strange party that trudged in from the forest.

"*Set him down here, Caymin.*" Enat had a soft blanket spread on the ground along with pots of herbs and salves.

"*Caymin?*" Broc looked up at her.

"*I will explain later,*" Caymin said as she gently laid Cuán on the blanket.

Together, Enat and Caymin examined Cuán and found a deep bite on his haunch. Enat frowned.

"*We need to clean it,*" Enat said to him. "*This will hurt.*"

She dipped a cloth in one of her salves, and then, as gently as she could, used a long bone needle to push it into the punctures made by the fox's teeth. Cuán gnashed his teeth and snarled, panting in pain.

"*Can we not heal it magically?*" Caymin asked Enat.

Enat shook her head. "*We will, but this wound is already infected. Feel it.*"

She placed her hands over Caymin's, guiding her. There, almost like a cauldron bubbling, Caymin felt the festering of the wound, deep inside Cuán's body.

"*If you were to try healing that as it is,*" Enat said, "*it could take all your energy for the infection alone, leaving you none left for the actual healing. We'll let this work, and then we'll finish with magic.*"

Cuán's panting eased as Enat finished packing the wounds with dampened leaves to draw the last of any infection out.

"*Help me now,*" she said to Caymin. "*He needs to sleep.*"

Caymin soaked a piece of bread with a strong tonic. "*Eat this. When you wake, you will feel better.*"

Cuán sniffed the bread and hesitated. Caymin laid a gentle hand on his head, looking him in the eye.

"*Trust me as you always did,*" she said.

He took the bread from her hand and ate it. Within a few heartbeats, his eyes began to close and his head dropped to the blanket.

"*He will sleep through the night,*" she said to Broc.

"*Thank you,*" Broc said to Enat.

"*You are most welcome.*" She looked at the other badgers who were huddled together, anxiously watching the two-legs gathered around them. "*You are all most welcome here.*"

Cíana sat down on the ground and gestured to the others to do the same. "*We have all been most eager to meet Caymin's clan.*"

"*You mean Ash,*" Gai said. "*They knew her as Ash.*"

"*You're right. I forgot.*"

Caymin felt a rush a gratitude to them for speaking so that the badgers could understand everything, rather than only a word here and there when spoken aloud. Daina and Diarmit could not join the conversation, but sat anyhow, looking around in mild bemusement.

Neela brought out a large basket of apples and root vegetables as well as some smoked fish. "*You must not have had time to do much hunting as you journeyed here. This will help until you can hunt for yourselves.*"

"*Thank you, Neela,*" Caymin said, for she herself hadn't thought about food. "*I have found a place, deep in the forest, that will make a good sett.*"

Broc huddled next to Caymin and ate a bit, as the other badgers tasted the food Neela had offered.

"*You must be very tired,*" Caymin said.

"*We are, little one.*"

"*I know where you can rest for now, until you can dig a sett.*"

Beanna hopped onto Caymin's knee. "*The tree?*"

"Yes. It will be warm and safe."

She got to her knees and carefully wrapped Cuán in the blanket. Standing with him, she said to the others, "I will show them where they can sleep for now."

Beanna led the way and the badgers all followed as Caymin carried Cuán to the hollow tree. Gently, she laid him inside, keeping him covered with the blanket.

"You can all rest safely here," she said.

The badgers sniffed and explored the interior of the tree. *"Can you stay with us?"*

She smiled. *"I will stay."*

She lay down and the badgers snuggled next to her, keeping her warm.

Broc nuzzled her cheek. *"It is good to see you, little one."*

She woke when Cuán stirred. Outside, snow had fallen overnight. She removed Enat's dressing and laid her hands on his haunch.

"This is ready to finish healing."

She closed her eyes and, as the badgers had seen once before, her hands glowed with her power as she completed the healing of his wound. Even with the infection gone, the healing demanded a good bit of energy. She took a deep breath and sat back.

"How do you feel?"

Cuán sat up. *"Hungry."*

She chuckled. *"I have some food for you."*

She laid out some of the food Neela had packed for them. To the others, she said, *"Do you feel up to hunting? You need not wait until nightfall here."*

"I will stay," said Broc.

The young badgers left the tree. Caymin leaned against the trunk and Broc settled against her thigh.

"You have not eaten," Caymin said. *"And you carry new cubs inside you."*

"I will hunt later. Tell us of your new name."

Caymin told them of the night of her spiritwalk. *"I saw my two-leg parents, and heard them call me by my name. And I saw you rescue me. You and Cuán and your sisters. Just like the story you told me when I was but a cub."*

Broc made a low, contented growl. *"You have grown. And you dress as a two-leg now."*

"Yes."

"You wear skins on your feet." Cuán sniffed Caymin's leather boots.

Caymin squirmed.

"I am not blaming you," he said. *"You are one of them now."*

"I am, and I am not," Caymin said.

"What do you mean?"

"I have always been apart from them. They were raised in two-leg families; I was raised by you. They know the two-leg stories and festivals; I do not. They speak of being matched with mates someday; I do not. But it is true, that I now wear skins and eat two-leg food."

Broc sat up. *"What troubles you?"*

"I do not wish to disappoint you."

"You could never disappoint us, little one."

Caymin stroked the sleek fur. *"I am glad you are here and safe."*

"Can you tell us more of this two-leg who is so dangerous?"

"He has powerful magic, and he wants something."

Broc turned as if sniffing for something. *"He wants what follows you?"*

Caymin looked at her in surprise. *"You can sense him?"*

"He is near. Can you call him?"

Caymin called to Péist, who was indeed very near. She'd felt his concern for her safety.

"Come. Meet my badger parents."

Within a short while, there was a rustling sound as Péist wriggled into the end of the hollow tree. Cuán growled and Broc backed up against Caymin, who said, *"This is Péist."*

Broc stretched her neck as long as it would go, sniffing as she circled Péist. *"This is what the magical two-leg wants?"*

Caymin smiled at the disdain in Broc's voice. Péist crawled nearer and dropped a dead vole at Broc's feet before moving to Caymin's side and pressing against her thigh. *"He knows you have not eaten and brought you a gift."* She laid a hand on Péist.

Broc came around to Caymin's other side and she and Péist stared at each other. *"He does not speak."*

"Not yet. He is a cub. And will have magical power of his own one day. That is why Timmin wanted him. I have been told he will speak someday. I… feel his thoughts. And he feels mine."

Broc gave a clear sniff of disbelief. *"He is the ugliest cub I have ever seen, but if you feel connected to him, little one, then we are as well."* She nosed the vole. *"Give him my thanks."*

Enat looked up from where she sat near the fire, sewing new soles on her boots as Caymin entered the cottage, shaking snow off her cloak. "Are the badgers pleased with the site you chose for them?"

"Yes. They will be busy digging for many days."

Caymin sat in front of the hearth. She stirred the fire and added a block of peat.

Enat set aside the boots. "Does something trouble you?"

Caymin stared into the flames for a bit before saying, "Broc did not know me at first."

"That's understandable. You've grown, and you look very different now."

Caymin nodded. "Péist came to meet her and Cuán while the others were out hunting."

"He honored them, as he felt what they mean to you."

A smile tugged at Caymin's mouth. "She said he was the ugliest cub she had ever seen."

Enat chuckled. "I daresay one day no one will call him ugly."

CHAPTER 18

The Secret Shared

A hard, bitter cold descended on the forest and a deep snow fell. Caymin had helped the badgers to lay in a supply of food in their new sett so that they could settle and rest after their long journey and Broc could give birth in peace.

"Call to me if you need me for anything," Caymin told them.

She concentrated on her lessons again, or tried to. She often found herself sitting in the meetinghouse with the other apprentices, her cauldron bubbling or some spell half-murmured, but then she would become distracted when she heard faint stirrings from the badgers, even when they weren't speaking directly to her.

"I never used to hear them from this far away before," she told Enat, rubbing her forehead. "And Péist is growing more insistent. He reaches out to me day and night now. I think maybe he is jealous."

Enat eyed her. "Perhaps it's a combination of how your power has grown and the forest magnifying everything."

"It is hard to focus."

"This might be a good time for you to learn to block your mind," Enat said. "It is a useful skill for all of us anyhow, and is normally saved for the older apprentices, but it will be especially good for you, with so many tugging at you."

"What do I do?"

"It is different for each," said Enat. "Some can clear their minds, but I find that exceedingly difficult. As soon I clear my mind, it fills up with all kinds of nonsense. I find it easier to focus so hard on one thing, that there is no room for anything else."

Caymin closed her eyes tightly, and then opened them again when she heard Enat's laugh.

"You'd best not learn to do this with your eyes closed," Enat said. "It would be most inconvenient if you had to close your eyes every time you needed to block someone. Aside from the practical aspect that you might have to do this in the middle of a confrontation, you'll want to master the skill in such a way that others will not know when you're blocking."

Caymin frowned. "This sounds very difficult."

"It can be," Enat said with a shrug. "For you, talking to animals comes naturally, while it doesn't for others. Some can block without even having to think about it, while you may have to work to learn to do this."

Enat prodded the fire. "Stare into the flames, find something to focus on – maybe a memory or something you see in the fire itself."

Caymin concentrated on the way the flames licked the blocks of peat, as if they were alive. She felt something pushing, almost a physical thing, pushing into her thoughts and she found herself remembering the end of the last winter when Enat came to find her.

"You're not blocking me," Enat said quietly. "You're letting me right in."

"But how do I stop you?"

"You must concentrate harder, do not let me in."

Caymin glared at the fire now, and this time, when the push came, she relived her spiritwalk the night she saw her mother for the first time.

"Try again."

She renewed her focus on the fire, trying to do as Enat said and fill her mind with what she saw, but time after time, Enat pushed through.

She heard Enat sigh, and the pushing stopped.

"This will not be easy for you," Enat said. "You've never tried to conceal your emotions from anyone. You never needed to, so it doesn't come naturally to you. We'll keep practicing, but not now."

The apprentices were given a free afternoon. They ate a mid-day meal and Diarmit announced he was going to the boys' cottage to sleep.

"Why is he so sleepy all the time?" Caymin asked.

Gai shrugged. "Because he's lazy? All he does is sleep and eat. I'm going to the forge with Ivar. Want to come along?"

Caymin shook her head. "I promised Broc I would come to visit."

Daina and Cíana accompanied Caymin to the sett, each carrying a small basket of carrots or dried venison or nuts. They walked through snow almost up to their knees.

"How old are the cubs now?" Daina asked, huffing along behind Caymin.

"Almost a moon."

They trudged for a while before coming to an area the badgers had cleared of snow.

"*We have come for a visit,*" Caymin called.

She dropped to her hands and knees and crawled down a long tunnel, enlarged to accommodate humans. Cíana and Daina followed. They came to a larger chamber where Broc lay with her four new cubs as they nursed.

"*We brought food.*"

"It's darker than night in here," said Daina. "How do you see anything?"

Caymin conjured a small flame to illuminate the chamber. "I forgot. I cannot see enough to be able to read, but enough to tell friend from foe."

The other badgers crowded around, greeting Caymin. Somewhat more shyly, they stretched their noses out to sniff Cíana and Daina, allowing them to stroke their heads.

"Thank you, little one," said Broc.

Cuán pulled a strip of venison from the basket and brought it to Broc.

"They're so cute," Daina said, looking at the newborn cubs. "May I hold one?"

Caymin translated for her, and Broc nudged one of the cubs in her direction. Daina picked it up, and it cried and wriggled. It settled as she snuggled it against her chest, keeping it warm.

"I never thought to have two-legs in our sett, beyond you, little one," Cuán said.

"I never thought to have you and my two-leg friends all together."

Cíana giggled. *"I like being called a two-leg."*

"I had to learn many new words when Enat came to get me," Caymin said, remembering how strange and new everything seemed back then.

"Please tell Enat again how grateful we are to her for sending help to us," Broc said. *"Has there been any sign of that two-leg, Timmin?"*

Caymin felt Cíana tense next to her, though Daina continued to croon and stroke the badger cub, oblivious to the unspoken conversation taking place around her.

"No," Caymin said. She waited a moment, but Cíana kept her silence. *"There has been no sign of him."*

The girls took their leave shortly thereafter, with a promise to come back soon. Caymin lingered for just a moment.

"Be well, little one," said Broc.

"And you."

As the girls walked back through the snow to the village, Daina chattered on and on about how she never thought she'd meet badgers and how cute the cubs were. Caymin stayed silent and noticed that Cíana said nothing.

When they neared Enat's cottage, Caymin veered off, but hadn't gone ten paces before Cíana circled around and caught up to her.

"I told Daina I'd forgotten something," she said. "I want to talk to you."

Caymin kept walking. Cíana grabbed her arm to pull her to a halt. "You know what I mean. Tell me about Timmin."

Caymin glanced around, but all near them was quiet. Still, she cast a spell to block any from hearing what they said.

"The elders know, but Enat asked me not to tell anyone else. If I tell you, you will not tell the others?"

"I won't. I give you my word."

Caymin bit her lip for a moment as she thought. "Do you know why Timmin left the forest?"

Cíana shook her head. "No one does. We guessed he had a disagreement with the other elders."

Caymin scoffed. "You are partially right. Timmin... he wanted something. And he tried to use me to get it. Enat and Neela saved me from him. At the circle of stones. They made him leave the forest."

"But what could he want from you that badly?"

"Péist."

Cíana laughed a little. "The worm-creature? The one who warned you the invaders were coming across the lake? Why in the world would Timmin want him?"

Caymin pulled Cíana down to sit under the shelter of a rowan tree where the ground was clear of snow. "Because Péist is a dragon cub. At least, Enat believes he is. And Timmin wanted him. Wanted to control him and use him to drive the invaders and the believers of the Christ from our land."

Cíana's mouth fell open and she said nothing for several heartbeats. "A dragon cub. You're sure?"

"I am not. But Enat thinks he is. The invader we caught had a dragon on the brooch holding his cloak and he said something about dragons in his speech. After the invaders were gone, Timmin asked me many questions, and then one day, took me to the circle of stones and made me call Péist. He tried to take Péist away, but his magic rebounded."

Cíana gasped. "Like the day Enat fought Ivar to make you protect her."

Caymin nodded. "I did not mean to, but my power rose to protect Péist, and Timmin was thrown back. Enat and Neela came then and made him leave the forest."

"But what has this to do with the badgers?"

"Enat thought Timmin might try to find them and use them to force me to do as he wishes. She sent Beanna to them first, asking them to come to the forest for protection."

Cíana's mouth fell open again. "This is why they're here?"

Caymin nodded.

"And was he after them?"

"It seems he was."

Cíana sat there, absorbing all of this. "Timmin must be desperate, if he would go to such lengths to get Péist."

"And Enat is worried that the protections around the forest may not be enough to keep him out."

"The forest and the elders are powerful."

Caymin's expression darkened. "So is Timmin."

The cold softened and the snow melted, carrying a hint of spring on the air.

"We celebrate Imbolc next moon," said Enat one evening as she and Caymin sat near the hearth. Enat paused her writing in the book she kept, her book of days, she called it. "It will be one year since I came to you and we started our journey here."

Caymin looked up from the arrow she was fletching. "You are right. I had not realized."

"How would you like to celebrate?"

Caymin tilted her head. "I do not understand."

"To mark the date. Humans often celebrate dates or occasions that are meaningful to them. I think 'twas very meaningful, the day I found you. I'd like to celebrate."

Caymin bent her head back over her arrow shaft, tightly pulling the thread she was using to bind crow feathers Beanna had brought her. "Everyone will celebrate Imbolc, will they not?"

"Aye, they will. But we can do something additional."

"Perhaps you and I could share a meal with the badgers?"

Enat smiled. "I think that is an excellent way to celebrate, since my coming took you away from them."

Caymin's stomach growled.

"You spoke of food," Enat said with a chuckle. "What would you like to eat?"

"Porridge?" Caymin looked up hopefully.

"Porridge it is."

"I will make it."

Caymin set aside her arrow. Just as she poured the ground grain into two bowls, her head snapped up.

"What is it?" Enat asked.

"Péist! He is in trouble."

Enat grabbed her staff and followed Caymin into the dark forest as she ran unerringly in the direction from which Péist continued to cry out.

"This way!"

Caymin scrambled over boulders and crawled under fallen trees, leaving Enat to follow. On and on she ran, following the sound of his cries in her head. She came to a small clearing, and even in the dim light from the quarter-moon, she could see that there had been a disturbance. Broken branches were scattered about, and the leaves and dirt on the forest floor had been dug and tossed over what remained of the snow. She knelt down and sniffed. Blood.

Caymin stopped to listen. She thought she heard running footsteps, but a moment later, Enat appeared and ran up behind her.

"What is it?" Enat gasped.

"I am not sure yet." Caymin pointed. "A fight? Someone was injured."

She and Enat paused, listening.

"Péist?" She called out, trying to hear him, but all was quiet now.

She closed her eyes, reaching out and felt... not Péist's thoughts as she had. It was different. "This way." She crept toward an outcropping of rock and dropped to her hands and knees. "I think he is in here."

She had to get on her belly to wriggle into the opening under the rocks. The pitch black of the crevice suddenly glowed with a faint light. She gathered her power, ready to throw a defensive spell if needed, but the light continued to pulse. Cautiously, she crawled forward and saw an orb, about the size of her head. It glowed with a white luminescence, waxing and waning from inside, as if some creature breathed within. She reached out and was surprised to feel that it was warm. She rolled it to her and gathered it in one arm as she wriggled her way back out of the crevice to where Enat waited.

"What is that?" Enat laid a hand on the object.

Caymin looked at her, her face illuminated by the light coming from the orb. "It is Péist."

CHAPTER 19

The Dragon Egg

Enat asked no more questions until they were well away from the clearing. Caymin carried the orb under her tunic to hide its light. She kept glancing behind them, fearful whoever had fought with Péist might be following them, but all was still.

They came to a dense thicket of blackthorn, a few white flowers already blooming. Enat whispered and the branches parted. They crawled under the hedge and Enat closed the wall of thorns around them again. She took the additional precaution of setting an enchantment to keep them from being overheard.

"You're sure this is Péist?"

Caymin nodded, setting the heavy object on her lap. "He is not communicating as he did before, but I can feel... things. He is injured, but healing. Whatever or whoever he fought with hurt him."

She looked up. "Did they, whoever they were, do this to him?"

Enat didn't answer immediately. She picked up the orb and held it, pulsing in her hands, its light illuminating their thorny enclosure. "I think not," she said at last. "I think Péist did this to himself." She looked at Caymin. "Dragon lore tells us that dragons hatch from eggs, and that's why no one recognized Péist for what he is. No one in our lifetime has ever seen a dragon egg. It may be that the worm-like Péist we have known is a stage dragons go through, much like a caterpillar. If so, then this is not truly an egg, but more a *khrusallis*."

"What is that?"

"Certain creatures encase themselves in a protective shell as they grow, in order to transform themselves," said Enat. "When they're ready, they emerge as something very different from what they were. Many winged creatures, not birds, but other winged creatures, such as butterflies, do this."

"You mean, when he hatches from this, this *khrusallis*, he will be a dragon?"

Enat shrugged. "I can't know for certain, but I believe so."

Caymin stared at the glowing sphere in Enat's hands. "How long will this last? When will he hatch?"

"I've no way of knowing. The tales tell of eggs being carried from place to place for many, many winters without hatching."

"How many?"

Enat shook her head. "I simply don't know, Caymin. Those tales are only that, stories. But one thing I know is that in those stories, none of those dragons had already bonded with a human."

The expression of wonder on Enat's face sobered as she handed the egg back to Caymin.

"The tales also tell of wars being fought over dragon eggs," Enat added.

"Then he is still not safe in this form."

"No, he is not."

Caymin hugged the sphere to her, feeling its warmth, feeling Péist inside. "What can we do to keep him safe?"

Enat thought for long heartbeats before saying, "This goes against everything we believe here, but I think we must keep this secret from everyone. Even Neela and Ivar. And you should not tell any of the apprentices."

"Cíana knows," Caymin said. "She heard Broc ask about Timmin, and she asked what she was speaking of. I know you told me to tell no one, but she asked and I did not know what to say."

"Tell no one else," Enat said firmly. "I know you don't know how to lie, Caymin, but this is very important. We cannot let anyone know that Péist is now an egg. He will become a target for any who want to steal him. We must both lie and tell any who ask that he has left the forest. Can you do this?"

"To keep Péist safe, yes." Caymin ran a hand over the smooth warmth of the *khrusallis*. "But where can we keep him?"

"Let's take him to the badgers." Enat nodded. "They'll protect him as they once protected you. Only a fool would take on an angry badger."

Caymin breathed a sigh of relief. "They will take care of him."

When Caymin joined the other apprentices the next day, she watched them to see if any showed signs of having been in a fight. To her dismay, both Gai and Niall had cuts and bruises.

"Boys," Una said with a shake of her head. "They were practicing sparring with staffs and didn't enchant them for protection."

"Why?"

"Because they wanted to see who was the better fighter, they said." She laughed, but Caymin did not.

Tucked deep in the sett, covered by a mound of dirt, leaves and moss, was Péist's egg. She couldn't hear him as she had before, but she felt him, like a heartbeat, low and steady, and it reassured her.

Diarmit limped into the meetinghouse.

"What happened to you?" Cíana asked him as he dropped onto the bench.

"He tripped in the dark, going to the latrine," Gai said, laughing.

Diarmit's cheeks reddened, but he chuckled along as he reached for an oatcake.

Caymin stared morosely at the table, her chin resting on her fist. Péist was in danger from someone here, or from some unknown person hiding in the forest. Lessons on making potions or learning to float feathers did not seem very important at the moment.

Ivar came in and the others all grew quiet. Caymin didn't bother to look up.

"Today, we are going to have you practice attacking and blocking one another," said Ivar. Caymin felt the boys shift eagerly. "Not with weapons, but with magic." At these words, she sat up.

Ivar moved around to better face them. "We have taught you how to use your power to move things, to call the elements, to heal. But sometimes, it is necessary to use magic to fight, to defend."

"Like Timmin did when the invaders came?" Daina said.

Cíana caught Caymin's eye. Caymin quickly looked down.

"Una and Niall have done this before," said Ivar. "They will show you, and then we will work with you as you practice."

They all went outside and watched as Niall and Una faced each other.

Niall smirked. "Ready?"

In answer, Una threw both hands in his direction as if she was hurling a stone at him. Caymin saw nothing, but felt the strength of her spell as it caught Niall squarely in the chest, throwing him onto his back.

Una put her hands on her hips. "You weren't."

She reached a hand out and pulled him to his feet. "Again?"

They faced off and, this time, Niall was prepared. When Una threw her spell at him, he blocked it. Caymin could feel the reverberation as it rebounded.

"You can't predict the type of spell someone may use on you," Ivar said. "But the same protective spell will work most of the time. Imagine you are throwing up an invisible shield in front of you."

The younger apprentices spread out. Ivar, Niall and Una attempted to enchant them with various spells while the apprentices tried to block them. Caymin was not quick enough to block Niall's whirlwind charm as he called up the air, picking her up in its vortex and tossing her like a bug. She stood up in time to see Diarmit tumbling head over heels from the strength of whatever Una used on him.

"Again," she said to Niall. This time, she got a partial block up as he aimed the same spell at her. Instead of being tossed by his whirlwind, she screwed her eyes up against it, but held her ground.

"Not bad." He let the air die. "But not good enough. Letting me through even that much and having to keep your shield up uses a lot more energy than if you can just stop me once and done, and then hit me with a spell of your own."

She reset her feet and prepared to bring up her protection. Niall looked down at the ground, scuffing at something with his toe, and suddenly sent a different spell at Caymin. She'd been expecting the whirlwind again and was so startled, that she threw up her protection out of instinct. Niall's spell knocked her backward, but her shield was so strong that it knocked Niall back also.

"Well done," he said. "You learn quickly."

"Not quickly enough. You still knocked me down."

He laughed. "If my full spell had gotten through, you would have been picking yourself out of a tree. Getting knocked down is nothing. Well done."

They switched partners and kept practicing. Caymin was attempting to jinx Ivar, who was easily blocking her.

"Let me attack you now," he said.

Caymin nervously prepared to put up a protective spell when she felt a push, inside her head, into her thoughts. It alarmed her and, without thinking, she threw up a blocking spell strong enough that Ivar was pushed back a step.

"I hadn't done anything yet," he said.

She looked around, but everyone else was busy practicing. She rubbed her forehead.

"Are you all right?" Ivar stepped closer.

"I am fine. Just tired."

He looked at the sky. "It's well past mid-day. We're all getting tired. That's enough for today."

Gai approached her. "Do you want to –"

"No." Caymin backed away. "My head hurts. I am going to rest."

She nearly ran back to the cottage, but Enat wasn't there. She headed into the forest, taking a direction away from the sett. She stopped frequently, listening for footsteps, but heard nothing. Overhead, she heard wings flapping and looked up to see Beanna landing on a branch.

"What troubles you, little one?"

The crow fluttered down to land on Caymin's shoulder.

Caymin hesitated. Enat had said not to tell anyone at all about Péist's change. *"There are strange things happening among the two-legs."*

"Stranger than usual with two-legs?" Beanna bobbed her head at her own joke.

Caymin smiled. *"Yes, even stranger than that."* She walked on, treading silently. *"You know that one of the apprentices was attacked at Samhain and that Timmin was made to leave the forest."*

"Yes."

"There is a feeling of unrest. Someone is trying to learn things they should not, and is willing to hurt others to get what they want."

"Is it the young two-leg male I spoke with? Gai?"

Caymin gave her a sideways glance. *"What did you see him doing in the forest?"*

"He was using magic to rip up bushes and blow bird nests from trees. He did not attack the trees, but he was testing his powers in ways that were destructive."

"Do you think him capable of hurting Péist?"

Beanna rode along on her shoulder for several steps. *"I think most two-legs are capable of great good or great harm. I do not understand them. You and Enat are among the few two-legs I trust."*

"I am beginning to feel the same."

Caymin skirted through the forest, coming around to the sett from the opposite direction. Beanna stayed with her, flying overhead to scout for any who followed. She reported back that she saw no one. Caymin crouched where she could see one of the entrances to the sett. One of the older cubs was cleaning, pushing soiled leaves out and away from the set. She called out as she approached, and the cub came to meet her. She went to her entrance and crawled inside while Beanna kept watch in a tree nearby.

The new cubs were crawling around, their eyes open and their little bodies now covered in fur, faint stripes visible on their heads. Broc came to greet her, nuzzling her cheek.

"*How are you little one?*"

"*I am fine.*" Caymin sat against the wall of the chamber and the cubs crawled into her lap.

"*You are not. What troubles you?*"

"*You have known me longer than any, and you know me better than any.*" She cradled the cubs in her arms. "*It seems there is another among us who is not honest. Someone is trying to read my thoughts.*"

"*To find the egg?*"

"*I believe so. Have any of you detected any two-legs about?*"

"*None.*"

"*How is Péist?*"

"*How is any egg?*" Broc whickered. "*It sits there until it hatches.*"

"*Can you take me to him?*"

Caymin set the cubs down and Broc told them to stay put as she led the way through a tunnel to another chamber. Not content to cover Péist's egg with leaves and moss, the badgers had dug a small crater and buried it.

"*To hide the light should any get in here to steal it,*" Broc said.

"*A wise precaution.*" Caymin laid her hands over the dirt covering the egg, and felt Péist there. She reassured him he was safe. "*I am going to add more layers of protection.*"

She raised her hand and whispered words, weaving a spell that would repel any except the badgers or Enat or her. She spread the boundaries of the protection to include the entire chamber.

"*If any make it this far, they will know he is here, but they should not be able to get to him.*"

Broc sniffed the dirt over the egg. "*Is it wise to let them know where he is?*"

"*If they come here, they already know where he is.*"

CHAPTER 20

Betrayed

The weather turned fierce as Imbolc approached. The apprentices were sent out to gather snowdrops and blackthorn, just as Caymin had watched Enat do near her sett the previous year.

They shivered in their cloaks as the wind tore through the forest, making the trees creak and groan overhead. Everything was wet as a heavy half-frozen rain fell.

"It doesn't feel like spring," Daina said through chattering teeth, her cloak drawn up over her head.

Diarmit cut blackthorn branches, stuffing them into a basket. "This is daft. We have magic. Why aren't we using it to shelter ourselves, or better yet, wait until this stupid storm has passed?"

"Because Imbolc is in three nights," said Cíana. "And you know better than to use magic for something so frivolous."

Gai glared out from under his hood. "It's not frivolous if it saves us from freezing to death in the cold."

"You were the one who got us in trouble using magic at the planting," Daina reminded him.

He scowled and bent to pluck a bunch of snowdrops bravely holding their heads up despite being battered by the slushy rain.

"Badgers welcome spring when it arrives," said Caymin, wet and shivering like the others. "And until it does, they are smart enough to stay warm and dry."

"Wish I was a badger," Diarmit grumbled. He shouldered the basket and they moved on.

They were all thoroughly drenched by the time they got back to the village, their lips blue with cold. Niall and Una sat in the meetinghouse stirring a large vat of stew, thick with barley and chunks of chicken.

"Thought you could use this," Una said cheerfully.

The apprentices dropped their baskets and took off their wet cloaks. They crowded around the fire, filling bowls with hot stew.

"Oh, this is so good," Diarmit said, his eyes closed.

No one else spoke as they all ate ravenously. When their stomachs were filled, they sat sleepily around the fire. Caymin sniffed. The wet woolen cloaks stunk. She used magic to dry herself and her cloak. The others did the same.

"That's better," Niall said. "You all were kind of smelly. Like wet dogs."

"You can laugh," Gai said.

"Yes, we can." Niall reached over to punch him in the shoulder. "We've been the ones doing the gathering. One year, the snow was up to our arses. Had to dig to find the snowdrops buried under the blasted snow. Just because it's Imbolc doesn't mean winter is ready to go away."

Caymin looked around. "Where are the elders?"

"Ivar thought it was a good time to sharpen swords," said Una. "And I think Enat and Neela are in Neela's cottage, brewing some potions to trade when they go on the next reaping."

"Reaping?" Caymin looked at her in bewilderment. "For new apprentices?"

"Yes," Niall said. "They have been feeling the stirrings of power, and will decide who to bring back here."

"Like Enat did with me?" Caymin wasn't sure why, but she felt a prick of jealousy to think of new apprentices coming. What if Enat wanted a new apprentice to live with her?

Una nodded. "Like they did for each of us. With three gone, we have room for new ones to come."

They sat inside, full bellies and fireside warmth making them drowsy as they listened to the howling wind outside the meetinghouse. Caymin contemplated going back to the cottage, but it was much warmer and dryer here... Her eyes drooped and she began to doze off.

She jumped when the meetinghouse door burst open. Ivar's huge form filled the opening as he stepped inside and pushed the door shut. When he turned around, Caymin saw that he held something.

He set a bedraggled hawk on the table. "Gai."

"It's Lorcan." Gai ran a finger over the hawk's wet head. "He belongs to our mage, Eachna."

"He carries a message," Ivar said.

Only then did Caymin see the scroll tied to the hawk's leg. She retrieved her cloak as Gai untied the scroll.

"Hold still and I will dry you," she said to the hawk as Gai unfurled the parchment. She gently rubbed the cloak over the hawk's sodden feathers.

"He is exhausted," she said to Ivar. "Fighting his way through the wind and the rain."

Ivar got a strip of dried venison and a small bowl of water. The hawk gobbled the meat and took a few drinks. He blinked his gratitude to Caymin.

"It's from my brother," Gai said. He sat heavily. "They went out to fight a neighboring clan who was encroaching on our land and my father was captured. They're holding him for ransom."

Cíana sat next to him. "What does that mean for you?"

"My brother wants me to return now."

"But you haven't completed your training," Una said. "Your staff."

Gai's jaw tightened and he tossed the parchment onto the table. Something on it caught Caymin's eye. She reached for the parchment and stared. There, at the top of the scroll, was a blue wolf with red eyes, holding a yellow sword in one paw.

"What is this?" Her voice was ragged and her finger trembled as she pointed.

Gai blinked and looked at the parchment. "It's our crest, the crest of our clan."

"Your crest." She stared at him. "Your father's warriors wear this crest."

"Yes. Why?"

Caymin said nothing, but shoved up from the table and jerked the door open. She ran through the slush and wind to the cottage, her mind in a complete jumble. She went to her bed where her old cloak lay folded. "*We'll keep it safe,*" Enat had said. She grabbed it.

She was breathless as she burst back into the meetinghouse. The others turned to her as, wordlessly, she held up the cloak.

"Oh, gods and goddesses," Ivar muttered.

Gai stood. "Where did you get that?"

He reached out to touch the red eyes of the wolf, faded, but clearly the same image.

"This is what the badgers wrapped me in the night they saved me," Caymin said, her voice breaking. "This is what the warriors wore – the ones who raided my village, the ones who killed my father and captured my mother, the ones who left me to burn."

Caymin's eyes swam with tears. Though her vision was blurred, she saw Daina raise a hand to her mouth and she saw Cíana's mouth move, but she couldn't hear anything through the roaring in her ears.

"You come from a clan of murderers! Your father, his warriors, all of you! You have no honor." She rounded on Ivar. "And you knew. You saw this when I first came. You and Enat knew."

She backed away, shaking her head as her tears spilled over. Hugging the cloak to her chest, she ran again, ran into the dark forest.

Caymin lay huddled in Péist's chamber in the sett, his egg still buried under its enchantments. She had set a protective barrier around the sett, but she knew Enat would be able to get through. She doubted it was strong enough to keep Diarmit out.

Broc and Cuán had asked no questions when she crawled into the sett earlier in the day, unable to stop crying. Night fell, but the badgers did not hunt, choosing instead to stay near her, Broc pressed to her side as her cubs nursed. Occasionally Broc nuzzled her cheek as she lay with her face buried in her old cloak.

Eventually, she slept. She was startled awake by the hissing of the badgers who surrounded her, their fur on end.

"It is I, Enat."

Caymin sat up and laid a calming hand on Cuán. *"I knew she would come."*

The badgers grew silent, but stayed crowded around Caymin while they waited for Enat to squirm down the tunnel into the chamber. Caymin conjured a flame and set it afloat.

Enat crawled into the chamber and sat. She allowed the silence to stretch on before finally saying, *"I don't need to read your thoughts to know how angry you are with me."*

Caymin stared at the white stripes on the head of the cub nearest her. She could not look Enat in the eye. *"You knew. From the beginning, you knew."*

"Not from the beginning. I did not know until we got here and washed your cloak and I saw the design woven into it." Enat closed her eyes and lowered her head. *"I should have told you then, perhaps, but I didn't know how."*

"Ivar knew." Caymin's eyes shot daggers. *"The morning he came to the cottage and thought I was sleeping. He saw it and asked if I knew. That is why you told me to keep my old cloak safe in the cottage – you did not want Gai to see it. You both lied to me. You have lied to me for a year."*

Enat nodded. *"Yes."*

"Why?"

"There were many reasons." Enat waited until Caymin unwillingly raised her gaze. *"The most important reason is that Gai is not his father or his brother."*

"But he is like them! We have seen him shoot innocent birds. Beanna told me he was harming animals in the forest. His clan burned my village and killed

my father. They took my mother prisoner and left me to die. And you defend him."

Cuán sat up at these words, a low growl in his throat.

"No," said Enat. "*I'm not defending him. Nothing defends what they did to your village and you. But Gai was but a babe himself when they attacked. He is not to blame. Caymin, I told you once that Gai was an empty vessel, capable of being filled with either good or evil. You reached out to him, befriended him when the others thought he had attacked Fergus.*"

"*I was a fool,*" Caymin said bitterly. "*A fool to think he did not do it. He is the one who attacked Péist. He is the one Péist feared. I know it. I will never trust him again.*"

"*And me? Will you trust me again?*"

Caymin lowered her gaze again, unable to bear the sadness in Enat's eyes.

When Caymin didn't respond, Enat said, "*My cottage is open to you whenever you are ready to come back.*" She turned and crept back up the tunnel.

"*Little one?*" Broc whickered, placing her front feet in Caymin's lap and reaching up to nuzzle her cheek. Caymin wrapped her arms around Broc and buried her face in the soft fur as she cried again.

For three days, Caymin stayed with the badgers, living as she had before. The storm had passed and the weather gentled, heralding the spring to come.

She foraged with the clan, unwilling to admit that the food available this time of year was lacking. The badgers, with their strong claws, tore through the frozen earth to find grubs and worms where they hid, sleeping their way through the winter. Caymin could only find the few dried up berries left on bushes. She went to the clearing where they had planted the year before, but the scattered leftover apples and turnips she was able to find had rotted and were not edible.

Her stomach was empty and complaining as she crept back into the sett. The young cubs crawled into her lap. They still nursed, but were eager to nibble on the bits of berry she had brought with her.

"Caymin?"

She heard Daina's voice echo faintly down the tunnel. She didn't answer.

"Caymin? We know you're in there." This time Cíana called so that the badgers could understand as well. *"Come out or we're coming in."*

Caymin glanced at Broc who gave her a push with her snout. *"Go, little one. Talk to the two-legs."*

Reluctantly, Caymin crawled up the tunnel. She emerged, wincing at the sunlight coming through the trees, to find Cíana and Daina sitting near the entrance to the sett.

Daina held up a small bag. "We brought you and your clan some food."

Caymin opened it and looked inside to find oatcakes and meat and cheese and bread. She hungrily stuffed an oatcake into her mouth. "Thank you," she mumbled.

"How long are you going to stay here?" Daina asked.

Caymin shrugged. "I do not know."

"Gai left." Cíana watched her with narrowed eyes as she delivered this news.

Caymin's head snapped up. "He left?"

"Yes."

Caymin suddenly found the woven pattern of the bag very interesting. She stared hard at it as she said, "Because of me?"

"You and the message from his brother."

"We're sorry," said Daina softly. "About your family. We didn't know."

"Why are you sorry?" Caymin asked, puzzled.

"Because it causes you pain," said Cíana. "I think Gai was sorry as well."

Caymin's expression hardened. "He should be sorry."

Cíana leaned forward. "It was horrible for you to find out that way, but Gai isn't the one who hurt you and your family."

Caymin thought about Enat saying the same thing.

Daina laid a hand on Caymin's knee. "Our circle feels as if it has broken. We miss you."

"What are you going to do?" Cíana asked.

"I… I do not know." Caymin felt lost. Just as when she'd become angry for the first time, she was unfamiliar with the things she was now feeling. She had no words to explain and didn't know how to resolve the turmoil inside her.

Cíana got to her feet and Daina followed.

"Tonight we celebrate Imbolc," Cíana said. "We hope you'll come and join us. We'll leave you now."

Caymin watched them go, feeling almost worse than before they came. She crawled back down the tunnel. She reached into the bag and handed out nuts and bits of dried meat to the cubs.

Broc came to her. *"What will you do, little one?"*

"I am not sure what to do."

"Enat has been kind to us."

"But she lied to me." Caymin wrapped her cloak around her, fingering the embroidered head of the wolf.

"I do not tell my cubs they may be hunted by two-legs, or die at the teeth of wolves," said Broc. *"They have much to learn and many things to fear. There will be time enough for them to know these hard truths. Perhaps Enat is the same. Perhaps she withheld this knowledge from you because you had much to learn, and she knew there would come a day when it was right to tell you about the ones who attacked your village."*

Caymin looked at her shadow in the darkness of the sett. *"You think I should go back?"*

"I think you should listen to what Enat has to say about why she did not tell you, and then you can make your decision. But think on this – if you do not go back, where will you go and what will you do? Do you know enough yet to leave?"

Caymin reached out to stroke Broc's silky coat. *"You have always been wise."*

"We will go with you if you leave," said Cuán.

"No!" Caymin sat up straight. *"You and Péist are safe here. I cannot put you in danger again."* She took a deep breath. *"I will go back. I will learn what I must to stop Timmin and protect you all."*

CHAPTER 21

The Traitor Revealed

Caymin lay on her bed, ashamed to admit how good it felt to have a soft, warm mat under her. She listened to Enat's breathing nearby and found it comforting.

They had all welcomed her back as they gathered around the fire in the village for Imbolc, but Gai's absence felt like a gaping hole in the celebration, more so than when Méav and Fergus and Ronan left, because they had left when they were supposed to. She had a hollow feeling in her stomach every time she thought of Gai – partly her continued rage at what his father's warriors had done, and partly a feeling of unease over how she had accused him.

She turned on her side and watched the dying flames in the hearth.

"You can't sleep?"

Enat's voice startled her. She sat up as Enat got out of bed and went to the fire.

"Neither can I," said Enat as she added a block of peat and prodded the flames.

Caymin joined her at the hearth.

"I'm glad you came back."

Caymin glanced at her, studying her face, the fine wrinkles visible in the dancing light from the fire. Enat turned and met her gaze. For long heartbeats, they stared into each other's eyes.

"You trusted me," said Enat. "You believed that I would care for you, look out for you, do what was best for you. Like Broc and Cuán did."

Caymin blinked. "Yes."

"And it feels to you as if I betrayed that trust by not telling you the cloak belonged to Gai's clan."

Caymin could no longer meet her eyes. Tears stung her own as she looked again at the fire. "Broc told me there are things cubs do not need to know when they are very young, that there is time later when it is right to tell them those things."

Enat smiled. "I've always respected the wisdom of animals, but I suspect Broc is wiser than most of the two-legs I know."

She heaved a heavy sigh. "I didn't know how to tell you, Caymin. When I saw the cloak, and the symbol on it, I hoped that somehow, it was a mistake, that somehow Gai's clan wasn't involved. But then you went on your spiritwalks, and you saw what happened." She rubbed her brow. "War between clans is a sad truth of our land. If we could unite under one king or queen, if we could accept one another's beliefs... but we're fragmented. We have many kings, and we have many gods and beliefs, and they each think they're the true and right one."

"Like Timmin?"

Enat nodded. "Like Timmin. And like the monks who fear the old ways. Not all are like that, but the ones there are stir up tensions and fuel the wars."

They sat side by side, staring into the flames.

"Did you feel anyone trying to push into your thoughts tonight?"

Caymin shook her head. She bit her lip to keep from blurting out that she didn't expect to with Gai not there.

"How is Péist?"

"He sleeps."

Enat sighed again. "I can't see what, but something else is stirring. I feel it. And I feel that Péist is tied to all that is happening."

Lessons continued for the apprentices under Enat's guidance, while Ivar and Neela left the forest to reap new apprentices.

They worked over their cauldrons. The four girls regularly made their monthly potions, but today all the younger apprentices were learning to mix a potion to ease childbirth.

"I don't want to make this," Diarmit said, wrinkling his nose.

Enat turned to him. "When you have heard a woman scream because she is being ripped in two giving birth to a child who is turned the wrong way, and an entire village is looking to you to ease her pain and save both lives, you will feel differently."

Diarmit's chubby cheeks reddened and he turned back to his potion.

"This potion needs to simmer. Keep stirring these until I return," Enat said, leaving them to work.

"How long will Neela and Ivar be gone?" Caymin asked. She hadn't counted the days she and Enat had traveled, but knew it had been close to a fortnight.

"They may not be back for two or three moons," Daina said. "Depending on how far they have to go."

"Una said she heard them arguing," Cíana said, stirring her potion. "She said it's not unusual for two elders to reap when they feel power stirring, but Ivar insisted they shouldn't both leave now."

Caymin paused, her hand suspended over her cauldron. "It is because of Timmin."

Cíana looked at her sharply as Daina said, "What do you mean?"

Thinking quickly, Caymin said, "I mean, before, two could leave at the same time because Timmin was still here as First Mage if he was needed. What if invaders came again while they were gone? Enat is First Mage now. She is alone."

Daina's eyes got big. "You're right. I hadn't thought of that."

"The invaders won't be back," Diarmit said.

"How can you know that?" Cíana asked. "When the prisoner we had here gets back to his people, what if he remembers and tells them of us? They may come back."

Diarmit scoffed. "What makes you think he got back to his people?"

Daina forgot her cauldron. "What makes you think he didn't?"

Diarmit's eyes darted from her to Cíana to Caymin and back again. He reminded Caymin forcefully of a fox she'd seen once, trapped by a handful of villagers when it was caught stealing chickens.

Enat startled them all by returning. "Let's see how you did." She checked their cauldrons, one by one. "You did well. We'll bottle these and keep them for when they're needed."

Carefully, they spooned their potions into glass bottles and sealed the lids with wax.

"You may have the rest of the day to do as you wish," Enat said as she placed the bottles on a shelf with their stock of other salves and potions.

A soft, misty rain was falling as they left the meetinghouse.

"Where are Una and Niall?" Daina asked.

"They said they were going to go hunting," Cíana said. "What do you want to do?"

Diarmit squinted as he looked up at the flat gray sky. "Sleep."

Cíana shook her head. "You always want to sleep."

He yawned. "I'm always tired."

"Or hungry," said Daina.

Diarmit grinned and shrugged, turning for the boys' cottage.

Caymin pulled her cloak over her head. "Ivar left me some arrows to mend. I am going to work on those."

The three girls walked together toward Enat's cottage.

Daina looked at her. "We have a free day to do what we want and you're going to work?"

"Well, what do you want to do?"

Daina looked around to make sure Enat was not within hearing. "Let's go find Timmin's cottage," she whispered.

"Why?" Cíana asked.

"To look around," Daina said. "Don't you wonder why he really left? Let's go see what's there."

"There is nothing there," Caymin said.

"How do you know?" Cíana demanded.

"I heard Enat tell Neela," Caymin said, lying deliberately for the first time.

Daina was watching her shrewdly. "Then there's no harm in going, is there?"

"Where is Timmin's cottage?" Cíana asked. "I never heard the other elders talk about it."

"I heard Fergus and Ronan talking after they had to go get Timmin. They said it's this way," Daina said, striking out into the forest in the direction Caymin knew would take them to the cottage.

Reluctantly, Caymin followed the others. She hung back, not at all sure they should be doing this. Daina grabbed her arm and dragged her along.

"Are you sure this is the way?" Cíana asked.

"I think so," Daina said, and Caymin knew the trail they were following would take them to their destination.

Caymin limped along with the others as they made their way through the damp forest.

Daina saw it first. She paused, pulling back some low hanging branches as she peered at the cottage. It seemed to Caymin that the moss had grown much more over the stones, as if the forest was swallowing the cottage, taking it back.

They all gasped as they saw Diarmit step out from behind the cottage.

"What's he doing here?" Cíana whispered.

He walked around the cottage, his hands held out before him.

"What are you feeling for?" Daina asked, stepping from the trees.

Diarmit jumped at the sound of her voice, and had his arm drawn back until he saw who it was. "You scared the life out of me." He eyed them. "Same as you. Curious about where Timmin lived."

"I thought you were going to sleep," Daina said.

He shrugged. "Changed my mind."

But Caymin's heart raced. *He knows. He knows there were protective enchantments in place, but he does not know Enat undid a portion of them.* She marched through the opening and straight up to the door. She pushed it open, juddering loudly on rusty hinges. She looked back to see Diarmit standing with his mouth open. The others came in behind her.

"What an awful, cold place to live," Cíana said, her nose wrinkling at the smell of damp and decay within the cottage.

Diarmit went directly to the table where the books and scrolls had lain. He let out an agitated breath as he moved the lamps and shuffled the few remaining scraps of parchment lying there.

"What are you looking for?" Caymin asked innocently.

Diarmit whirled, his eyes wild for a moment. As he met her gaze, understanding dawned on his face and he immediately composed his features.

"Nothing."

Something shifted and the sleepy boy she'd known was gone. In his place was someone who suddenly appeared large and powerful, rather than fat and lumpy. His eyes held hers as her heart pounded in her chest and she couldn't seem to look away. Vaguely, she heard Daina and Cíana talking, saying something about how cold and damp the stone cottage was. Diarmit's face became a mask and he turned from her.

Caymin felt dizzy with the speed of the realizations that raced through her head. But they battled with what she knew of Diarmit – the boy who couldn't work spells, couldn't talk to animals, didn't do anything but eat and sleep.

"I must go," she heard herself say as she backed toward the door.

A loud bang made her jump as the door slammed shut behind her. Another bang and Daina and Cíana crumpled to the floor.

Caymin gasped, looking at their still bodies. "What have you done?"

Diarmit took a step toward her. "Where are they?"

"Who?"

He pointed to the table. "The scrolls and the brooch. Where are they?"

"I do not –"

She stopped abruptly as she felt a push, a familiar intrusion into her thoughts. She still couldn't block her emotions as Enat had tried to teach her. Reflexively, she threw up a protective spell that knocked Diarmit back a couple of steps.

"It cannot be you." She shook her head. "Gai..."

Diarmit laughed. "Yes, he seems much more likely, doesn't he? Arrogant, proud, selfish. Who would suspect me, the boy who can't do anything right when Gai so conveniently made himself so unlikeable? No one looked at me twice."

"But why?"

He smiled and, for the first time, Caymin saw a cruel glint in his eyes. "Timmin and the other elders think things are so simple – the old ways or the new, magic or the Christ. True power lies in knowing both, using both."

"Beanna? I need help. Get Enat!"

Diarmit laughed again. "Calling for help? From the crow?"

Caymin's eyes widened. "You can understand?"

Diarmit stepped sideways and Caymin circled, facing him.

"It's amazing what others say when they think you can't hear or understand," Diarmit said. "And the crow says they'll tell tales of you one day? I'll be the one they speak of someday, in whispers because they fear me."

"But why are you doing this?"

Diarmit tilted his head. "My master recognized the power in me from a young age."

"Your master? Who is your master?"

"A monk who understands how to use power, how to control it and the people under him."

"A monk?"

"He has power of his own, but he was smart enough to see

which way the wind blows. He knew the followers of the Christ were gaining control and the old ways were dying out. He uses both and taught me to do the same. I learned more from him than I have from these buffoons this entire past year. I had seen the white worm. I didn't know what he was at first, and then the invaders came. I remembered the northman's brooch, and when I saw Timmin's interest in the worm, I knew what it meant. If I can harness the power of a dragon, and bring it back to my master, we could be invincible."

Caymin stared at him, not quite believing what she was hearing.

"It was you," she breathed. "You were the one who hurt Péist."

Diarmit's eyes were wild. He picked up a heavy iron poker leaning against the hearth.

"Enough of this. Before Enat comes. Where are the scrolls, where is the brooch and where is the worm?"

"You would hurt me?" Caymin eyed him, placing her hand on the knife at her belt.

"If I have to."

Her fists balled up as he laughed. She drew herself up. "Then you will have to hurt me, for I will tell you nothing."

Diarmit's eyes narrowed. He reached into his tunic and pulled out a small bottle as he stepped nearer to Daina's and Cíana's motionless forms.

"I don't have to hurt you." He knelt next to them. "A few drops of this in their mouths, and they'll sleep until you're an old woman."

He kept an eye on Caymin as he wiggled the stopper loose with his thumb. He bent over Daina.

"NO!"

Caymin threw all of her power at him, slamming him against the stone wall. The bottle shattered as it hit the flagstones. Diarmit slumped to the floor, unconscious. Caymin wrenched the door open and reached for Daina, grabbing her under the arms and dragging her out to safety. Cíana was stirring as Caymin went back inside.

She groaned as she sat up. She saw Diarmit. "What happened?"

"I will tell you later," Caymin said. "We must get you out of here."

Cíana revived a bit in the cool, misty air outside. Together, she and Caymin picked Daina up and dragged her farther into the forest.

"Enat? Beanna? Cuán?"

Caymin called repeatedly. Daina began to come round and sat up, rubbing her head.

All at once, Beanna burst through the trees. She landed on Caymin's shoulder.

"Enat is coming. What is it, little one?"

"It is Diarmit. He has betrayed us."

Enat ran to them, breathless and clutching her side. She quickly took in Daina and Cíana's disheveled appearance. "What happened?"

Caymin pointed. "Diarmit. He is the one. It was never Gai."

Enat stared just for a moment and then sprinted to the cottage. Caymin followed.

"He isn't here," Enat said.

"He must be." Caymin stepped inside to look for herself. "There is no other door and I did not see him leave."

"Remember, I showed you that I could hide myself, make myself appear to be invisible," Enat said. She looked around carefully, listening for a moment before turning back to Caymin. "He's not here. Apparently, he knows a great deal more than we realized."

"I feel as if we're being invaded again," Una said as the remaining five apprentices huddled in the meetinghouse while Enat placed protective enchantments around the village perimeter. Beanna had taken a message to the badgers for Caymin.

"Please ask them to take extra care," she begged. *"I do not want him to use them to get to me."*

She half-listened as, for what felt like the hundredth time, the others went back over the various ways Diarmit had fooled them all.

They had moved beds and clothing to the meetinghouse, stocked up on food, alerted the animals to be on the lookout for the traitor.

"He's clever, though," Enat had reminded the apprentices. "Clever enough to fool us all this time."

Without Ivar and Neela, Caymin knew Enat felt the full responsibility to keep Diarmit from doing any more harm.

"I hope he does come back," Niall growled. "I'd like to teach the weasel a lesson."

"He will not fight you openly," Caymin said. "He was ready to poison Daina and Cíana."

"I don't think he'll chance an open confrontation," Enat said. "Not now that we know what his true motive is. But if you encounter him, don't let him tempt you into using dark magic. Use defensive spells to keep yourself and others safe, and send word to the rest of us as soon as you can. Whatever you do, don't allow him to draw you into the forest alone. Caymin is right, he won't fight you fairly."

Days passed and there was no sign of Diarmit, but another worry nagged at Caymin. She pulled Enat aside.

"I accused Gai of things he did not do. I accused him of being the one to hurt Péist."

"You were angry and hurt over learning that it was his father's warriors who sacked your village," Enat said. "You were looking for other reasons to be angry with him. It was a normal reaction."

"But I was wrong," Caymin fretted.

"Someday you can tell him you were wrong."

Caymin doubted she would ever have that opportunity, but she voiced something else that had been worrying her. "You and the others are in danger while Péist and I are here."

Enat laid a hand on her shoulder. "Listen to what I say, Caymin. We'll help take care of you and Péist. You're safer here than you would be anywhere else. I'll have your word that you won't do anything foolish, like leaving the forest."

Caymin looked up at her.

"Your word," Enat said.

Caymin nodded.

"Come then, let's make some porridge for everyone. Nothing seems as dire with a full belly."

CHAPTER 22

Enemies Everywhere

After a fortnight of being corralled together, the apprentices were snapping at one other.

"I told you to stay off my bedding," said Niall, yanking his blankets and causing Daina to tumble under the table.

"I didn't mean to step on your bloody bedding," scowled Daina. "But there's no room to turn around in here."

"Enough, all of you," said Enat, her own temper growing short. "I need to check the forest protections. I'll be gone the entire day. I'll raise the enchantments around the village, and you may all go where you wish, but you must go with at least one other person. And I want you to have weapons with you at all times."

"Weapons?" Caymin asked. "You would have us use weapons on Diarmit?"

Enat did not look at her as she replied, "I would have you do what you must to protect yourselves and the forest."

The apprentices went together to gather weapons from the storehouse. Caymin chose her favored bow, while Una and Niall chose staffs and Cíana and Daina chose spears.

"I wish to visit the badgers," Caymin said. "Will one of you go with me?"

"I'll go," said Niall. "I fancy some fresh air and a long walk."

Caymin had to jog to keep up with him. Spring sunshine showered them with golden light. They kept a sharp ear for any unusual sounds as they moved through the forest, which was full of sound as new life burst forth all about them. Trees flowered and budded, and birds flew frantically, searching for materials for their nests. Caymin heard the whispers of new cubs lying in dens and burrows – foxes and voles and stoats – while squirrels chattered overhead in the trees.

"Enat is worried," Niall said as they walked.

"She is." Caymin wondered how much the others had seen. "This is a bad time for Neela and Ivar to be gone."

"And Diarmit knows it," Niall said darkly. "To think I shared a cottage with him for over a year."

That was what troubled Caymin as well. Diarmit knew them – their routines, their strengths and weaknesses. He could use that when and if he chose to attack again.

Niall glanced down at her. "I feel bad that we accused Gai when Fergus was attacked."

"I accused him of far worse than you," Caymin said.

He dropped a hand onto her shoulder. "Don't let it trouble you, little badger. I –"

But whatever he had been about to say went unsaid as Timmin stepped out from behind a tree, his staff leveled. Without a word, he blasted Niall off his feet, sending him crashing against a tree where he fell motionless to the ground.

"Don't," Timmin said to Caymin, turning his staff on her as she unslung her bow from her shoulder. "Drop it."

She let the bow fall to her feet. They stood looking at each other. Timmin was nearly unrecognizable; his hair was long and tangled, his clothing stained and torn. His face was thinner than Caymin remembered, but his eyes burned like coals, sunken in their sockets.

He approached her warily, keeping his staff aimed at her.

"Where is he?"

"Where is –"

"Don't toy with me!" Timmin looked quite mad, his eyes ringed with white and spittle flying from his mouth. "I must have the dragon!"

His eyes narrowed and his voice became dangerously quiet. "I will have him."

Caymin stood still, though her heart was pounding in her chest. She flinched as Timmin raised his staff and drew a circle in the air. He rested his staff on the ground.

"Where is he?"

Caymin felt his push into her mind. Closing her eyes, she pushed back with a protective shield.

"You think to stop me? I, who have worked magic you can't even dream of?" Timmin laughed, a crazed laugh that raised goosebumps on Caymin's arms as she listened.

"I will hurt you if I must," he said.

"Enat! Beanna!"

Timmin shook his head. "You'll not call for help this time."

Caymin felt her words echo back at her from the barrier Timmin had cast. Again, he aimed his staff at her chest.

"I'll only ask one more time."

Caymin pressed her lips together as she braced herself. She saw Timmin's mouth move, but heard nothing beyond her own screams as unbearable pain tore through her. He stopped only when she fell to her knees.

"Call him to you, or tell me where he is."

Caymin peered at him through watery eyes as she gasped for breath. "He will not bond with you."

Timmin pointed his staff at her again, and again, Caymin felt as if she were being torn apart, the pain was so intense. She tried not to scream, but the cries were ripped from her throat as she writhed on the ground.

She lay face down, sobbing as the pain continued to throb. Even the distant memory of the agony of her burns seemed mild compared to this.

She panted against the earth, her body trembling as she tried to brace herself for his next assault, when she heard a horrible snarl rip through the forest. She blinked away her tears to see a whirlwind of fur and teeth. It took her a moment to realize that badgers were attacking Timmin from all sides. It seemed the entire clan was snapping and biting at him. He spun, aiming spells at them, trying to fend them off, but they kept attacking from every side.

The air rang with a bugling cry, and an enormous shadow flew over Caymin as she lay there. The ground shook as huge hooves landed between her and Timmin. The great antlers slashed as Ríordán charged, stomping and kicking, while the badgers savaged Timmin from below.

More shadows passed overhead, and a flock of birds – crows, hawks, owls, thrushes – led by Beanna, struck from the air.

With loud curses, Timmin turned and ran with his arms covering his head, leaving a trail of blood littering the ground. Caymin tried frantically to focus, tried to call out, but all went black.

Enat walked as silently as possible as she made her rounds of the forest. It was too vast to check the entire boundary, but she'd felt a breach, two nights before. Since then, she'd listened – as best she could through the squabbling of the apprentices as they stayed cooped up together. There had been nothing more, but she knew better than to ignore what she'd felt. Someone was here, and she was fairly certain it was Timmin.

He knew what this time of year meant. Ivar and Neela had already put their departure off nearly a full moon after the rift between Caymin and Gai. They had discussed not reaping at all this year, but with the three eldest gone, and Niall and Una due to take their trials this coming Samhain, they needed new apprentices.

They were still out there, young ones with power, but it wasn't like the old days, when the air almost buzzed with it. Enat remembered when mothers and fathers had welcomed the news that one of their young was blessed with magic. Oftentimes, they had seen glimpses of it, and they were eager to have a mage in the family, one who would come back to their village or clan and do them honor.

These days, the reaping had to be approached much more cautiously. All of the elders had experienced the result of the fear the monks had spread, and all had, at one time or another, barely escaped with their lives. Forgotten in those villages were the gods and goddesses, the old festivals and their seasons. Oh, there were remnants, and Enat could see that there always would be – May Day dances, harvest festivals.

What they couldn't entirely stamp out by fear mongering, the monks had turned into something Christian, like their recent claims that the Christ had been born in the winter, so the people could have a Christian reason for their continued celebration of the Yule.

She'd even seen statues to the mother of the Christ. Those monks were canny, giving the people a woman to take the place of the goddess, though they'd had to make her a virgin to do it.

She snorted and shook her head as she walked. She'd considered trying to send messages to Ivar and Neela, calling them back after Diarmit revealed his true intentions, but it was impossible to know where they were now.

She walked along, so intent in her thoughts as she checked the magical protections of the forest, that when she heard the sound of a twig snapping behind her, she knew it was too late.

"Drop the staff on the ground and step away from it."

She let the staff fall and stepped aside. "Diarmit." She turned around to see him holding a sword with both hands. "You don't want to do this."

He leaned forward and grabbed the staff, breathing hard at his own daring as he let the sword fall and pointed the staff at her. "You don't know what I want."

She tilted her head and smiled. "You look hungry. Come back with me and –"

"Don't talk to me as if I'm an imbecile!" He poked himself in the chest with his thumb. "I was smart enough to fool all of you.

You thought I was slow, but I know more than the others put together. I know things they'll never know."

"Like how to torture harmless creatures?"

Diarmit flushed.

Enat clasped her hands and faced him. "I know you didn't learn those things from us. Who taught you?"

"His name is Angus. He's the priest in our village."

"A priest?" Enat's eyes widened but then she smiled. "Ah, he has power himself."

Diarmit stood a little taller. "He does and he recognized the power in me. He taught me himself. Showed me how we can use both."

Enat took a step closer. "But to what end, Diarmit? To control people? To hurt them? Is that really how you want to use your power? You obviously have a great deal of natural ability. Let us teach you how to use it for good."

"For good?" Diarmit sneered. "Power doesn't know good or evil. It just is. And the one who has it, controls others."

"Is that what Angus told you?" She shook her head. "He's wrong. When you use force - magical or otherwise - to dominate others, it ends up controlling you."

He laughed. "How can it control you?"

"Because you live in constant fear of losing it."

He jabbed the staff in her direction. "Stay back. Stay back or I'll use this."

The tip of the staff sparked.

"You don't want to be doing that."

"Why?" Diarmit twirled the staff once and aimed it at Enat again. "I could've earned one of these without even trying."

Enat smiled. "You think you earn a staff simply by being able to use magic?" She shook her head. "No, 'tis much more than that. And that's what you'll never learn from Angus. Come back to us, Diarmit."

She took another step toward him when there was a sudden flutter of wings overhead. It seemed birds burst into flight from nearly every tree and Enat felt the forest floor shudder so powerfully that it knocked her off balance. She fell to one knee.

"No," she whispered. She stood. "Give me my staff."

Diarmit also looked around for the cause of the disturbance. "No! Stay back or I'll use this."

"Enough. I've no time for this." She raised one hand and the staff in Diarmit's grasp glowed white-hot.

He dropped it with a yelp of pain, and with one more gesture, she knocked him to the ground, immobile. She conjured ropes out of thin air and tied him tightly, adding another layer of magical power to bind him in place.

"I'm sorry to do this, but I can't have you interfering again."

She grabbed her staff and ran as fast as she could toward the village.

Enat was out of breath, clutching a stitch in her side by the time she arrived to the strangest sight she had ever seen.

Ríordán was walking slowly with Niall cradled, unconscious, across his great antlers while his mate, Osán, walked behind with Caymin draped over her broad back. The entire clan of badgers accompanied the elk, spread out, their heads up, sniffing the air as they kept guard. Beanna and a large flock of birds circled overhead. Enat heard them talking to one another as they kept watch. The other apprentices stood dumbfounded at the procession.

"*What happened?*" Enat asked.

"*Timmin,*" Beanna said as she landed on Enat's shoulder. "*He attacked Caymin and other two-leg.*"

Ríordán lowered his head so that Una, Cíana and Daina could pull Niall off the antlers and lay him on the ground. Una placed an ear over his chest.

"He's alive."

Enat went to Osán and reached up, lowering Caymin also to the ground where she cradled her head in her lap. Blood ran from Caymin's nose and ears.

Broc approached. "*Little one?*" She nuzzled Caymin's cheek until her eyes fluttered open.

"Stay still a moment," Enat said when Caymin tried to sit up.

"*Timmin?*"

"*He ran,*" said Beanna.

"*He is a coward,*" Cuán said with a growl. "*He attacked the two-leg cubs without warning, and then fled when we came to their defense.*"

Enat looked around, her brow furrowed. "*He is not gone. What did he do to you?*"

"*He still wants Péist. He...*" She shuddered with the memory. "*He used a spell to cause pain.*"

Broc placed a paw on Caymin's leg. "*The egg is waking.*"

"*What?*" Caymin sat up, swaying as she wiped the blood from her nose with her hand.

"*What egg?*" Beanna asked.

"*Péist,*" said Caymin.

"*When we heard your screams, it began to shake.*"

Caymin turned to Enat. "*I must go to him.*"

"*Give me a moment.*"

Enat went to Niall, placing her hand over his chest and murmuring words. She instructed Daina to retrieve one of the potions stored in the meetinghouse.

"Give him four drops only. No more. I'll return as quickly as I can."

She went to Ríordán and Osán. "*Will you stay to keep watch until I return?*"

"*We will.*"

She picked up her staff, and she and Beanna accompanied Caymin and the badgers to the sett. As they approached, Caymin stopped, rocked by the strength of the images and sensations she was receiving from Péist. She glanced up at Enat.

"*He is waking.*"

As soon as they entered the tunnel, they could see the illumination, rays of light emanating from the chamber where Péist had managed to dislodge his *khrusallis* from where it was buried. Wobbling within its crater of earth, the egg glowed and pulsed. Slight cracks had appeared in the shell with shafts of blinding light beaming from them.

"*The worm is in there?*" Beanna asked as she hopped around it.

Caymin tried to pick it up. "*I cannot lift it.*" She looked at Enat in bewilderment. "*It is the same size. How is it so much heavier?*"

Enat also tried lifting it and could not. "*I don't know.*"

Beanna strutted closer and peered into one of the cracks. "*I do not think you want him to hatch in here.*"

Caymin quickly rolled the egg back up the tunnel, aided by the badgers as they pushed with their paws. Outside, they all gathered round the egg, keeping watch for any sign of Timmin.

Caymin turned to Enat. "*We cannot stay here. You know it as well as I. We bring danger to all the forest while Péist is here. Timmin will not stop, and Diarmit knows too much.*"

"*Diarmit is not a threat at the moment, as he's lying where I left him, tied up,*" Enat said.

She held up her hands to stave off any further questions. "*You're right. I'm not worried about us, but you and Péist will be targets as long as he's this vulnerable. I hate to see you go, but I'm afraid you must.*"

Caymin looked down at the egg, still rocking where it lay, and too heavy to carry. "*But how? And how long will this take?*"

Enat shook her head. "*To my knowledge, no one alive has ever seen the birth of a dragon. I've no idea how long this can take or what will happen once he's out of there.*"

She thought for a moment.

"*We're going to need help.*"

She cast a spell to help make the egg light enough for her to carry, and the motley group made its way back to the village, the badgers circling them as their guard.

When they arrived, the giant elk were lying there placidly, while the apprentices waited in agitation.

Niall was sitting up, holding his head, but the girls were pacing.

"What is it?" Una asked when she saw the glowing orb in Enat's arms.

"I'll tell you all more later, but for now, we need your help."

Enat groaned a little as she set the egg down. She turned to the apprentices. "Cíana and Daina, can you gather a large bag of food, enough for a full moon cycle? Una and Niall, I need for you to gather a large quiver of arrows if you would."

"I can do that myself," Niall said.

"No!" Enat took a breath. "I don't want any of you going anywhere alone just now."

They left to do as she asked, and she went to the elk. *"May we ask a great boon of you? Caymin and Péist need safe passage from the forest. His egg is very heavy now, too heavy for us to carry, but I believe you can."*

Osán inclined her head. *"We will help."*

Broc whickered, and Caymin dropped to her knees. *"Where will you go, little one?"*

"I do not know," Caymin said, her voice cracking as she buried her face in Broc's fur. *"I just got you back, and now I must leave you again. But you are not safe while Péist and I are here."*

Caymin sat on the ground with the badgers gathered close, nuzzling her. In a short while, the others were all back – Niall and Una with a quiver bristling full of arrows, Daina and Cíana with a soft woven bag stuffed with food.

"Thank you," Caymin said, standing to accept the things they brought.

Suddenly, the full realization that she was leaving the forest forever came over her and her eyes pricked with tears.

"We'll see you again," Cíana said, enfolding her in a hug. "I know it."

Caymin didn't see how that could happen, but didn't trust her voice. She simply nodded. Daina hugged her also.

She climbed up onto Ríordán's back, and Una and Niall together wrapped Péist's egg in a cloth and hoisted it onto his back in front of Caymin. The giant elk got to his feet. Osán stood beside him.

"I can't leave the others," said Enat. "But I'll walk a way with you." She turned to the others. "Stay vigilant. Timmin is here and may return."

As the two elk led the way out of the village, she said, "*I wish to stop by our cottage first.*"

There, she disappeared inside, returning a moment later with Caymin's old cloak and a bundle wrapped in a cloth.

They walked through the forest, Caymin having to bend almost flat against Ríordán's back occasionally as he walked under low hanging branches that caught on his antlers and snapped back at her. The badgers accompanied them, and Beanna perched on Osán's back.

They climbed the hill to the standing stones.

"*This is as far as I can go with Timmin still here,*" Enat said. She handed the cloak and the bundle to Caymin, saying, "*I've been saving this, but I think you should have it now.*"

Caymin unwrapped the cloth to reveal Enat's bow, polished and carved with runes and spirals. "*I cannot accept this. It is yours.*"

"*I want you to have it.*"

"*It is so beautiful.*"

"*One thing more.*" Enat pressed something into Caymin's hand.

Caymin stared at the dragon brooch Timmin had taken from the northman.

"*I cannot think of anyone more worthy to wear this than a dragonmage,*" Enat said.

Tears spilled from Caymin's eyes as she looked down at Enat. "*I cannot find words enough to thank you for all you have done for me.*" She looked at the badgers gathered around, staring up at her. "*Take care of one another. I will return if I can.*"

She could see nothing as Ríordán ambled down the far side of the hill, taking care to place his hooves so as not to jar Caymin and Péist. Tears fell freely down her cheeks and she did not try to stop them. She only pressed her old cloak to her face to stifle her sobs.

"*Do not cry, little one,*" said Beanna, flitting over to sit on her shoulder.

"*I will miss all of you so much,*" Caymin said.

"*You will not miss me. I am going with you.*"

Caymin raised her tear-stained face. "*You are?*"

"*You need someone to look after you and the worm.*"

CHAPTER 23

Nowhere to Hide

The western sky was streaked with reds and purples, and still the elk walked on. Caymin looked around in a daze.

"*Where are we going?*"

Osán glanced back at her. "*Enat asked us to take you toward the setting sun. She said you would be closest to the endless water there.*"

Caymin pressed her hands to the wrapped egg cradled between her legs on Ríordán's broad back. It was growing warmer. "*Why would we need to be near the endless water?*"

"*I do not know.*"

Beanna sat nestled securely on Osán's back. "*She must know something we do not.*"

Caymin's stomach growled, but she did not wish to eat while the elk plodded on without stopping to graze.

Ríordán must have heard. "*You should eat, little one. You do not know what you will face when we leave the protections of the forest.*"

Caymin reached around to the bag of food, and pulled out some bread and cheese. She offered some to Beanna, and ate as darkness fell completely. Behind them a sliver of a moon rode high enough to be seen through the trees.

She tried to remain vigilant. Enat said she had taken care of Diarmit, but he had escaped before and Timmin was still a threat. If he knew they were on the move, he might be desperate enough to attack again.

Despite the danger, the rhythmic sway of Ríordán's walk lulled her to sleep. She did not know how much time had passed when her head snapped up.

"*Rest while you can,*" said Beanna. "*We will wake you if we sense danger.*"

Caymin shifted Péist's heavy *khrusallis* to relieve the pressure on Ríordán's back. It felt even warmer. She peeled back the cloth covering it and was blinded by the radiant beams of light that shot out of it. She flung the cloth back over the egg, but it was a long time before her eyes adjusted to the darkness again.

The sliver of moon had shifted so that it was ahead of them, and the stars had wheeled through the sky, and still they walked.

Dawn began to break through the clouds behind them.

"*We must stop,*" Caymin said. "*You need to rest and eat.*"

The elk didn't argue. Ríordán knelt so that Caymin could slide off his back and lower the egg to the ground. She placed her hands on his back, rubbing and kneading the muscles. She whispered a spell of healing to ease the soreness from the burden he'd carried. He groaned in delight, his eyes closed.

She sat with Beanna while Ríordán and Osán grazed hungrily.

"*How goes it with the egg?*" Beanna asked, hopping up onto the wrapped bundle and settling on it as if she were roosting.

"*He continues to be agitated, restless,*" said Caymin. "*I wish someone knew to tell us what to expect.*"

"*I would guess that any who have witnessed what is coming are long dead.*"

"*Do you think he is dangerous?*"

Beanna tapped the egg with her beak. "*I think he is a dragon.*"

A cold rain had begun to fall as Caymin grunted to hoist the egg. Even using magic to lighten it, it was almost heavier than she could lift. She straddled Ríordán's back with the egg clamped securely between her legs and grabbed a handful of hair to steady herself as he got to his feet. She pulled her cloak over her head. It didn't keep her dry but, combined with the warmth from Péist and Ríordán, at least she wasn't shivering with cold.

They trudged through a gray, lightless world as the rain fell more heavily. Beanna hunched down into a ball of tight, black feathers on Osán's back, letting the rain run off her in rivulets.

Caymin sat engrossed in her own thoughts as the day passed with no letup in the rain and no change in the flat, dull light. She ate from her bag of food, offering bits to Beanna, and encouraged the elk to graze as they walked. They stripped leaves off trees and reached for mouthfuls of leafy branches from bushes they passed, but they kept moving through the steady downpour.

Caymin was just starting to wonder whether she might dare to start a fire for the night when she was startled by a sudden crack. The sound reverberated sharply through the forest. Ríordán and Osán stopped abruptly, their great heads high in the air as they sniffed for danger. Caymin looked around wildly for the source, her bow at the ready with an arrow nocked and half-drawn. Beanna flapped into the air, circling.

"*What was it? Can you see anything?*" Caymin asked her.

"*No.*"

Another resounding crack broke through the thrum of the rainfall, and Caymin realized what it was.

"*It is Péist.*"

Ríordán knelt and Caymin rolled the egg to the ground. She pulled back the cloth and had to shield her eyes with one hand. The light coming from within the egg was blinding in its brilliance.

"*It is opening.*"

The gaps in the shell had widened, and Caymin saw Péist writhing inside the *khrusallis.* The shell cracked again and the gap widened. They all stared transfixed as the pieces of the shell slowly, excruciatingly opened.

Caymin kept her bow in one hand. They could go nowhere now. If Timmin chose this moment to attack, there would be no escape. She scanned the woods around them and asked Beanna to fly circles overhead.

"*Nothing,*" said the crow, flapping back down to where pieces of the shell lay on the ground. "*It is taking him forever. My fledglings hatched in half this time.*"

As if spurred by her comment, a taloned foot emerged, stretching. They moved back as more of Péist came out of the shell.

"*How is this possible?*" asked Osán. "*The egg was not that big.*"

Caymin wondered the same thing as more and more dragon kept unfolding from the confines of the *khrusallis.* One tightly furled wing expanded, a length of tail, a haunch, all covered in white scales so iridescent, they caused the raindrops to light up in rainbow colors as they fell.

At last, an enormous body, larger even than the giant elk, lay on the wet ground as Péist clawed at the remains of the egg. A long neck rose sinuously and, with a vicious shake of his head, the last remnants of the shell flew off. Péist raised his head to the sky and took his first breath of air as a dragon. He stood on legs too wobbly to hold him, his head and neck weaving as he tried to keep his balance. He snorted, blowing his nostrils clear, and sparks flew.

Caymin stood suddenly and turned to the elk. "*You must go!*"

"*What is wrong?*"

"*His hunger. I can feel it. It is bottomless now, and he will hunt soon. You must leave. I cannot have him harm you, but I will not be able to stop him.*"

She placed her hands on their shoulders as they hesitated. "*Go, Osán. Take word back to Enat of what has happened. Tell her we will send word when we can. Please, Ríordán. You must leave us.*"

He nuzzled her, his great antlers making a temporary shelter from the rain. "*Take care, little one. You and Beanna. You are certain he will not harm you?*"

"I am certain. We are safe, but you are not."

The elk retreated into the forest, looking back reluctantly as Péist stretched out both wings and roared to the sky.

Caymin and Beanna sat side by side, listening to the crashes coming from the forest. For two days, they had waited while Péist hunted, clumsily launching himself after deer, foxes, even voles. With the ruckus he made, the game had fled, leading him farther and farther from Caymin as he hunted.

"I do not understand how he is catching anything with all the noise he is making," Beanna said, perched on Caymin's knee as they sat beside a fire.

Caymin would have agreed, but she had seen his head dart upward through the trees so fast that he had snagged a hawk in midflight. His strength and hunger were prodigious, even if he was completely lacking in grace.

At first, she had followed him, her bow nocked and ready, afraid Timmin would make an appearance, drawn by the commotion. But Péist was so ravenous and moved so quickly, that she soon realized Timmin was likely to be eaten if he did show himself. She figured Timmin was wise enough to have figured this out, based on the dragon lore she and Enat had found in his cottage. If he was near, he was biding his time, as even Caymin could not penetrate the all-encompassing hunger that drove Péist now.

Sometime in the night, a sudden silence woke Caymin from an uneasy sleep. Beanna, too, had her head up, listening to the quiet.

The circle of light cast by their fire seemed pitifully small as they tried to pierce the darkness around them. A light seemed to be moving through the forest, and Caymin gasped as Péist appeared. He still glowed white in the night, but he seemed even larger than he had when he tumbled out of his egg. A few feathers stuck to the scales of his face, and his talons were stained with blood.

Uncertain as to whether his terrible hunger had been sated, Caymin tucked Beanna under her arm as Péist approached. He crouched near her and reached his snout out to sniff her, his warm breath puffing on her face.

Caymin laid a tentative hand on his jaw. "*Have you eaten enough?*"

She was startled when he replied, "*For now.*" He had never used words before.

"*I will need to eat again soon, but we must travel.*" He lifted his head, looking to the west. "*That way.*"

"*Why? What lies in that direction?*"

He snorted and sparks flew into the sky. "*I do not know, but we must go there.*"

Beanna wriggled loose from Caymin's protective grasp. "*And how are we supposed to travel with a great white worm without all the two-legs seeing us?*"

He looked down at her, and tilted his massive head to fix one green eye on her, its vertical pupil contracting. Almost more quickly than Caymin's eye could follow, he snapped his great jaws, missing Beanna by a hair's breadth.

With a squawk, she flapped and fell onto her back.

Péist opened his jaws in unmistakable laughter. "*I am a worm no longer and you would not even be a mouthful.*"

With as much dignity as she could muster, Beanna ruffled her feathers to settle them back in place and eyed him balefully. "*You will always be a white worm to me.*"

They traveled for three more days. Occasionally, Péist stretched his wings, flapping them, testing them as they walked. When they reached the forest boundary, Caymin hesitated.

"*If I cross this threshold, I will not be permitted to re-enter.*"

Péist thrust his long, white neck skyward. "*We must go on.*"

And so, they walked through the magical barrier protecting the forest. Just as when she had entered, they passed through a mist until they emerged on the other side. She tried to retrace her steps, but the mist led her directly back to where Péist and Beanna waited for her.

Beanna flapped to her shoulder. "*Do not worry, little one. When it is time, I can fly back to Enat.*"

Caymin sighed and turned to the west. They traveled now by night. Beanna flew ahead as Caymin and Péist walked, and then she circled back to tell them which route would take them past the fewest villages. Caymin had tried various spells to dull Péist's luminous glow, but none worked. He had rolled in the soft mud of a stream, but nothing clung to his scales. They shed the mud as easily as Beanna's feathers shed water. Caymin could shed neither without using energy to cast a spell, so she traveled wet and dirty, wishing for a bath and a warm, dry bed to sleep in. Péist provided as best he could.

By day, they sheltered in remote places where he offered protection from the rain as Caymin slept. He did not need to sleep – "*I slept long enough in my egg,*" he said – but instead fell into a waking trance. Caymin could sense his mind and his feelings during those times, but it was as if from a distance.

A few times they had to stop while Péist hunted again. Caymin asked him not to snatch livestock.

"*They are easy prey,*" Péist grumbled.

"*But the villagers depend on them,*" Caymin argued.

"*Are you a dragon or a worm?*" taunted Beanna. "*Go hunt.*"

He was learning to be stealthier, and could now catch prey without waking the entire forest. His appetite was appeased with less food than when he had first hatched, and usually a half-night's hunt could sate him enough that they could journey on.

Péist's great bulk proved to be a problem in some places where the trees grew tightly. He solved that problem by simply pushing through them.

"*Must you make so much noise?*" Beanna asked. "*The two-legs will hear us.*"

Caymin glanced back at the trees, lying broken and split like twigs. She shrugged. "*The villagers will make up some story about a magical creature.*"

Péist sniffed. "*And they would be right.*"

They walked on, a new moon providing welcome darkness, but

Péist's silvery form glowed all the brighter for the dark night. Here, outside the magical protections of the forest, Caymin felt more exposed. Timmin was still a danger, but she knew any people they encountered would prove to be more dangerous still.

Two nights later, a crescent moon was just beginning to show herself when they heard men's voices.

Beanna flew to a high tree branch. *"Two-legs. They are coming your way."*

"Over here. I saw a light."

Caymin saw the flicker of torches approaching through the trees.

"I don't like this. What if it's the woodfolk?"

The progress of the torches paused.

"You think it's woodfolk?"

"Don't be daft. There's no such thing. Whatever's out there is flesh and blood."

"There! I see something glowing in the forest. Are you sure it isn't faeries?"

"Stay silent," Caymin said. She raised her hands and conjured a concealing spell. She had practiced this only on small objects, and had never made them completely disappear. She could hear the men's voices coming nearer. She concentrated, drew the power, tried again to conjure the spell, but Péist's head and tail shone like the drawings of sea serpents in Ivar's scrolls.

"There," one of the men said. "I told you I saw something."

Suddenly, she felt energy draining from her like water pouring from a pitcher. The spell, incomplete and unable to hide Péist completely, was drawing every bit of energy she had. Her knees buckled and her eyes rolled back in her head. Péist shifted to touch his foot to her leg and she felt his energy combining with hers. With the surge in power, she completely shielded the dragon and herself. She cast another spell to confound the men, sending them in another direction. Beanna flitted from tree to tree, following them to make sure they wandered away from the dragon and girl.

Caymin and Péist sat hunched, scarcely daring to breathe, until the men's voices and footfalls faded into the night. With a gasp, she ended the spell.

"Do not do that again," Péist said as Caymin slumped against him.

For long heartbeats, Caymin did not answer. *"I am sorry. That was foolish. I did not think about what that spell would cost me."*

"And it nearly cost you everything."

Beanna flew back to them. *"Follow me."*

Caymin got shakily to her feet and they resumed their journey.

"What would we have done if they had found us?" she asked.

"I could have eaten them," Péist offered.

Caymin gave him a look. *"No villagers. No villagers' livestock. We would be hunted for certain."*

"The sooner we arrive at our destination, the better," Beanna said. *"Do you know yet where we are bound?"*

Péist snorted sparks as he walked, his tail leaving an undulating track in his wake. *"I will know when we arrive."*

CHAPTER 24

Over the Endless Water

Their journey took them over a fortnight, traveling by cover of night, with several narrow escapes from villagers drawn by the curious glow in the dark. Each time, Caymin combined her power with Péist's to conjure a spell of concealment.

"*This is dangerous,*" Caymin said. "*We may not always be able to hide from them.*"

"*We are getting closer,*" Péist said. "*Soon.*"

Caymin heard the water before she saw it. There were no trees to provide cover as they approached the edge of a cliff. Caymin gaped at the sight below her, waves crashing on rocks below, the stars and moonlight rippling over the constantly moving water stretching into the darkness.

"*The birds told us of this when I lived with the badgers, and I saw it on Ivar's maps, but never could I have imagined so much water. It is truly endless.*"

"*This is where we must go,*" Péist said, stretching his neck out as he sniffed the breeze blowing in from the sea.

"There is nowhere to go," said Beanna. *"Unless you hunt prey from the water as some birds do."*

But Péist's eyes were fixed on the horizon. *"We must go."* He turned to Caymin. *"Climb on."*

"What?" Caymin stared up at him.

"Climb on my back. There." He twisted his sinuous neck around to indicate a space at his withers where there was a gap in the spikes transitioning from his neck to his back.

When Caymin hesitated, his pupils suddenly contracted to mere slits. He picked her up by the neck of her tunic as Broc picked up her newborn cubs and swung her over his back, dropping her into position.

Before she could protest, he stretched his wings. The air rising off the water filled the leathery white expanses and, without warning, he launched himself off the cliff.

Caymin's yell was whipped from her mouth by the wind as they plummeted toward the water. With one great whoosh, Péist beat his wings and they rose into the air. He flapped several times to gain altitude, and then suddenly found an air current he could ride. Behind them, Beanna flew madly to catch up. Caymin snatched her out of the air as Péist gave another downward thrust of his wings, accelerating over the water. His wings dipped and twitched, feeling and catching the currents as if he'd been doing this for ages.

"He'll leave you behind," Caymin said to the crow, who nestled in her lap.

Beanna looked down at the water flashing by far below them. *"So the worm knows how to fly."*

Caymin's eyes watered as they streaked through the air. She looked back and already the land behind them was sinking into distant shadows.

"Where are we going?" she asked, but Péist only shook his head and flew on.

They flew through what remained of the night. The sun rose behind them, throwing their shadow down onto the water. Beanna stayed tucked against Caymin's body as she held tight to the spike in front of her, occasionally shifting as Péist flapped his wings to lift and find another air current. No land was to be seen in any direction, but still Péist flew, away from the rising sun, toward a destination known to him alone.

On and on they flew as the sun arced over them, settling toward the far horizon ahead. Péist began to tire. Caymin felt his fatigue and laid her hands on either side of his neck, giving him some of her power and strength. He glanced back once in gratitude. Beanna stayed tucked against Caymin, her head pulled in between her wings as she hunched against the cold wind.

They were all hungry, but Caymin didn't dare twist around to try and pull food from the basket slung over her shoulders. She wondered how much longer Péist could fly without eating.

Just before the sun began to sink below the endless expanse of ocean in the distance, the flat line of the horizon was broken by a jagged mass. Caymin, weary and droopy-eyed, sat up, alert. She felt Péist's heart quicken at the sight and knew that this was their destination.

As they approached, a craggy peak rose out of the water, its sheer face home to a few birds clinging to the rock. As they drew near, Péist flapped to gain altitude, and when they rose higher than the peak, Caymin saw that what had looked like the point of a needle from the distance was actually a very large plateau with scattered scrub trees. Péist spread his wings wide and landed with a jolt. Beanna immediately fluttered to the ground, flapping her own wings as she shook her head.

"I never want to do that again. Crows are not made for flying over the endless water."

"You did not fly. I did," Péist said.

Caymin looked around. *"What is this place?"*

"The home of my kind," said Péist. He turned to look at her. *"You have food?"*

She unslung her bow and the woven basket from her shoulders. *"Yes,"* she said, reaching in to pull out the last of the bread and cheese.

"I will hunt for all of us." With a great thrust of his wings, he leapt into the air and disappeared over the edge of the precipice on the side opposite from which they had approached.

Caymin and Beanna hurried over to see him soaring over a large expanse of forested land. In the light from the moon that had risen in the east, she could see that it was a steep drop from their cliff-top site down to the flatter land below. Péist hovered for a moment, and then dove through the dark canopy of the trees, disappearing from view.

The trees up here, exposed to the wind and weather, were twisted and gnarled, their roots dug tenaciously into the thin soil. Caymin gathered deadwood from the ground under them and lit a fire. The wind blew steady and cold up this high, and she was already chilled from their flight over the water. Beanna huddled next to her as they both ate.

When Péist returned, he brought with him a haunch from a deer. Caymin gave thanks to the spirit of the deer, and used her knife to carve chunks of meat off, offering some to Beanna and skewering others on a stick to put them over the fire. She watched Beanna a little enviously as the crow tore at the pieces of meat, gobbling them down while she waited impatiently for her own meat to cook sufficiently to be able to eat it. As soon as it was half-done, she plucked the chunks of venison off the skewer and ate.

At last, with her belly full and her body partially warmed by the fire, Caymin sat back against Péist's side.

"What now?"

"I am not sure. We wait."

"Wait for what?"

"If I knew that, we would not have to wait."

Caymin gave him an elbow in the ribs and heard a deep rumble as he laughed.

The night wind howled and whistled around the edge of Péist's wing as it sheltered Caymin and Beanna. They lay together against his body for warmth, Beanna tucked against Caymin under her cloak.

Caymin's restless sleep was disrupted sometime in the middle of the night by a vibration coming from Péist. She felt it against her back.

"Péist?"

He did not respond.

She threw off her cloak and crawled out from under his wing. His head was stretched to the sky, his eyes closed as he hummed.

"What is he doing?" Beanna asked, hopping along beside Caymin.

"I do not know." She stepped around to look up at him and called to him again. The humming continued, but he did not open his eyes or answer.

Caymin shivered in the damp wind blowing off the sea as she stood looking up at him. Tears pricked her eyes. She was alone in the middle of the endless water with a dragon and a crow, cut off from all she knew, everyone she loved. At this moment, she almost wished Péist had bonded with Diarmit or Timmin.

As soon as she thought it, she regretted it. None of this was his fault.

With a sigh, she turned to Beanna. *"We may as well stay warm."*

They crawled back under his wing.

The sun when it rose shone through the filmy skin of the dragon wing. Caymin squinted as she opened her eyes, enjoying the increased warmth. Behind her, Péist still hummed. She got up and stirred the coals of the fire into life. She and Beanna ate more of the venison from the night before.

"What do we do now?" Beanna asked, waddling around Péist and looking up at him.

"As he said, we wait."

"Must we wait here?"

Caymin considered. *"I do not see why. We can explore while we wait."*

Beanna immediately took off, flying off the edge of the precipice while Caymin slung her bow and a water skin over her shoulder and wandered the perimeter of the clifftop. The seaward side made her dizzy as the rock plunged many times Péist's length into the crashing waves below. The other sides gave her a view out over the forested land below, stretching farther than her eye could see. As she crept along the edge, looking down, she found a worn trail, barely visible against the side of the cliff. She picked her way gingerly down the trail, climbing over piles of fallen rock and jumping gaps in the narrow path. It wound its way down from their landing place to the forest below. Caymin entered the shadows of the forest and listened.

It was ancient, older even than the forest they had left. It was a place of massive power, buried deep in the earth like the roots of the trees. She stepped to an old tree and placed her hands on it, listening. She asked permission to be there.

The tree registered mild curiosity at her presence. Caymin got vague images of people in the long-ago past, and knew it had been many, many lifetimes since a two-leg had been here. She stepped into the forest and explored, sensing many animals. She reached out with her mind, but they were wary after Péist's hunt the night before. She gathered as she wandered, digging up wild turnips and onions for later. She found asparagus and wild cabbage as well as herbs and roots she could use for potions if she got sick or hurt.

Glancing back up at the cliff where Péist was, she craned her neck. The cliff-face had several holes, high above the trail.

Beanna saw also. She landed on Caymin's shoulder. "*What are they?*"

"*I do not know. Can you fly up there?*"

Beanna took off, flying higher until she was a tiny black speck. She was gone for a while before she flew back down to where Caymin waited next to a spring, filling the water skin.

"*They are caves. I think other dragons hatched there,*" Beanna said. "*I saw pieces of shell, like Péist's. All colors – blue, green, red, black.*"

Caymin looked up sharply. "*Are any recent?*"

"*No. They all look very old. The fragments of egg had dust on them. They have not been disturbed for a long time.*"

"*Is there any way for me to get there?*"

"I do not think so. They are very high and there is nothing for a two-leg to climb."

"That is why the dragons used them." Caymin smiled. *"There, the eggs could have stayed safe as long as they needed to until the dragons were ready to hatch."*

Beanna clicked her beak in the direction of the forest. *"Do you think there are more worms here?"*

Caymin turned. *"I do not know."*

A sudden call made her jump.

"We must go back. Péist is awake."

Caymin was halfway up the trail, breathless and panting, when a sudden shadow darkened the trail and a great gust of wind buffeted her. Péist hovered, his wings beating the air against the cliff-face as he flapped. His front feet reached for her, each grasping an arm, and he hoisted her into the air. She looked down at the forest far below her dangling feet as he flew her back to the top of the precipice. Afraid to struggle lest she loosen herself from his grip, she closed her eyes tightly until she felt her feet hit solid ground again.

"Why did you do that?" she demanded angrily.

"I know." Péist lowered his head to look her in the eye.

Caymin shook her twisted tunic back into position. *"You know what?"*

"I know why we had to come here."

His pupils were wide, almost round, in a sea of brilliant green. She felt his excitement and some of her irritation abated.

Beanna flapped down to alight on Caymin's shoulder. *"Do tell us, oh great dragon."*

He snorted a blast of hot air that ruffled all of Beanna's feathers. With a loud caw, she rose into the air.

"Stop." Caymin held out an arm for Beanna who grudgingly accepted. *"Tell us. What was happening in the night?"*

"This is one hatching place of my kind," Péist said. *"There are others,*

scattered in safe places where we can hatch in peace. The only two-legs who have been here are the mages who have bonded with us." He spread his wings and raised his head to the sky with a trumpeting roar. *"All the knowledge of my kind, our history, our deeds, all has been given me."*

"How can that be?"

"I do not know. During the night, I was pulled into a place not of this world, a place in between."

"In between what?"

"I am not certain. It was a realm where I could see my ancestors."

"Like my spiritwalk?"

"Perhaps. But they spoke to me, and told me of my kind. The dragons who hatched here came to this world knowing all, because there were other dragons with them, but I did not." He looked down at her. *"I must take you with me."*

"Where?"

"You will see. Climb on my back."

Caymin did as he asked and he leapt into the sky. Beanna followed as he dropped off the edge of the cliff, over the ocean, his wings tightly folded against his body. For several heartbeats, Caymin was certain they were going to plunge into the water, but then, he spread his wings and, instantly, they soared upward. Caymin felt the utter joy of flight emanating from Péist as he turned from side to side. She gripped the spike in front of her, wondering, if she fell off, whether Péist could fly fast enough to catch her.

Beanna flew along behind them, and Caymin heard the joy in her cries as well. Péist rose along the cliff-face high over the water, and Caymin saw that there were more caves here. Flapping hard, he aimed for one of them. What had looked like a small opening in the rock proved to be enormous as they entered. Caymin slid off his back and peered over the lip of the cliff, looking down at a sheer drop to the ocean below.

"No two-leg could get up here," she said.

"This was our place of safety."

Beanna strutted back into the recesses of the cave. *"Look."*

Caymin and Péist followed. The cave got darker as they retreated farther into the mountain. Caymin conjured a ball of fire to illuminate their way. The passage opened into a large room carved into the rock, large enough for a dragon three times Péist's size.

"*What is this?*"

Caymin went to a huge boulder draped with a large piece of supple leather with several straps attached to it.

"*It is for you,*" said Péist. "*A saddle to hold you on my back as we fly. I saw others do so.*"

She struggled to pick up the saddle and saw that there were holes for his spikes. She cast a spell to lighten it enough to lift it and place it on his back. As it touched him, it glowed and formed itself to fit him perfectly. Two straps secured around his chest and his girth, holding the saddle fast. Small loops of leather provided footholds for her to climb up. Once on his back, she saw that there was a stout belt to cinch around her own waist, attached to the saddle by four other straps so that no matter which direction Péist twisted or turned, even upside-down, she would remain firmly anchored.

"*Shall we try it?*" she asked as she buckled the belt in place.

Péist trotted eagerly to the mouth of the cave, jarring Caymin's teeth. He spread his wings and launched himself out over the water. Without the need to hold to the spike in front of her, Caymin lifted her arms and shouted with joy, matching Péist's writhing and twisting as he tried his wings, carving sharp turns through the air, flying spirals so that the water and the sky switched places and then switched back again.

Looking back at the cliff, Caymin saw Beanna, a tiny black spot against the gray rock.

"*Take us back to the top.*"

Péist flew to the top of the mountain.

"*So, the worm can truly fly,*" Beanna said as she joined them.

Caymin unbuckled the straps securing her and slid to the ground where her legs refused to hold her. She flopped to the earth and lay on her back, breathless and flushed.

"*No wonder Timmin wanted this so badly.*"

Péist's lip curled, revealing a tooth nearly as long as Caymin's arm. *"I would never have consented to bond with him."*

She sat up. *"You can choose?"*

"Of course." He settled on the ground, tucking his legs neatly under him. *"You think it was an accident that we bonded in that cave?"*

"I... I did not know." She surveyed him as the sunlight reflected off his white scales. *"Why me?"*

"I sensed that you were different from other two-legs, just as I am different from other four-legs."

"Did you have to bond with someone?"

"No. I did not know then what I know now, but I could have remained unbonded."

"You would have been free," said Beanna.

"I would have been alone."

Nights spent in the cave were much more comfortable than on the exposed cliff top. Caymin found torches and old bottles of oil, and so had light in the darkness of the cavern without having to use magic. There was a bed that had belonged to some mage long ago, as well as a hollowed place in the cave floor, padded with several soft skins, that fit Péist perfectly. Just as his insatiable hunger when he first hatched had abated, his ability to go without sleep had waned so that he now fell into a deeper trance at night, while Caymin and Beanna slept.

Days were spent exploring. While Péist hunted, Caymin gathered more root vegetables and other edible plants to store for the future.

"How long will we be here?" Beanna asked.

But none of them knew the answer to that question.

During their flights, they realized they were on an island they guessed to be about the size of their old forest. They found a few crumbling ruins of buildings, stone walls and circles overgrown with vines and grasses. In the middle of the island was a circle of standing stones. Like the circle where Caymin had claimed her name and Timmin tried to wrest Péist from her, this circle was very, very old. The stones were mottled with moss and lichens, but carved into the stones were spirals, connected three by three. Standing in the circle, Caymin felt the power gathered there as it vibrated through her body.

Beanna flew on her own when they explored the island, but when they flew over the ocean, soaring on Péist's broad wings, she rode tucked inside a sling Caymin fashioned to keep the bird snug against her body.

They explored some of the other caves and found mountains of scrolls, written by former dragonmages, containing much of the wisdom and history of the dragons and their riders. The writing on many was faded and difficult to make out. The island had once been home to scores of dragons and some mages.

As Enat had done for her, she read so that Péist and Beanna could hear and enjoy the stories as well.

"*This scroll tells of a dragon, Ríona was her name, who lived for hundreds of winters,*" Caymin read.

"*Was she bonded to a mage?*" Beanna asked as she preened her feathers.

"*Yes,*" said Péist. "*Her name was Ailill. Together, they protected Éire from invaders and other dragons.*"

Beanna looked up from her preening. "*Did she live as long as her dragon did? I did not think two-legs could live so long.*"

"*Dragons can live forever, and so, too, their mages,*" said Péist. "*They can be killed in battle, but they do not die of old age as others do.*"

Every so often, Péist came forth with these insights about dragonkind, bits of the knowledge he had gleaned during his spiritwalk, for Caymin was convinced that that was what he had experienced.

"*If they do not die, where are they? What happened to all of them?*" It made Caymin sad to look at the drawings of fierce and beautiful dragons, and to think they were no more, that Péist was the last of his kind.

"*I do not know,*" Péist said. For all he had seen, there were things he had not been shown and Caymin felt his sadness at this unknown.

Caymin did not speak of her own sadness. Lying in her bed at night, she wondered what Enat and the others were doing, if they were safe. She thought of Méav and Ronan and Fergus, out in the world somewhere, and she thought of Gai, home with his clan. She wondered what was to become of herself and Péist and Beanna. They could not stay here, hidden away on this island for hundreds of winters, like the stories in the scrolls. Sooner or later, they would have to either return or move on in search of other lands.

CHAPTER 25

Alone No Longer

"D*o you see anything?*"

Caymin had learned that Péist's eyes were much sharper than her own. She squinted into the distance as they flew over the ocean, looking for any break in the flat line of the horizon.

"*Nothing.*"

Beanna was snug in her sling against Caymin's belly, only her head sticking out. "*I do not see anything, either.*"

Every day the weather permitted, they had been flying, searching for other lands, going in any direction but the one from which they had come.

Péist had been flying farther and farther, but always staying within a day's range of their island, even if they found their way back by the stars.

"*If we cannot find any other land,*" Péist said, "*we will have no choice but to go back.*"

Caymin knew from Ivar's maps that there were other lands to the north and east of Éire, but none of his maps had shown any lands to the west.

They were far out to sea when another raging storm blew in from the west, black clouds rolling over one another with lightning sparking across them and down to the water. They'd encountered similar storms often. The first time, they had underestimated the speed at which it moved and had endured a miserable flight back to the island, wet and surrounded by dangerous spikes of lightning.

They raced this one back to the island, arriving at their cave as the first rain fell. Waves pounded the base of the cliff far below. Inside, they stayed dry and warm, but could feel the tremors from the relentless battering of the sea.

Sitting around the fire, they discussed what they should do, what their future held. Péist was not afraid to face Timmin.

"But you have not seen what he is capable of doing," Caymin fretted, remembering the pain Timmin had inflicted. *"His magic is powerful."*

"So is ours. You were powerful before, but together, we are even more so."

Caymin poked the fire with a stick, sending a shower of sparks toward the smoke hole. *"Do you think the forest needs protection from him? We have been here for more than a moon. Surely Ivar and Neela have returned by now to help Enat safeguard the others."*

"But what of those at risk outside the forest?" Beanna said. *"Timmin is not the only danger. People like Diarmit and his master are perhaps more dangerous, because they are not afraid to deceive all to achieve their end, whatever that may be."*

Péist shifted his head to fix Caymin with his unblinking gaze. *"I think Éire needs a new Ríona and Ailill."*

The storm passed, leaving a crystal clear sky in its wake. Caymin's mind churned as they flew over the empty sea, searching for lands that were not there. All day they soared. Péist had grown stronger, no longer tiring as he had when first he flew. Giving up for the day, they made their way back to their island, the sun sinking low in the sky behind them, when Péist was suddenly alert.

"What is it?" Caymin squinted at the horizon.

"On the water."

She looked down and saw something small bobbing on the waves. Péist flew lower and they could see that it was a small boat, its mast splintered. A man lay in the boat, motionless. Péist dove to get closer. Still, the man did not move.

"*What should we do?*" Péist asked.

Caymin leaned over as they circled. "*Can you carry him?*"

Péist reached down with his back feet, picking up boat and all, and flew toward their island. He circled around to the far side, away from the mountain and the caves. There, a small inlet provided a safe landing point. He gently deposited the boat on the shore, and then landed beside it.

Caymin uncinched her tethers and climbed down off Péist's back. Cautiously, she approached the boat. The man was lying on his side, half-submerged in water that had gathered in the bottom of the vessel during the storm. A bundle lay beside him, wrapped in oiled cloth. Beanna perched on the side of the boat and cawed loudly. He did not stir.

"*Is he dead?*" she asked.

Caymin leaned near enough to place a hand on his chest. A rough wooden cross fell out of his robe. She withdrew her hand as if stung.

"*He wears a cross. He is a follower of the Christ.*"

"*The ones that Timmin wanted to war against?*" Péist craned his neck to get a closer look.

The man groaned and stirred.

"*We cannot let him see you,*" Caymin said. "*Fly up to the cave. Beanna and I will stay with him for a while.*"

"*I do not like this,*" Péist protested. "*What if he tries to hurt you?*"

"*I do not think he is strong enough to hurt anyone right now,*" Caymin said, looking at him. "*And I have magic to protect me if I need it.*"

"*I can always put his eyes out if he does see the worm,*" Beanna offered.

Péist snapped his jaws, but Beanna just bobbed her head.

"Go," said Caymin. "*I will come later to a place where you can fly down and get me.*"

Reluctantly, Péist walked a short distance away and leapt into the air. Beanna flew up into an overhead tree where she could keep an eye on the stranger.

Hovering her hands over him, Caymin ran them down his arms and legs, stopping when she came to a break in his leg. She hesitated. She could easily heal this injury without it costing her greatly, but she wasn't certain she wanted him whole and healthy enough to wander the island. She used just enough magic to ease his pain a bit, and then tipped the boat, dumping the man onto the sand, along with all the water from the bottom of the boat.

Magically erasing her footprints, she retreated into the trees as he sputtered and opened his eyes.

Dazed, he looked around at his twilit surroundings as he wiped the water from his face. He tried to get to his feet, but fell back to the sand, grabbing his leg and grimacing. He tried again, balancing on his good leg as he uprighted his boat. He muttered as he inspected the shattered mast, the useless sail and ropes lying in a heap.

"I must have washed up here."

He closed his eyes and touched his hand to his forehead, chest and each shoulder as he muttered more words Caymin couldn't hear. After a moment, he opened his eyes and looked around again. With darkness nearly upon him, he apparently decided his priority was to create some shelter for the night. He pushed his boat up on its side again, using a broken fragment of the mast to prop it so that he could crawl underneath.

Silently, Caymin backed away until she could safely walk. Beanna joined her a moment later, landing on her shoulder.

"*We will have to bring him food,*" Caymin said.

"*Why? If we do not feed him, he may die or try to leave.*"

Caymin shook her head. "*We cannot leave him to that fate.*"

"*Do not feed him too much. He will be easier to subdue if he is weak.*"

"*Why would I need to subdue him?*"

"*I do not trust this two-leg.*"

"*You do not know this two-leg.*"

Beanna clicked her beak in response. "*I do not want to know him.*"

Caymin sighed as she looked up at the mountain where Péist waited. "*We are on an island. His boat is damaged. We may not have a choice but to get to know him.*"

Caymin became the ghost-child again. She crouched and slunk around the stranger, keeping mostly out of sight, giving him only glimpses of her. She brought him meat and some of the edible roots she'd dug. At first, she deposited the items near the edge of the forest at the inlet, staying out of sight. She watched as he struggled to make a fire to cook the meat, hobbling around with the aid of a stick he'd found. All of the wood was still damp from the recent storm, and he had no firestarters. She waved her hand to ignite a branch and placed it where he would find it. He stood holding the branch, looking around for his benefactor. When he saw nothing, he carefully fed the flames with bits of twig and fibers he tore from his robe. She watched with satisfaction as he laid in a supply of wood and bark and made certain he never let the fire die away.

He was nearly as tall as Ivar, broad-shouldered and strong, despite his injury. He had already been trying to determine whether the mast of his boat could be repaired, sizing up some of the nearby trees. From the oilcloth pack in his boat, he had produced tools and a sword. He moved off the little beach of the inlet into a clearing in the trees. There, he built himself a sturdier shelter, using a combination of stacked stones and leafy branches hacked from the trees with his axe. Caymin winced at the sound of the iron hitting the trees.

"I know you're there, watching me," he said one evening as he sat by his fire. "I thank you for the food. I've no desire to hurt you. You can show yourself."

She eased out of the underbrush, staying a cautious distance away. He eyed her curiously. A momentary look of repulsion flashed across his eyes as he gazed at her. It was the first time in a very long time that she was reminded of her scars.

"My name is Garvan," he said. "What's yours?"

She stood silent, ready to throw up a protective shield if need be. Beanna, she knew, was nearby, also standing guard. She could feel Péist, listening anxiously from the mountaintop, ready to pounce.

Garvan, obviously thinking she didn't understand his language, touched his own chest. "Garvan. Garvan." He tapped his chest as he spoke, then held his hand out to her.

She hesitated. "Ash." She was not ready to trust him with her true name.

"Ash," he repeated, sitting back and smiling. He pointed to a chunk of meat roasting over the fire, a part of Péist's last kill. "Thank you."

He eyed the knife at her belt and the bow slung over her shoulder. "Did you hunt?" He mimicked the action of drawing the bow.

She nodded. Better for him to think it was her than to wonder who else could have hunted.

When she simply stood there, he asked, "Where are your people? What land is this?"

She shook her head.

He reached into his robe and pulled out his cross. "Do you know this?"

She took a step back, eyeing the cross warily. He sighed and looked back at his fire. "God help me. You sent me here; grant me patience."

Caymin hid a smile. *"Should I tell him his god had nothing to do with it? He was brought here by a dragon and a mage."*

"I think that would not be wise," Beanna said. *"Amusing, but not wise."*

Garvan tried again. "Where do you live?" He pointed at her and then gestured with his arm, sweeping it in a wide arc.

She pointed vaguely in a direction away from the mountain, but his gaze was drawn upward. She retreated into the woods, and he turned back to her.

"Don't go!"

But she was already creeping away from him, deliberately picking a trail away from the mountain. She walked until she was far enough away to call to Péist.

The cave was dark when Caymin woke. Silently, she rose from her bed, trying not to disturb the others. She padded to the back of the cave. Flicking her finger, she conjured a small bit of flame and set it afloat. Here, propped against the rock wall by a former inhabitant of the cave, was a flat plate of glass and silver, polished and gleaming. She'd found it by accident, scaring herself when she thought another person was there with her. She'd avoided it since, not wanting to look at herself. But she approached now. When she stepped in front of it, she saw her image reflected back at her in the glass.

She turned her face, studying first her scarred side and then the other. When her scars weren't visible, she looked just like anyone else, like Gai or Daina or Cíana. She combed her fingers through her hair. It had grown, as no one had cut it since she left Enat. Pulling at the strands, she separated her hair into small bunches, braiding them. When she was done, she smiled grimly at her reflection. She would never be beautiful like Méav, but she thought she looked fearsome, and fearsome would have to do.

Caymin sat with Péist and Beanna on the cliff top, looking down at the pinprick of light that was Garvan's fire.

"*You are giving him too much of our food,*" Beanna said.

"*If I do not give him food, he will go in search of it,*" Caymin countered. "*I want him to stay in one place.*"

"*His leg is healing. Already, he can walk without his stick. He will not stay in one place for long.*"

Beanna was right. He was healing. He still limped, but was walking farther, exploring the area around the clearing on his own.

More than once, Caymin had brought down thick fog to confound him and keep him close to his fire.

She observed him sometimes from the concealment of the forest, watching as he knelt with his eyes closed, his lips moving. She knew he prayed to his god, but she didn't know what he asked for.

Sometimes he hit himself across the back with the knotted end of the rope he wore around his waist.

When she brought him food, he plied her with endless questions. In response to where they were, she answered truthfully, "West." It was as much as she knew. He seemed to have decided she was alone, and she let him think her boat had sunk in a storm similar to the one that had brought him there, drowning her people.

He pressed to find out where she lived, where she slept, and she avoided answering, pretending not to understand, but she could tell by the look in his eyes that he didn't believe that. Again and again, his gaze was drawn to the mountain.

"*How can we get him to leave here?*" Péist asked now as they saw his shadow move across his fire.

"*We cannot, unless he can fix his boat,*" Caymin replied.

"*Has he said yet why he was in such a small boat on such large water?*"

"*No. He has not. When I try to ask him, he evades answering. He is hiding something.*"

"*What of us?*" Beanna asked. "*We have not flown in search of land for nearly a moon because we cannot fly during the day. Are we to stay here all our days? We could leave, and let him fend for himself here.*"

Caymin stewed as she listened, knowing Beanna was right about this as well. Péist had taken to flying over the ocean at night to keep his wings strong. They were all chafing at how Garvan's presence had restricted their activity.

"*If you will not let me eat him,*" Péist said, "*I think I should pick him up and carry him far out over the ocean and drop him in.*"

"*We cannot do that.*" Caymin lay back in frustration. She watched the stars filling the sky above her. "*Why did he have to come here? We were better on our own.*"

"*Something has to happen,*" said Beanna. "*We cannot continue like this forever.*"

Péist flew Caymin down from their cave, landing in an open area outside the forest, as close as they dared to Garvan's clearing. *"I will hunt while you take the last of this meat to the two-leg."*

No sooner had Péist taken off than Garvan appeared. Startled, Caymin had her hands up, ready to cast a protective shield before he could take a breath.

"Stay!" He held up both of his hands. "'Tis I."

She lowered her hands, her heart still pounding. "What are you doing here?"

He cocked his head at the sound of Péist landing in the forest a distance away.

"What in the name of heaven is that?"

She shrugged but didn't respond.

"Are you a druid, then?"

She stared at him. "A what?"

He picked up a stone, rubbing it in between his palms. "I know you healed me, at least some." He wiggled his leg. "This should have been much worse than it was."

Still, she said nothing, but guarded her mind in case he had the skill to try and push into her thoughts.

"How do you get to the top of the mountain?"

"Why would you think I go to the top?"

He looked at her, and she couldn't decide what she saw in his eyes – curiosity that wouldn't be satisfied with vague answers, or calculation, like what she'd seen in Diarmit's eyes when he finally admitted all he knew. Either way, she had the feeling he knew more than she'd realized.

Apparently, Péist thought so as well, because she felt him, just a heartbeat before a huge shadow blotted out the sun and he crashed down, landing with his front legs braced on either side of her.

Garvan fell back, his eyes huge, his mouth open in a silent scream as Péist bared his teeth in a fearsome snarl.

"Holy mother of God," Garvan managed to whimper as he stared up at the dragon.

"What are you doing?" Caymin asked.

"Do not be fooled," Péist answered. *"He knows. Don't you, holy man?"*

Garvan's mouth gaped. "You... you can talk."

"He can hear you?"

"When I choose to let him. All dragons can do this." He stretched his neck out until his muzzle was just a hair from Garvan's face. *"Just as all dragons could eat any two-leg with no more than a snap of our mighty jaws."*

"Holy mother of God," Garvan said again, making the sign of the cross.

Péist raised his head. *"Luckily for you, holy man, my mage took pity on you, so I will do the same. For now."*

Garvan placed a hand over his heart and took a few deep breaths. "Your mage?"

Caymin laid a hand on Péist's leg and drew herself up to her full height. "You asked if I am a druid. I am not. I am a mage, born to bond with this dragon."

Garvan stared at them. "But... but those are only children's tales, told round the fire. And there are no such things as mages."

A deep rumble sounded from Péist. *"Do I look like a fable told to children? And my mage has powers you cannot dream of."*

Garvan's mouth opened and closed a few times. He rubbed his hand over his eyes, and then opened them again as if hoping the sight before him would have disappeared. When it did not, he sat up. "May I stand?"

Péist dipped his head. *"You may."*

He scrambled to his feet as Beanna fluttered down to Caymin's shoulder. He pointed. "I've seen that bird everywhere, watching me."

Caymin ran a finger down Beanna's sleek breast. "She has been keeping watch."

Garvan stood looking at them. "What now?"

"Now we talk."

Péist refused to allow Caymin to walk with Garvan where he could not follow. He flew her back to the inlet where the boat sat on its side, while Garvan retraced his path through the forest.

By the time he arrived, Caymin was waiting at his fire. Péist could not fit his body into the clearing, but his head rested next to Caymin. Garvan sat opposite her, still eyeing Péist with a mix of fascination and disbelief while Beanna hopped around them. As he gazed at her, Caymin could tell he was trying to reconcile the ignorant ghost-child she'd seemed with what he now knew.

"Now," Caymin began, "it is time for truth. We found you on the ocean after a storm. Your boat was damaged, as you were. We brought you here. Saved your life. You will tell us what you were doing out there."

Garvan fed the fire, his bearded jaw working as he considered. "I was exiled. By my abbot."

"For what?"

He looked at her, his eyes hard. "For killing a man."

She stared at him for a moment. "You killed a man? Why?"

He tilted his head, regarding her. "I just told you I killed a man, and instead of being afraid of me, you want to know why?"

"I have no need to fear you," she said calmly. "I could subdue you myself with magic if I needed to, and Péist could easily kill you."

Garvan threw his head back and laughed. "If I didn't know I was awake, I would swear the devil was playing me."

Caymin waited.

Garvan ran his fingers through his beard. "He was a brute. One of the landholders near our monastery. He had a wife and children, but was lusting after another young woman. I caught him trying to force her –" He stopped, looking at Caymin. "He had to be stopped. I didn't mean to kill him. He fell over a watering trough and his neck snapped. But I was the cause."

"And they sent you away for this?"

"Aye. He was kin to the king, and the king was threatening to seize our lands if I wasn't dealt with."

Caymin looked into his eyes. *"He tells the truth."*

"I agree," said Péist.

"I planned to sail to a land where I could bring word of our Lord or perhaps start a new monastery." Garvan chuckled. "Instead, I landed on an island with no other men, just a girl and a dragon."

He shifted. "What of you? Why are you here?"

Caymin looked at Péist. *"How much to tell him?"*

"Not all. Do not tell him of my life in the forest. Begin when I was an egg."

And so Caymin told of bonding with Péist's egg, and the danger they were in as others sought to use him for their own goals. She told of their fleeing the forest and Péist's hatching and their flight to this island.

Garvan listened raptly. "There are places where mages are taught?"

"Yes."

His eyes narrowed. "What manner of magic are you taught?"

Caymin wondered how much to say. "We are taught the use of plants to make healing potions and salves."

He rubbed his leg. "You didn't heal me with a potion or salve."

Caymin smiled. "We are taught to do a bit more."

"Do you serve the devil?"

Caymin tilted her head. "What is the devil?"

"The tempter, the bringer of evil."

She laid her hand on Péist's jaw. "Do we seem evil to you?"

"We saved your life, holy man," Péist said, speaking so Garvan could hear. *"When we could have left you adrift to die."*

Garvan frowned.

"Is anyone wholly good or evil?" Caymin asked. "One or the other? We are taught to do no harm with our power. I did not grow up among humans, but I think perhaps mages are no better or worse than others."

He stared into the fire, thinking about what she'd said.

"Your baseless fears that we are evil is what drove Timmin to do what he did."

Garvan looked at her. "And you say this other mage, Timmin, tried to steal the egg?"

"He wanted to use Péist for his own purposes."

"As if I would have done what he wished," Péist said, snorting sparks.

"He may have had a way of forcing you to do his will," Caymin said.

"Did the boy, Diarmit, tell you the name of the monk he served?"

Caymin tried to remember. "No. He never told me who his master was."

Péist raised his head. *"And yet you question whether we are evil."*

Garvan sighed. "I have much to think on, to pray on."

Caymin stood. "Pray all you like. You and your god do not change who we are."

CHAPTER 26

Back to the Forest

Péist continued to hunt for them all, but Garvan also fished, wading out into the water of the inlet and casting a net he had packed in his boat.

"*Fish are good, but it would take a boatful of them to satisfy me,*" Péist said, using a talon to pick a fish bone from his teeth.

With no further need to keep Péist's existence a secret from Garvan, they took to flying during the day again. Caymin had nearly forgotten the joy and freedom of being strapped to the dragon's back as they soared over the ocean. But still, there was no sign of any other land.

"I have heard tales of lands far, far to the west," Garvan said as they sat around his fire one evening while Péist hunted. "But those who tell the tales do not know for certain where they are. And the travelers went in ships, much larger than my boat, with provisions for the journey, enough to be on the water for many moons."

He looked across the fire at Caymin, studying her scars. "You told me you were not raised by humans. What did you mean?"

"My village was attacked, ransacked by another kingdom."

Caymin heard the bitterness in her voice as she spoke, but she couldn't help it. She raised a hand to the ridges on her face. "I was left to die. I called out and a family of badgers rescued me. They took care of me, taught me, raised me."

"What do you mean you called out?"

"I speak to animals. Not just Péist and Beanna, but all."

He looked beyond her to the forest. "You can speak with all the animals out there?"

She nodded. "I can. Most of them do not speak back to me here, because Péist has been hunting among them."

"It is always our choice," Beanna said.

Caymin smiled and translated, for Beanna could not make herself heard by Garvan as Péist could.

"And other mages can do this also?"

"Not all. Some are gifted with this ability, some can learn, and some cannot."

Garvan stirred the fire. "Do you know who attacked your village?"

Caymin's eyes flashed. "Yes. I have a cloak with their crest. It was the clan of one of the other apprentices. His father's warriors were the ones who attacked us."

"I'm sorry, child." Garvan watched her. "They killed all your family?"

"They killed my father, but they took my mother."

"How can you know that?"

"I saw it. In a spiritwalk."

"A spiritwalk?"

Caymin nodded. "Enat gave me a potion and guided me the first time. I went again, on my own. I saw the attack. I saw them kill my father as he tried to protect us, and I saw them drag my mother away, leaving me in the fire."

"You saw all of this?"

Tears stung her eyes and she turned away, not wanting Garvan to see her weak. He was quiet for long heartbeats, giving her time to collect herself.

"So your mother might be alive?"

Caymin swiped a hand over her eyes. "I do not know."

"Do you have this cloak with you? The one with the crest?"

"Yes."

"Let me see it one day. It may be I'll recognize it."

"What good will that do?"

He laughed. "You've a dragon, haven't you? If your mother is still alive, I'm thinking you'd be able to find her."

"You think we should go back?"

"Lass, you've turned my thinking on its head since I met you. I've no answers for what you and Péist should or shouldn't do, but it seems to me that you were bonded for a reason. And leaving people like Timmin and whoever it is that the boy Diarmit serves running loose is not a good thing for others."

She tilted her head. "What about you? You said you were sent away for killing a man who was trying to harm another. Is it right for you to stay away?"

"I'm vowed to obey my superior."

"Even when the superior is wrong?" Caymin had listened as he spoke of his god and the god-son, and decided his stories didn't sound that different from Neela's songs and tales of gods and goddesses. She didn't believe in any of them, but kept those thoughts to herself. "I thought your Christ made enemies because he did what he knew to be right even when it angered those in authority."

He chuckled. "I should bring you back to argue with my brothers. You make more sense than all of them." His expression sobered. "But you may be right. While I was on the sea, I realized I let myself be driven away for the wrong reasons."

"Perhaps one day we will all go back," Beanna said.

As the days shortened, and the sun traveled a lower arc through the sky, the weather began to worsen. Caymin had lost track of the days, but estimated it must be between Lughnasadh and Samhain.

Caymin, Péist and Beanna sat huddled in their cave while a heavy fog blanketed the island. The fog had moved in from the sea four days ago, and was showing no signs of abating. They had flown down once to bring Garvan some meat and make sure he had all he needed. Caymin had asked Péist if they should bring him with them.

Péist refused to fly Garvan to the mountaintop or to the caves. "*Some things are for us alone,*" he told Caymin.

Secretly, she was relieved. She liked having the caves to themselves. With the entrance to the cave magically sealed to keep the fog and damp outside, they were warm and comfortable. She sat under the light of a torch, reading more of the scrolls they'd found.

"*How did you come to be in our forest?*" she asked.

Péist lay curled up in his bed. "*I do not know.*"

"*Do you remember anything from before you were a worm?*"

He closed his eyes. "*No. My earliest memory is of hunting in the forest, and then bonding with you.*"

She frowned down at the book. "*It speaks of the hatching of the* khrusallis, *but nowhere does it say where dragon worms come from.*" She looked at him. "*You must come from somewhere.*"

"*What of the different colors?*" asked Beanna. "*Does it say aught of that?*"

Caymin shook her head. "*No. It does not.*"

"*Crows are all the same color.*"

"*How boring.*" Péist opened one green eye. "*From the shell fragments we have found, dragons come in all colors, but I do not know if there is a reason.*"

"*It makes me sad, to think of all those dragons that were here at one time,*" she said, closing the book. "*Where have they all gone?*"

Outside the cave, the fog formed a solid wall against the night. She doused the torch and lay down on her bed. Beanna waddled over to curl up against her under her cloak. Lying in the dark, Caymin fingered the pattern of the crest woven into the fabric.

Something awakened her. She sat up, but the cave was in complete darkness. At the entrance, the fog beckoned. She got up, leaving herself asleep with Péist and Beanna, and walked to the mouth of the cave. Whispers coaxed her, calling to her. Trusting the voices, she stepped out, into what should have been thin air, but her feet met solid ground. Like before, the mist parted just in front of her, only enough to lead her step by step, away from the cave. On and on she walked, following the whispers.

When the fog parted, she found herself standing on a knoll overlooking a broad valley. Large birds flew through the sky, circling, wheeling – and she realized they weren't birds. They were dragons. Dragons of every hue under the sun – green and yellow and blue and gray and bronze and crimson. Some had riders, but most did not.

She stood in amazement at the glory of them.

"Welcome, Caymin of Péist."

She turned to find a huge dragon beside her on the knoll. The voice that sounded in Caymin's head was that of a female. Judging by the size of the ridges and horns growing from her head, she must be very old. Her scales gleamed black as onyx and her eyes burned yellow.

"Where am I?"

The dragon chuckled, a deep rumble from her chest, and geysers of steam blew from her nostrils.

"You are where all dragons and dragonmages have gone – all except you and Péist. This is a land far to the west. There is no place for us now in the world you inhabit. Our time there has passed. Here, we can live without war, without fear of being hunted."

Caymin watched, transfixed, as dragons walked the valley below her, their great tails leaving undulating trails behind them.

She turned to look at the one beside her. *"Who are you?"*

"I am Ríona of Ailill."

Caymin gaped. *"I have read of you. I did not know you still lived. Does Ailill live as well?"*

"Aye. She lives. You will meet her one day."

"Why was Péist left behind?"

Ríona sighed. *"It was a great sadness to us, but if we had taken him with us to this land, he could never have bonded with you as he was meant to. We had to place him where he would be protected and safe until you came to him."*

"He was not safe there. One of the mages, Timmin, sought to use Péist for his own gains in a war against the Christians."

Ríona glowered. *"A mage should know better than to tamper with a bonding, and he should know that no dragon would consent to be used in that way."*

"Enat said he had been twisted by hatred."

"Aye, that can happen to the wisest among us. Even dragons and riders are not immune."

"What do you mean?"

"Sadly, our last war was initiated by a mage, Scolaí. His hunger for power became a madness, a madness he shared with his dragon, Tuala. Together, they wreaked devastation on much of the land beyond Éire."

"When was this?"

"A thousand winters ago, or longer," said Ríona. *"They thought all the lands should be ruled by a mage and dragon. They were not alone. Some among us agreed and joined them to depose the non-magical kings of the day. Many of us died in that war, but some still alive here fought them. That was the beginning of the end of our place in the world of humans. They did not trust those with magic or power after that, and we cannot blame them. Not long after, the followers of the Christ began to spread their word, and magic became more and more feared. It has been a hundred winters since we left to come to this land."*

"A hundred winters? And Péist was left alone all that time?"

"Aye."

Caymin looked around at the towering mountains in the distance. *"How is it that I am here and Péist is not?"*

"In the old days, you both would have been brought to Inishbreith to be trained."

"Inishbreith? Is that the island Péist flew us to after he hatched?"

"Aye. He was driven to return to his home."

"But we are alone here. We have nothing but the scrolls you left behind."

Ríona lowered her head. *"It is our biggest regret, that we cannot train you as you should be. Some you will learn from the scrolls; some you will learn by bonding with us as you are now."*

"In a spiritwalk?"

"Of sorts."

They stood together, watching the dragons around them, and Caymin wished she and Péist could be with them always.

"There are two things I must tell you," Ríona said. *"Péist cannot leave Inishbreith until he enters the firechamber. If he does not, he will never be able to breathe fire."*

"What is the firechamber?"

"He will know. It is a test for both of you."

Caymin looked up at the dragon. *"A test of what?"*

"Of your bond. Your trust in each other." Seeing that Caymin was about to question further, Ríona said, *"Do not worry. You will know what to do when the time comes."*

Caymin frowned but held back the questions that filled her mind. *"You said two things."*

"Other than the mages who have bonded with dragons, no two-leg has ever set foot on Inishbreith. That island has been a sanctuary for our kind for ages beyond even my memory. You must see to it that the two-leg there now can never tell any others about it. Humans who are not bonded to us cannot be trusted."

"And how do I do that?"

Ríona raised her great head and gazed far out across the valley. *"You must silence him."*

Caymin gasped. *"You mean, I must kill him?"*

"You will do what you must to keep our island a secret."

Ríona lowered her head again. *"You must know, Caymin of Péist, that great things are needed of you. Another war is on the horizon, and you and your dragon will have to end it before it starts, or the damage will be unending."*

Caymin looked up at the ancient dragon. *"How can we stop a war?"*

Ríona focused one gold eye on her. *"You must begin by forgiving."*

"Forgiving? Whom must I forgive?"

But the mist returned, obscuring the dragon from Caymin's view. She called out, but there was no response.

The fog parted before her, and she knew she had no choice but to walk on, following where it led. The mist still surrounded her as she heard panicked voices calling, screaming. She hurried forward and stumbled onto a scene that made her heart go still.

She was in the forest, her forest. The meetinghouse was on fire, and outside it, Niall and Una stood back to back, fighting heavily armed warriors. Swords and staffs sang through the air, landing with clashes and thuds. Una took a blow to the arm and Caymin heard the bone snap as she cried out and dropped her staff. Caymin yelled and ran forward to stand between her and the warrior towering over her, but Niall's sword jabbed through her from behind as if she wasn't there – and she remembered she wasn't.

Helplessly, she looked around and saw Ivar fighting three warriors at once, a sword in one hand, his other conjuring a line of flame to hold them at bay. Two children cowered behind him, holding their swords feebly.

She spotted Daina and Cíana aiming arrows from the cover of nearby trees. One of the invading warriors yelled and fell to the ground with an arrow through his neck. His gurgling cries were muffled by the noise of the fighting going on around him, but Caymin watched his blood soak into the soil beneath him.

A scream to one side made her whirl as Cuán and the other badgers ran snarling from the forest, attacking the warriors, biting and clawing at their legs and feet.

"NO!" This time, the scream erupted from Caymin as she saw a warrior plunge a spear into Cuán's body. He fell, quivering, his eyes glazing over.

Dazed, she turned and saw Neela standing over a prone form on the ground, her staff shooting jets of light as she fended off yet more attackers. Caymin looked more closely and saw that the crumpled body on the ground was Enat.

She stumbled over, falling to her knees next to Enat who lay bleeding from a gash across her belly. Her bloody hands grasped her middle, but her gaze fixed on Caymin.

"We need you. Help us."

Caymin tried to reach out to touch Enat's face, but her hand was no more than smoke as it passed through.

The mist returned, and all sound was obscured. Caymin struggled to her feet, barely able to breathe for her grief.

"You must forgive."

Ríona's voice sounded in her ears.

"You will need to gather forces, allies who can help, who will follow a dragon and his mage. You must forgive."

When Caymin opened her eyes, Péist was awake, waiting for her.

"You went to them."

"Yes." She sat up, dazed. Beanna ruffled her feathers at the disturbance.

Outside, dawn was breaking. The fog had lifted.

"Ríona was waiting for me. She said Ailill is still alive. They have lived for over a thousand winters."

"What else did she say?"

"You and I must go to the firechamber."

"I have dreamt of it," Péist said.

Caymin wiped tears from her cheeks.

Beanna hopped onto her knee. *"Why do you cry?"*

"I saw Enat and Ivar and all the others fighting. Warriors have invaded the forest. War has come. We must go back. And I think I must find Gai and his clan."

"Why?"

She picked up her cloak and conjured a ball of flame to illuminate the cave as she looked at the crest of those she had always considered her enemies.

"We need their help."

"Do you know it?"

Caymin paced as Garvan examined her cloak, studying the insignia woven into the cloth.

"Part of it." He looked up at her. "The wolf is the symbol of the kingdom of the Eoganacht. But the rest, I think, is from the clans to the west, those who claim and protect the coastline."

He reached down and dragged a finger through the dirt at his feet.

"There is a large protected bay here," he said, drawing a map that Caymin recognized as Éire. "Just to the south of it, you will fly over three small islands and, beyond them, you will come to steep cliffs that drop into the sea. This is the land you seek."

He eyed her closely. "What did you see?"

Her eyes shimmered with tears as she looked at him. She could not tell him of the dragons – no human could know they still existed somewhere to the west. And Ríona's warning still echoed in her head – the warning that he would have to be silenced.

"War. War has come to the forest where live all those I love."

"Are you sure 'tis happening now?"

She threw her hands up. "I do not know."

"You told me you've seen things from the past, the attack on your village and the death of your father. Perhaps on these spiritwalks, you can be shown what is to come, or what might come."

She paused her pacing. "Do you believe that?"

He shrugged. "Why would they ask you to come and help if it was all done?"

For the first time since she'd awakened from her spiritwalk, her heart slowed a bit. "Perhaps you are right. Perhaps I was shown those things now so that I may have time to alter what is coming."

"What were they wearing, these warriors who were attacking your friends?"

Caymin frowned, trying to remember. She'd been so focused on the fighting that she hadn't paid much attention to what the enemy was wearing. "Some wore robes, like yours. Others wore fur capes, like the northmen who invaded our forest last winter."

Garvan's expression darkened and he closed his eyes for a moment. "I've no magic to offer, Ash, but you have my aid, if you want it. I will come with you and help in any way I can."

"Thank you, Garvan."

It was the first time Péist had spoken his name, and his face flushed.

Péist nudged Caymin. *"You should tell him."*

"Tell me what?"

She looked at him. "My true name. The badgers called me Ash, and it was my name for many winters, until Enat came for me. When I went on my first spiritwalk, I learned my true name." She laid a hand on Péist's neck. "I am Caymin. Caymin of Péist."

As it had the night she first claimed her name, the earth trembled. The very air shimmered with their power combined with that of the forest. Garvan looked around in fear and awe.

"Truly, you and your magic must be from the one God," he whispered. "Never have I seen or felt such things, but I no longer believe them to be evil." He knelt before her, pressing the hilt of his sword against his forehead and then holding it out to her. "My sword is yours to command."

Touched, she placed a hand on his head. "Thank you, Garvan."

"And how does he think we will all get back to our land?" Beanna asked.

"I am bigger and stronger than I was when we came here," Péist said, masking his voice from Garvan's hearing. *"I can carry all of you."*

"Are you sure? There will be no place for you to rest once we leave Inishbreith."

"We must, so we will," Péist said.

Caymin thought for a long moment and then turned to Garvan. "You promised me your sword. Will you also promise me your silence?"

"What do you mean?"

She considered what she was about to do. "No human can learn of this island. You know that."

"Aye. I know that." His eyes narrowed as he regarded her. "You're supposed to kill me, aren't you?"

She looked away. "I am supposed to silence you. If you give me your word, that is good enough for me."

He still knelt in front of her. "I give you my vow. No one will ever learn of this island from me. But you haven't told me how we're to get back to Éire."

Caymin smiled. "You will ride on the back of a dragon."

CHAPTER 27

Trial by Fire

It took two days for them to prepare – two days of worry and frustration for Caymin as she fretted the attackers would get to the forest before they could.

"*Remember,*" said Beanna. "*You were shown what might come so that you could gather forces to aid us. There is time.*"

Garvan insisted they travel with enough food to supply them for several days.

"You don't know that you'll be welcome with Gai's clan," he pointed out. "We may have to observe them from a distance or seek help elsewhere. We should be prepared."

Péist hunted and Garvan fished, and then they spent time drying and smoking the meat while Caymin gathered as many roots as she could.

"*It is time,*" Péist said.

"Time for what?" Garvan asked as he built up the fire on his makeshift smokehouse.

Caymin stood. "I do not know when we will return."

Garvan sat up and looked at her. "What do you mean?"

"There is something we must do before we leave the island."

Beanna flapped to Caymin's shoulder.

"*No,*" Caymin said. "*You must wait here as well. I do not know what we will face, but it is for dragons and their mages only.*"

Beanna fixed her with a baleful eye. "*Very well, but I am waiting in the cave, not with the two-leg.*"

Caymin smiled. "*I promise, we will seek you first when we return.*"

She climbed up into the saddle and Péist spread his wings, launching them skyward. He soared over the island, circling. She wondered where they were destined when she felt something pull at them, taking Péist into a waking trance. He flew out over the sea. Suddenly, he banked and dove, aiming for the cliff-face. She opened her mouth to yell just as the magical façade of rock in front of them melted away, revealing an opening larger than their cave. Péist flew straight in, flying deeper into the mountain. Torches ignited as they passed, illuminating a tunnel that took them down, down into the bowels of the mountain. The torches became more sporadic, the tunnel darker until the only light was Péist glowing white in the darkness of the mountain.

"*It is hard to breathe,*" Caymin said, covering her mouth with her sleeve against the hot, toxic air.

"*Just here,*" said Péist, landing with a jolt.

He walked now, still following the tunnel as it angled downward. Caymin was certain they must be far below the island by now. They saw a red glow ahead of them, and a hot wind blew Caymin's braids off her shoulders.

Cautiously, they rounded a bend in the tunnel to find themselves in an enormous chamber. In the center of the floor was a pool of thick liquid, white-hot where bubbles were sluggishly belching while crusts of glowing red and orange covered the remainder. As the surface undulated, it burst with more bubbles splashing white liquid that sizzled as it landed on the solid rock they stood on.

"*What do we do now?*" Caymin looked around.

"*We go in.*"

"*In?*"

"This is our test." Péist twisted his head around to look at her. *"You must shield us and I must take us into the fire."*

Caymin stared in horror at the mass of liquid fire in front of them, gurgling and spitting.

"We must do this, little one."

She took a deep breath. Drawing her power from deep within her, she laid her hands on either side of Péist's neck, adding his power to hers. She murmured the incantation and created a shield to protect them as Péist stepped forward.

Gingerly, he dipped one talon into the liquid and then pushed on, wading into the pit. The liquid fire rose higher around his legs, to his belly. Caymin felt her shield waver and drew deeper to summon more power for her spell. Her lips moved incessantly as Péist strode farther into the pool. She felt a warmth that wasn't altogether unpleasant, but knew they would be incinerated in an instant if her protection failed. He stopped in the middle of the pit, with the liquid bubbling just below Caymin's feet. She fought the instinct to draw them higher out of its reach.

They stood still, waiting. She felt a vibration from under the saddle as Péist began to hum, his neck stretched upward. A thick bubble spattered her leg, burning a hole through her legging, and she quickly renewed the energy of her shielding spell.

Suddenly, Péist bugled a roar that echoed within the walls of the cavern and then he dunked his mouth into the molten fire. Caymin swallowed a cry of alarm as he drank from the pool. She felt a churning under her as his body absorbed the scorching liquid. He gulped down mouthfuls of the stuff.

At last, he lifted his head, fiery red drops clinging to his muzzle. He shook his head, sending them flying, and backed out of the pit. Once again on solid rock, Caymin let the shield drop, sagging with the drain on her energy.

Péist, though, was exhilarated. *"I am now a full dragon!"*

"What do you mean?"

In reply, he roared, and a geyser of fire erupted from his throat, filling the tunnel. Caymin closed her eyes as they charged through, but they emerged unscathed as the last licks of flame winked out behind them. Again and again, as Péist trotted back up the tunnel, he burped flames.

"Drinking the liquid fire ignited something within me."

"Will you need to replenish it to keep breathing fire?"

"I do not think so. I do not know for certain, but I believe, once it is ignited, it will never go out."

When the tunnel widened enough, he spread his wings and flew them back out, announcing his arrival to the outside world with another burst of flame.

Beanna was watching for them in the mouth of their cave. "*So the worm can now breathe fire?*"

Péist belched and sent a tiny ball of flame in her direction. "*Take heed, little bird, or you may end up roasted.*"

At last, they were ready. They planned to leave so that they would return to Éire under cover of night, with the moon and stars to guide them. They had food enough gathered, all stored in Caymin's basket, which Garvan slung over his shoulders. He had his sword strapped to his belt, while Caymin wore her cloak, fastened by the dragon brooch, with her bow slung over her back, her quiver and knife fastened to her belt. Péist preened as he wore his saddle, occasionally sending out little bursts of fire, simply because he could. Caymin hid a smile. He looked magnificent and he knew it.

Caymin climbed up, strapping herself to the saddle. Beanna snuggled herself into her sling, tucked against Caymin's body.

Garvan took a deep breath and climbed up behind her, wedging himself between two of Péist's spikes where they came up through the holes in the saddle. "This could change my life forever," he muttered, grasping the spike protruding between his legs.

Péist spread his wings. "*Are you ready?*"

Garvan could only laugh in answer as the dragon leapt into the air. It took him a bit longer to gain altitude under the extra weight.

He circled the island once. Reluctantly, Caymin looked down at the mountaintop and the caves, where she'd left all the scrolls and books they'd found.

"*We will return one day,*" Péist said. "*But for now, we must find Gai's clan and convince them to help us.*"

"*You are right.*"

Péist banked away from the island with the setting sun at their backs.

Caymin took one last backward glance and then turned to face the open ocean before them. "*Take us to our destiny.*"

THE END

Character & Pronunciation Guide

Ailill – (ah LEEL) – dragonmage, bonded to Ríona

Angus – (ANG gus) – fanatical Christian monk

Bealtaine – (BELL tān) – Celtic summer festival, traditionally May 1st

Beanna – (B'YAWN nuh) – crow, friend to Caymin, Enat, and Péist

Broc – (brawk) – badger sow, Caymin's badger mother

Caymin – (KĀ min) – orphan, rescued by badgers, dragonmage to Péist

Cíana – (KEE ah nuh) – young mage apprentice

Cuán – (KOO awn) – badger boar, Caymin's badger father

Daina – (DĪ nuh) – young mage apprentice

Diarmit – (DEER mit) – young mage apprentice

Dughall – (DOO gull) – Gai's father, king of the Eoganacht clan

Eachna – (AHK nah) – mage to the Eoganacht

Éire – (AIR uh) – Gaelic for Ireland

Enat – (Ā nut) – mage, teacher

Eoganacht – (OH ga naght) – Gai's clan

Fergus – (FER gus) – older mage apprentice

Gai - (GĪ - like the English word 'guy') - young mage apprentice

Imbolc - (IM molg) - Celtic spring festival, traditionally February 1st

Inishbreith - (IN ish breth) - island where dragon young hatched and grew

Ivar - (EE var) - mage, teacher

Lughnasadh - (LOO nuh suh) - Celtic harvest festival, traditionally August 1st

Méav - (māv) - older mage apprentice

Neela - (NEE la) - mage, teacher

Niall - (NEE ull) - older mage apprentice

Osán - (Ō sawn) - female giant elk, mate to Ríordán

Péist - (Pesht) - white male dragon, bonded to Caymin

Ríona - (REE ah nuh) - black female dragon, bonded to Ailill

Ríordán - (REE ur dawn) - male giant elk, mate to Osán

Ronan - (RO nan) - older mage apprentice

Samhain - (SAH win) - Celtic winter festival, traditionally the night of October 31st to November 1st

Scolaí - (SKUL lee) - dragonmage, bonded to Tuala

Timmin - (TIM min) - mage, teacher

Tuala - (TOO ah la) - bronze male dragon, bonded to Scolaí

Una - (OO nah) - older mage apprentice

EXCERPT FROM
THE PORTAL
THE CHRONICLES OF CAYMIN

CHAPTER 1
To the Enemy

With the coming of dawn, Caymin crawled out from under the shelter of the dragon's wing. She shivered in the cold damp of the morning, and was joined by a crow, who flapped her wings to land on the girl's shoulder. Together, they made their way to the top of a hill. Below them, sheep huddled on the hillside, but there were no signs of dwellings or other two-legs. In the distance, they could see cliffs rising from the mist that covered the surface of the sea under a sky tinged with pink and purple.

"There is the land of Gai's clan," said Caymin.

Beanna fluffed her feathers. *"But will they be friend or foe?"*

"That is what we will have to see."

Caymin limped back down the hill to where the white dragon lay. Péist opened his eyes as a man crept out from under his other wing. Garvan straightened his monk's robes and looked up at Péist who stretched his long neck to the sky.

"I'm going to pray before I break my fast," Garvan said, scratching his beard. "Don't wait for me."

They watched him disappear over the same hill Caymin and Beanna had climbed a moment before, while Caymin retrieved a woven bag and pulled out some smoked fish and meat, along with a few of the roots she had harvested from Inishbreith before they left. She passed some of the meat to Beanna.

"Are you rested?" she asked Péist.

"Somewhat. The flight here was tiring, with Garvan's extra weight."

"Do you need to hunt again?"

"I will soon. There is nothing on this rock but sheep." Péist picked at his teeth with a talon. *"Their wool catches in my throat."*

"I am afraid sheep is all you will have until we get to Éire," Caymin said.

"And when will that be?" Beanna asked.

"I do not know."

When Garvan rejoined them, he ate hungrily. He pointed to the south, where two other small islands could now be seen as the mist cleared. "These three islands are the last points of land this side of Éire. No humans live on them now, only sheep left to graze and breed, but the humans come over in boats in spring and autumn, before the sea gets too rough, to gather the sheep." He looked at Péist. "Until you're ready to show yourself, you can hunt among these islands."

"Eating sheep is not hunting," Péist grumbled.

Garvan chuckled. "I'm afraid your choices are limited out here."

He led them all back to the crest of the hill that shielded them from the mainland. "All the land you see here is under the control of clan Eoganacht."

He glanced at Caymin, and she realized she was unconsciously touching the scars that ridged the side of her face. She immediately lowered her hand.

"I know they raided your village and killed your father, but there are answers to be had there. See that tower?" He pointed to a place where a round tower could be seen rising above the cliffs. "That is one of their outposts. Péist will only be able to fly at night, or they'll see him. Even then, a white dragon will be easy to spot."

"If Péist carries us there," Caymin said, indicating a stretch of cliffs well north of the tower, "can we approach them on foot?"

Garvan nodded. "Aye, but we'll want to be wary. If they think we're a threat to them, they'll lock us up before we can speak to anyone and we won't learn what we need to. We should rest today, and then tonight, we fly back to Éire."

The endless water rippled below, tiny points of light reflecting the moon and stars back from the waves. Silently, great white dragon wings soared over the water, catching currents of air and riding them closer and closer to Éire.

Péist came to ground in a remote stretch of grassland above the cliffs. Caymin unstrapped herself from the saddle while Garvan slid down off his back. Beanna wriggled out of her sling tucked against Caymin's belly. She flew to a thistle bush and flapped her wings.

"We can walk from here," Caymin said, untying her bow and quiver from Péist's saddle and slipping them over her shoulder.

"I do not like this," Péist said with a growl. *"I do not want to leave you unprotected."*

"You and I will remain connected, no matter how far apart we are," Caymin said. "If I am in any trouble, you will know and can get there quickly. But it would be best not to let them know we have a dragon in our midst in the beginning. Not until I know whether they will help us or no."

Garvan patted the sword hanging from his belt and said, "I promise, I'll protect her."

Péist lowered his head to look him in the eye. *"You had better, holy man."*

Caymin drew herself up. "You both forget, I do not need protecting."

Péist raised his head and glared toward their destination. *"That remains to be seen.*" He shielded his voice from Garvan. "*Come with me.*"

Caymin walked a short distance away, and Péist lowered his head again to touch her face with his muzzle.

"*I do not like leaving you, little one.*"

"*I know,*" she said, pressing her forehead to his. "*It will not be for long. As soon as we know whether Gai's clan will help us, we will move on. In the meantime, rest and rebuild your strength. We may need to flee, and I will need you to be ready.*" She backed away. "*Go now, while it is still dark.*"

Péist fanned his wings and allowed the wind blowing in from the water to lift him off the cliff. Caymin watched him fly back in the direction of the small islands far out on the sea.

Beanna flew to her shoulder. "*Shall we see what we will see?*"

Walking as quietly as possible, the trio made their way south. Caymin was able to keep up with Garvan despite her scarred leg. The day was beginning to brighten when Garvan suddenly pulled Caymin to the ground. They heard voices nearby, and soon after, saw a band of five warriors tramp by, all armed with spears, swords strapped to their belts. The cloaks they wore all bore one insignia—a blue wolf with red eyes, holding a yellow sword—the same image woven into the cloak that Caymin wore.

They followed the band from a safe distance and hid behind a hedge of blackthorn to watch the warriors approach a sentry guarding an entry through a stone wall. The stones were stacked taller than two men, and the gate was broad enough to allow four men to pass shoulder to shoulder. The sentry, armed as the other warriors were, questioned them briefly and then let them pass through a small door set into the massive gate.

The wall extended left and right, gradually curving out of sight as it encircled the buildings within. Outside the walls were fields, half of them nothing but stalks, while the others were filled with men and women harvesting.

"They're on alert," Garvan whispered. "The men we followed were probably coming off night patrol. They won't be eager to let strangers enter."

"Gai told us, before he was called back here, that their clan had been battling another. His father was captured and being held for ransom, but I do not understand what that means."

Garvan pulled her down to sit beside him. "It means Gai's clan will have to pay a small treasure to get their king back. This could give us the opportunity we need to bargain with them."

Caymin looked at him in bewilderment. "What do we have to bargain with? We do not have a treasure."

Garvan smiled grimly. "You have a dragon."

"Stay!"

The sentry barred their way, leveling his spear at them. Garvan pulled back his monk's hood.

"Pray, grant us entrance," he said. "We've traveled far and are weary."

The sentry eyed them suspiciously. He jabbed his spear at Caymin. "You, too. Off with your cloak."

When Garvan gestured for her to lower her hood, the sentry stepped back, a look of repulsion on his face as he took in her scars. "What happened to you?"

When she simply looked at him, he glanced at Garvan. "What's the matter with her?"

"She's deaf and dumb," Garvan said, laying a fatherly hand on Caymin's shoulder. "The scars are from a fire. She was burned when she was but a babe."

The suspicion on the sentry's face lessened a bit. He made her turn around. "Where'd she get that cloak?"

"One of your warriors took pity on her. That's what her mother told me before she died and left the lass in my keeping." Garvan bowed his head. "I am but a poor man of God and have no means of caring for a child. I was hoping she might find a place here. She's a good worker."

"I don't know," the sentry said, looking over his shoulder.

"May we petition your lord directly?"

The sentry barked a laugh. "Would that you could."

Caymin looked up at Garvan and rubbed her stomach.

"She's hungry," said Garvan. "Might we enter and look for a bite or two to eat?"

The sentry hesitated, eyeing Caymin and her scars. "Oh, go on then."

He stepped aside, opening the small door.

"God bless you," Garvan said as they passed through, Caymin limping more than usual.

"*That was well done,*" said Beanna from atop the wall where she had observed the entire exchange.

"*Keep watch,*" said Caymin. "*Let me know if you see Gai.*"

She looked around in wonderment as they walked through the village enclosed within the stone walls. In the distance, built into the far portion of the wall, was the largest building Caymin had ever seen, taller than a tree. She saw more warriors on a walkway built into its upper levels, standing guard.

People were stirring, cooking over fires in front of their dwellings. Like the fortress, most of these were built of stone, but with thatched roofs. The villagers watched the strangers with open curiosity, some with expressions of revulsion at the scars marring the right side of Caymin's face, while others took pity and offered a bit of bread or cheese.

Garvan accepted with a blessing and thanks.

"I have never been in the midst of so many two-legs," Caymin muttered as she shoved a bite of cheese into her mouth.

"You'd best not be calling them two-legs while we're here," Garvan muttered back. "In fact, you're not supposed to be talking at all. I'd feel better if we had our weapons."

"We had to hide them. The sentry never would have let us enter with weapons." Caymin looked around. "Most of these people are not armed. I can protect us if need be."

Garvan stopped and nodded toward a stone building with a wooden cross affixed to the roof. "A church. Stay here and let me go talk to the priest there." He glanced at her. "Stay to yourself and, remember, you're the ghost-child again. You can't speak or hear."

Caymin pulled her cloak back up over her head and sat out of the way against the wall. This place felt... strange. It wasn't just the presence of so many two-legs; it was the absence of trees or plants. She dug her fingers into the soil and felt nothing. No hum of life, no power. It felt dead. With a shiver, she brushed the dirt off her fingers.

"*Do you see anything?*" she asked as Beanna perched on top of the wall above her head.

"*I see many things. Do I see anything useful? Not yet.*" She hopped along the wall. "*Wait. I see a man carrying a hawk on his arm. Did you not tell me their mage has a hawk that is bonded to him?*"

"*Yes. It was the hawk who brought the message to Gai that his father had been captured. Is the man you see the mage here?*"

"*I do not know. Mages look like other two-legs, but... wait. He carries a staff. I think it is he. He is coming in this direction.*"

Caymin glanced up. "*We must stop talking now or he may hear.*"

Beanna flew away, flitting to another nearby rooftop where she could keep watch.

Caymin sat with her head bowed, her cloak pulled low over her head while she watched the people milling about. She spotted him—a small, thin man, striding away with his staff in one hand. The hawk was no longer with him. She listened, but heard no unspoken conversation between mage and hawk. She felt Péist's unrest as he waited anxiously on the island.

She was just considering whether to warn Beanna to be on the lookout in case the hawk attacked from the air, when the hawk suddenly landed in front of her.

"*Greetings,*" said the hawk.

Caymin blinked. "*Greetings.*"

The hawk tilted his head as he regarded her. "*You dried me and fed me when I brought a message to young Gai.*"

"*I remember, Lorcan. I am Caymin.*"

"*My mage wishes to meet you, Caymin.*"

"How did he know I am here?"

"We felt you. Will you come?"

Caymin looked around, but there was no sign of Garvan. This village wasn't so big that she wouldn't be able to find him later. *"I will come."*

Lorcan spread wings that tip to tip were nearly as long as Caymin was tall. He thrust into the air.

"The crow may come as well."

Beanna flew down to Caymin's shoulder. *"The crow was going to come whether the hawk gave permission or no."*

Caymin smiled. They followed Lorcan as he flew from rooftop to rooftop, leading them to an unassuming stone cottage, thatched like most of the others. The only thing that made this cottage different from the others was the small garden of herbs outside its door. Lorcan swooped through the open door. Caymin hesitated for a moment and then followed.

Standing inside near the fire was the man Caymin had seen. Slight of stature, he turned as she entered. Lorcan perched on a stout tree limb that had been dragged inside and propped in a corner. The mage's staff leaned against the hearth.

"I am Eachna." The mage approached, taking Caymin by the chin and turning her head so that he could see her scars. "You are Caymin."

He smiled when she tugged her chin from his grasp. He gestured toward a stool near the hearth. Caymin sat, and Beanna flitted over to a table where she could keep an eye on Lorcan and the two-legs. The inside of the cottage was sparsely furnished with a table and shelves stacked with many bowls and jars. Bunches of dried roots and flowers hung from the rafters—much as Enat's cottage used to be.

Caymin studied him. He was clean-shaven, with short-cropped hair the color of a sword's blade. "How do you know me?"

He didn't respond immediately, but bent toward the fire where he had a kettle sitting. He poured hot water into two cups. As he worked, she felt a push into her thoughts. Without thinking, she cast a protective spell, but the intrusion continued as if she had done nothing. Alarmed, she tried again, to no avail. Against her wishes, she saw images of the mages she had trained with—Enat and Neela making potions, Ivar teaching her how to use a sword, the other apprentices she had learned with.

When the image of Péist formed in her mind, she stood, knocking her stool over.

"Stop!"

"I apologize." He glanced up at her. He didn't look sorry. "That was rude."

He held out a cup. She watched him angrily for several heartbeats before righting her stool and accepting the cup.

"Why did you do that?" she asked as she sat.

"Why couldn't you stop me?"

Caymin felt the heat rise into her cheeks, as she had been thinking the same thing. She wondered if he could have cast some type of spell to nullify her magic within his house.

He scrutinized her, but there was no further pushing into her thoughts.

She took a sip of her drink, realizing only after she swallowed that he could have poisoned it or put a sleeping potion in it. She waited, but nothing seemed to be happening.

"How do you know me?" she repeated.

"Gai spoke of you. And Lorcan and I felt you when you arrived."

"I do not understand."

"Your magic. It's powerful."

Caymin blushed again and looked down into her cup. "Not so powerful. I could not stop you pushing into my thoughts."

"You've been in a place of power."

She stared up at him. Had he indeed read her thoughts again without her feeling it?

His smile did not quite reach his eyes. "You've never had to use magic outside a place of power, have you? It's not so easy."

She realized he was right. Enat had warned her when she was first brought to the mystical forest to be trained that using magic would be easier there because of the power of the forest. From there, she and Péist and Beanna had fled to Inishbreith, which had power even greater than that of the forest. When she had used magic on their journey, Péist had had to bolster her power with his own.

"Your magic is like an aura around you, but you've yet to refine it, to learn to control it. If you're here, you left the forest much earlier than you should have." He narrowed his eyes as he studied her. "I wonder why that was?"

She said nothing, but suspected he already knew the answer to his question.

He turned back to the fire and said, "You're probably curious to know how Gai is."

"You said he told you about me."

He shrugged. "It's more what Gai didn't say rather than what he did."

"What do you mean?"

"He's been... different since he returned." Eachna reached forward to stir the fire. "You changed him."

"I? How?"

Again, Eachna didn't answer. Instead, he said, "Gai told me of the cloak you wear, the cloak that was taken from the warriors who attacked your village and killed your family, leaving you to burn." He eyed her curiously. "Your arm and leg are burned as well."

Caymin said nothing, only looked at him.

"You accused him of being a murderer."

Caymin flushed furiously. "I was wrong to accuse him so."

"Were you?" Eachna tilted his head to stare at her again. "Is that why you're here? To tell him you were wrong?"

"Caymin."

She turned to Beanna just as a shadow darkened the doorway. Her mouth dropped.

"Gai."

Made in the USA
Monee, IL
24 January 2021